From the Ashes

An Alternate History Novel

Sandra Saidak

Uffington Horse Press San Jose, CA

ISBN: 978-0-9863385-2-6

Other books by Sandra Saidak:

The Seal Queen

Books in the Kalie's Journey Series:

Daughter of the Goddess Lands
Shadow of the Horsemen
Keepers of the Ancient Wisdom
Oathbreaker's Daughter (short stand-alone, set in the same universe)
In the Balance (Short story collection; title story in set in Kalie's universe)

Acknowledgement:

Thanking everyone who helped with this decades-long project would be impossible, but I'll do my best. First and most important, my husband Tom, who worked with me every step of the way, helped write the battle scenes, and came to know the characters as well as I do. Heartfelt thanks to my mother, Charlotte Fisher, and to all the members of three different writers groups: the Whensday People, the Over the Hill Gang, and that group who met at the Coffee Factory in the late 1990s (sorry I don't remember the name) who read and critiqued its many drafts. And again, special thanks to the very talented team of George MacDonald and Donji Columbine for making the physical reality of the book possible. But, as in the real story of the Holocaust, the stories contained in these pages came to me from countless sources, I am unable to name. From stories overheard at conventions, to the tales of WWII veterans I met while working as a cocktail waitress in my college days, to the books I read in my middle-school library, to survivors who spoke at my high school, this novel is the result of everything I've ever heard or imagined about a piece of human history that has always sounded more like science fiction/ horror than fact.

This novel is dedicated to ALL of the victims of the Holocaust. The millions who died and the hundreds of thousands who survived. The righteous who risked everything to help friends and strangers, and those who stayed silent in violation of their conscience, and then had to live with that for the rest of their lives. And above all, to the children, who never had a voice in any of it.

Book I

CHAPTER 1

"In the beginning, there was chaos!"

Adolf paced the small room while his father yelled.

"Then, He came to us! We have order now; we have a future! The Golden Age of the Thousand Year *Reich* is just around the corner! So I come to see how my first-born son is preparing for that great destiny, and what do I find? You! Reading books in a stuffy dormitory! What's the matter with you? Your first year at Berlin's finest university! A brilliant future ahead of you! You should be living it up. Look out there!" Helmut Goebbels pushed his son to the small window.

Adolf looked, feeling both longing and fear as he watched the groups of students holding outdoor study sessions, or drinking beer and chatting in the late autumn sunshine. He already knew what would happen if he tried to join them. He should keep silent; just wait until his father got tired and left. Yet, *for the last time* he told himself, Adolf tried to make his father understand.

"I don't fit in here, Father! I try, but I feel like there's a wall between me and everyone else. No one likes me for myself--just my family name. I joined all the clubs you told me to, but...they're boring! They're full of braggarts and boot-lickers...."

Although every girl who attended the University was officially a Domestic Engineering major, there to receive a bit of polish before making the best possible marriage, many came here hoping to be discovered by the film industry. Talent scouts rarely bothered looking anyplace but campuses these days. The girl beside Josef would probably soon be a star.

Once past the park, Adolf headed for the nearby civic center, hoping to find something there to take his mind off his troubles. Party sponsored cultural events and art exhibits occurred there almost every day.

People made way for Adolf as he moved through the crowded street. Even at eighteen, without his illustrious family around him, others deferred to his natural superiority. Or perhaps, he thought bitterly, it's the expensive clothes and platinum *Hitlerjugend* badge that does it.

Seeing nothing of interest, he walked past the civic center toward an older part of the city. Now the streets were cracked and dirty. Adolf paused as a truck full of Enemies of The State roared by, the war vintage Puma armored car smoking badly from its ill maintained engine. Probably on their way to the Colonies in Africa, he thought as he coughed from the fumes.

Adolf wandered through progressively rougher and dirtier streets, ending up in a nearly deserted plaza. Boards covered all the buildings but one so Adolf drifted over for a look.

It was one of the smaller museums, maintained by the Department of Education. It was just one room, small and cluttered, and for a moment, Adolf thought it was deserted. But when his eyes adjusted to

Book I

CHAPTER 1

"In the beginning, there was chaos!"

Adolf paced the small room while his father yelled.

"Then, He came to us! We have order now; we have a future! The Golden Age of the Thousand Year *Reich* is just around the corner! So I come to see how my first-born son is preparing for that great destiny, and what do I find? You! Reading books in a stuffy dormitory! What's the matter with you? Your first year at Berlin's finest university! A brilliant future ahead of you! You should be living it up. Look out there!" Helmut Goebbels pushed his son to the small window.

Adolf looked, feeling both longing and fear as he watched the groups of students holding outdoor study sessions, or drinking beer and chatting in the late autumn sunshine. He already knew what would happen if he tried to join them. He should keep silent; just wait until his father got tired and left. Yet, *for the last time* he told himself, Adolf tried to make his father understand.

"I don't fit in here, Father! I try, but I feel like there's a wall between me and everyone else. No one likes me for myself--just my family name. I joined all the clubs you told me to, but...they're boring! They're full of braggarts and boot-lickers...."

Adolf clenched his teeth at the sting as Helmut slapped his face, wishing for just a moment, that he could get his hands around his father's throat. "That is the cream of the National Socialist Party you're slandering! Grandsons of heroes--like you, Adolf! Your grandfather stood at the right hand of the First *Führer*. His speeches--"

"'Moved millions and knocked the old United States out of the war.' Yes, I know! And I spend every day of my life trying to live up to that image that you cram down my throat!"

"And this is how you glorify his memory? Wasting your time with books--" Helmut grabbed the collection of poetry Adolf had been reading and hurled it against the wall. "Why can't you be more like Josef Heydrich? He comes from lesser stock than you, Adolf, yet look what he's done with himself!"

Adolf tried to laugh, but it came out as a groan. Only two years ago, when Josef first was first accepted into the University, Helmut had stormed about the degeneration of standards that would allow lower stock into the hallowed halls for which a Goebbels was destined. Now, as the Heydrich family continued to rise, their eldest son a top student, Helmut had begun comparing his son to theirs—always to Adolf's detriment.

"You have a duty to your race," Helmut said, as the familiar speech wound down. "And your family as well."

Adolf set his jaw and stared out the window until he heard his father's footsteps lead to the door. Then he turned, already at attention. "*Heil* the *Führer*," Helmut said formally, clicking his heels and saluting. Adolf limply returned the salute.

When the door finally shut, Adolf sat heavily on his hard bed, fighting tears--and the shame and horror that any Aryan man would feel at such weakness. Once he was back under control, he picked up the book his father had thrown, surprised to feel the same urge to throw it--or anything else he could get his hands on. Suddenly claustrophobic, Adolf left the dorm.

Hitler University was very old, and Adolf had heard that long ago, like so many places in the *Reich*, it once had a different name. The autumn air was growing cold, but Adolf found comfort in the sensation as the stinging chill dried his face.

Next to the campus was a beautiful park, one of the many public works commissioned by the First *Führer*, to be enjoyed by all Aryan citizens. Several young men were running along the track, while others worked out on the par course. A multi- aged group of women sat on benches, chatting, while a pretty blonde woman from the Party's *Kinder-Korps* led their children in a game of capture the flag. Behind them, some older boys were playing *Wermacht*. Adolf smiled briefly as the rat-a-tat-tat of their toy assault guns brought back memories of his own childhood.

Then he noticed Josef Heydrich holding court with a group of fellow academic and athletic stars. For a moment, jealousy tore through Adolf, hotter and more painful than even his anger at his father. Like Adolf, Josef was tall, blond and muscular, but from Adolf's perspective, the whole package fit better on the older boy. As if it was all Josef's by right, but Adolf's only through some accident of nature.

Josef had his arm around a girl Adolf recognized as a campus beauty pageant winner.

Although every girl who attended the University was officially a Domestic Engineering major, there to receive a bit of polish before making the best possible marriage, many came here hoping to be discovered by the film industry. Talent scouts rarely bothered looking anyplace but campuses these days. The girl beside Josef would probably soon be a star.

Once past the park, Adolf headed for the nearby civic center, hoping to find something there to take his mind off his troubles. Party sponsored cultural events and art exhibits occurred there almost every day.

People made way for Adolf as he moved through the crowded street. Even at eighteen, without his illustrious family around him, others deferred to his natural superiority. Or perhaps, he thought bitterly, it's the expensive clothes and platinum *Hitlerjugend* badge that does it.

Seeing nothing of interest, he walked past the civic center toward an older part of the city. Now the streets were cracked and dirty. Adolf paused as a truck full of Enemies of The State roared by, the war vintage Puma armored car smoking badly from its ill maintained engine. Probably on their way to the Colonies in Africa, he thought as he coughed from the fumes.

Adolf wandered through progressively rougher and dirtier streets, ending up in a nearly deserted plaza. Boards covered all the buildings but one so Adolf drifted over for a look.

It was one of the smaller museums, maintained by the Department of Education. It was just one room, small and cluttered, and for a moment, Adolf thought it was deserted. But when his eyes adjusted to the gloom, he saw a young woman seated behind a desk, polishing a strangely wrought candlestick.

She was strikingly attractive, tall with blue eyes, and he thought her blond hair might even be natural.

Adolf looked around and saw piles of books, unframed paintings, and artwork of iron, brass and cloth. The woman continued to sit at her desk, seemingly oblivious to his presence. "What is this place?" he finally asked.

"A *Judenmuseum*," the woman said, looking up.

"A what?"

"A museum of Jewish artifacts. The Jews were enemies of the Fatherland; an inferior race. They no longer exist, but these objects are kept as curiosities."

Adolf nodded. "I read about that race in school. But I didn't know there were places like this."

"Oh, yes. It was Himmler's idea, begun during the War. There are thirty-eight of these, scattered throughout the world. Hardly anyone comes to them anymore."

Adolf smiled winningly. "So why is a beautiful girl like you wasting away in one?"

Instead of answering, she pulled her arm away from her desk, but not before Adolf saw the red bar code tattooed on her forearm. He stiffened. That color was reserved for the *missgeburt;* the people outside of the gene pool. Originally, it meant severe physical or mental defects. Those had long since been terminated. Today, it could only mean...

"Infertility," said Adolf, wishing he could melt into the floor. "I'm so sorry. I..."

"Do not concern yourself."

"What is your name?"

"Ilsa."

"I am Adolf. Goebbels."

"Such an important personage to grace my humble museum. What brings you here?"

"A desire to avoid my Political Science text, perhaps."

"Is that your major at the University?"

"For the moment. Until my father decides another major will further the brilliant government career he has planned for me."

"And what would you do if it were up to you?"

Adolf glanced sharply at the woman. Was there a mocking note in her voice? And even if there wasn't, why discuss his private dreams with a total stranger? *Because sometimes it's easier to open up to a stranger than someone you know,* Adolf answered himself.

"If I could choose, I would be a teacher," he said, half afraid she would laugh.

But Ilsa only nodded. "A worthy profession. And your family might even approve, if you planned to become a professor at some great university. But that's not the kind of teacher you'd be, would you?"

Adolf raised an eyebrow. "You are most perceptive, *fräulein.* No. I would be a humble village schoolmaster. I would teach the young ones, before they grew obnoxious."

"'Woman's work,'" snorted Ilsa.

"So my father would say if he knew. So he won't." Adolf looked away. "Are all father's bastards, or just mine?"

"I suppose none of them start out with that

intention. But most of the parents I have known make me grateful I shall never be one." Ilsa shook her head. "Come, *Herr* Goebbels. As long as you are here, let me show you around. After all, it's my duty."

Ilsa pointed to a portrait of Heinrich Himmler in a corner. "Our Illustrious Leaders," she began, "saw that the body of Germany was riddled with disease. Unchecked, they would have utterly destroyed our glorious civilization." Her voice, suddenly mechanical, startled Adolf. This was not at all how she had sounded before.

Ilsa continued what was clearly a memorized speech about the Jews and their inevitable destruction. Adolf noticed that Ilsa was more than bored by the words she mouthed; her voice dripped with sarcasm. He also noticed that the portraits of Himmler, Eichmann and other heroes of the Fatherland, were gathering dust in a dark corner, while the Jewish artifacts were extremely well cared for. The metal vessels and sculptures showed signs of constant polishing, and the books, though worn, were free of dust and dirt, even those that were probably centuries old.

They stopped by a small table, covered with photographs. "You can tell from these pictures," the speech went on, "that Jews were of another race entirely. Inferior, and nothing like ours."

Adolf picked up a photo. It was of a little girl, picking flowers in a beautifully kept garden, in front of a house very much like his family's home. The girl bore a strong resemblance to Adolf's youngest sister.

"I don't think they look so different," said Adolf. "How were they rounded up in the first place?"

"Synagogue records, passports, tips from neighbors." Ilsa's voice had changed again. Her words were her own now, and looking into her mysterious blue eyes, Adolf had the strange feeling that he had just passed some kind of test.

Ilsa went to the table of dishes and candlesticks. "Do you know they weren't really a race at all, in the technical sense of the word? The only thing that set them apart was their religion. Perhaps 'way of life' is more accurate."

"How do you know so much about them?" asked Adolf.

Ilsa smiled. "I've little enough to do all day but read. That certainly wasn't part of Himmler's plan when he began these archives, but they have a fascinating history. Did you know ours was not the first attempt at exterminating them? It was tried over and over, all around the world, for five thousand years. They always endured. They lost their homeland, wandered the world, built up wealth and had it stolen...all for a belief in one God."

"What's so special about that?"

"Maybe nothing. But think about it. How many cultures on earth have survived for five thousand years? We've only been promised one thousand--if we can last that long."

Ilsa went back to polishing that curious candlestick. "What is that?" asked Adolf.

"A *menorah*. There are several here, but this is my favorite. An ordinary *menorah* has seven branches."

"This one has nine. What's the difference?"

"It's for a holiday called *Hanukkah*." Ilsa pointed to a book on the edge of the table. "I've just been reading about it. It wasn't their most important holiday, but there's a lovely story behind it, about a light in the darkness that never went out. A lot of their folklore seemed to be about that; about keeping the light alive, even in the darkest times."

Adolf took the *menorah* from Ilsa and examined it. The workmanship was impeccable, and Ilsa's polishing had given it a soft glow. "It isn't gold, is it?" he said.

"Of course not. Those are long gone."

"But they did have them once?"

"Oh, yes. Many of their holiday vessels were made of precious metals, but those were taken early on, and melted down. You might have a bit of them in the coins in your pocket, *Herr* Goebbels. Every so often, the *Gestapo* comes here, to see if there's any they missed. That's how I know things are worse than broadcasts say they are."

"Things are always worse than the broadcasts say," said Adolf. "I expect we'll be having shortages again. Crop yield is down again in North America."

Ilsa nodded. "In the Ukraine, too, I've heard."

Adolf sighed. "Well, I should be going." But he didn't move.

"Good luck with the Political Science study," said Ilsa.

He looked around again. The poor lighting seemed to imbue the room with an air of mystery; of treasure waiting to be found. The stacks of ancient books and alien artifacts beckoned him. "I wish I could stay," he said suddenly. "Just do nothing but read and talk to you."

Ilsa picked up one of the books on her desk. "Here, scholar. Take this with you. You may find it interesting."

She gave him a thick, paper bound volume, probably close to a century old. Its title was *The Debate*.

"Can you do that? Just give books away?"

Ilsa shrugged. "No one cares what happens to the books in here. Besides, I have to make room. There's a shipment coming in soon from the digs outside of Palestine."

Adolf whistled. "That region is still radioactive. Are you certain the artifacts will be safe for you to handle?"

"No. Did you think that would concern my employers?" She laughed. It sounded like glass breaking. "Farewell, *Herr* Goebbels."

"*Heil* the *Führer*," he responded automatically.

Adolf tucked the book under his arm, and headed back to the university.

CHAPTER 2

At the Student Activity Center Adolf bought a newspaper. A thick black headline shrieked "Would-Be Assassin Believed to Be American!" Various articles beneath it described yesterday's attempted assassination of the *Führer*, assured citizens that those responsible would be caught, and showed grizzly pictures of the interrogations of suspects.

For no reason that he could name, Adolf wandered down to the *Judenmuseum*. He did not know if it would be open on a Sunday, but it didn't matter. He needed the exercise.

Life at the University had improved for Adolf in the two weeks since he had stumbled across the place. Although he still had no real friends, his classes were going well, and his father had not visited again.

The rush of pleasure Adolf felt when he saw Ilsa surprised him. She was behind her desk again, repairing a damaged book with great care. He was nearly at the desk, book in hand, when he realized that this time, they were not alone.

Three young men sat on the floor among the stacks of books speaking in low voices. A dark haired young woman sat in one of the few well-lit areas, staring at a stained and crumpled painting. She had a sketchpad on her lap, and Adolf could see she was attempting to copy the painting. It depicted an old man on a mountain, holding what looked like a pair of tombstones.

"Nice to see you again, *Herr* Goebbels." Ilsa's voice startled Adolf. Conversation stopped, and the three men regarded Adolf curiously.

"I wanted to return the book you loaned me," he said, setting <u>The Debate</u> on Ilsa's desk.

"Finished so soon? Or perhaps it did not hold your interest?"

"On the contrary, I finished it in one night." He glanced curiously at the others in the room, wondering if he should leave.

Ilsa smiled mischievously. "Some of your classmates?"

Puzzled, Adolf looked again, and realized that the other visitors were all students at Hitler University. The tall, muscular man was Franz Krueger, a senior who assisted in Adolf's Chemistry class. The other two men were vaguely familiar.

"They're semi-regular visitors," said Ilsa. "I get a few others, from time to time."

"They probably just come to look at you."

"Of course we do," said the woman doing the sketch.

The men laughed, but Adolf gaped. Even joking about homosexuality could be dangerous.

"Actually," said Franz, "we're a bunch of people who have nothing better to do on a Sunday afternoon."

Adolf smiled in spite of himself. "Sounds like my kind of group."

"So come join us," said a short upperclassman with a beckoning wave. "Maybe you can add something to this discussion."

Curious, Adolf joined the group on the floor, and peered at the open book before them. "It's a book on Jewish laws," said Franz. "This chapter talks about duties to the poor."

"Duties *to* the poor?"

"*Ja,* strange thought," said the boy next to Franz. "They had this thing called 'gleaning'. It required every land owner to leave a section of his fields for the poor to harvest--and keep."

"Frederick here," said Franz, nodding to the boy who spoke, "thinks it's literal; that the Jews actually got rid of starvation altogether. Karl thinks it's just some kind of fable."

"What do you think?" asked Adolf.

"I think if we tried it in the Ukraine, we might prevent a few food riots."

"Any governor who tried something like that would be shot," said Karl.

"Yes, but it would mean dying for an original thought," said Adolf. "That almost makes it worth it."

The others laughed. "You're Adolf oebbels?" said Franz.

"That's right."

"What brings you here?"

Adolf shrugged. "I just…stumbled upon it one day. The place seemed interesting so I came back. How about you?"

"About the same. And, as you can see, we're not the only ones. Lately, we've been coming here on weekends, reading and discussing…"

"And painting!" called the woman in the corner. She rose and walked to where the men were sitting.

"Krista, here, is an artist," said Karl.

"But the Party thinks I'm here to become a Domestic Engineer. So that is what I must be. I guess

I should be grateful to be here at all."

"I know how you feel," said Adolf, trying not to stare at the eyeglasses she wore or her unusually short stature.

"Go ahead and say it," she said quietly. "I don't look like the future mother of Aryan supermen. But I am pure Aryan. That's why I got this scholarship. I think the government finally realized that when you knock everyone out of higher education but one small ethnic group, you better use everyone you have."

"And once the thrill of this great honor wore off, you realized you had interests and talents that the Party doesn't encourage?"

"I don't think anyone in this room is studying what we want," said Franz. "We're here to fulfill our father's dreams."

"And studying the Jews is supposed to help?" said Adolf.

"It takes our minds off the rest of it, at least, and gives us something new to talk about. I think all of us are drawn here by an interest in forgotten ways of life."

"And a strong disgust for our current way of life!" said Frederick.

"I'm sure we can agree that the glorious life our grandparents were promised hasn't materialized," said Franz. "We might as well look to the past."

"And you expect to find answers among inferior races?" asked Adolf.

"We haven't had much luck with the innately superior," said Franz.

Adolf smiled. "Touché."

"There's something about this place," said

Krista. "It's like stepping into another world. There's an entire history here; one you'll never find in the campus library."

"Has there ever been any trouble?" Adolf asked Ilsa.

She shook her head. "Officially, nothing's happening here. There are no formal meetings or scheduled discussions. The *Gestapo* has better things to do."

"Government paranoia has its advantages," said Frederick. "As long as they're busy hunting conspirators behind every American curtain, and partisans in every Russian forest, they don't tend to worry about what dissatisfied college kids are doing between classes."

"And if this sort of thing isn't to your liking," said Franz. "You could try the Communists down the street, or the Environmentalists--I think they meet in the park--or..."

"Yes," said Karl bitterly. "The young of today would truly make Hitler proud. When he was our age, he vowed to redeem Germany from the ashes; then he built an empire from its rubble. Look at us. A bunch of spoiled brats, playing at being radicals."

"Considering what we have to work with," said Krista. "We're not doing so bad."

"Come on," said Franz. "Let's go to Rolf's Beer Garden."

Adolf was about to make a polite departure-- then realized from the others' expectant faces that the invitation included him. Feeling good for the first time since arriving in school, he followed.

CHAPTER 3

The Friday night meeting at the *Judenmuseum* had not yet started. About a dozen people sat in groups, casually conversing. Adolf brushed the snow from his coat and closed the door behind him.

"*Shabbat Shalom*," he called to the group at large.

"*Shabbat Shalom*," returned several voices.

He nodded to various friends, then immediately noticed the new face in the crowd. The newcomer looked young; probably a freshman like himself.

"Adolf, meet Peter," said Klaus, a handsome blonde sophomore, majoring in Physical Education.

Peter smiled shyly, glancing around nervously, as if expecting the *Gestapo* to come barging in at any moment.

Adolf shook the smaller boy's hand. "So, Peter, what brings you here?"

"Klaus thought I might like it. He's my roommate; he says I don't get out enough."

"Actually," said Klaus. "I'm tired of him reading in the middle of the night, with all the lights on."

"It's the only way I can get back to sleep," Peter said apologetically.

"Sounds like one of us," said Adolf.

"What you told me so far is interesting," said Peter, "But how can you speak so freely here?"

Ilsa appeared beside him, silently as always. "Listen. Do you hear the music?"

Everyone nodded. A scratchy recording of Beethoven's Pastoral Symphony played on the museum's speaker system. "The phonograph is located directly below the only working listening device left in the building."

Adolf smiled. From what he had learned about Ilsa so far, there was no cause for doubt.

"I hope you change the music occasionally," said Franz. "I'd hate to think how bored our friendly local agents must be, hearing the same recording day after day."

Klaus nodded. "Those moments in my dorm when I stop and wonder if there's a listening device planted, I have to feel sorry for the poor guy who's assigned to listen to my boring life. So to relieve the tedium, I sing Wagner's entire Ring Cycle, at least once a week."

"He does," Peter confirmed through shut teeth.

"I just go through life assuming everything I say is being recorded somewhere," said Karl. "That way, I never have to worry about it."

"I've heard that some enterprising soul in the Engineering Department is selling jamming devices," said Adolf. "He guarantees up to three hours of privacy."

All the upperclassmen in the room laughed. "There's one every semester," said Franz. "I tend to judge the quality of their work by how long it takes them—and their customers—to disappear. Usually, it's a matter of weeks."

Peter gulped audibly.

Frederic shook his head. "Everyone knows, the only place for real privacy is the showers. Running water is the only effective jamming device we have left."

"I certainly hope that's true," Krista muttered as she examined a stack of photographs. Adolf glanced her way, curious about what kind of conversations she'd had there recently—and with whom.

"Is it true you're learning to read Hebrew?" asked Klaus.

Adolf felt embarrassed. "I'm just dabbling. It gives me something to do during Professor Schultz' lectures."

"Other than sleeping, you mean?"

Adolf smiled, wondering if they guessed that it began as an excuse to spend more time with Ilsa, who was nearly fluent in the ancient language. But since then, he had discovered a genuine interest--and talent--for it.

"Hey, look!" said Krista, holding up an old picture. "Recognize this place?"

Adolf took the photo carefully. "That's the Mengele mansion. I was there last year with my family. What's it doing here?"

"Oh, many of Germany's finest houses once belonged to Jews," said Ilsa.

"Yet another benefit reaped for us by our grandparents' ideas of ethnic cleansing," said Frederic.

"Let me see those," said Klaus, scooping up the stack of photos. "I want to see if my house is here!"

"We might as well get started," said Franz. "Adolf, why don't you share your translations?"

Adolf grunted with surprise. "I don't have much translated, and I'm not sure if any of it's accurate. Isn't Heinrik supposed to read something tonight?"

"He won't be coming," said Krista. "He had an accident at weapons practice this morning."

"Anything serious?" asked Adolf.

"No permanent damage."

"Good." Adolf shrugged, and took a battered notebook and an even more battered book from his knapsack. He went to the lopsided lectern that occupied the only clear space in the tiny museum, and spread out his materials.

Adolf glanced nervously at the people gathered before him. Eight men and two women sat on folding chairs, while Ilsa leaned against her desk across the room, watching with interest. They were his friends, but public speaking was not one of his strengths. Then Krista winked at him, and Heidi, the stunning women next to her, gave him a smile that could have sent any man into combat without a second thought. Adolf smiled back.

"I guess it's appropriate that I've been working with writings on the subject of *Shabbat*, or Sabbath," he began. "I still haven't found out why the Hebrews began their day at sundown, but I did find quite a lot about the importance they placed on the idea of a day of rest."

"I wish some of our professors would place some importance on it, too!" said Karl.

"I wish my parents would," said Heidi.

"Actually," said Adolf, "our professors have the right idea, according to the scriptures. *Shabbat* was meant to be a time of study and contemplation. Back when most people spent all their time just trying to stay alive, the idea of setting aside one whole day

out of every seven to do nothing physical--just to read
or think or pray-- must have been pretty radical."

"Sounds pretty boring to me," said Klaus.

"That's because you have no one to pray to,"
said Franz.

"I think the problem is just the opposite,"
said Frederick. "We have a whole pantheon: Odin,
Thor, Loki--plus our Beloved First *Führer*."

"And a new one added each time a *Führer*
dies," said Heidi.

"I should have said no one *worth* praying to."

"Now you're getting picky!" said Karl.

"Give them time," said Klaus. "Those gods
have been out of work for over a thousand years.
They're probably just a little rusty."

Adolf watched his friends, enjoying their
banter as he always did. Yet underneath he felt a
prickle of irritation. Was it because they weren't
listening to his brilliant oration?

No, he decided. It was like so much of what
he felt in this building: something entirely new.

"Let's try it," he said suddenly.

"What?" asked Franz.

"Prayer. The Jewish way."

Several people exchanged nervous glances.
Then Krista said, "Okay. Ilsa, how many prayer
books do we have in German?"

Instead of answering, Ilsa glanced up at Adolf.
*Is it possible she understands what I'm trying to say?
he wondered.*

"I don't mean from books. The Jews believed
in just one god, and that each person had to find their
own path to Him. Part of the *Shabbat* was spent in
groups, but even there, time was set aside for silent,

individual prayer. And what you said to God during that time, was just between you and Him."

"What, you mean they didn't have a priesthood?" asked Heidi.

"I'm not sure."

"They did have a priesthood," said Ilsa. "But Adolf's right about the individual relationship with God. It was one of the cornerstones of this religion."

"Don't tell the *SS*," laughed Klaus. "They make little enough money from church attendance as it is. An idea like this could put them out of business!"

"I'd still like to try it," said Adolf. "Here, now, on a Friday night. Like they used to."

Karl and Frederick looked a little embarrassed, but Krista, Franz and Klaus all said "okay".

"What do we do?" asked Heidi.

You're asking me? Adolf wanted to say. But it was his idea, so he improvised. "Close your eyes, and think about whatever is most important to you right now. Try to imagine a person--no--a presence out there that cares as much about that thing as you do." If they needed more direction, or were still waiting expectantly, Adolf didn't know, because he, too, had closed his eyes.

For a moment, he felt stupid, standing in front of a group of people with his eyes closed. Then, frightened, because when he tried to focus on something that was important to him, all he found was a huge black void.

Then something seemed to flicker behind his eyes as if he had shut them too tightly. Adolf felt a sense of expectation, as if lightening had struck nearby, and he was waiting for the sound of the thunder.

Then the moment passed, and he was once again a university student; a poor little rich boy with nothing better to do on a Friday night then play occult games in a moldering museum.

But when he opened his eyes, about to offer a joke as an apology to his friends, Adolf saw eleven people with their eyes closed--some with very intense expressions.

One by one they opened their eyes.

"What *was* that?" asked Krista, looking around.

"What do you mean?" said Karl. "Nothing happened."

"Well, I think that's enough for tonight," Ilsa said quickly.

"Let's go to Rolf's," said Frederick.

Everyone began to put on their coats.

"Ilsa, won't you come with us, this time?" asked Krista.

Ilsa rubbed the long sleeve that covered her tattoo and seemed about to say no.

"Please," said Adolf. Then, to his pleasure, the others in the room took up the cause.

"Come on!" said Franz. "Just keep your coat on."

Ilsa seemed surprised. "All right," she said. "Just for one drink. I'll have to lock up first."

Adolf sensed her pleasure, and wished he had thought of inviting her long before now.

CHAPTER 4

The bookstore was crowded. Adolf fought a wave of claustrophobia and pushed his way in.

Classes had already ended, but Adolf would not be leaving for home until tomorrow, allowing him one day to buy gifts for nearly a dozen family members. And, of course, one more evening in the *Judenmuseum*.

He found a book on the history of film for his father. As Adolf expected, his grandfather's work was prominently displayed. He smiled at the subtle revenge of giving a book to one of the most anti-intellectual men in the *Reich*. For his youngest sister, he bought a *Children's Illustrated Mein Kampf*, and a history of space exploration for his uncle.

He would have liked to have gotten all his shopping done here, but knew that this was as far as he could push books. No one else in his family was even remotely interested in reading, and to buy more would have been asking for trouble with Helmut.

"I should have gotten my shopping done weeks ago," Adolf muttered as he stepped into the purchase line that stretched across the store.

"You and everyone else here."

Adolf turned and saw a short, gray haired man smiling at him. He recognized the man from the university; one of the senior professors.

"Including you, *Herr* Professor...?"

"Hoffman. History Department."

"Ah, yes. I hope I shall be one of the privileged few to attend your senior seminar," Adolf said politely.

Professor of History Hoffman waved the flattery away with one hand, balancing an impressive load of books with the other. He glanced at the books Adolf held. "Holiday gifts, I see?"

Adolf nodded.

"Buy what you can now. Fewer and fewer books are being printed these days," said Hoffman.

Adolf glanced around at the crowded shelves. Not wishing to contradict an honored teacher he said only, "Oh."

Hoffman followed his gaze and laughed. "I should have said new books. Most of what you see here are old standards, 'appropriate for loyal Party members.' Which is not a complaint. I shall always love the classics. And even among the older books, one can still find delightful surprises. For example..."

The professor reached over to a nearby display of colorful volumes bound in imitation leather and chose one. "I find it a sign of great confidence among our leaders that this one is back in circulation."

Adolf read the title: "Sorrows of Young Werther." The author was Johann von Goethe. "I've never heard of it," he told the professor.

"Not surprising. It was written over two hundred years ago. Brilliantly written, I might add. It tells the story of an angst ridden young man, who eventually commits suicide."

"That sounds like a subject that would always have an audience. At least for a short time."

"A shorter time than you might think," said Hoffman. "You see, each time this book has been available to the general public, it has attracted a cult following of gloomy young men. They adopt the protagonist's dress and mannerisms--then there are enough Werther inspired suicides to result in the banning of the book. Then, a while later, it comes back."

Adolf laughed. "Sounds absurd."

A sudden commotion in the front of the store cut short any comment Professor Hoffman might have made.

The owner was ejecting an old man, with the strong and eager help of several customers. The man, dressed in neatly pressed, if shabby clothes of the middle class seemed to be trying to explain himself, but his words soon turned to pleas for mercy.

Adolf turned to glance at the professor, only to find him moving purposefully through the crowd.

"What has he done?" inquired Hoffman.

"He said he wanted to buy a 'Christmas' gift," said a woman, disgust in her voice, but glee in her face as she watched the beating.

"So for that they beat him?" Adolf demanded. He had not intended to raise his voice, but it carried throughout the store. As people turned to look at him, he added lamely, "That's simply one of the older names for the Yule."

A pair of soldiers, entering the store, looked Adolf up and down. "It's more than that, sir," one of them finally said, while the other hauled the old man to his feet. "It's an insult to good Party members who follow the true German faith of our ancestors. If the proprietor of this establishment won't allow such talk from customers, he has the right to eject them."

Adolf looked at the old man, who, though bruised and bleeding did not seem to need immediate medical attention. "I am sure," he began, wondering why he had gotten involved in the first place, "that he was only momentarily confused. If he must be escorted out, please, allow me."

The soldiers glanced at each other, then at the owner of the store.

"If you let him go, he'll likely create more trouble," said the merchant.

"I have a car and driver waiting outside," said Professor Hoffman. "If you would allow me, in the spirit of the season, to escort the man home, I shall do so."

It was clear from the expression on the owner's face that Hoffman was well known in this shop. "As you wish, *Herr* Professor," he said tightly, and then turned back to his customers as if the whole incident had not happened.

"Give me a hand, please, Adolf?" Hoffman asked as he guided the hobbling old man out of the store.

At once, Adolf set down his books. "Yes, *mein Herr*," he said. To the store owner, he added, "I'll come back for these."

Hoffman shook his head, "The store will close in an hour. Put them on my account," he told the merchant, indicating both his own books and Adolf's. "And have them sent to the University."

That evening, at the *Judenmuseum*, Adolf related the events of the day to his friends. The group was small, as most of the regular members had already left for home. Ilsa had put up the government required holiday decorations, but also lit candles on the largest *menorah*. Franz had brought a bottle of wine and Klaus had brought cookies. The air was festive, if a bit melancholy.

"So, you actually helped escort an Enemy of the State home?" asked Ilsa.

"I wouldn't exactly call him that," said Adolf. "After all, there's nothing illegal about being Christian. Half the rural population of Germany is still Lutheran."

"Still," said Franz, "in Berlin..."

"And the Professor just *bought* your books for you?" said Krista. "What kind of car did he have?" Adolf smiled. Here on a scholarship, Krista did not grow up with cars and drivers like the rest of them.

"A Mercedes." Adolf shook his head. "Being with Hoffman was almost as weird as being here. He wouldn't tell me how he knew my name, or why he was helping the old man, or why he wanted me with him."

"Did you ask?" said Ilsa.

"You don't ask a senior professor anything," said Adolf. "You just listen."

"Well? Did he say anything?"

Adolf nodded. "That was the really great part. He lectured."

"Lectured?" said Franz. "To an underclassman and some old guy who's not even a Party Member?"

"And why would a lecture be great?" said Klaus. "It's vacation time!"

"But that's just it! Professor Hoffman was interesting! I hope I get him next year--he says he'll try to arrange it! He talked about all these different names people have had throughout history for the winter solstice holiday: Christmas, Yule, Saturnalia--some others I can't remember. He said every society

in history celebrated the winter solstice, and that what
we're doing today is just another derivation."

"I don't suppose he mentioned *Hanukkah*, did
he?" asked Krista.

"No, but I almost asked him!" The others in
the room laughed and whistled.

"That would have really been some ride, if you
had!" said Franz.

Adolf poured himself another glass of wine.
"Not to mention a more interesting vacation. Possibly
better than going home."

His friends, unaware of how serious he was,
laughed and joked until the wine was gone. Then they
made polite, yet heartfelt wishes for happy holidays,
and headed for their rooms.

Only Adolf and Ilsa remained.

"Let me help you clean up," Adolf said,
gathering up napkins and paper cups.

"Thank you," said Ilsa, folding the chairs and
returning them to the closet.

"Perhaps I could walk you home," said Adolf.
"It gets dark so early this time of year--"

"Thank you, no. I can manage. And there are
plenty of police and soldiers about."

"That's what worries me." He didn't want to
say anything more, as if that might give his fears
power. But this was one of the few times during the
year when alcohol flowed freely among the entire
population. The sight of an attractive, working class
woman walking alone at night might initially attract a
chivalrous escort from the soldiers. But once they saw
her bar code, they might just as easily use Ilsa for an
evening's entertainment, without fear of reprisal. It
was not something Adolf would have thought about a

few months ago. Now, it enraged him.

"I won't be leaving until much later, anyway,"
said Ilsa. "I'm going to let the candles burn out, as the
book says they must." She drew the chair from her
desk into a better-lit spot, sat down and picked up
some sewing.

Adolf looked at the *menorah*, and was once
again struck by the beauty of the nine white candles,
still an inch or so tall. "Those candles must have been
expensive."

Ilsa shrugged.

"If you would, please, allow me to buy the
candles next time. Or--anything else you need."

"You are most generous. But there is little I
need. My salary covers my room and board, with a
little to spare. I do not buy cosmetics or hair dye. I
have no family to support, nor any dowry to save for."
At that, the thread under her fingers snapped. Ilsa
looked startled, and then returned more carefully to
the stockings she was mending. "My only hobby is
reading, and, as long as I remain here, it costs
nothing."

"Strange," said Adolf. "The Party branded
you as '*missgeburt*'--useless-- and stuck you here, in
this dead-end 'career'. Yet, they put you in the right
place. By accident, of course."

Ilsa smiled. "I have often thought about that."

"Why--?" Adolf faltered. "Why does it matter
so much to you?" His gaze took in the whole
museum.

"I'm not always sure myself. Love of the
dead, perhaps?"

At Adolf's quizzical look, she continued. "I
am dead--or might as well be; so says the Party. The

Jews are dead. Yet what they left behind--the art, the poetry, their way of understanding the universe--is so powerful. So alive. Perhaps I still hope that, even without having children, I can leave something behind as well."

"You will probably leave more behind than I ever will," Adolf said.

"Why do you say that?"

He stood, and began to wander about the room. "This place, you, there is more life...more *meaning* here than in any part of my life. It may be that I will have a parcel of children, but what of it? Will they hate me, as I hate my father?

"I may rise in the government, but will I ever do anything that matters?

"But when I'm here, I feel *something.* Something I don't have, but that I want. It's like there's a hole inside me, aching to be filled, and I don't even know what it is I'm supposed to fill it with!" Adolf broke off, gazing at Ilsa, as if she could somehow fill that place inside him.

"I feel that way, too, Adolf," she said. "Just because I revere the dead, doesn't mean I don't yearn for life."

"But what do you hope to find here?"

"Understanding, perhaps."

"Of what? The Jews? Or of the world that destroyed them—and now tries to rob you of your life and humanity?" Adolf wondered what was happening to him. His words bordered on treason. His feelings, if he dared to speak them aloud to another Party member, could get him arrested.

"Of myself, I think." Ilsa shook her head. "I'm not sure that I can explain it. Only that, since I

first began reading their books, I started believing that
these people, if they were here today, would
understand me. The loneliness, the anger, the feelings
of the outcast—" Ilsa broke off, as if fearing she had
revealed too much. Then, making a decision, she
plunged ahead.

"If I can't be loved, or valued, or respected,
it's nice to at least be understood. Or maybe even,
eventually, part of the understanding of something
wonderful. Something that once belonged to the
human race, but is now gone." Ilsa shook her head.
"No. Not gone. Hidden. Waiting for the chosen few
to uncover it."

"Yes! And I want to be one of those chosen
few!" Adolf's voice shook with the heresy of his
words. On this night, with just the two of them,
Judaism didn't seem like a game.

The candles sputtered, then flickered out, one
by one, plunging the room into darkness. Adolf
thought about the rest of Ilsa's words. And perhaps
because of the darkness, or the magic of the longest
night of the year, he found the courage to say
something he hadn't even imagined thinking of yet.

"You're wrong if you think you can't be loved,
Ilsa. Or any of those other things the Party tells you
you're not worthy of."

And then, without giving himself time to think
and change his mind, Adolf found Ilsa's hands in the
darkness, pulled her close, and kissed her. Her eyes
widened, but she did not pull away. She returned the
kiss, chastely, Adolf thought, but did not care.

Later, as he walked Ilsa home, Adolf thought
about his family, awaiting him in Munich. He hoped
the faulty train system might for once work in his

favor, and strand him in Berlin for the entire season.

CHAPTER 5

"Isn't it wonderful how all the trains are running on time again!" The large man leaned across his seat toward Adolf, and winked. "You know, when I was a boy, you could set your watch by the trains; anywhere in the *Reich.*"

Adolf wanted to point out to his companion that this was the fourth time he had mentioned it, but it wouldn't do for the son of Helmut Goebbels to speak so to a soldier of his father's generation. So he kept a smile pasted on his face, and tried to look admiringly at the medals and ribbons that adorned the older man's decommissioned uniform.

"You know, everyone *says* they'd give their right arm for the Fatherland, but not many of us actually *do* it!" He laughed heartily and clapped Adolf on the back with his one remaining arm. "Lost it in '92, I did, in Africa. But we made those *swinehunds* pay! That region won't be livable for centuries now! And the Party never forgot me. Even like this, I get a place to live, and all the privileges of my old rank, everywhere I go. Yes, son, we truly live in the best place on earth."

Adolf sighed with relief as the old man settled into a silent reverie. He tried not to think about what it was like for the old soldier, with nothing to do all day but ride the trains or sit in the parks, looking for anyone who would listen to him. Sure, he could travel anywhere in the *Reich* for free, get front row seating at any game or rally, but when was the last time

someone invited him to dinner? It frightened Adolf
more than he cared to admit that it would only take
one accident, one injury that couldn't be repaired, to
render him physically imperfect, and turn him into a
pariah.

Like this pathetic old man.

Like Ilsa.

The train pulled into the Munich Station, just
as Adolf's seatmate was beginning the story of how he
ended up in Africa in '92. Adolf saluted him in the
name of the *Führer*, then hurried out of the car and
into the comforting warmth and cavernous space of
the station.

Adolf saw his mother at once. She wore a fur
coat with a matching hat that must have cost his father
at least a month's pay. The collar was turned back,
displaying the bronze star which signified the woman
wearing it had born at least three children. Despite
her best efforts, Elena Goebbels had never been able
to trade it in for one of silver, signifying six births.
Her bleached hair was long, but modestly braided and
pinned about her head as befitting a matron of the
Reich.

"Adolf!" He was swept into his mother's
embrace, as she breathed a kiss on each of his
cheeks. "Oh, you're so skinny! Don't they feed you
in that expensive university?"

Adolf murmured something in response,
smiling down at his two younger sisters, who stood
demurely behind their mother.

"Do you mean to tell me mother let you miss
school to come meet my train?" he teased.

Twelve year old Leisl giggled, but little Marta,
who had even less of a sense of humor than their

father said, "School is out for the holidays, Adolf.
Our last day was yesterday."

"I'll put your bags in the car, sir," said a voice
at Adolf's shoulder. He turned to see Otto, one of the
family's drivers, already loaded down with Adolf's
suitcases. Adolf never ceased being amazed that
someone so large could appear and disappear so
silently.

Leisl was dancing on her toes now, plying
Adolf with questions about college. Not even a stern
look from their mother could restore Leisl's properly
demure behavior.

"The whole family will be at dinner," Elena
said, once they were seated in the quiet and comfort of
the Daimler Benz.

Adolf leaned back into the cushioned seat and
sighed with relief. The whole family meant his
maternal uncle; maybe even his older sister and her
husband. The knots in Adolf's stomach began to
untie. Seeing his father was never as bad an ordeal in
large groups.

The Goebbels mansion seemed smaller than
Adolf remembered it. That, at least, he had been
warned to expect during his first trip home from
college. What surprised him was the way he kept
wondering if this beautiful home in which he had
grown up had once belonged to a Jewish family.

As he stood in the doorway of his mother's
immaculate parlor, Adolf imagined the room filled
with books; *Shabbat* candles and a *menorah* on the
shelf where the tea service now stood; a painting of
David at his harp in place of the Edicts for Party
Women on the wall.

While supper was being prepared, Adolf

watched snow falling in the darkening garden and
imagined a creative banker or doctor planting palms
and fig trees, trying to bring a piece of the ancient
homeland to life in this northern refuge. What was it
like for them, he wondered, always starting over in
strange, often hostile, new lands? How often were
they the most educated or talented of their neighbors?
And was that, perhaps, their only real crime?

"Adolf?" He was shaken from his reverie by
Leisl, who stood dressed for dinner in a full-skirted,
pink dress with lace across the bodice. Her honey
brown hair was braided and tied with pink ribbons.
"It's time for dinner."

Adolf bowed gallantly. "May I escort you,
most beauteous maiden?"

Leisl laughed at their old childhood game.
"Very well, noble warrior." Adolf took her arm.
Leisl matched his long strides easily. "Do you think
Father will let me start bleaching my hair in time for
New Years Eve?"

"Don't you think you're a little young, yet?"
said Adolf.

"Helga Schmidt bleaches hers, and she's the
same age I am!"

Adolf grimaced. "Helga Schmidt is so ugly,
her parents would let her try anything! Besides, I'll
bet she looks even worse as a blonde."

"Well, now that you mention it, yes," said
Leisl.

"In fact..." Adolf gazed at his sister's lustrous
brown hair, for the first time noticing how lovely it
was.

"What?"

"I'll bet if you let it stay its natural color,

you'll get noticed more. With everyone trying to look blond--and lots of them turning out like Helga Schmidt--people with dark hair like yours will really stand out. You could start a new trend in modeling."

Leisl laughed, and a moment later, a servant flung open the door to the formal dining room. Adolf found his family arrayed before him, all wearing their best. He gulped, hoping his school uniform would pass muster.

Apparently it did. Helmut Goebbels stood at the head of the table, and glanced at Adolf with the snarl of approval. His wife beamed proudly at their only son, as Adolf escorted Leisl to her chair. At a nod from Helmut, everyone sat down.

Servants brought in the first course, while the men began typical dinner table conversation.

"How is life at University?" Uncle Gustav asked as he slurped his soup.

"Very challenging," said Adolf. "I made high marks in everything--except mathematics."

"As usual," Helmut muttered.

"A family trait," said Gustav easily. "Nothing to worry about. It never held you back, eh, Helmut?"

Gazing at the two men, Adolf found it hard to believe they were family, even through marriage. Gustav was as jolly and easy going as Helmut was cold and rigid. And he never seemed to resent the fact that his sister's husband was the shining star of their combined family; the power broker who moved in the inner circles. Gustav seemed content to serve the Fatherland as a humble and, Adolf had to admit, mediocre, engineer.

"You will get a tutor, I suppose?" said Adolf's father.

Adolf ground his teeth. To say yes was admitting weakness; to say no would be to risk failing a class. Before he could answer, however, Gustav surprised Adolf by calling out, "It worked for you, Helmut. I'm sure Adolf will be no different."

"I was eight," Helmut said. "Not eighteen."

Adolf decided to steer the subject back to the one thing all four men at the table held in common: University. "I'm being considered for Professor Elias Hoffman's select sophomore class next year."

"Hoffman?" said Gustav with a bark of laughter. "Is he still teaching? That man was ancient when I was there!"

"Rumor has it that he's immortal," said Adolf.

"Watch your back in his class," said Helmut. "I always hated the bastard."

Adolf would have liked to hear more, but knew better than to question his father about anything.

"Do you get to drill with real weapons?" asked Kurt, Helmut's son by one of his mistresses. At thirteen, Kurt was Helmut's only such child to be raised in his father's household. The others remained with their mothers.

"Not until second year," said Adolf. "But I'll be fencing in a saber tournament in early spring. Perhaps you can come see me."

At this, all three of Adolf's sisters nodded eagerly and looked at Helmut with hopeful eyes, but their father remained impassive.

"If there's time while you're home, we can practice," said Edwin, Adolf's brother-in-law.

"I doubt I'm up to your level," said Adolf. "But I'd appreciate the chance to work out with a provost."

"Well, I'm not a provost," said Edwin. "Not yet."

Seated next to her husband, Adolf's sister Frieda looked small and pale. Adolf noticed that she kept her eyes down and said little all evening. Frieda and Edwin had married shortly before Adolf left for college, but five months later, Frieda was still not pregnant. Naturally, she was concerned.

Strange, Adolf thought, that while no woman could legally marry until tests had verified her fertility, their husbands could divorce them if they failed to get pregnant within a year. A woman in such a position could be shipped off to the Colonies, unless her family was willing to take her back. He hoped things would never reach that point for Frieda.

After dinner, Helmut went to his home office to make a phone call, while Adolf and Gustav retired to the smoking room. Adolf sat in one of the leather chairs, drumming his fingers on his father's favorite ashtray. It stood nearly three feet tall, decorated with figures of marching soldiers and huge inlaid swastikas. Gustav stood before the trophy wall, and gazed at the family's many accolades.

"I suppose it could have been worse," said Adolf.

"What do you mean?" asked Gustav.

"Dinner. At least my father didn't launch into one of his speeches. And my mother didn't try to set me up with another 'beautiful young girl from a fine family.'"

"Your father really is proud of you, Adolf," Gustav said. "Though I know he doesn't always show it."

Adolf sighed. "Thank you for trying, Uncle,

but we both know I don't measure up. Maybe he'll
have better luck with Kurt."

"Kurt is a fine boy, but you are your father's
heir. I don't know why Helmut is so hard on you. I
don't even know how he became so driven; so serious.
Helmut was really quite a clown when we were boys."

Adolf shook his head. He'd hear that before,
but still couldn't quite believe it. "I've always
assumed it came from being the only son of the Right
Hand of the First *Führer*," he said.

"That and growing up with five sisters," his
uncle added. "But that driven side was always there,
too. Helmut...he always had to achieve more; be
noticed more. And now, with times so uncertain...."

"Have times ever been anything else?" asked
Adolf.

Gustav stopped in front of a shelf that held a
commemorative coin from 1983, struck in honor of
the Fiftieth Anniversary of the *Reich*.

"Did you know that only one hundred of these
coins were ever made?" asked Gustav. "And I was
there, Adolf. In Berlin for the festivities. You don't
remember; you were just a baby. But that year, Adolf.
I look back on that year and say, 'that was when it was
perfect.' It was the year we reached the moon! We
held the world--the universe, even!--in our grasp.

"I stood beside your father when the Third
Führer presented this token to him and I thought, 'this
is what all of it was for: our parent's sacrifices, the
awful years of war, the terrible choices that had to be
made." Gustav stared at the coin in its red velvet case,
and seemed to forget Adolf was there. "I don't think
I've felt that way since that day."

Coming back to himself, Gustav added

quickly, "But those days will come again! Greater days, even! It will be young men like you, Adolf, who will do it: quell these silly rebellions; get the economy back on track. Who knows, maybe even get our space program going again."

"I know how much you loved working there, Uncle. The Department of Space Conquest was lucky to have so dedicated an engineer."

"Too bad my wife didn't agree. Too many nights alone while I worked, I suppose." Gustav sighed.

Adolf suppressed a twinge of discomfort. While Gustav had handled the ugly divorce well, no one in the *Reich* spoke of women who deceived their husbands. It had been Gustav's right to kill her and her lover, although he had not, something Adolf had always admired about his uncle, while Helmut had only added it to his long list of weaknesses.

It was, perhaps, easier for Aryan women, who had no expectations of fidelity from husbands whose duty it was to father as many children as possible. Adolf tried to imagine his father's reaction if Elena were to have an affair. Then nearly laughed when he realized that Helmut would never believe such a thing were possible.

Gustav continued talking with no sign of distress. "But no matter. It is my privilege to serve the Fatherland. In any capacity."

Even inspecting waste disposal units? Adolf wondered.

The door opened and Adolf's father marched in, followed by Elena. Automatically, Adolf jumped from his chair and stood at attention.

"Good news," said Helmut. "I have secured

for our family an invitation to attend the Winter Ball in Vienna this year."

Adolf made appropriately impressed murmurs. His mother dimpled with pride. "Helmut?" she said. "You didn't forget that other matter, did you?"

"Of course not." Wilhelm turned to Adolf. "Also in attendance with be the Mauser family, lately of Amsterdam. Bruno Mauser has just been appointed senior advisor to the Department of Commerce and shows every sign of having a brilliant future. He also has a daughter, in her last year of secondary school. I have arranged for you to be her escort to the ball--and her guide for the season. See that she enjoys herself."

Adolf was careful not to meet Uncle Gustav's eye. It would not do for them to both break up laughing in front of Helmut.

The rest of the season proceeded quietly. Gretchen Mauser turned out to be a lovely girl, with pale golden hair and china blue eyes that were so huge Adolf wondered if she were taking belladonna. She was a skilled dance partner, never once stepping on Adolf's feet, even as she avoided being stepped on by him. She laughed at his jokes, asked him about himself, and listened with a look of practiced intensity.

She was, in short, the perfect match for a future Aryan power broker like himself.

And, Adolf admitted to himself, if things had not changed, he might well have rated Gretchen as the top choice of all his mother's selections.

But things had changed. Or, more accurately, Adolf had.

When they sat in his family's box at Wagner's

Ring Cycle, Adolf found himself wondering what Ilsa would have thought of it; of all the meaning she would draw; the symbols she would catch. Gretchen's only comment was, "A great triumph of German culture!"

At a movie starring Heinz Heinie, a famous comedian, Adolf put his arm around Gretchen's slender shoulders. She snuggled easily into his embrace. But her constant giggling annoyed him. He thought of Ilsa, and how her scathing review of the film would be more entertaining than either the movie, or the girl who sat next to him.

One night, after a party at the Mengele mansion, Adolf found himself unable to sleep. He went to the kitchen for a glass of milk, smiling at the childhood memories this simple act stirred up. As he starred out the window at the searchlights and the marching soldiers, he heard the creak of floorboards behind him. It was yet another scene from his past: Leisl had joined him in the kitchen.

"Still having trouble sleeping?" he asked.

Leisl poured milk for herself, and sat opposite Adolf at the table. "Mother took me to another doctor a few months ago. He gave me more pills."

"I take it they don't work?"

"Oh, they make me sleep, okay, but they give me bad dreams. I quit taking them. Don't tell mother, okay?"

"Okay."

"So what are you doing up, Adolf?"

Adolf sighed. "Gretchen Mauser. Every time I start to fall asleep, I hear her stupid giggling. It gets under my skin."

"Adolf, I don't think that's how it's supposed to work," said his little sister. "I think *you're* supposed to get under *her* skin. Or at least between certain folds of it."

"Leisl!" Adolf looked around, then lowered his voice. "When did you start talking dirty?" He didn't know whether to be amused or outraged.

"I'm not a little kid anymore, you know! And I know—certain things." Even in the shadows, Adolf could see Leisl blush, as she walked the line between showing off her adult knowledge, and fear of where it might take her. Steering the conversation back to safer territory, she said, "So what's wrong with Gretchen? She seems nice."

"She is. Nice. Pretty. But so stupid! And so…empty! And don't say it's my job to fill her up, or I'll wash your mouth out with soap, young lady!"

Leisl laughed. "Don't worry, I won't. But you can't be too surprised she's stupid. After all, Mother picked her out."

"True." Adolf starred moodily into his empty glass.

"Anyway, I hope you won't be in too much of a hurry to get married. After you, it'll be my turn."

Adolf laughed. "There's six years between us Leisl; you've got lots of time."

"Maybe not." Leisl's playful mood had vanished. She was awake because she was worried about something, Adolf realized. Leisl worried a lot, despite the popular myths about the carefree years of childhood that all Aryan children enjoyed.

"What's going on?" asked Adolf.

"I overheard Father on the phone a few days ago. Nothing is certain yet, but he's trying for an alliance with the Heydrich family. He's considering marrying me to their oldest son."

"Josef?" Adolf asked in horror. Leisl nodded. "That's insane! He despises that entire family! Calls them upstarts—"

"You know how fast things like that can change," said Leisl. "Some guy; one of the Bormanns, who Father sponsored, was arrested just before you came home."

Adolf whistled. That was serious. A typical enough occurrence in the Inner Circles, but for someone like Helmut…of course he would be scrambling to control the damage and bolster his position in any way possible.

The Heydrich family was the *Führer's* new golden boy; Josef their shining star. In the shifting sands of Third *Reich* politics, Helmut was behaving normally.

But…Leisl? Married to Josef?

"Father can't marry you to anyone until you're sixteen," Adolf said. "A lot can change between now and then. And girls aren't being married off that young anymore. At least two years of Domestic Engineering is becoming a requirement in our circles. An ambitious little snot like Josef won't want to wait that long to be married."

"He'll do whatever his father tells him to," Leisl said glumly.

It was a truth Adolf could not refute. And he was painfully aware that it applied to himself as well. For all that he might be the daring rebel at school, Adolf was about as likely to defy Helmut as to sprout wings. Though he might wish it with all his might, the power to save Leisl from a horrendous marriage, or to court the only woman he was interested in was beyond him.

"Hey, Adolf?" He looked up to see Leisl peering at him intensely. "You're in love, aren't you? Someone you met at school?"

"Well—" As Adolf stammered, Leisl slapped her thigh through her pink nightgown. "I knew it!"

"Shh! Look, I'm not sure I'd call it love, but there's this girl—"

"What's she like? Tell me all about her!"

Then Adolf imagined himself bringing Ilsa—beautiful, blonde, intelligent Ilsa—home to meet his family. Oh, yes, they would love her—until they saw the bar code on her wrist. After that—it didn't bear thinking about.

"She's not someone I could bring home," he said. Leisl's eyes filled with sympathy. No more explanation was needed.

"I'm homesick," he said. "I want to go back to school."

"Home sick for school? Isn't that kind of a…what's it called? Oxymoric?"

"An oxymoron," said Adolf. "Maybe. Or maybe 'homesick' really means something else."

"Like being sick of home?"

"Yeah."

"I know just what you mean," said Leisl.

CHAPTER 6

The New Year arrived at last, and with it, the new semester. Although he kissed his sisters farewell with genuine regret, Adolf felt only relief when the train carried him away from Munich.

Back at school, the flurry of new classes, deadlines, and lectures washed away all memory of Gretchen Mauser, formal dinners and his father's endless demands. The Friday after his return to Berlin was Adolf's first opportunity to visit the *Judenmuseum*. The familiar room, crowded with books, relics and friends, enveloped him like a warm blanket.

"...So there I was," Klaus was saying, "The wedding about to start, my cousin the groom, looking for his best man--me--and I'm locked in the tool shed. I finally get us out, and she says, "Best man, hah! You weren't even the best man in that shed!""

Karl, Franz, Heidi, and Peter all exploded with laughter. Adolf smiled as he joined them. "I guess I don't have to ask how *your* holidays were, Klaus," he said.

"I don't believe you for a minute," Heidi said. "But you tell a great story."

Klaus gave Heidi an extravagant bow and grinned. "I can arrange a private performance for you, anytime you like."

Ilsa appeared from the shadows carrying a stack of books. Krista was at her heels, taking excitedly. "I wish I could have brought it with me," the dark haired girl was saying. "But it belongs to my grandfather, and bringing it here probably wouldn't have been safe. Hi, everybody."

"So what's this big discovery you've been telling Ilsa about?" Heidi asked.

Franz and Peter began setting up folding chairs. Krista, too excited to sit, spoke quickly. "At my grandparents house, over the holidays, I found this book. In the back, it has the names of everyone in my family, going all the way back to my great-great-great grandparents, in the 1800s! But what's really weird is that the stories in the beginning of the book are almost exactly the same as the stories we've been reading in the Jew book--I mean *Torah*," Krista corrected herself proudly.

"Written in German?" asked Frederick.

Krista made a face. "Of course it's in German! Do you think my grandparents could read anything else? Anyway, it's got the same people: Adam and Eve, Jacob and Joseph, that stuff in Egypt--"

"What was it called?" asked Adolf.

"*Die Bibel*," said Krista.

Franz nodded impatiently. "Yes, yes, that's the old name for the Lutheran Prayer Book. You can find one in any--"

"I know what a Lutheran Prayer Book looks like! But this book was at least five times as long, and some of the words were just like *Torah*."

Ilsa stood up from behind her desk, holding out a thick, dusty book. "Was this what you saw, Krista?"

Krista opened the black volume, whose crumbling gold letters proclaimed with words "*Die Bibel*" on the cover. After a moment, Krista nodded.

"Look here," she said passing the book to Franz.

When Adolf's turn came, he let out a grunt of surprise. He was not scanning the first pages, but rather the tops of all the pages. "Genesis, Exodus, Leviticus...what are these doing in a German Christian bible?"

"And what is an outdated Christian bible doing in a *Judenmuseum?*" asked Franz.

"I can answer your question first, Franz," said Ilsa. "Though I think it is connected to Adolf's. Several of these books were mixed in with the Jewish relics that came here in the last few years. I'm not sure of their origins. Others came more recently, from the Palestinian digs."

Karl, who had just picked up the book, suddenly dropped it. "*Sheisse!* How do you know it's not hot?"

"Relax," said Ilsa. "I keep a Geiger counter in the back. Only safe items remain here."

"What happens to the ones that aren't safe?" asked Heidi.

Ilsa smiled a small, and, Adolf thought, rather frightening smile. "As I was saying, this book, and a few others like it, came here years after the new translations of the bible came into use. My guess is that when books like these are found, they make their way to some kind of depository where some bored clerk--my counterpart in another city, I suppose--flips through them. They check their contents against lists of censored material, or something particular that the Party is looking for--in this case, Jewish relics. Since the verses are similar to *Torah*, they are assumed to be related. The clerk just sends them to the Department of History, who sends them here."

Adolf nodded. "Of course. Even those clerks who are practicing Christians would never have seen a bible this old." He picked up the book that Karl had dropped. "And no Aryan alive today would imagine any connection between the teachings of a dead, inferior race, and a faith that was once the cornerstone of civilized Europe."

"But what *is* the connection?" asked Krista.

"I'm not altogether sure, yet," said Ilsa. "But look here." She opened a lower drawer in her desk, and took out a thin volume entitled Lutheran Prayer Book.

"Oh, are you a Lutheran, Ilsa?" asked Heidi.

"No. This was here when I took the job. The current translation has two hundred pages." Adolf opened the earlier version. It had nearly one thousand.

A murmur went through the room.

"This one appears to be fairly typical," said Ilsa. "Most of the others are in different languages, and of course, size of type varies. But from what I've read and translated so far, huge sections have been removed or rewritten."

"Nothing new about that," said Karl. "Books are always being 'corrected' these days."

But Adolf could see where Ilsa was going. "Not every book needs corrections for having identical script with Jewish writing,"

"Their most holy writing," added Franz.

"What would the Party do," Adolf continued, "if it were revealed that a religion practiced by nearly a quarter of the world--with strong German roots-- shared its beginnings with Judaism?"

Tension was suddenly palpable in the room as

the students thought about Adolf's question.

Then Krista said with a grin, "I don't know, but it sounds like a great new project! Want some help with it, Ilsa?"

"Sign me up, too!" said Adolf. After the initial shock, this new discovery was just one more daring defiance of their parents world; an attack on their stodgy sacred cows. Still, Adolf could see from several expressions, Karl in particular, that for some of his friends, this could be crossing a line.

It didn't matter, Adolf realized suddenly. He had crossed that line long ago.

"How about Monday afternoons?" he asked Ilsa and Krista, who both nodded.

The process of uncovering the changes in the Christian text proceeded slowly, but Adolf had no complaints. It kept him in close contact with two of his favorite people, and brought much of what he had learned of Judaism into a whole new light. It also left him in awe of the intellectual abilities of the women he worked with.

Like most Aryan men, Adolf believed that even the brightest women were inferior to their male counterparts. Yet, as he listened to Krista translate Greek, Latin and English texts into German, or watched Ilsa study a two thousand page tome, and suddenly zero in on three paragraphs that were missing from a similar book she had read the week before, more than just his beliefs were shaken.

"Oh, come now," teased Krista, as they sat in the *Judenmuseum* one icy February evening. "You came here to question everything you believed in! Don't let male pride get in the way of finding the truth. We thought you were different."

"I thought so too," said Adolf. "I just didn't realize that exploring new ideas would mean discovering that every girl I associate with is smarter than I am!"

"Not every girl," said Ilsa. "I'd say you and Heidi are about equal in I.Q. points."

"Thanks a lot," said Adolf. He grinned, but inside, he didn't feel very humorous. All his father's doubts--quiet for so long--were starting to stir. *I should be working harder on my studies, not wasting my time here*, he thought.

At that moment the door flew open, bringing the cold fury of a rainstorm into the room. Franz and Karl, both soaking wet, hurried inside. "You two had better get back to campus," Karl said.

"What's up?" asked Krista.

"Don't know," said Franz. "But the proctors are nervous, and the word is there's going be a bed check at 2100 hours."

Adolf checked his watch. "We should make it if we hurry." He stood, and helped Krista to her feet. "Any idea what they're looking for?"

"No, but we've all been told to report with our text books to the practice field tomorrow morning," said Franz.

"Our textbooks?" said Adolf. "All of them? Outside in the freezing cold? What for?"

Karl shrugged. "I suppose another purge."

For all of Adolf's nervousness the night before, the morning went quickly and smoothly. All five thousand University students assembled in the field, and were directed by proctors to place their textbooks in various piles, according to subject. When this was completed, the piles were bulldozed into one. The headmaster of the University, helped by two officials from the Department of Education poured kerosene over the huge mound, and then set it alight.

Adolf watched in disbelief as the accumulated knowledge of four years of University study blackened, turned to ash and blew away. As he marched with the others to the library, not really sure what for, a single leaf from an unknown book drifted by on the wind. Adolf could not take his eyes off the singed edges; at the handful of words, still visible in the middle.

In front of the library, the students lined up and proctors gave then new books for each subject.

Then they all went to lunch.

"You mean this has happened before?" Adolf asked over an untouched bowl of cabbage soup. The smell of burning paper still filled his nostrils.

Karl nodded. "Two years ago, in my sophomore year. It was the same thing: no explanation, no discussion--"

"And no questions if you're smart," said Frederick, setting his tray down and joining them.

"Of course," said Adolf. "But...it just doesn't make any...how could they have had these new books ready--"

"If you ask me," said Franz, "I'd say the printers didn't have much time to throw them together. They're not very well made. Look at this Science book. The page setting is canted. And the illustrations--"

"What illustrations?" said Frederick, pointing at the black and white sketches, which replaced the colored photographs taken with electron microscopes in the old book.

"I call it an improvement," said Klaus. "This History text is only half the length of the old one."

"They didn't even give us a book for Mathematics," said Adolf.

"Like I said," said Klaus. "An improvement."

"For us it's an improvement," said Karl. "But what does Adolf care? With his photographic memory, books are his friends!" Karl sounded unusually bitter, Adolf thought. But then again, with his poor grades, Karl was in serious danger of not graduating.

He shook his head, still at a loss. "All those books--"

"Quiet," whispered Franz, as two assistant professors walked by.

"We should suspend meetings for a while," said Franz. "And avoid certain...places. Until things settle down."

Everyone nodded reluctantly.

Things didn't settle down.

Classes were held as if nothing was amiss, yet students disappeared at an alarming rate. Always, it was the same: don't ask questions; don't appear overly concerned; and if anyone asks, say you hardly knew him. Rumors of conspiracies and treason flew far and wide, but nothing official arrived over the daily broadcasts; no assembly was held to inform or reassure the students. Tension was heavy in the air. Adolf wondered how long it would be before one of the museum crowd disappeared, and what that would mean for the rest of them.

A letter from home brought Adolf his first bit of happy news since the purge: Frieda was pregnant. Adolf felt almost smug as he walked off campus to a nearby toy store, his mother's letter tucked neatly into his breast pocket along with his identification papers. If he were questioned, he needed only to show the letter, and the soldiers would have no choice but to respond with congratulations and suggestions for a gift: to do otherwise would be unthinkable for any true Aryan man.

As it turned out, none of the half dozen soldiers patrolling the street in front of the shop stopped him, and only cameras surveyed the activity within. *Maybe things were settling down*, thought Adolf.

He bought a handmade blanket and a cuddly stuffed wolf. Leaving the shop, Adolf briefly considered stopping at the *Judenmuseum* and seeing how Ilsa was doing. His thoughts were interrupted by screams from a nearby alley. Guards hurried over, but after a few moments, continued on their way. One appeared to be telling a joke, for a few steps later, the whole group burst out laughing.

The screams intensified, followed by the meaty thud of flesh striking flesh, then broken sobs and harsh laughter. Against his better judgment, Adolf ran into the alley.

A young woman lay on her back on the filthy pavement. A man was on top of her, trying to pry her legs apart. Five other men surrounded the pair, cheering on their friend, for despite her battered face, the woman was putting up an impressive fight.

The red bar code on her arm was all the explanation Adolf needed for why the soldiers had passed by.

Red was also the color that bathed everything in Adolf's vision as he leapt at the rapist. He was only peripherally aware that the other young men present were known to him: all were fellow University students.

His opponent went over with a surprised grunt, and then whirled to face Adolf. The others all stared, their laughter cut off in unison. Still, two of them recovered fast enough to grab the woman and prevent her escape.

Then it was Adolf's turn for surprise when he saw his opponent was Josef Heydrich.

"Just what the hell to you think you're doing?" Heydrich demanded.

"I was about to ask you the same thing," said Adolf.

"All *missgeburt* are under a curfew these days," said Heydrich. "We caught this bitch out on the street with no good explanation. Her papers say she works for a jeweler across town."

"I was sent to deliver a watch," cried the young woman. She was in her mid twenties, heavy boned and dark haired. Not the type to catch most men's eyes, but her vulnerability made her attractive enough. To one type of man, at least. "I was on my way back to work. Ask my employer! Ask *Herr* Schindler—"

"Shut up," said Heydrich, hitting her in the face again. He turned to Adolf. "We're just doing our part to keep order in difficult times. Want a turn, Adolf? Upper classmen first, of course. Being a freshman, you'll have to go last."

"It's nice to know everything I've heard about

your charm with women is true," Adolf said, smiling over shut teeth. "Tell me, Josef? Is this how you plan to treat my sister as well? That is, if my father has failed to regain his sanity, and could still consider marrying her to the bastard whelp of a *swinehund*!"

All around Adolf there was total and complete silence. Even the sobbing woman caught her breath and held it.

Heydrich released her and stood to face Adolf. "I would take that as an attack upon my honor, but you so defiled your own sister by comparing her to this *missgeburt*, that instead I challenge you on behalf of my bride to be!" He slapped Adolf twice across the face in the age-old challenge.

"I will fight you only for your own honor—if you can still claim to have any!" said Adolf. "As for Leisl, you may have her over my dead body— whatever my father or yours may say on the matter!"

Heydrich grinned. "At dawn then." At a signal from their leader, the other men fell in step behind him, and marched away. Thus, Adolf learned that preparation for a campus duel was more important than rape.

He turned to offer the *missgeburt* woman what assistance he could, but only caught a glimpse of her disappearing form as she fled down the alley.

"Oh, Adolf, how did you get yourself into this?" asked Heidi.

"I've been asking myself that all night," said Adolf.

They were in the practice field behind the gymnasium. Krista was lacing up Adolf's boots, while Franz waited to take the shirt that Adolf was

now unbuttoning. The chill air of the late February
morning raised goose flesh on his naked arms and
chest.

"There's two other duels this morning," said
Karl, arriving late. He rubbed his hands together,
though whether from cold or anticipation, Adolf didn't
know.

Krista nodded. "As stressed as everyone is,
fights are breaking out everywhere. People are using
duels to release the tension. The headmaster is
actually promoting it, since it keeps them out of worse
trouble."

"Which is a good thing for you, Adolf," said
Franz. "In the current climate, you don't want it
generally known that this whole thing started with you
defending the honor of a *missgeburt*."

"It's more than that," said Frederic. "Josef
Heydrich is a public nuisance. I wish this duel was to
the death!"

Adolf gagged on a sip from the water bottle
Heidi gave him. "I assume that means you have great
faith in my skill?" he asked Frederic.

"Of course," said Frederic, looking puzzled.

Adolf had to smile. Here he was, about to
make a fool of himself by dueling the best fencer on
campus, yet he could only stare in wonder at how
much his life had changed in just five short months.
Last fall, no one could have penetrated his isolation
enough for even an argument.

Now he was surrounded by friends who had
been willing to give up sleep and risk the scorn of the
rest of the student body—all to stand with Adolf.
When he had told them of the duel, everyone present
had offered to be his second—including Heidi and

Krista. In the end, Adolf had chosen Franz, simply because Franz had done it before. But he was touched beyond words. The support of his friends more than made up for the humiliating defeat he was about to suffer.

But nothing could block from his mind the sight of that poor woman in the alley, nor stop the thought that had been haunting him ever since: *that could have been Ilsa.*

"*Herr* Heydrich has arrived," Franz said in the formal voice of a second. "We may proceed."

Josef, surrounded by his friends (all male, Adolf noticed) stopped midway across the field. One of them, a lanky, good looking senior, detached himself from the group, and walked to the designated area. Franz went to meet him.

Adolf moved to follow, but Karl stopped him. "Wait until Franz gives you the signal. The seconds have to observe certain protocols."

"I just want to get it over with," sighed Adolf. The duel would end with first blood. Since every Aryan man belonged to the *Führer*, no duel to the death could be fought without his permission. To do so was a grave offense, since it meant depriving the *Führer* of a valuable asset. Of course, accidents still happened.

"Okay, that's it," said Krista, nudging Adolf. He had failed to notice Franz gesturing to him.

As Adolf started across the field, his friends fell in step behind him—except for Klaus, who was asleep on the bench. Karl and Frederic went back, pulled him upright and dragged him along.

"Why do they have to start these things so early?" Klaus muttered.

"Because we're not allowed to miss class for them," said Karl.

Adolf took his place across from Heydrich. Both men wore only black pants and boots. Legal target area consisted of all exposed flesh. For all that their dress was identical, Heydrich's tanned, muscular form seemed to tower over Adolf. His perfectly cropped blond hair shone like gold, despite the fact that the sun wasn't yet up.

Adolf raised the special student's dueling sabre and saluted his opponent. A fraction of a second later, Josef did the same. They dropped into en garde and took each other's measure. Josef lunged, almost lazily. Adolf parried easily. Too easily. Heydrich was playing with him.

After a few more exchanges, which served only to tire Adolf, Heydrich lunged, panther quick. Adolf retreated, and barely got the parry in time.

Heydrich recovered from his lunge, slowly. Without thinking, Adolf attempted a riposte to the head. Too late, Adolf saw Heydrich spring his second intention attack. At the last second, Heydrich sped up his lunge recovery and retreated just out of Adolf's reach. Adolf instinctively leaned forward in a vain attempt to connect with Heydrich's body. Off balance, Adolf could only swear as Heydrich finished him off, with a moulinet as the parry, and the final insulting move as the moulinet finished with the blade cutting Adolf's back.

The game was over, Adolf realized. Heydrich's plan had been to amuse the crowd, then cut Adolf on the back—a legal target, but not a normal place for a dueling scar: it would look as if Adolf had been running away.

Adolf, to his and everyone else's surprise, hadn't stopped moving. He fell back to the classic en garde, stopping his blade's motion a centimeter from Heydrich's throat. Had Adolf kept moving, his blade, dulled as it was, would have slashed the carotid artery, killing his opponent. Heydrich's second screamed "Halt!" trying to prevent Adolf from hitting Heydrich, but Adolf had already stopped moving.

Both men leaned over, panting heavily. Franz hurried to bandage Adolf's back, which stung fiercely, but the cut was not dangerous.

Heydrich raised his arms to the ragged cheering of the small crowd. The sun had risen without Adolf being aware of it. They had all missed breakfast, and would have to hurry to get to morning classes on time.

"You could have killed me," Heydrich whispered, before his friends pulled him away.

"That wasn't allowed in this contest," said Adolf.

Heydrich laughed harshly. "What you mean is that you didn't have the stomach for it! And you never will. Face it, Adolf, you'll never be one of us; the Master Race has no use for cowards."

Josef was carried from the field on the backs of his minions, while Adolf's friends surrounded him.

"That was amazing!" said Krista.

"You should have killed him when you had the chance," said Karl.

"Then what would have happened to Adolf?" demanded Frederic. "Scum like Heydrich isn't worth a black mark on his record." He turned to Adolf. "For what it's worth, I'd rather loose like you than win like him."

"Same here," said Franz.

"I've heard that watching a duel causes sexual arousal in the spectators." Klaus draped one arm each over Krista and Heidi. "Care to comment?"

Adolf took time for a shower and arrived late to class, but it didn't matter: he didn't hear anything his teachers said all day.

And that afternoon, despite the risk, he went to the *Judenmuseum*.

It looked the same as ever, despite the political turbulence that churned the world around it. The entire district seemed even more run down than it had when Adolf first saw it, or perhaps it was just the dark gray clouds of February.

Few soldiers patrolled this nearly deserted part of town, and Adolf was allowed the luxury of his own thoughts as he made his way down the crumbling stairs to the tiny building.

Ilsa was mending socks at her desk when he stepped inside. She jumped at the sound of the door, and then relaxed when she saw who it was. "*Shabbat Shalom*, Adolf, though it's not quite sunset."

That it was Friday took Adolf by surprise. He'd been away from the rituals of this room for too long. "Are you all right?" he asked Ilsa, feeling a bit foolish, since she obviously was.

"Shouldn't I be asking you that? You're the one who fought a duel today."

"How did you know that?"

"Word gets around, even here. It was wrong of me, since it exposes you to danger, but I was hoping you'd come by. I haven't seen many friendly faces since the latest assassination attempt, or whatever's happened to get everyone so riled up."

Adolf pulled up his shirt and turned to show Ilsa the bandage. "My first dueling scar. My last as well, I hope."

"You must tell me all about it, so I can tell Clotilde," said Ilsa. "I know she hopes she can thank you in person, someday."

"Clotilde? Oh, the girl in the alley. Strange, I never even knew her name."

"Yet you fought a duel for her." In the dim light, Adolf could just make out Ilsa's ironic smile.

"It was more than that."

"I know."

"How is she?"

"Far better than she'd be without your intervention, Adolf. It's always hard for the lower classes, but when fear walks, it's much worse."

"I almost killed a man today, Ilsa. Maybe I should have."

Ilsa shook her head. "That wasn't why you met him on the field today. Why let him bring you down to his level?"

Adolf relaxed a little. He'd been hoping she would say something like that.

"Shall we discuss what the Jews had to say on the subject? As long as you're here?"

"I'd love to," said Adolf. "But you know how we always lose track of time, once we get going. Maybe I could borrow some books. I really just wanted to see you—and know that you're all right." Ilsa smiled reassuringly, but Adolf thought of Clotilde, and heard again the voice in his head: *it could have been Ilsa.*

She went to her desk and picked up a stack of books by the knot of the twine that held them together. "Here's a portion of what the Jews had to say about fighting. Since you asked."

Adolf glanced sharply at Ilsa, even as he eagerly took the books. How did she always know what he was going to do or think or need before he did?

"Oh, and there's one more." She began hunting around her desk, finally locating an open book buried beneath her mending. "Since *Hanukkah* was such a success, I thought you might like to try another Jewish holiday. There's one coming up that looks really great. It's called Purim. See what you think."

Adolf sighed. "A celebration sounds like just what we need. The headmaster's been encouraging parties almost as much as duels: anything to ease tensions and boost morale. We could probably hold it in the Student Activity Center without anyone even noticing." He looked down at the book Ilsa had given him, not willing to admit how hungry he was for ritual; for anything that would separate him from Josef Heydrich—and from Helmut Goebbels.

"It won't be the kind of party the Party who runs the place has in mind for the center," Ilsa said with a grin. "But fortunately, they won't be there."

"We hope," said Adolf. "I just wish you could be there."

"I'll be there in spirit," said Ilsa. "But to be honest, it's not really my kind of celebration."

His curiosity piqued, Adolf hurried back to his dorm to read the book, and get the preparations underway.

Two weeks later, Adolf stood in the doorway of the private party room in the Student Activity Center and surveyed the chaos inside.

Franz staggered over and handed him a noisemaker and a cup of something fermented. "*Chag Purim Sameach!*" he shouted over the din.

Heidi, too drunk to stand, reached up and pulled Adolf onto the sofa on which she was sprawled. "This was a great idea, Adolf!" she said, planting a reeking kiss on his mouth.

Adolf disentangled himself as gently as possible and stood up again. "Thanks," he said. "But this wasn't quite what I had in mind."

"Come on," said Franz. "Join in. Call it a spiritual duty."

"But everyone here is shit faced!" said Adolf.

"Of course we are," Klaus said, waving a tattered book. "Because we're good little Party members who always follow orders. And it says right here that we're supposed to drink until we can't tell if we're cursing Haman and blessing Mordecai--or doing it the other round away."

Adolf took the book from Klaus. "This is your Biology textbook."

"It is? I must need more to drink." Klaus wandered back to the punchbowl, which sat between two plates of homely little triangular pastries.

Adolf sighed. "I suppose a choral reading from the Book of Esther is pretty much out of the question?"

Frederick blew a noisemaker in Adolf's face.

"Get with the program! It's Purim! We're commanded to rejoice! Stop being such a wet blanket, Adolf!"

At that moment, Heidi pulled Frederick onto the sofa with her. He made no effort to disentangle himself.

Franz, looking on, shook his head. "Really Adolf, you're far too serious for such a young man. Remind me to do something about it when I'm sober."

"I just hope everybody here sobers up before they venture outside!" he shouted at no one in particular. "At least enough to refrain from inviting the *Gestapo* to join us!"

Krista came by with a fifth of gin in each hand. "Hey, Karl, where do you want this? In the punch?"

Karl, wearing a ridiculous hat and plastic glasses with a rubber nose attached, took the liquor from Krista. "No. The punch is full of schnapps. This is for a game. Okay, everybody, this is what we're going to do! Each player takes a shot of gin, and then says a sentence in Hebrew. If you flub it, you have to try again."

"And also," said Klaus, using the wall to remain upright, "when you're finished, turn over your shot glass. Anything drips out, you gotta do it over again."

Adolf went to the opposite side of the room, righted a toppled chair and sat down. He gazed at the cheap paper decorations on the walls, then down at the two hundred year old book in his hands. He turned the pages, past engraved illustrations of the ancient Persian capital; of the heroic Jewish queen as she defeated a plot against her people; of the villain Haman on the gallows.

Then he looked at his drunken friends. Karl left the game quite suddenly and ran to the adjoining bathroom to throw up. A few people made jokes about men who couldn't hold their liquor, and the game continued.

Adolf wanted to leave. He thought about going to the *Judenmuseum*, but knew he shouldn't push his luck—or hers—again so soon. So he sat and stared, growing more and more morose, and confused as to why.

"Is this all it is?" Adolf asked aloud. "Everything we've been doing for the past six months? The faith that millions of people thought was worth dying for? It's just a dumb new excuse to get drunk?"

"I didn't know you had started taking it so seriously."

Startled, Adolf looked up. Krista, looking a bit green, stood before him—though none too steadily.

Adolf stood and hurried to get her a chair. She sat down carefully.

"Why aren't you in the game?" Adolf asked.

"I started feeling sick. I've never been much of a drinker, and I decided I didn't want to end up like Karl, over there. Or like Heidi, for that matter."

"Sorry," said Adolf, "but I'm not good company right now."

"So I see. So when did you start taking this stuff seriously?"

"Good question. I'm not sure myself."

"If it makes you feel any better, it's sort of been growing on me, too. But if you don't mind, can I give you a word of advice?"

"Sure."

"Don't make it public. This religion; this Judaism…it's taking on a life of its own. To be safe, it's best if it just stays a game; officially anyway."

Adolf looked into Krista's earnest face, and felt his spirits lift a little. "Thank you," he said. "That's good advice. And you're a good friend."

Krista actually blushed, bringing a little color back to her face. "I think I'll go now," she said.

"Would you mind sticking around for awhile? I'm going to read from the Book of Esther, and I could use an audience."

Krista looked around. A fight had broken out between Karl and Frederic. Franz and Klaus were breaking it up. "You're going to read it here? Now? The whole thing?"

"It isn't very long. And you can read half if you like."

"Thanks, but I'll just listen."

Adolf opened the book and began to read. "'Now it came to pass in the days of Ahasuerus who reigned from India even unto Ethiopia over a hundred and seven and twenty provinces...'"

They paused once early on for a debate over the circumstances that made Esther the Jewish queen of the ancient Persian empire.

"Let me get this straight," Krista said, stopping Adolf in the middle of the second chapter. "This king orders his wife to appear naked before his drunken party guests. She refuses, so he has her killed. Then he has a beauty pageant that Esther happens to win, so he makes her the new queen—and the Jews think this is something to brag about?"

"It gets better," Adolf said carefully, keeping an eye on Krista's hands. They weren't balled into fists yet, which was a good sign.

"I'm sure it does. I'd just like to make a case that the real hero of this story is Queen Vashti! She had the courage to stand up to that pig of husband—even if he was king! What does Esther do? Use sex to get her way?"

"No, she does more than that," Adolf said, uncomfortably aware that beyond the use of her body and the influence of her cousin Mordecai, Esther wasn't really in the book that much.

He went on reading, relating the story of the heroic Mordecai, who saved the king's life, the jealous Haman who sought to destroy, not just Mordecai, but all his people, and how Haman used the king's seal to send out an order to wipe out all the Jews of the empire on a given day. How Esther denounced Haman to the king, and how Mordecai convinced King Ahasuerus to send out a second decree, this time to the Jews of the empire, telling them to arm themselves and stand against those who would slay them.

Adolf reached the end of the saga, which described various great deeds of King Ahasuerus—with Mordecai as his right hand man. "'For Mordecai the Jew was next unto King Ahasuerus, and great among the Jews, and accepted of the multitude of his brethren, seeking the wealth of his people, and speaking peace to all his seed.'"

Adolf looked up and was startled to see that his audience had grown. Though not all were fully conscious, and few were comprehending very much, all attending party- goers were gathered in chairs or on the floor in front of Adolf.

"So that's what this party is all about?" said Heidi. "We're supposed to dress up and get drunk—because a bunch of people who were about to kill the Jews got killed by them instead?"

"Sounds good to me," said Klaus, slugging down another cup of punch.

"I'll admit it's kind of morbid," said Adolf. "Still, it was the first time in history that the Jews fought back—and won. I can see why they thought that was worth celebrating to excess."

"Let's hear it for excess!" said Frederic. He threw back his head to drink a toast, but ended up falling over backwards. Fortunately, he was sitting on the floor rather than in a chair.

"How could an idiot like that Ahas...Ahsarsass...whatever his name was, hang onto an empire?" Karl grumbled. "He never seemed to know who was sending out orders under his name! And the massacre of the Jews was supposed to happen in the twelfth month of the year! Esther blew the whistle on the plot in the third month! He had plenty of time. Why didn't he just cancel the order?"

"He couldn't," said Krista. She picked up the book, and leafed through it carefully. "It says right here in chapter eight, '...for the writing which is written in the king's name and sealed with the king's ring, no man may recall.'"

Franz nodded thoughtfully. "So he righted one wrong—the annihilation of one group of subjects, by letting them kill—what was the number, Krista?"

She flipped another page and scanned the text. "Seventy-five thousand."

"Depending on the number of Jews, not to mention which group provided more revenue...Yes, I'd say he was a typical king. Compared to some of our Illustrious Leaders lately—"

"I wonder," said Adolf suddenly.

Franz's eyebrows shot up in surprise. Adolf

seldom interrupted anyone. "What?"

"If there was something else he could have done. Karl's right..."

"I am?"

"He is?" Karl turned to take a swing at the person who said that, but it turned out to be three different people. He settled for shoving Frederic, who had finally gotten up, back to the floor.

"I mean," said Adolf, ignoring the interplay, "the king had a terrible situation, but several months to solve it. The decision he made was to save the Jews by sacrificing the people who were only following orders to kill them. Before they even attempted to carry out those orders. It really doesn't seem fair. I wonder if there was another way."

Heidi stood up, yawning. "Well, Adolf," she said, clumsily patting his shoulder. "If there was another way, I'm sure you'd have thought of it. Come on, guys. I'd say the party's over."

People filed out, calling out slurred goodbyes, and congratulating each other on what a great idea it was to celebrate this Jewish holiday. No one, Adolf noticed, stopped to pick up garbage or straighten the room on their way out.

"You read with great power," Franz said as Adolf and Krista began to gather up trash.

"Say that when you're sober and I'll believe you," said Adolf.

"Someday I will. But my earlier opinion remains unchanged: you're far too serious for such a young man."

Adolf smiled and said nothing. From where he stood tonight, he could take that as a compliment.

CHAPTER 7

Eventually, things calmed down as they always did. Whatever conspiracy or threat the Party had been worried about had presumably been taken care of. By the middle of April, tension had eased considerably on campus and elsewhere, and now, most people were caught up in the spirit of celebration.

The One Hundred Twelfth Anniversary of the Birth of the First *Führer* would be celebrated on April 20th. Berlin, of course would be a major center, but not the largest. The *Führer's* birthplace of Braunau Inn in Austria--now a shrine--would be where most of the movers and shakers gathered.

Adolf's parents would be there, but not any of the children, nor Uncle Gustav. Adolf's mother explained that tickets were harder to get this year, and Adolf would surely have more fun just staying in Berlin. He sensed a strain in his mother's voice, and knew something was going on, but he couldn't argue with her second statement.

School was closed for a whole week, and was nearly deserted, as everyone who had any place to go hurried to get there. Adolf was looking forward to spending the entire week at the *Judenmuseum*. With him would be Krista, who could not afford to travel home, and Ilsa, who had nowhere else to go.

The week began just as he hoped. Saturday morning, Adolf's footsteps echoed in the deserted halls of the empty dormitory. Few professors had assigned work over the holiday, and Adolf had already finished what little there was. Taking only a knapsack full of books, he left campus, stopping at an expensive pastry shop, where he bought an impressive selection of breakfast rolls and breads. Then he went to a butcher for roasted beef, avoiding foods that had been blamed for several deaths lately, such as fish and pork. Seafood had become especially risky, as more and more toxins were washed into the oceans.

Adolf hadn't really planned to miss all the festivities--had in fact hoped he could convince Ilsa to come with him to see the fireworks, or some of the parades. But he ended up spending the next four days at the *Judenmuseum*, leaving only to buy food, or return to his dorm to sleep. Then he gave up going back to sleep, deciding the floor of the museum would be more restful than the silent, empty dormitory.

Ilsa was not there when he showed up Wednesday morning with a pillow and blanket.

"Planning on moving in?" asked Krista, as she looked up from her sketch pad, her dark hair still damp from her morning shower.

"Why not? It looks like you already have. How do you get here so early? I walk you to your dorm every night, but you're always here when I arrive in the morning."

"I haven't been sleeping well. It's easier for me to just leave at first light. I can nap later if I need to."

"What are you working on?" Adolf asked, reaching for the pad.

Krista pulled it away from Adolf, clutching it protectively. Then she sighed and turned it toward Adolf.

It was a sketch of Ilsa.

She was standing by a window--probably the single window in the front of the museum--staring outside with a far off gaze. Her blonde hair, fine features, and shapely limbs were all rendered with great skill.

"This is magnificent!" said Adolf. "Why were you reluctant to show it to me?"

Krista shrugged, but couldn't make it look natural. "Oh, nothing. I just--" Then she burst into tears and ran to the bathroom.

"What did I say?" Adolf asked the sketch, wondering what was wrong with Krista.

Not her talent, that's for sure. Adolf leafed through the tablet. There were landscapes from around campus, copies of illustrations from books, and portraits of everyone who came to the meetings. Even Adolf was there. He had to admit he was flattered--even though his big ears were a little too true to life, and his smile was goofy. Klaus, too, seemed to be drawn more for comic relief than beauty, but, come to think of it, Klaus really *was* comic relief.

Then Adolf came upon another page full of sketches of Ilsa. All of them were nude. Feeling like he had just placed his foot on what he thought was a step, only to fall down a shaft, Adolf could only stare. Why had Krista done these? *How* had she done these? From imagination or...

Adolf shook his head. That was unthinkable. And yet...people posed naked for artists all the time. But Ilsa? That didn't seem like her style. Yet everything he knew about art and anatomy suggested that this was not the work of Krista's imagination.

He remembered the joke she had made that

first day they met in the museum, about only coming there to look at Ilsa. It had been a joke, hadn't it?

The door flew open and Ilsa ran in, out of breath and flustered. The pad slid from Adolf's fingers, scattering pages all over the floor.

"What's wrong?" he asked as Ilsa bolted the door. From outside came a kind of chaotic rumbling.

"There was an explosion in the square. Some kind of bomb. I'm not exactly sure..." She took a deep breath, striving for her usual calm.

"Here, sit down." Adolf helped Ilsa into a chair. He went to the bathroom to get her a glass of water, nearly colliding with Krista.

"What happened?" she demanded.

"It was at the Boulevard of the Fathers. There was nothing important going on; just a parade of cavalry troops--" Ilsa shivered. "I've never seen a horse die before. People, yes, but horses? It seemed...indecent. It was their screams that got to me."

"How big was the explosion?" asked Adolf. They could hear sirens outside, getting closer. "Were there many casualties--other than the horses?"

"Some riders, I suppose." Ilsa didn't sound too concerned about them. "Maybe a few people in the crowd. Most of the damage I saw was the statues."

"Oh, right, the Boulevard," said Krista. "The square just in front of Party Headquarters. Oh, that's terrible! Those are some of the finest works of sculpture in the *Reich*!"

"Maybe that was the idea," said Adolf. "Some kind of symbolic terrorist statement."

"Or, maybe just a disgruntled ex cavalry

officer with a score to settle," said Krista.

"It probably wasn't smart of me to run back here, but if they started looking for suspects, and found a *missgeburt*... I don't know what they would have done to me. I don't want to find out--"

"Were you followed?" asked Adolf.

"I don't think so. I'm usually so careful, but--"

"Don't worry, you're safe now." Adolf wished he could have said something more intelligent—or at least more truthful.

"Is there any hot water left?" asked Krista. "I'll make you some tea--"

"No!" Ilsa stood. "You two have to get out of here, now!"

"Why? Even if they search this place, what will they find? Two students visiting a museum and a dutiful curator."

"The museum is officially closed this week. I've only kept it open for us because, normally, no one notices. But with a bomb exploding down the street, and a terrorist on the loose, I think they'll damned well notice!"

Ilsa gulped some water and took a deep breath. "If we're searched, they're going to find the son of a highly placed Party member consorting with a lower order of life, and an Aryan throwback, who could not possibly be his girlfriend. Sorry Krista, but it's true. It would be suspicious under normal circumstances, but now, it's dangerous!"

She took another deep breath. "Leave here, and head for the nearest crowd. Join in; ask questions. Even if they do stop you for questioning, you should be okay: you're just a couple of students, there to watch the parade."

"I don't want to go," said Krista. "I don't like crowds and I don't like police."

"I don't want to leave either," said Adolf. He glanced around the warm, dimly lit museum. It felt so safe. Outside was chaos and death. Staying here seemed like the sanest thing anyone could do.

"Just lock the door, and we can all three hide in the back," said Krista. "This neighborhood is mostly deserted anyway. If anyone comes by, they'll just give it a cursory glance and move on."

"Besides," said Adolf, "if anyone *is* out there now, they're going to see us leave, and that will be even more suspicious."

Ilsa looked from one to the other, seemingly undecided. Finally she sighed and said, "I hope you're right." With that, she went to work with impressive efficiency, locking doors, dimming lights, then disappearing into the back of the museum. From there, Adolf heard the sounds of things moving. Furniture? Equipment? What exactly was back there, anyway?

"Let's go see if we can help," Krista said.

Adolf pushed open a door holding a lopsided "employees only" sign. Inside was a small room, mostly taken up with a lumpy sofa with no legs and stacks of boxes. Ilsa was pushing some of the boxes and a few damaged artifacts through another door, probably a closet. When she was finished, there was enough floor space exposed for one person to stretch out on--although the carpet didn't appear to have been vacuumed lately.

"Krista, why don't you take the couch first?" said Ilsa. "I'd prefer the floor now anyway. Adolf, you'll have to start out wedged in a corner, but you and Krista can trade off every couple of hours."

"Two people can sit on the couch," said Adolf. "Great Thor, it's not like we haven't sat in close quarters together before!"

"We're not going to be sitting," said Ilsa. "We're going to be lying down. It will be easier not to move that way." She nodded toward the skylight overhead. "There will be light enough for reading until late afternoon. There's box full of books that arrived last week; I haven't had time to go through them, so that should keep us busy awhile. When the light's gone, I suggest we sleep."

"I was thinking we could talk," said Adolf. "Maybe help you with paper work; set up new displays. As long as we keep our voices down, and walk without shoes, we should be able to--"

Ilsa sighed and shook her head. Krista was looking from her to Adolf and back again, but she seemed to be agreeing with Adolf.

"I don't think you understand what's going on here," said Ilsa. Hearing her tone, Adolf found himself coming to attention. "These walls are thin. There's a street out in front, and an alley behind this room. Any sound can be heard by anyone outside; any movement can be seen through the skylight by someone on the roof. And if we're caught in an obviously closed building, we will have no alibi. And no one will believe that we didn't hear the noise of the crowd, or at least the sirens, and leave to investigate, like good citizens."

Adolf stared at her, the seriousness of the situation starting to sink in. "What about...what about using the facilities?" he asked lamely.

"You'll have to find your way in the dark. And no flushing."

"You talked about trading the sofa every couple of hours," said Krista. "How long will we need to stay?"

"Until tomorrow morning, I would assume," said Ilsa. "Don't you two understand what's going on?"

"I'm beginning to," said Krista.

"This is like being Jews for real," Adolf said suddenly. "Hiding from the Nazis."

"It's not quite that extreme--" Krista began.

"Yes it is," said Ilsa harshly. "And while you're at it, just remember what happened to those Jews when the Nazis caught them!"

Unconsciously, Adolf backed away from Ilsa, and Krista did the same. There wasn't far to go, and they both landed against the wall, Adolf nearly stumbling over a box.

Ilsa forced a smile. "Look, I'm sorry; maybe I'm getting carried away. I just don't think we can be too careful. Do you?"

Adolf and Krista shook their heads without a word. Ilsa slipped out of the room silently. She returned a moment later with Krista's sketch pad and the remains of their food supply: half a loaf of bread, some pastries, an unopened block of cheese and a jar of fruit preserves.

Krista began smoothing the bunched up sheets of art paper, and went to work drawing. Ilsa opened the box on the floor.

"This stuff was found in a warehouse in Amsterdam," she whispered. She took out a small cardboard bound book and gave it to Adolf. "That's

the diary of some girl who hid out for years before
getting captured."

"Ironically appropriate reading material,"
Adolf murmured. He curled his tall body into a
relatively comfortable position on the floor with his
back against the wall, and began to read.

An hour later, Adolf was not remotely
comfortable, nor could he ever remember being so.
He had lost interest in the diary, and couldn't read in
such poor light anyway. Krista was asleep on the
sofa. Ilsa lay on the floor reading.

He fidgeted for a few moments, not aware of
how noisy he was being until Ilsa slithered over to
him. Silently, she indicated he should take her place
on the floor. Grunting, Adolf heaved himself over--
both legs were asleep--and tried to get comfortable on
the dirty carpet. With unbelievable grace, Ilsa neatly
folded herself into the corner Adolf had vacated.

The next thing Adolf remembered was waking
from a light doze, feeling cramps in parts of his body
he didn't know had muscles. Ilsa and Krista were
both asleep.

Sighing, Adolf rose carefully to his feet and
tiptoed to the bathroom.

He switched on the light without thinking.

He turned it back off, silently cursing his
carelessness. Almost at once, however, he grew
angry. Why was he so worried? Why were he and his
friends putting themselves through this kind of ordeal
in the first place? No one was going to bother them
here. Wasn't that why they all came to the
Judenmuseum in the first place?

He left the bathroom, and wandered into the

front of the museum, stretching sore muscles. Evening light came through the room's single window. Ilsa had not covered it, evidently fearing someone was already watching from the street when they decided to hide.

Hard to believe it's not even dark yet, thought Adolf. I feel like I've been stuck here for days. He drifted over to the window, and considered going back to his dorm. Ilsa and Krista probably wouldn't even notice he was gone.

He looked outside, where a pair of blue eyes met his, and then widened in surprise. A moment later, the shrill sound of a whistle pierced the silence of the museum.

CHAPTER 8

The *Waffen SS* private who stood outside the *Judenmuseum* was about Adolf's age. He continued to blow shrilly into the whistle he wore around his neck, until two other, slightly older soldiers hurried to the front of the building. The *Scharführer* pounded on the door, barking orders that it be opened.

Adolf stared, as if in a dream. This could not be happening. Then he heard sounds from the back room; terrified shouts as Ilsa and Krista came rudely awake, and knew it was all too real. And his fault.

Feeling a rush of heat as adrenaline surged through his body, Adolf hurried to the door, opening it with one hand, pulling ID papers from his vest pocket with the other.

"Good day, sergeant," he said, scanning the first rank insignia that swam into view as the soldiers pushed their way in. Was his voice shaking?

"*Scharführer* Schultz. You papers, please, *mein Herr*." Adolf's hand was steady as he handed over his ID. Schultz's eyes widened as he read the name, quickly handing the papers to his superior.

"Might I inquire as to what you are doing here, *Herr* Goebbels?" asked the captain.

Adolf froze as the door behind them opened. But as Krista limped out of the back room, leaning heavily on Ilsa, he felt like kissing both of them.

"Ah, I see you're well enough to walk," he said, hurrying to assist Krista, while Ilsa melted into the background. "My friend and I were on our way to the parade this morning," he said to the men, smoothly pulling Krista's papers from her vest pocket and presenting them to the senior officer. "We heard that horrible explosion and--" Krista promptly dissolved into tears, throwing herself against Adolf.

"When Krista collapsed, I thought she'd been shot. Then I saw it was only shock. I think it was seeing the horses dying that did it. I tried to get her away but she could barely walk. The kind curator of this museum allowed us come in and rest."

While Adolf spoke, the two junior guards were methodically searching the place, while the captain listened intently to Adolf's every word.

Schultz stopped in front of Ilsa, and barked a command Adolf barely understood. Ilsa held up her right forearm, and Schultz became even less personable--if that were possible. He roughly grabbed the papers she held--Adolf's and Krista's had been returned neatly folded--then shoved Ilsa in the captain's general direction. The officer glanced at Ilsa's ID papers and said, "This museum was to have been closed today. Why is it open?"

"I received a shipment of new artifacts from America last week, *mein Herr*," Ilsa said. "Along with orders to have them in place for the week following the Celebration. Since I had nothing else to do today, I came here to get extra work done, as I often do. I wish never to fall behind in my work."

Schultz emerged from the back room carrying the blanket Adolf had brought that morning and the box of food. He exchanged a look with his superior officer that made Adolf's skin crawl. *Why?* He wanted to shout. *There is absolutely nothing dangerous about food and a blanket in the back room of a museum.* For a normal German citizen, at least.

But Ilsa lived in a different world; a world Adolf had never really let himself think about until now.

"I see no reason to detain you, *Herr* Goebbels, or your *friend*." The captain's last word came out as a hiss. He obviously did not like deferring to ugly women. But, as she was in the company of someone like Adolf, he had no choice. "*Scharführer* Schultz will escort you back to your dormitory."

"And the museum *fräulein*?" Adolf struggled to sound casual.

"We have a few more questions for her."

Fighting for control, he led Krista to the door where Schultz waited. Glancing back, he spoke to Ilsa. "Thank you for your assistance, *fräulein*. I hope I have not placed you in any difficulty. I shall never forgive myself if I have." He shot the captain a look which he seen his father perfect and then left.

It was all he could think of to do to help Ilsa.

They walked through silent streets. As usual in these circumstances, a curfew was in effect. All the windows they passed were shuttered. Light leaked through very few of them.

"So, sergeant," said Adolf. "Has anything been learned about this terrible assault on the body of the *Reich*?"

"The man who planted the bomb was caught about two hours ago," said Schultz. "Of course this is only the beginning. It will be some time before all facts are known."

"What do we know so far?" asked Krista.

"The bomber was Russian, but with a very good German cover. He must have had a great deal of help. The explosion has been an isolated attack--so far." Schultz glanced at Adolf. "I regret to inform you, *Herr* Goebbels, that Schatwall's masterpiece, the statue of your grandfather, was destroyed."

"How terrible!" Adolf struggled to achieve an appropriate facial expression.

They had reached the university. Schultz left them at the door of the commissary/ lounge, which stood between the men's and women's dormitories. The light and noise that enveloped them as they walked inside was a soothing balm. Although curfew was in effect here, too, it was limited, requiring only that students be indoors.

Everyone who was still on campus was gathered here, watching the news on the large wall screen, playing cards or talking in groups. They were not Adolf's friends, but that didn't matter. No one wanted to be alone right now, and for once, Adolf felt the same way everyone else did.

He and Krista murmured greetings and exchanged "where were you when the bomb went off?" stories with a dozen or so fellow students. Then they found an unoccupied sofa and sat down.

"Are you hungry?" Adolf asked Krista. "We could get snacks downstairs--"

Krista shook her head. "Maybe we should go somewhere and talk?"

"What for?" Adolf blurted out, and then was instantly ashamed, when he saw Krista's expression. "I mean...I already know that I messed up. And that Ilsa could be in danger because of me."

"That's not what I meant."

Adolf pulled his jacket back on and stood up. "I'm going back. I have to know how she is!"

Krista's small hand gripped his arm with surprising strength. "You can't and you know it!"

"You don't understand!" Adolf's voice came out as a hiss.

"I understand plenty!" Krista's voice was nearly a shriek. Casting a nervous glance over her shoulder, where the few people who looked their way were now turning back to what they had been doing, Krista took a deep breath. "I understand that you're in love with her, too," she whispered.

Adolf opened his mouth, closed it, and tried again. "You're right," he said, swallowing hard. "We need to talk."

"Let's go take a shower," Krista said, and led the way.

A few minutes later, Krista, wearing a blue swimming suit, and Adolf, in a pair of faded green shorts, were sitting side by side on a green tile bench, enjoying the caress of warm water from several shower heads above them. But it was the noise they came for.

As often as Adolf had seen pairs and small groups headed for the showers for private conversation, he had never staked his life on the popular belief in the security they provided. But tonight, he guessed, he was about to do so.

"How long have you known?" Adolf asked.

"About you or about me?" Krista responded dryly.

Adolf almost smiled. "I'm an egotist, so let's start with me."

"It's been pretty obvious to me since, oh, I guess the time we started translating the old bibles."

"Does everyone else know?"

"I haven't discussed it with anyone. If you're wondering if you've been obvious, I'd have to say no. I just have--shall we say--a kind of kindred spirit radar."

Adolf took a deep breath. "And you Krista? How long have you known you're a...that is...assuming you really are--"

"A lesbian? Go ahead, you can say it. I guess I've sort of known my whole life. I pretended not to."

"Understandable, since discovery tends to equal death."

"Right. But when I met Ilsa...when I started going to the meetings...I don't know. I finally just knew it."

Adolf shook his head. "I wish I knew what to say."

"That you won't turn me in would be a good place to start."

"Oh, come on, Krista, you know I wouldn't! Neither would anyone else in the group."

"No one else in the group is in love with the same woman I am!"

Adolf ran his hands through soggy hair, and then stared up at the ceiling, rather grateful for the spray of water that temporarily blinded him.

"I really don't know how to ask, but I have to know. Does Ilsa...? Are you and she...?"

"What? Oh, no! *Sheisse*, you men are so slow! Ilsa isn't that way at all! She's been great with me, of course. Understanding. Sympathetic. And completely unavailable! I was so stupid! When she didn't reject me right away, I thought I had a chance, and really pushed. She finally had to make herself painfully clear this morning. God, was it just this morning? It feels like years!"

"I know what you mean. Did she say why?"
Adolf leaned forward eagerly, almost bumping his wet
face into hers. "Did she say anything about me?"

"Sorry, your name didn't come up," Krista
said coldly.

Adolf felt himself blush. "Sorry. It's just--
look, I don't know what to say in this situation! Do I
challenge you to a duel? Or do we just shake hands
and say, 'may the best man win?'"

"How typically male! Creating an edge for
yourself, even in your platitudes!"

Adolf thought about what he had just said.
Suddenly, he burst out laughing. After a moment,
Krista joined him. In the echo chamber of the shower,
their laughter multiplied, louder even than the sound
of running water. "They can probably hear us
outside," Adolf gasped when he had enough breath.

"Good, maybe a few of them will come in and
join us. Then we can both look at the girls!"

Their laughter slowly subsided; they made eye
contact and looked away. Finally, Adolf said, "I
really hope everything works out for you, Krista.
That, someday, you find someone, and stay safe."

"Thank you. You'll never know how much
that means to me. For what it's worth, I think that if
any guy has a chance with Ilsa, it's you."

"Really?" For an instant, Adolf felt a rush of
hope. Then he thought about the situation and shook
his head. "Even if I did once, I lost it today. It's my
fault she's in trouble." He tried not to think about
what might be happening to her now.

"It was an accident, Adolf. You couldn't have
known--"

"Yes I could have! If I had listened to her! She lives with it, every day: danger, fear, degradation. Having no protection from anything--"

"Yes, Adolf, she lives with it! And she still chose to let us stay, even though she knows that if she insisted, we would have left. She chooses to open that crumbling museum to us, every day, and every Friday evening. To us, it's a game. To her, it probably means death or deportation if some bureaucrat decides to look at what we're doing as seditious or contributing to delinquency or some other nonsense."

Adolf was silent while Krista's words sank in. "So why does she do it?" he asked finally.

Krista shrugged. "I think her aura of mystery is what draws me to her. There's more to her than meets the eye. But a lot if it is anger."

The hot water was nearly gone. Shivering, Adolf and Krista turned it off and went to the dressing room outside to wrap themselves in towels.

"We should try to get some sleep," said Krista. "Tomorrow...will probably be busy."

The next morning showed every sign of business as usual. The curfew was lifted; celebrations continued as planned, with only an extra heavy military and paramilitary presence to indicate anything had happened the day before.

The broadcast station alternated coverage of the First *Führer's* Birthday Celebrations with scenes from inside the interrogation rooms where three suspected accomplices of the bomber--two men and one woman--were questioned with the help of thumbscrews and electrodes.

Adolf was up at first light, trying to pull himself together after a night without sleep. He stopped in the commissary for breakfast, where he discovered the smell of food made him sick.

He gave up and walked to the *Judenmuseum*, terrified of what he would find when he got there, and heaving a sigh of relief when he arrived and saw it was open. The front window was now boarded up like all the others in the plaza, but once inside, he saw the glass had been swept up. A few displays were in disarray, but other than that, the place looked good. Ilsa, however, was nowhere to be seen.

Adolf went into the back, to the room where they had hidden. It was empty. Then he heard noises: faint crackling sounds, then the scrape of a chair on a floor. They were coming from the closet or whatever was on the other side of the door he had noticed yesterday.

He opened the door carefully, and found a cramped, cluttered office. Ilsa sat at a small desk, running a Geiger counter over a series of small objects. She was wearing full protective gear: helmet, gloves, leaded suit and goggles. Adolf felt underdressed.

"What are you doing?" he finally asked.

Ilsa pulled up the goggles and looked up at him. "Hi, Adolf." She pointed to a large empty crate, marked 'Haifa.' "New shipment. Like I told you before, I check to see what's safe and what's not." She pulled a heavy cloth, probably lead- filled, over the desk, got up, and began stripping off the protective gear.

"Are you all right?" he asked. With the opaque layer removed, Adolf could see a bruise on

Ilsa's left cheek. Other than that, she seemed
unharmed.

She hung the suit on a hook in the back of the
room, tucking the gloves into the pockets. "I'm fine,"
she said. "How about you? And Krista?"

"Fine," said Adolf, growing angry, although he
was not sure why. "What happened after we left?"

"They questioned me. Messed the place up a
bit. It wasn't bad, really, Adolf. I'm still employed;
still free to roam--as much as before, at least. It could
have been much worse."

"I know. I just wish it didn't have to be that
way for you."

"I'll go make some tea," said Ilsa. "You
should come out of there. It isn't safe without the
proper precautions."

Adolf knew that. Every school child did.
What he didn't know was where and how Ilsa had
obtained a military grade hot suit--for that is what it
was--and why she even opened boxes that came from
obvious hot spots, and how he could believe that any
of the regular visitors here were safe. And although
he knew he should be moving in the opposite
direction, Adolf found he was curious enough to walk
up to the desk, and pull off the cloth with nothing to
protect his hands. And then stare at what lay beneath.

It was an assortment of Jewish artifacts. Most
were small and all were damaged: a *dreidel,* a half
melted *menorah*, several pocket sized books, two
yarmulkes and a crumpled, but colorful *ketubah*,
sealing some long dead couple's marriage. Beside
each item lay a scrap of paper, where Ilsa had
scribbled the number of rads; they ranged from 3 to
50.

On the floor beside the desk were a dozen similar items, each one mounted in a cheap, clear plastic mold, or set in an attractive wooden box.

"Adolf, get out of there!"

He turned to see Ilsa, holding his favorite tray, the glass mosaic patterned with blue and green Stars of David. A pair of steaming teacups lay on it.

Adolf stepped out of the doorway. "Quite an operation you have here, Ilsa. Care to tell me about it?"

She closed the door and took the tea to her desk. Adolf took his cup and perched on a stool, waiting, not sure what he would do if she said nothing.

"One never knows when a little extra money might come in handy. And old war trophies still trade very well on the black market."

"How are Jewish relics trophies? They were made by a dead race; subhuman by official Party standards. Who would want them?"

Ilsa sipped her tea. "In the final days of the Final Solution, it was mostly young boys who were recruited to run the termination camps; everyone else was needed to do the actual fighting. Many of them are still alive, old men now, who missed their chance for glory on the front lines. A few of them thought to take souvenirs at the time, but most did not, or lost what little they took. So they buy them, as reminders of the greatness of their youth, or to illustrate the stories they tell to anyone who will listen.

"Others, who did nothing at all in the War, buy whatever souvenirs they can afford, to convince everyone else that they did something. They would probably prefer pieces of the Washington Monument or the Great Wall of China, or Dresden glass, but I sell cheaper than most, and a lot of these elderly trophy hunters are of limited means—they simply can't pass up a bargain."

"Quite a bargain," said Adolf, gazing at the closed door, as if it led to a death chamber--which, in fact, it did. "You're willing to take smaller profits, for the satisfaction of sending your customers to their deaths."

Ilsa smiled. "Just doing my part," she said.

Adolf gulped his tea, nearly choking. He remembered the time that Ilsa had assured the group that she only kept relics that were safe. He had asked what she did with the rest. Now he had an answer. For a crazy instant, he wondered if would leave this room alive. *Forget the late night movies*, he told himself.

"No one checks the merchandise?"

"The people I deal with directly don't hang on to it long enough to be at risk, and don't particularly care about what happens to anything after it leaves their hands. As for the customers--if they had brains enough to check for themselves, they probably wouldn't have had such dismal careers in the first place."

"Why do you do it?" Adolf asked.

Ilsa stared into her empty cup. "Perhaps for the same reason I host *Shabbat* services every Friday night. A way to be someone. A way to bring meaning into an otherwise empty existence."

"A way to strike back at those who have wronged you?"

Ilsa looked up, eyes ablaze. Yet her voice was ominously quiet when she spoke. "No one has wronged me, *Herr* Goebbels. Your father or your professors could explain that, if you are confused. 'Only by sacrificing the imperfect can we hope to achieve perfection.'" Her fingers tightened around the teacup. "Those of us who are not killed outright should be grateful to serve our overlords in any capacity. I am treated this way because I deserve it. I am unable to bring forth life. Should anyone be surprised that I chose to bring forth death?"

The teacup shattered in her hand.

Adolf leapt over to her, gently pulling tiny shards from her fingers, relieved to see few cuts. He found a first aid kit in the bathroom, and put antiseptic ointment on each of them, and bandages on the worst. Ilsa showed no reaction at all.

"Did they rape you?" he blurted out.

"What?" Ilsa started as though waking up.

"Those soldiers, last night?" Adolf realized he was very afraid of the answer, because he knew that if they had, he was going to kill all three of them with his bare hands, or die trying.

Ilsa looked away. "What does it matter? Others have in the past. Others will in the future. And if you can't learn to live with that, Adolf, it will, eventually, mean your death." She turned to face him. "And that would be a great loss. One I do not wish to be part of."

Adolf bit his lips, but tears leaked out anyway. He wanted to lash out--at anyone. If he couldn't get the men who had hurt her, or the government that made it happen, then he'd settle for strangling Ilsa-- just for being so damned complacent about it!

He felt her hand on his shoulder. He looked up, and saw no judgment in her eyes. "It isn't your fault Adolf."

He took a shuddering breath. "Krista said you were angry. She didn't know the half of it."

Ilsa smiled--with real amusement this time. "If Krista says *I'm* angry, I say that's the pot calling the kettle black."

Adolf thought about that for a moment. "I don't want to go there," he said.

Ilsa nodded. "Good idea."

Adolf took a deep breath. "I know this isn't the time, and that you already know it anyway, but I love you, Ilsa."

Ilsa's breath caught. "I...was rather hoping you wouldn't say that."

"I'm sorry."

"Don't be. Adolf, I...I don't know what to tell you. I like you...more than I expected to. More than is safe for me. But I don't know if I can love anyone. At least in the way you mean."

"You can, Ilsa. Maybe not me, but someone. As much as you hate, you can love."

"That philosophy makes good poetry, but I'm not at all sure it's accurate."

"Not for everyone. But it's true for you. If all you had was hate, you'd be exploring careers in assassination and information extraction--and believe me, you'd be good! But you spend your days with Judaism and angst-ridden adolescents. There's a kind of love in that. And I think...that's just the beginning."

It was one of those rare moments when Ilsa looked surprised. "You're a good friend, Adolf. I'm sorry I dragged you through my private hell, just now. You didn't deserve it."

"Anytime you want company there, give me a

call." Hesitantly, he put his arm around her shoulders, and left it there while she sat stiff and undecided. Then slowly, she relaxed into his hold. After a moment, her hand sought his.

They sat that way quietly for over an hour.

Finally, Adolf gave her a gentle hug and straightened up. "I'll go now," he said stretching the kinks out of his neck and back. "But if there's anything I can do for you, ever, please let me know."

"Keep coming to see me," she said.

Adolf suppressed an urge to jump with joy. "I will. And, hey, look at it this way: you have at least two college students pining for you. Third class citizen or not, you're making conquests."

Ilsa grinned. "And what I lack in quantity, I make up for in quality--and variety."

"I'll see you Friday."

"I'll be here."

Book II

CHAPTER 9

"These are the names of the curators of the other thirty-seven *Judenmuseums*, and their addresses. Those who can be trusted are highlighted in red."

Adolf took the list from Ilsa. He was not surprised to find only four names highlighted.

"Do you really think the Party will close them all?" asked Brigitta, a petite freshman who still wore her blond hair in schoolgirl braids.

Ilsa tapped the official notice on her desk. "You can read as well as I can."

"It's reading between the lines that you're so good at," said Peter. "Phrases like 'new head of the Department of Education' and 'review of all resource allocation' could mean so many things. And these museums are not the only public works facing the ax. It could take them years to actually shut us down. Or maybe never."

"True," said Ilsa. "And these scares have happened before. But something tells me this time it's for real. In that event, I want to make sure that as many books and relics as possible are safely stored, and all records doctored."

"So the number of relics they burn will appear to be all there ever were?" said Briggita.

"Right," said Ilsa.

The door swung open, and Franz, now an assistant professor, came in, his stylish black overcoat snapping in the cold March wind. "I knew you'd all lose track of time! It's 1100 hours, and we all have to be in the quad at noon--with our books. Let's get going."

Briggita gasped and leapt to her feet. The others, used to the purges by now, were more relaxed.

"We're graduating in three months!" said Frederick, indicating himself, Adolf and Krista and Peter. "What's the point of giving us new textbooks?"

"Orders, my friend," said Franz. "Just because my status has changed from student to faculty, doesn't mean I can start questioning them."

"Let's go," said Krista. "We'll come back and help you with this tonight if we can, Ilsa."

"You all go on ahead," said Adolf. "I'll catch up with you soon."

Everyone exchanged knowing looks. Ever since Adolf and Ilsa had been declared a couple, over two years ago, other members of the rapidly growing group had been careful to give them as much privacy as they could--and speculated at length at what the two of them did when they were alone.

The group filed out, Franz holding back. "I almost forgot, Adolf. Congratulations on your winning essay. You're a sure thing for valedictorian, now."

"I'm still surprised it's creating such a stir," said Adolf. "Now, if the Party knew where I got the ideas for it, *that* would create a stir."

"Remember when you first thought of suggesting gleaning laws as a form of economic management?" said Ilsa, smiling. "You thought it would get you shot."

Adolf laughed. "As it turns out, all I had to do was change the names, translate some Hebrew and add three pages of fancy sounding gobbledygook! And now, they think I'm a genius."

Franz stopped at the door and looked back. "Don't stay too long," he said.

As soon as he heard the door shut, Adolf wrapped his arms around Ilsa. He kissed her once, but then pulled away, despite the ardor of her response.

"Have you thought about what you're going to do, if they close the museums?" he asked. He hated to bring it up, as if talking about it would make his worst fears come true.

Ilsa looked away. "Word among the other *missgeburt* is that reassignment is not likely. Unemployment in occupied territory is dangerously high. The Party will need all its jobs for them--even jobs once reserved for the lesser beings."

"So what will happen to the...*missgeburt*?"

Ilsa shrugged. "Hard to say."

"How can you be so calm?" Adolf paced the cluttered room, wanting to hit something.

"What would you have me do? Work myself up to burst blood vessels, like you're doing?" Adolf opened his mouth to retort, but Ilsa put a finger on his lips. "Stop. We'll deal with each crisis like we always have--as they come up. Now, I have work to do, and you have a book burning to attend." She kissed him forcefully. "Get moving."

Adolf clicked his heels and saluted her.

Another book burning. Another set of textbooks purged, and new ones assigned. For how long this time? The last one was just the past October.

This time, the seniors probably wouldn't even get new books. The professors would simply give final exams based on lectures. Students who made it this far were not likely to fail. Adolf felt a pang as he thought of poor Klaus, expelled in his third year for poor grades and a frivolous attitude. He was in the army now; his unit somewhere in Northern Russia.

Karl, at least, had graduated--though just barely, thanks to his taste for schnapps and his increasingly depressive attitude-- and moved on to an entry level job in the Department of Commerce. Franz and Heidi both remained on campus teaching. *And*, thought Adolf, *if I can only manage to secure that position as assistant speech writer for the Minister of Communications, I could maybe do something to help Ilsa.* It was an excellent job for a young man just out of University—though not as impressive as Josef Heydrich's first post within the *Führer's* Honor Guard, as Adolf's father kept reminding him. Still, all the top ranking students were vying for this speech-writing job. With this latest award, Adolf felt he had a chance. And since one of the privileges included was an apartment, he might be able to hire Ilsa as a maid, or at least acquire the influence to get her a job somewhere.

He would miss the museum crowd. In the four years that Adolf had been here, their numbers had grown to more than fifty. For some, it would always be a game, but more and more, Adolf sensed the presence of those, who like Franz, and Krista and himself, took it more seriously. It was still mostly a male crowd, although this year, at least, there were a few more girls.

Just as Adolf reached the edge of the

campus district, an Opal produce truck passed in front of him and pulled to a stop in front of a large grocery store. Eight heavily armed *Wehrmacht* soldiers stood before the store. Six more got out of the truck while it was being unloaded. While the crowds of people gathered at the entrances were well behaved today, Adolf crossed the street to avoid them. Trouble could start without warning, and he couldn't afford to be late for the campus purge.

Soon he would be going home, where the pantry never ran low, and no one thought to ask where all the meat and bread and fruits and vegetables came from. Even Adolf, who knew the servants better than most of the family, wasn't clear on where they shopped, or why they needed no armed escort, or what would happen if someday, finding safe and abundant food would become too great a feat even for the Goebbels household.

On a more positive note, Adolf would soon be meeting his nephew for the first time. He needed to think of a gift. Something that wouldn't remind Frieda and Edwin of their first child, born without an immune system, as so many were, these days. She had lived only three weeks. At least little Paul Joseph seemed inclined to thrive.

When at last he reached the quad, Adolf saw all the students gathered as usual. He slipped into the back of a group of seniors, among the young men he knew. The Headmaster's speech was just ending. Then titles were called out. Adolf was surprised when they started, not with textbooks, but with novels that had been popular on campus of late. The first book to be called was "Sorrows of Young Werther," by Johann von Goethe.

More than thirty students, all of them male, and all wearing identical blue coats, yellows breeches and jackboots, came forward sullenly. They stacked their books in a pile, then to Adolf's amazement, peeled off their clothing as well. The students were made to stand in the cold March wind wearing only their underwear while the books and costumes burned. Only after three more novels were collected and burned were the Werther followers allowed to return to their dorms.

Adolf was grateful that senior textbooks were collected next. While he would not be free to leave until all the books were burned, with his arms empty, he could at least wander around the crowd. He spotted Professor Hoffman standing apart from the rest of the faculty, his mouth drawn into a tight grimace. Edging carefully in that direction, Adolf approached him.

"It seems you are a prophet, *Herr* Professor," Adolf said.

"Excuse me?" the teacher looked startled.

"Three years ago last December. We saw the return of Young Werther at a bookstore. You told me the book's history, and predicted its future. Today, you are proven correct. As always." Adolf smiled.

Professor Hoffman acknowledged the praise with a nod, but did not return Adolf's smile. "Sometimes, I would prefer to be wrong. Banning the book is one thing; even burning it, for that is the Party's way of banning something. Very symbolic, like everything else in the *Reich*. But humiliating the followers that way? I see no good in that."

It had bothered him as well, but Adolf was

surprised to hear a professor say such a thing.
Although he knew none of the group personally,
Adolf felt an affinity for any group of rebels with an
identifying theme. It was like Judaism for him. But,
of course, he couldn't say that to Professor Hoffman,
so he said, "It is a standard form of discipline. And a
good way to set an example." He looked cautiously at
his favorite teacher. "Isn't it?"

Hoffman sighed. "I could quote you statistics
and cite schools of thought dreamed up by great men
whose names can no longer be spoken aloud in this
land. But what of it? In the final analyses, it always
remains that those who know not history are doomed
to repeat it."

Adolf thought about that and nodded slowly.
It seemed like an interesting notion. He wondered if
the professor had been quoting someone and said,
"Without textbooks, I shall look forward to your
lectures even more, for whatever time remains."

For a moment, Hoffman's eyes narrowed.
Then he smiled pleasantly. "I see the party is
breaking up. You'd better go study your notes, young
Adolf, if you expect to pass my course!"

Adolf filed out of the quad with the rest of the
students, shaking his head, as he reflected that
conversations with Professor Hoffman were always a
little strange.

Adolf waited for Ilsa to finish cataloging the
last of the books. Then he picked up her valise. "I'm
glad you decided to visit my home," he said.

"I decided a change might be good for me,"
Ilsa said, locking the *Judenmuseum* behind them. "I
haven't been out of Berlin in some time. I only hope I

don't create problems for you. Even in disguise--"
Ilsa held up her arms, swathed in the blue silk of the
dress on which Adolf had spent most of his prize
money "--your parents will probably figure out what I
am."

"They're only going to be in town the first two
days. Then, they're off to Austria for the Anniversary
celebrations. But we can stay in Munich the whole
week if you like. I know my sisters will love you."
As I do, he wanted to add, but restrained himself.

For all the gossip surrounding Adolf and Ilsa,
what none but the two of them knew was that their
relationship was a chaste one.

Sometimes, Adolf wondered if there was
something wrong with him. Ilsa was willing enough.
And he surely desired her. But every time things
moved in that direction, Ilsa grew detached, as if she
were offering her body--but taking the rest of her
away somewhere. Someplace safe, he guessed. And
then they would either fight over the subject of trust,
or Adolf would suddenly remember an appointment
he had somewhere else.

They walked to the train station, dodging
between heavy construction equipment and gangs of
slave laborers. "The streets are so much cleaner now,"
said Adolf.

"That's what happens when the new *Führer*
has the head of sanitation shot," said Ilsa. "He's very
efficient, this one."

They reached the train station. Ilsa stopped on
the front steps and took a deep breath. "The
Judenmuseums are to be shut down," she said. "I
received word this morning."

Adolf's head jerked up. "All of them?" he

asked.

"Yes, all. By the end of this year. The Department of Education has decided that maintaining relics of a dead race is a waste of resources."

Adolf had been prepared for this, but he cursed anyway. "And what about you, Ilsa? Have they--?

"Yes, Adolf, they have. I've been assigned work in a brothel. In Hamburg."

"What!" Adolf's voice was loud. People turned to stare. Ilsa led him to a bench near the ticket counter, silently commanding him to get a grip.

"They can't do that here!" he hissed as they sat down. "Only in occupied lands! The government cannot force German women..."

"Normal German women," corrected Ilsa. "But, being barren, I am without the protection of citizenship. It isn't just me, you know. My guess is, within a few years, all people with physical defects will be removed from society. Just as the mentally defective were removed in the first years of the *Reich*.

"In the mean time, some of us *missgeburt* can still be useful--or at least used. They won't send me to an *SS* brothel; those are for fertile women, who can serve as vessels for the cream of the Aryan crop, but..."

"How can you be so cool about this?" demanded Adolf. "Stop talking that way! You know I would never let that happen to you."

Ilsa stood and stared down at him with piercing blue eyes. "How would you stop them, Adolf?"

Adolf looked into her eyes. "I could marry

you."

For so long, he had dreamed of saying those words to Ilsa. Generally, he imagined a more romantic setting than a train station.

"It would ruin your future, Adolf."

"So what? My father can take my career and stuff it up his ass! If you think I'm going to stand by and let something like that happen to you...Have you seriously considered what you'll do if they send you--?"

Ilsa sat back down and gazed up at the ancient clock tower above the station. "When France was first taken," she said, "a Jewish girls boarding school was turned into a brothel for the infantry. It made sense: there were beds; there were girls. They were Jews, so no hand would be raised to protect them. But it was only in business for one night."

"What happened?" asked Adolf, but he thought he knew.

"The Nazis had neglected to secure all the gasoline and matches before sending the first crew of soldiers there. No one got out alive."

Adolf wondered if he would have even cared a few years ago. Now he felt a surge of pride. And fear. "Is that what you will do?" he asked Ilsa.

"Perhaps."

"Damn it, Ilsa! Sometimes you scare me!"

He might have said more, but a gesture from Ilsa silenced him. He followed her gaze through the crowded station to where two nondescript men stood talking. With them was Heidi.

"Quickly," Ilsa whispered.

Adolf barely had time to follow her as she melted into a shadowy alcove where heavy equipment stood.

"What is it?" asked Adolf.

"Those men with Heidi. They are *Gestapo*."

"What?" Adolf peered around the corner, trying to see. The men certainly *could* have been *Gestapo*. Anyone could be. That was what made them so frightening. But why would they be talking to Heidi? "Do you think she's in trouble?"

"No," said Ilsa. "I think we are."

CHAPTER 10

Adolf felt a curious sensation of duality; of the world suddenly turning upside down, only to be righted again, simply because it had to. He was in Berlin's beautiful old train station, on his way to see his family for a last visit before graduating the *Reich's* finest university. Then in six weeks, he would receive his diploma, begin a promising career in government, and maybe, finally make his father proud.

But right now, to look into to Ilsa's white and terrified face, was to realize that life as he knew it had just ended. So he tried not to look in her face. He tried to look at the mobs of people in the station, at least half of them students like himself. And at the men who Ilsa thought were *Gestapo*, but probably weren't.

Finally, he looked back at Ilsa. She was still staring at the men with Heidi, but he could see from her expression she was thinking frantically.

"Why do you think they're *Gestapo*?" he asked.

"I recognize one. We have had—dealings--in the past. But it's the other one I'm worried about. See that badge on his hat?" Adolf could see some kind of ornamentation on the younger man's expensive leather hat, but had no idea what it was.

"It's an award given very rarely, to members of one of the most secret enclaves in the *Gestapo*."

"For what?" Adolf asked, his mouth dry.

"The Cleansing of Internal Enemies of the *Reich*."

Then the man put his arm around Heidi. She

laughed at something he said, and looked into his eyes with an expression that could be read as adoration even from where Adolf and Ilsa stood.

"We are dead," Ilsa said, very softly.

"Don't jump to conclusions," Adolf said, wishing his voice didn't shake so much. "Heidi probably doesn't even know--"

Then he saw Franz and Peter, with his arm around Brigitta, enter the station. It was only chance that he happened to glance back at Heidi the very next moment. And because he did so, he saw her stiffen. He saw her pull away from her lover. And he saw her raise one beautiful white hand, and point to three of the people Adolf loved most in the world.

A moment later, the older *Gestapo* agent intercepted them. Three uniformed men moved in from out of nowhere. Adolf saw the disbelief, then terror on his friends faces as they were led outside with a minimum of noise and fuss. The few people who glanced their way, hurried away from them, and to their trains.

Then Franz, Peter and Brigitta were gone. Adolf knew he would never see them again in this life.

But is wasn't over. Heidi and the other agent remained where they were, and Adolf realized she was going to identify every member of the *Judenmuseum* group who came to the station--which was more than half of them. The others would doubtless be rounded up on campus, or in their family homes, if they had made it that far.

This cannot be happening! screamed a voice in his head.

"Over here," whispered Ilsa, and he saw she had squeezed between a broken ladder and a piece of twisted paneling, where a door stood locked. A window, thickly coated with dust, was set high in the door.

Adolf didn't even wonder as he wrapped his jacket around his fist and broke the window. He didn't hear a sound as the glass shattered, but he was sure he could hear the sound of pursuit behind them, over the pounding of blood in his eardrums.

The door led to a small storage room, which in turn led through a door and into an alley. It was filthy, but unguarded, and it got them out of the train station. Adolf followed Ilsa, who led the way with grim confidence. He moved as one in a nightmare, all the while, trying to find some way to explain everything; a way to see it so that everything could go back to being the way it was this morning.

A few hours later, Adolf and Ilsa sat in relative safety in what had once been part of Berlin's old sewer system. They had risked a quick stop at the boarding house where Ilsa lived, gambling that it would be low on the lists of places searched. They had won that throw of the dice, and emerged safely with a few supplies; mostly books, clothing, and the money that Ilsa had put aside.

She had nothing for Adolf to change into, so here he sat, in his holiday best, in a service alcove off an ancient tunnel, populated by rats. Adolf couldn't tell if it was cold or not, because he had been hivering since they left the station. He guessed they were directly beneath the warehouse district, about five miles from campus. Five miles and a lifetime.

These tunnels, it seemed, led everywhere, including into the new sewer system, which would

have been a much less comfortable way to travel.
Here, at least, it was dry and relatively clean, and it
didn't smell any worse than the neighborhood above
it.

Which was bad enough, thought Adolf.

But now, finally, there was time. Time to sort
out what had happened. If Adolf was never going to
see his family again, never draw a breath without
looking over his shoulder, he at least had to know
why.

"Was Heidi a spy all along, you think?" he asked.

"Probably. It's so arbitrary, we sometimes forget
about it. But generally, anytime more than three people
gather together on a regular basis, someone in the Party
sends an agent."

Adolf nodded. He knew that. Everyone did.
But the *Judenmuseum*? It was so...unimportant. A
homely little building lacking even the funds for a new
paint job. Filled with books and pictures that no longer
meant anything to anyone. "So what happened? A
handful of students, playing around with a forgotten
religion? It shouldn't have mattered to the *Reich*,
anymore than kids playing with tarot cards and Ouija
boards."

"But the numbers were growing. Over fifty in
Berlin. I can't be sure, since so many of them wouldn't
talk to me, or else I was suspicious of them, but--I think
people have found their way to the *Judenmuseums* in
every city that has one. And possibly elsewhere. Mostly
students, but others as well. I'd guess our numbers were
in the hundreds. Maybe higher."

For a moment, Adolf forgot about the danger he
was in, and thought with awe--and even a little pride—
about what that meant. "The Jews," he whispered.

"Someone, somewhere, must have thought they'd returned. And been afraid."

"Were they right?" asked Ilsa. "Have the Jews returned?"

"I wish I could think clearly enough to give a straight answer." Adolf thought back across the years, trying to find the moment that it had become more than a game to him. That first *Hanukkah*? The day he began translating the Christian bibles to find their roots in Judaism? The first time he questioned the righteousness of a government that did so many things that were wrong? "I suppose, in the sense that so many people are about to die for the faith described in *Torah*, we are Jews."

He had meant it as a joke, but Ilsa grabbed his hand, and gripped it with painful force. "Then maybe there is hope."

"What?"

"If it's worth dying for, do you think it's worth living for?"

"Maybe for you Ilsa. You've always been stronger than me. But for me..." He trailed off, afraid of where the thought led. "For all that I've found in the *Judenmuseum*, with you, with the heroes of old, I find that I'm still trying to die like a good Nazi. It's really all that's left to me."

"You've always been one to underestimate yourself, Adolf. But I guess that's a trademark of everyone who found their way to the museums. Krista, Frederic, Klaus--even Franz, who was certainly the most 'normal' of the bunch. Gifted, intelligent--but always tripping yourselves up."

"That's a real comfort now," said Adolf, closing his eyes, and leaning back against the rough stone of the tunnel wall.

"It should be!" Ilsa was angry now, and somehow, that was more daunting than the specter of death. "Look, I'm sorry about Franz and the others! Especially those poor kids like Brigitta, who were still just playing! But we're alive, Adolf! We've got to make that count for something!"

"Like what? Running and hiding until they find us? Dying as traitors?" Suddenly Adolf was angry too, and it felt so much better than being afraid. "My family is ruined because of me! My old friends, my teachers! Everyone! They're going to be interrogated; probed for the answer to what made me go bad! If I were a nobody, a younger son of an intelligent technician, sent off to University, it might not matter!

"But I am the grandson of Paul Joseph Goebbels! The son of one of the Party's inner circle. They can't afford to let me escape! They'll find me no matter who they have to kill to get to me!"

And suddenly, the reality of that statement struck, and he collapsed against Ilsa, sobbing and shaking, his stomach heaving. Ilsa held him, and for all her icy demeanor, her cheeks were as wet as his own.

Then, his sobs changed to hysterical laughter.

Ilsa slapped him.

"How dramatic!" gasped Adolf. "I knew you'd seen too many movies.

"But what I was laughing about," Adolf's breath turned into a harsh wheezing and he stopped. He took a few deep breaths and tried again. "What I was laughing about was that for all that I loved

Judaism, I never really hated Nazism! I mean, I hated
the injustice and the paranoia, and the waste, but I
never really wanted to overthrow it! I hoped I could
take what I learned from the Jews and make things
better. Less unfair, less cruel, but never really less
National Socialist! In my heart, I never, truly, turned
against the *Reich*."

"Well," said Ilsa thoughtfully. "Don't you
think it's about time you did?"

In the near total darkness of the abandoned
sewer tunnel, Adolf's eyes sought Ilsa's. The
passionate glow he found only confirmed what he
already knew: she was serious.

"Listen to me," she continued. "Our friends
are going to die, but not all of them. If we've escaped,
then so have others. And yes, a lot of innocent people,
including your family, are going to suffer--but that
isn't your fault, Adolf!"

"Then whose fault is it?"

"If I had a hundred years, I couldn't name
them all, or explain what each one did to bring this
about. For me, it's enough to say that this system of
running the world is just plain evil! And maybe, just
maybe, it's been evil since its accursed inception, and
maybe it's time somebody did something about it!"
She was shouting now, her words echoing eerily in the
endless tunnel.

"What do you suggest?" asked Adolf.

Ilsa's voice dropped back to her usual
unearthly calm. "Personally, I plan to devote every
moment I have left to overthrowing the current world
order." She sighed. "Face it, Adolf, it's falling apart
anyway. I'll help, just like thousands of others
who've lost everything, or simply can't get used to

living under a yoke. And one day, soon, the Thousand
Year *Reich* will fall. And I'd be there to cheer, except
that whatever replaces it will probably be just as bad."

"Wow. You even know how to make
martyrdom suck."

Then his head exploded in pain, and he yelped
and realized that Ilsa had just hit him with a copy of
Torah.

"Maybe if we had something worth replacing
it with; some leaders worth following, martyrdom
wouldn't suck so much!"

Adolf stared at her, daring her to continue,
while swearing to himself that if Ilsa named him the
next world savior he would run screaming from the
tunnel. But she only wrapped her arms around her
body, shivered a little and lowered her head. Calm
again, she raised her eyes to Adolf's. "Sorry. I got
carried away. I guess we should be concentrating on
getting out of here."

"On that subject, at least, I'm open to
suggestions."

"Believe it or not, we do have friends, Adolf."
She dug into her jacket pocket, and pulled out a scrap
of paper. From one of the bags they had gotten from
her place, she took a flashlight. In its weak light,
Adolf saw three names. The first was followed by a
Berlin address; the other two were in distant cities.
"Some contacts I have reason to believe the
authorities don't know about. Memorize each
address, then destroy the paper."

"Ilsa! Look at me! Do I look like some kind
of comic book hero to you? I'm ready to throw up!
You might know all there is to know about how to
disappear and live in the shadows but I don't! I'd get

myself killed, along with anyone who tried to help me." He stuffed the paper down the front of her dress. "Find yourself another hero. Or better yet, use these contacts yourself."

"I've already got a place to hide," she said, extracting the paper, and pushing it firmly into his vest pocket. "Live or die, it's up to you Adolf. But if you die, I'll never forgive you!"

Adolf rubbed his throbbing head. "I don't want to die, either. I just don't know how to live anymore."

"I'll help you. So will others. Judaism isn't the only underground. There are places we can hide, and maybe, someday, come back. With a vengeance."

"And do what?"

"Build a new world. Find out firsthand what freedom and justice and equality really are. Get married." She smiled. "You did ask me to marry you, remember? In a better world we could. And if you turn me down now, I can sue you for breach of promise."

Adolf suddenly saw an image of Ilsa hauling him before a *Bet Din*, the religious courts of the ancient Jews, and burst out laughing. "Now that might be something worth living for," he said. He began to think about living again. His chances were pretty bad, but if he managed to, there were some things to look forward to. "We'd be social equals, at last," he said.

"I could live with that," said Ilsa. "As long as you don't start thinking we're intellectual equals."

"Never," said Adolf. "So, what about it? Will you marry me?" This was the second time today he had proposed to her in a less than ideal setting.

Ilsa's blue eyes were solemn. "Yes, Adolf, I will." Then she smiled again. "I can't think of a better incentive to get through all this alive."

Adolf shook his head. "No. Not when it's all over. Will you marry me now? Here?" From the last finger of his right hand, Adolf pulled a battered gold ring, inscribed with words whose meaning and origin he had never learned. An ancient ruby sparkled in the flashlight's beam.

"According to at least one source I've read, one way Jews could be married was for the man to give the woman a token worth more than ten *zloty*—I think that was a Polish coin—and for her to accept it. This ring has been in my family for over two hundred years. Will you take it as a bride gift?"

Without a word, Ilsa took the ring, and slid it onto the fourth finger of her left hand.

He kissed her then, and for a moment forgot all about where they were and what had happened. Perhaps it was their shared danger, or perhaps it was their new found equality, but this time, Ilsa stayed in her body while they kissed. And she stayed while Adolf unbuttoned the dress he had bought her, and while he caressed her soft breasts.

By the time Ilsa began tearing Adolf's clothes from his body, he stopped thinking altogether, and just enjoyed her ferocious attention.

Had he ever really used words like "cold", "distant" or "detached" to describe the woman he now held in his arms? Writhing beneath him, wrapping herself around him, she seemed to be made of fire. Adolf felt himself consumed, as if he too burned; as if they would consume each other.

Afterwards, as they lay in each other's arms,

Adolf said, "We're not going to be leaving together, are we?"

Ilsa shook her head. "It would be too dangerous. But we will be together again, Adolf. I believed it before, but I'm sure of it now."

Adolf smiled. "Divine inspiration?"

"Something like that." Ilsa sat up, and began getting dressed.

"Well," said Adolf, extricating his clothes from the tangled heap beside them, "I'd call what just happened divine, but I don't think the God of the Hebrews was personally involved."

"No?"

"Not His style."

"Sure it is," said Ilsa. "Remember Moses? All that stuff about his long life, still enjoying his juices up 'till the end?"

"True. Sounds kind of one sided, though. It never said if his partners enjoyed them too."

"That's what happens when men write the history." Ilsa shone the flashlight over herself, then Adolf. "Damn! We could have gotten more money for these clothes if we hadn't just messed them up so much."

Adolf sighed. "I knew your practical side would resurface eventually."

"Until now, no one's been able to disconnect it even temporarily."

"I'm flattered." Letting go of the magic with a final sigh, he straightened and asked, "So, now what?"

"Now, we follow this tunnel about a half mile to an access point on the street above." Ilsa peered at her watch. "It's eight o'clock. That means it's dark. I'll go up first, and make my way to a contact I know.

You wait until midnight, and then get to the first
address on that list I gave you." Adolf dug it out of
his pocket. "You'll talk to a man named Hans. Give
him your clothes, that platinum pin you have, the
silver cuff links--everything you got. He'll swap them
for some cheap, working class clothes and a fake ID.
It won't be top of the line, but it'll get you out of
Berlin."

Adolf studied Ilsa's map of the city--both
above and below ground. "I'll have to walk at least
two miles above ground to get there! How am I
supposed to do that, dressed like this, with half the
Reich looking for me?"

"That's why I'm asking you to wait until
midnight. I'll create a distraction."

"And assuming I make it to this dealer? How
do you know he he'll settle for my possessions? He
could collect more money turning me in."

"This man has reasons to avoid the authorities,
no matter how much they're offering for information
about you."

They stood and embraced, then walked to their
exit point in silence. Adolf spent the entire time
wondering if he would ever see her again. Just before
they climbed the ladder that had been worked into the
brick pillar, she turned and kissed him. "Good
journey, Adolf. Until we meet again." Then she was
gone.

Adolf settled down in the darkness to wait.

At the stroke of midnight, Adolf emerged from
the tunnel.

He was in a narrow street in the warehouse

district, standing beneath a crumbling, deserted building. He had memorized his route, but even as looked around, he saw at least two guards between him and the street he needed to get to.

Suddenly, the sound of breaking glass shattered the night. Something came tumbling off the roof of the building across the street, stopping about ten feet off the ground.

It was a body, hanging from some kind of rope or cord. Guards began yelling, people boiled forth, and Adolf knew he had only a matter of seconds to take advantage of Ilsa's "distraction."

But he wasted some of that time just staring at the body that swung through the night before him.

It was Heidi. Her throat and belly had been slit open. It was, Adolf thought, remembering his childhood visits to the country, the way one slaughtered and dressed a swine.

CHAPTER 11

Adolf paused at the muddy track that led to the dilapidated farmhouse. He tried to summon a smile at what his mother's reaction would be to the prospect of spending the night in such a place. Then he gave up: he was simply too tired.

In the three days since fleeing Berlin, Adolf had slept approximately four hours. He had eaten well enough: sausage from a vendor on the road; bread from a baker in the village just past, apples from a man who had probably stolen them from some farmer's tree. Ilsa's money had seen to that, at least.

And, thanks to the I.D. that Hans had provided, and a few cosmetic changes in his appearance, Adolf was still a free man.

"Free to live like a hunted animal for a few more days," he muttered.

The dye that made his hair as dark as Krista's also made his scalp itch. The short--almost shaven--style was hard to get used to as well. His eyeglasses had a cracked lens, which was helpful for getting people to dismiss him without a second glance, but they were also giving him a headache.

Adolf reached the front door, and cast his gaze around the yard, deserted but for a few scrawny chickens. Just as he was about to knock, the door creaked open a few inches. A red haired young man about his own age peered out from behind the door.

"Stefan?" asked Adolf.

"Who wants to know?"

"Adolf." He smiled disarmingly, and then added, "I need a place to stay for a few days. I can offer my services as a farmhand, and maybe trade some old books and curios." He held up the battered valise he carried. "Ilsa told me you might be interested."

Stefan's expression slowly changed from suspicious to hopeful. "Ilsa? From the Berlin museum?" he asked.

Adolf's gut twisted as he answered, wondering if he would ever see her again. Or his family. Or Munich. Or anyplace that showed on a map. "I had to leave there in rather a hurry. And I'd prefer not to stand out in plain sight for long. If you don't let me in, I'll understand. I'm in serious trouble."

"So who isn't?" Stefan swung open the door and ushered Adolf inside.

The inside of the farmhouse wasn't much better than the outside. A once elegant sofa sagged against one wall. A pile of dirty laundry sat in a corner. By an open sewing box on a rusted metal coffee table, a stack of clothes waited to be mended. A large fireplace dominated the end of the main room. Adolf guessed it provided the house's only source of heat. He hoped he would not be spending the winter here.

The mantle above the fireplace was crowded with photographs. Some sat in little gold frames, but most just leaned against the wall, faded edges showing where frames had once been.

"As you've probably guessed," Stefan said, "we don't get many visitors."

Adolf shook his head, trying to stay awake. "I gather that things used to be better for you, but Ilsa didn't tell me anything specific."

Stefan took Adolf's suitcase and knapsack and led him to the kitchen. "I'll tell you all about it. My sister and I, we never pass up a chance for conversation. We get it so rarely, and we get tired of each other. Sit down; you look like you could use a meal."

Adolf chose a padded folding chair from the three mismatched chairs that surrounded the long wooden table. Stefan brought him a piece of brown bread and a hunk of yellow cheese, and then dipped a glass of water from a bucket that sat beside a pump by the kitchen door.

"Thank you," said Adolf, wishing for more, but saying nothing. He ate slowly. The bread was coarse and hard, but the cheese was soft and buttery. "So what happened to you, Stefan? And why are you risking even worse fortune by helping me?"

Stefan laughed. "Things couldn't get much...but, no. We never say that, do we? My father was a businessman and a landowner; what they used to call a *burgher*. We were doing well enough that between his connections and my brains, I got a University scholarship. That's why you and I are talking to each other today: I got into studying the Jews, and running with the local museum crowd.

"Then, three years ago, my father was arrested."

Adolf winced. "What for?"

Stefan shrugged. "They never said; just took him away and asked everyone a lot of questions. But that was enough to ruin us. They confiscated everything worth having, and of course, all of our neighbors suddenly realized they'd never actually met us."

"How do you still own the farm?" asked Adolf.

"We don't. We're allowed to stay here and work it, as long as we keep up our quota. And, technically, we're being allowed to 'buy it back.' That means, we sell everything we can to make payments that will never get us back the land. Unless of course, the next *Führer* decides my father is innocent of whatever his supposed crime is, and pardons him. One can but hope."

"This cheese is very good," said Adolf, not knowing what else he could say just then.

Stefan brightened. "Thank you. Anna makes it. She's a great cook, but the dairy is her pride and joy."

As if on cue, a young woman, red haired like Stefan, came running into the kitchen. She was out of breath, her face so red that her freckles were barely visible. "Mother's gone off again!" she said, wiping her hands on a stained and faded blue gingham skirt.

"What now?" Stefan demanded. At that moment, a naked, middle-aged woman went running past the kitchen window. She was shrieking something that sounded like the Edicts for Party Women, interlaced with obscenities. The three young people watched as the woman collided with a clothesline full of linens, and proceeded to thoroughly entangle herself.

Stefan sighed. "Come on, Anna, let's go."

But Anna made no move to follow. "There's a

man in my kitchen," she said, staring at Adolf with wide eyes.

"Oh, yes. Adolf, this is my sister, Anna. She and mother and I are all that's left of the family, which should explain why we're so happy to have you here. Anna, this is Adolf, a fugitive of some kind, who we'll be helping for a few days."

"Pleased to meet you," said Anna, still staring, while Adolf took her hand.

"Charmed," said Adolf, pressing her hand to his lips.

"Come on, Anna," said Stefan.

Then Adolf was alone in the kitchen. He went to the bucket and refilled his glass, then sat down trying to drink until his stomach was full. Next he tried to think of something useful to do...

He awoke to the sensation of being lifted from the only solid thing in the universe.

"Aagh!" he screamed, kicking over the only solid thing in the universe—which turned out to be a chair.

"It's okay!" yelled Stefan, fending off Adolf's fist. "It's just us!"

"I told you we shouldn't have tried to carry him to bed without waking him up!" said Anna.

"I *tried* waking him up!"

"Sorry," Adolf muttered, standing and working the kinks out of his back.

"Come on upstairs," said Anna. "I'll show you a more comfortable bed. Slightly more comfortable, anyway."

Adolf stumbled after her as she led him up creaking stairs, devoid of carpet. The second floor contained several closed doors on either side of a hallway. Anna opened the last one on the left. The room was small and musty smelling. A small bed--the only furniture in the room--was covered with only a sheet. At least it was clean. Adolf took off his shoes and shirt, then stretched out, delighted to discover Anna was wrong. The bed was much more comfortable than the table.

The last thing he recalled was Anna dropping a blanket over him.

When Adolf awoke, he was alone in the dark. He sat up feeling stiff and hungry. His head ached fiercely, but at least, for once, he was well rested. He left the bed, feeling for a light switch along the wall. He found one, but nothing happened when he flipped it. As his eyes adjusted to the gloom, Adolf began to search for a bathroom. Stymied once again, he was about to get dressed when the door opened.

"Oh, good," said Anna. "You're awake."

"How long--?"

"Almost fourteen hours. It's just after five,"

"Morning or evening?"

Anna laughed. "The sun's just coming up." She set a bundle of clothes on the bed. "These are Stefan's. They should fit you all right, except for the pants being too short, but no one will see you except us."

"Are you sure? I'd think the appearance of a stranger among pariahs would attract a lot of attention."

"They'll just assume you're another dispossessed wanderer looking for work and a meal. There's an awful lot of them around these days. But if anyone does come by, don't say anything. That

cultured speech of yours would be a dead giveaway."
She gazed thoughtfully at Adolf. "We should give
you a scar on your throat. You can pretend you're
mute."

Adolf nodded absently, his attention focused
on more pressing matters. "Is there a bathroom here?"
he asked.

"Of course. In the yard out back. It's the little
building with the half moon on the door."

Adolf laughed, embarrassed. Of course he
should have realized that no family out of favor with
the State would have running water. Still, he wasn't
used to thinking in those terms.

"Uh, how about aspirin?"

"I'll make you some willow bark tea." Anna
left, and Adolf hurried downstairs and out the back
door.

Returning to the farmhouse--at a much more
relaxed pace--Adolf found Stefan sitting on the floor
by the fireplace with Adolf's valise laying open beside
him, and the contents spread neatly before him.

"Can I help you find anything?" Adolf asked,
trying not to sound angry.

Stefan looked like a child caught with his
hand in a cookie jar. "Uh--sorry. I didn't know
how long you'd be asleep, and it's been so long since
I've had anything new to read--" He gestured
helplessly at the papers on the floor.

"That's all right," said Adolf sitting beside
Stefan. "After all, I brought them to share."

"This is incredible!" Stefan held a stained and
torn book of seventeenth century rabbinical teaching
as if it were made of gold. He put it down carefully
and picked up a fragment of someone's diary. "I've

never seen such a wealth of knowledge in one place;
not even the *Judenmuseum*! You've got--what? At
least three scholarly texts--"

"With pages missing," Adolf pointed out.

"And a *Torah*--"

"Several of them. I think if you put the
various pieces of them together, you get one complete
one. I haven't had time to try it yet."

"And what are these?" Stefan reverently
spread out notebooks with missing covers, and loose
papers with writing in various languages scrawled
across it. "Medical research notes; personal journals;
plans for some kind of resistance movement--" He
stared at Adolf as if he were an alchemist. "Your
curator must think very highly of you, to trust you
with treasure like this."

"And here I just thought she wanted me to
have something to read when I got bored," Adolf
said, scratching his neck where the course
homespun shirt chaffed his skin.

"What do you say when you're searched on the
road?" asked Stefan. "Doesn't it look rather odd for a
penniless wanderer to be carrying this much reading
material?"

"Not anymore," said Adolf. "Paper's in short
supply. Recyclers are paying a penny a pound for any
kind. I just tell the soldiers I'm on my way to sell it."

"I didn't know about the paper shortage," said
Stefan. Then, glancing worriedly at Adolf, "You
wouldn't really sell this for recycling, would you?"

Adolf sighed. "No. I--" He faltered, wanting
to say that sometimes he blamed those books and
stories for ruining his life. But how could he tell that
to someone like Stefan? Someone who had lost as

much as Adolf, yet still found the energy for enthusiasm and faith? "I wouldn't. I just hope someday, these pages will mean something to more than just us."

"They will," said Stefan with a certainty Adolf envied.

"Speaking of earning your keep, you two--" They looked up to see Anna in the kitchen doorway. "Time's a wasting. Get some food in ya' and get to work. Adolf, you ready to learn to be a farmer?"

"As ready as I'll ever be." They went into the kitchen, and sat down at the table Adolf had fallen asleep on the day before.

Anna brought them plates of bread along with eggs scrambled with some of the excellent cheese she made.

"Drink this," she said, handing Adolf a cup of steaming liquid. He took a careful sip, and nearly choked. It tasted awful. "Drink it," she insisted. "It will help your headache. This is all you'll be seeing in the way of medicine from now on. We don't have Medical Priority Points, or a pharmacy down the street."

Adolf shuddered, but drank the tea, trying not to think about what getting a serious illness would mean out here.

His mouth was full when he noticed Anna and Stefan's mother--with clothes on, this time--peering at him from the doorway. He swallowed and tried to make some kind of polite greeting. The woman turned and ran, disappearing up the stairs.

"I'm sorry," said Adolf. "I didn't mean to scare her--"

"It's not you," said Stefan.

"She's been like this since they took Father away," said Anna.

"That must be difficult," said Adolf, wiping up the last of the egg with his bread.

"Usually, it's not a problem. She only has violent episodes about--"

"She's not ever violent!" said Anna.

"All right: *energetic* episodes, like yesterday, every couple of months. The rest of the time, she just sits in her old rocking chair."

"Or stays in bed."

They were silent for a moment. Then, Stefan clapped Adolf on the shoulder. "Come on!" he said. "Let's make a farmer out of you!"

Over the next twelve hours, Adolf learned more than he ever wanted to know about farming. He helped Stefan plow a field with an ill tempered ox, repaired a fence, weeded a garden patch that was mostly weeds to begin with and unsuccessfully chased after a chicken that escaped while Adolf was learning how to spread feed.

He returned to the house tired, sore, filthy, and dismayed by his performance.

"Don't take it so hard," Stefan said, clapping Adolf on the shoulder. He nearly collapsed from the pain. "Sorry. What I meant was: you did well for a first day. And we caught the chicken eventually, so no harm done."

The aroma coming from the kitchen almost made Adolf forget how horrible he felt. *Food*, thought Adolf. *Food and then sleep*.

"Hold it right there!" said Anna, looking like a hallway monitor from back in primary school.

"You're not coming into my kitchen looking and smelling like that. Wash up first."

"Come on," said Stefan, steering Adolf towards the pump.

"Actually, being clean sounds wonderful," said Adolf. "I don't suppose a hot shower is a possibility?"

"Shower, no," said Stefan, stripping off his shirt, and pouring a bucket of water over himself. "But you can have a hot bath after supper, if you're willing to carry water from the stove to the tub upstairs."

Adolf hefted the bucket Stefan held out to him, and tried to calculate how many trips up and down stairs filling that tub would mean. *Forget it*, he thought, as his overworked muscles screamed in protest just holding the one bucket, half filled.

Supper consisted of cooked turnips, fresh baked bread, and chicken stuffed with onions and rutabagas. Anna insisted on giving Adolf the largest portion of everything, which he protested in earnest, once he discovered how tough and stringy the chicken was. Still, considering how rarely these people probably ate meat of any kind, and what an honor it bestowed on a guest, Adolf ate it all, lavishly complimenting Anna's cooking.

After supper, while Anna cleared the table, and Adolf tried to muster the energy to climb the stairs to bed, Stefan bounced to his feet and announced, "I'll help you with the dishes, Anna."

"Does he do that often?" Adolf asked her.

"No. But he's so anxious to start the reading and discussion, he'll do anything to hurry it along."

"Reading? Discussion?" said Adolf. "I was

thinking more along the lines of sleeping."

"Oh, Adolf, please," said Stefan, almost dropping a stack of plates. "Those books and papers you brought...It's been so long since...couldn't we--?"

"You're welcomed to do all the reading you like," said Adolf. "But--"

"I know we don't have a *minyan*," said Stefan. "But still, just having four people present would be something."

"And mother loves being read to," said Anna. "That and having her hair combed. Those are about the only things that get her to smile these days."

Adolf could only stare. "I didn't realize how seriously you were taking Judaism," he said.

Stefan smiled bleakly. "We've got to have something to make sense of all this shit, don't we?"

"Stefan," said Anna. "Adolf's probably read most of this, but it's still new to us. Why don't we let him get some sleep while we do some reading. Maybe he'll be up for a discussion tomorrow night."

"You're right," said Stefan. "That would probably be better."

Adolf glanced at the old woman in the corner, then at his benefactors. "No, that's all right. There's plenty here that I haven't read, and I'd like to hear your thoughts."

Anna and Stefan cleaned, while Adolf rummaged through the books. Soon after, they all gathered around the hearth, and despite the balmy April evening and the enormous cost of fuel, lit a fire, and by its light, read from the book of Daniel. Adolf and Stefan took turns reading, while Anna combed her mother's long gray hair.

"Don't you want to read?" Adolf asked her at

one point.

Anna smiled dreamily. "I'd rather listen to you, Adolf. There's such power in your voice."

"Yes," said Stefan. "I feel it too."

Adolf yawned. He certainly didn't feel powerful. Yet he could admit to feeling less lost and less helpless than he had since fleeing Berlin. Whether it was the fellowship or the ancient words, he did not know.

But for now, he was content to remain that way.

CHAPTER 12

Adolf stayed two weeks with Stefan and Anna.
After that, they filled his knapsack with food and gave
him directions to his next contact: a former
Judenmuseum curator who now traveled the
countryside as a tinker and storyteller.

"I wish you could stay longer," said Anna, as
they walked toward the gate at the end of the lane.

"So do I," said Adolf. "But Stefan is right:
wandering laborers don't stay this long. And you
don't need the extra trouble suspicious neighbors can
bring."

"Thank you for all you've done," said Anna.

Adolf laughed. "All *I've* done? You're the
ones who fed, clothed and sheltered me! Not to
mention teaching me enough about my new life to
give me a shot at survival."

"You gave us plenty in return and you know it.
We'll be discussing your ideas for days. Not to
mention all those books you're leaving behind. Won't
you take something more in trade besides that book of
Hebrew folktales?"

Adolf shook his head. "I'm grateful to you for
lightening my load." He paused, uncertain of what
Anna expected. Finally, he kissed her hand, and then
started down the road.

"Hey!" she called. He turned.
"Remember us!"

"I'll do more than that!" he called. "I'll see
you again someday!" Adolf had no idea why he made
her such a promise, but he sensed he had just made

Anna and Stefan both very happy.

Late that afternoon, Adolf sat beside a
handsome Aryan man just a few years older than
himself. They rode in a rickety cart, pulled by a half
lame horse. Adolf's companion seemed to find the
jolting and bouncing relaxing.

"So then, about twelve years ago, the scientists
came up with a way to test for late stage multiple
sclerosis. Now, of course, they test in utero; anyone
with the defective gene just isn't born. But back
then...well, you know how excited the Third *Führer*
was about new scientific techniques."

Adolf nodded. "And then, when they found
they had whole cartloads of attractive, pure blooded
Aryans with hidden defects--"

"Yes. It was either kill them all--and many
were children--or find some sort of quiet 'retirement'.
After sterilization, of course."

"How old were you then?" asked Adolf.

"Fifteen. When my school was called out for
testing, I hardly gave it a thought. Then the results
come in and: surprise! They tell me I'm a
carrier. Suddenly, everything changes. I can't
get married or father children--"

"--Which translates into no longer being part
of the Body of the *Reich*." Adolf sighed.

"They were very nice; very sympathetic, all
those nurses and technicians and councilors. But in
the end it was the same for me as everyone else: my
family disowned me, and the other two members who
turned out to have the same gene. Actually, I was
luckier than either of them. I'd been at the top of my
class at school. Education plus good looks got me a

job as museum curator once my 'retraining' was completed. It could have been worse."

"And now you don't even have that. I'm sorry, Markus."

"I'm not. I've always wanted to travel. And thanks to all those books I read—*torah*, numerology, the *kabbalah*—my new career was ready the day the museum closed."

"And people actually pay you for storytelling?"

"Not in money. Some places, I can get a meal and a night in a barn in exchange for telling stories. It's the fortune telling that's really lucrative."

Adolf laughed. "But anyone wanting a horoscope or psychic reading just has to go to an official Party Soothsayer! Why risk their life and coin with some roving wanderer? A *missgeburt*, no less? Uh, no offense."

"None taken," said Markus. "But, see? You've hit the nail on the head. No one believes official Party *anything*, anymore. Especially in personal matters. But a wanderer, with claims to ancient knowledge? People desperate enough will believe. Will pay to believe, as a matter of fact. Being an outcast makes me even more credible--and less of a risk, since I stand more to lose than my customers if we're caught."

Markus turned the horse down a nearly invisible track. The forest darkened around them. "You know," he continued, "Jews weren't the only race to be eradicated by our grandparents. There were people called Gypsies. From what I can tell, most of our popular conception of fortune telling and influencing Fate comes from them."

"Is that why they were wiped out?" asked Adolf. "Competition with the New Order?"

"Don't know. I found scraps of tantalizing information, but so much more was missing. One thing I have learned, though: when a society is undergoing great stress, fortune tellers thrive."

"I suppose people see it as a last resort; a way to exert at least the illusion of control over their lives and fears."

Markus nodded. "And, at the moment, ancient Judaism is selling really well. Ah, here we are!"

They stopped in front of a burned out farm. It was very old, and far enough away from the nearest village to have been isolated even in better times. Now, the forest had reclaimed field and garden, and only the foundations poked out from the trees.

Markus stood with his hands in plain sight, and whistled three shrill notes.

"Let's see your friend's hands," came a gruff voice from the tree behind them.

Adolf tucked the valise under his arm and held out his hands without turning around. The owner of the voice, a middle aged man wearing the remnants of a military uniform and carrying a rusty Luger, came into view. "Drop the bag," he said.

Adolf dropped the valise, then slid his knapsack from his shoulders and let it fall. A boy of about ten darted out from the bushes and took them both, searching them quickly and efficiently.

"What are all these books and papers?" asked the boy.

The man with the gun looked interested. "Who is he and why did you bring him?" he asked

Markus.

"A onetime rich boy who had to disappear," said Markus. "He and I have several...associates...in common. I can vouch for him."

"He looks like a rich boy," growled the older man. "Still, we need all the help we can get." He looked Adolf up and down. "So what'd you do? Seduce your father's mistress? See something you weren't supposed to? Join the wrong side of a coup?"

"A fondness for dead religions, I think," said Adolf.

The man glanced again at the books and papers. "Judaism?" he asked. Adolf nodded. "Great! Just what we need! Another preacher!"

Adolf opened his mouth, both to protest the title and to ask how many others like him might be found here, but the gruff man spoke again. "And so now you want to join the Revolution?"

Before Adolf's expression could turn to bafflement, Markus spoke. "I haven't told him about your organization. For now, he's only looking for food and shelter--"

"We're not a charity, Markus!" He looked at Adolf. "And we're not a social club, either. We're an underground, dedicated to the overthrow of the Evil Empire. And thanks to this one," he threw a disgusted look at Markus, "we're your new family. At least until we change locations or decide to kill you."

"Pleased to meet you," said Adolf wearily. *When is this crazy roller coaster that used to be my life going to slow down?* "I'm Adolf--"

"Don't give me your name--!"

"Schmidt," he finished with a smile. That

much, at least he had learned.

The other laughed. "Nice to meet you, *Herr* Schmidt. I got two of your brothers working for me already! I'm Reinhardt."

Later, in the cellar of the ruined farm, Adolf met the two-dozen members of Reinhardt's cadre. They were a fairly even mix of dedicated idealists, former members of the upper and middle classes who blamed their ruin on the Party, and unsuccessful criminals. From the first two groups, Adolf discovered six others who shared his interest in Judaism. While the rest of the cell remained wary, this group warmed to Adolf at once.

"Have some more soup," said Lena, a young woman of about twenty. Adolf had learned she was the only survivor of a once prosperous merchant's family.

"I'd snuck out of the house to see my boyfriend the night they came," she said as she ladled out more of the thin broth floating with carrots and peas that the group called supper. "When I came back, the whole family was being loaded into the truck. I hid in the greenhouse for three days. I didn't leave until the new family moved in."

"And you never knew that your father was trafficking in censored reading material?"

"Only vaguely. But after that, I made up my mind to find out about it. After all, he felt it was worth his life--and the lives of his children. So, since then, I've read all the suppressed writings I can get my hands on."

"And what have you decided?" Adolf asked, setting down the empty bowl.

"That it's worth my life as well. I just don't intend to die before everyone on the planet finds out what the Party tries so hard to hide." She began gathering up the empty bowls.

One of the differences between this group and the Berlin museum crowd was the number of women. Nearly half this base was female. Of the male half, Adolf counted at least five under the age of sixteen.

The cellar, though cold, was surprisingly comfortable, which told Adolf the group had been here for some time. There were cots and sleeping bags, dishes and utensils of all kinds, a decent latrine, with a well-ordered rotation for cleaning, and a large assortment of second rate weapons.

Reinhardt, Adolf discovered, was once a staff sergeant. When his unit was sent to pacify food riots in Latvia, he decided he was on the wrong side. "Currently," he told Adolf that night, "I'm the only one in the cadre with real military training."

"Leader by default?" asked Adolf.

Reinhardt laughed bitterly. "You could say that. We had two other guys, Navy, but still good guys. Lost 'em three months ago trying to blow up a base, just across the border, in Belgium."

Adolf, who had been wondering exactly where he was, felt better now that he had an idea. He decided asking for a more specific location wasn't a good idea. "Is there a chance you might know some of my friends?" he asked. "Klaus Feiffer? He was in the Tiger division in Russia?"

"Sorry. Doesn't ring a bell."

Adolf knew it was a long shot. The military was huge. And even if this guy knew Klaus, he might not tell Adolf. So far, his attempts to learn the fate of his friends had led nowhere. Even Ilsa, who he had expected to see, or at least get a message from, seemed to have disappeared.

It felt strange to be surrounded by people, and yet completely isolated from any news that mattered. Anna and Stefan had a radio, rationing it to only one hour a day to save batteries. While Anna preferred listening to music, she graciously tuned in the news broadcasts for Adolf's sake. He had learned of trouble in the Ukraine and new outbreaks of polio, but nothing about a sinister Jewish underground—and nothing about his once newsworthy family. It was as if they'd just disappeared. Maybe they had.

"You better get some sleep." Reinhardt pointed to an empty sleeping bag in one of the draftier corners of the cellar. "Tomorrow, we'll figure out what you can do. I figure a college boy's had some military training, right?"

"Four years worth."

"We don't need much help learning to march on parade or light ladies' cigarettes, but maybe you can help teach the kids to shoot."

"I'll give it a try," said Adolf.

Adolf spent the next six weeks teaching what little knowledge and skill with weapons he had to several unruly teenagers, and listening a great deal. For all that he admired the courage and, admittedly, lunacy of anyone who thought they could overthrow the Third *Reich*, he quickly became disenchanted with the rebels with whom he now lived. Their days seemed taken up entirely with two activities: locating food and talking.

Their talking fascinated Adolf at first. They

hatched plans to assassinate every high ranking official in the *Reich*; to kidnap the wife of the *Führer*; to seize control of the central broadcasting station in Berlin and eloquently shout out a message of truth to all people, before dying gloriously.

And the truth they wanted to shout was cause for even more discussions--and arguments.

Adolf began volunteering for foraging detail. At least fighting the brambles for a handful of berries and stealing eggs from farmers gave him a sense of accomplishment.

"Don't be so hard on them," said Schuller, as he showed Adolf how to set snares. At fifty, Schuller was the oldest of the group, and he reminded Adolf of Professor Hoffman. "They've accomplished the impossible just by forming this group and keeping it together for this long. Miracles take a little longer."

"I admire your faith," said Adolf. Then, ashamed, he said, "I admire them, too. I'm certainly in no position to judge. I just don't see these people ever actually *doing* anything!"

Schuller gazed shrewdly at Adolf. "Maybe they remind you too much of yourself."

Adolf stood motionless for a full minute, and then smiled. "Bull's-eye," he said.

"Want to talk about it?"

Adolf slowed his pace to match Schuller's pronounced limp as they headed back to base. "I guess this place reminds me of the *Judenmuseum*. We talked; all the time. We read ancient texts and argued about what they meant. We found great truths, and thought about how someday, we'd use them to save the world.

"And all we accomplished is...this. Me, barely

making it as a fugitive. My friends, dead, or in labor camps, or on the run like me. It's so discouraging. Almost...insulting."

"Insulting to whom?"

"To the Jews. To anyone who could create such history and live and die with such honor. To receive the gift of their knowledge --at the price of their lives-- and then fumble around like this; spinning our wheels; it...it...insults their memory."

Schuller stopped and looked at Adolf again. At his full height, he barely reached Adolf's chest. "Young man," he said. "With a tongue like yours, I don't see that gift ever being wasted. Maybe you just need to talk and walk at the same time. Once people start following you, who knows what will happen?"

"Following *me*?" Adolf laughed. "Don't you think I'd better figure out where I'm going first?"

"Why bother? From what I can see, few of history's great leaders ever did."

They reached the ruins, where they found a man Adolf had never met engaged in animated discussion with Reinhardt and several of his lieutenants.

"Do you know him?" Adolf whispered to Schuller, as one of the women took the foodstuffs from them.

The older man nodded. "Braun. He's a liaison between us and one of the larger cells. When he's involved, it usually means something is actually going to happen."

Interested, Adolf moved close enough to hear what was being said. Braun looked his way, stopped talking and looked at Reinhardt, who nodded. Braun shrugged and continued. "...so it's either now or never. Finster's leaving in two weeks for the summit conference on land allocation. We take him out—we might have a shot at a more moderate voice in the *Führer's* ear."

"Or at least a marginally competent one," said Reinhardt.

"Finster?" said Adolf. "Rupert Finster? The Chairman of the Department of Agriculture?"

"The good friend of the *Führer*, who thinks farmers can live on good thoughts and prayers to the gods," said Lena. "The one who thinks education is bad for peasants—and especially bad for women."

"So how will we get close enough to kill him?" asked Reinhardt.

"We're going to substitute one of our agents for one of his maids. I'm going to all the cells, looking for a suitable candidate, and as much back up as I can get. We need a young Aryan woman who can pass for a maid and knows how to kill. Obviously, it's a suicide mission, but Finster is the greatest threat to the survival of the ordinary people to date. And I think we stand a good chance of pulling this off."

"I'd like to volunteer," said Emilie, the girl who sat next to Lena.

Again, Braun glanced at Reinhardt.

"Maybe," said the leader. "She's learns fast and stays cool under fire. But she's never killed anyone."

"But like the man said," said Emilie. "I learn fast."

"Wait a minute," said Adolf. "How are you planning on duplicating the servant class bar code on her arm?"

"We've matched the color of the yellow dye

they use," said Braun. "The pattern, too. Obviously, it won't pass a scan, but once she's inside the house, it won't matter."

"The hell it won't!"

"Keep out of this, rich boy!" snapped one of the younger men. "No one's asking you to risk your neck—"

"I just thought you might like to know that Finster has code readers installed in every doorway of his house. And he's not one of those paranoid types who constantly changes staff; he's one of those paranoid types who knows every servant better than their own mothers do!"

"What makes you the expert?" demanded the same man.

"I've been to his house," said Adolf. He noticed then that he had everyone's attention. "And when he came to visit my family, he brought his own cook! My father used to joke that he was the most anal retentive man in the *Reich*; the kind who notices every little detail."

Everyone in the circle seemed to deflate.

"Anything else you know about the man that you'd like to share with us?" Adolf couldn't tell if Reinhardt was angry with Adolf, or just situation.

Adolf tried to remember. He'd only met the man a few times. Maybe he should have kept his mouth shut. "My uncle once said that you could set your watch by his daily routines. And that he'd kick out the *Führer* himself if he tried to stay past ten at night."

"What happens at ten?" asked Lena.

"He listens to 'Mystery Theater' on the radio in bed. Drinking a glass of warm milk, I believe."

Braun glared at Adolf, as his brilliant plan collapsed under the weight of reality. Reinhardt's expression was hard to read. But the meeting was definitely over.

"I can't believe you actually knew these people," Emilie whispered as she rose to leave. "Oh, and by the way. Thanks for saving me from dying stupidly. When I die, I want it to mean something."

"Glad I could help," Adolf said to no one in particular. But he wondered if he really had.

The next day, a messenger arrived. He was about twelve years old, slightly built, and apparently very good at surviving on his own.

After speaking with the boy at length, Reinhardt sent him to the cellar for a meal and some rest, and called a meeting of the entire camp.

"Our intelligence has confirmed the latest rumor: several of the old wartime extermination camps have reopened for business."

"So who's being exterminated this time?" asked Lena.

"Officially, only mental and physical defectives who were somehow missed earlier. But we've got witnesses who say it's a lot more than that. Mostly very old and very young; non Aryans who aren't worth shipping to the Colonies. Also, they say, healthy looking adults; *missgeburt* or other undesirables."

Adolf felt his stomach tighten.

"I've been asked to send a half-dozen volunteers to Dengler. He's planning on blowing up the rails and taking one of the trains. At worst, we'll be making a statement. At best, we'll be recruiting a few more members.

"I want to hear from all interested volunteers by this afternoon. I'll decide who's going by nightfall. The mission leaves at dawn."

People began to disperse, speaking quietly among themselves. Adolf was trying to catch Shuler's eye, when Reinhardt intercepted him. "There were some private messages as well," the leader told him. "I believe one of them is for you, but you'll have to ask the boy yourself."

Keeping a tight rein on his emotions, Adolf hurried to the mess area, where he found the messenger boy gulping down a day's worth of rations.

"I'm Adolf," he said. "I hear you might have a message for me."

The boy met his gaze with hazel eyes that seemed far too old for such a young face. "Someone named Ilsa gave me a letter. Tell me who she is to you. If it's the right answer, you get the letter."

Adolf released a breath he didn't know he'd been holding and he whispered, "My wife."

"Then I guess this is yours." He took a crumpled, weather stained envelope from an inside pocket of his jacket and gave it to Adolf, who just stared at it without making any move to open it.

"If I give you a letter to give to her, do you think you could deliver it?" he asked.

"Sure."

The boy's easy confidence startled Adolf. "What's your name?" he asked.

"Wolf."

"Where are your parents?"

"Dead."

"The rest of your family?"

"Right here." Wolf swept a hand in a circle to indicate the base.

"And when it's time to deliver the mail, you can find a fugitive that the entire *Reich*, with all its resources, can't find?"

Wolf half smiled. "I have my ways." Then he stood, wiping his hands on his pants. "But it's still a good idea to be careful about what you write. *I* never get caught. But I can't vouch for what happens to the mail after I deliver it."

Adolf walked a long way into the woods before stopping beneath a huge oak, and unfolding the letter with shaking hands. It was dated May 15; less than a month after their flight from Berlin. Adolf squinted into the deepening shadows, trying to guess at what day it was now. Late June was all he could be certain of.

Dear Adolf,

I hope this note finds you well, whenever and wherever it reaches you. For me, the sun shines brighter, the wind is warmer, and food (when I can get it) tastes sweeter.

Such is freedom. I think I should have left my life as a missgeburt and joined the resistance years ago, but for you and our friends at the museum. Now that time is over; the decision made for us all.

Each day I think of you, Adolf, and wonder how you are faring. I believe you are still seeking your place in all this. In my travels, I have met many formerly privileged young men who are too angry at their change in fortune to be of any use to the

revolution. I think of you and say, "Not my husband!"
("Husband." It still feels strange to say!)

Whatever your circumstances, Adolf, I know
you're involved in all this for a reason. Yours is a
special role, and no one can take your place. If you're
feeling lost, remember that nearly all the ancient
prophets were lost at first too. They all did their time
in the desert--or among lions, or inside whales. Think
of this as your time of wandering.

Until we meet again in the flesh, know that we
are joined forever in spirit.

All my love,

Ilsa

Adolf read the letter a dozen more times. Then
he went to find Reinhardt and told him he wanted to
be part of the next morning's mission.

"So what is this Dengler like?" Adolf
whispered to Lena as they made their way through the
forest.

"His group is more experienced; better armed.
They've done more successful actions against the
Reich than any other cadre I know of."

"So what do they need with us?"

"Their last action wasn't so successful," said
Wolf. "They need replacements."

Lovely, thought Adolf.

Adolf and the other five volunteers, including
Lena and Schuller, crossed the woodland without
incident. Wolf, acting as their guide, would stay only

long enough to deliver messages. Adolf had been spending what little spare time he had working on a letter to Ilsa.

Dengler's camp turned out to be hidden in the middle of a city. "Best place to hide," Schuller explained as they crawled through a shaft in an abandoned coal mine, then into a network of sewer pipes beneath the factory town whose name Adolf did not even know. Despite the memories of his last night with Ilsa that the journey dredged up, the sense of déjà vu was not a pleasant one.

Darkness had fallen while they were still underground. Wolf led the others through silent streets to the back door of a modest house.

Wolf exchanged passwords with someone at the door. Then they were all ushered inside. The place seemed to be without electricity. Someone shone a flashlight on each of them, keeping himself in the shadows. Adolf, exhausted from a day of marching, crawling and climbing with little food, found the whole thing unnerving.

"So this is what Reinhardt sends me?" sighed a man's voice. "Let's hope they look more impressive once they're cleaned up."

"Don't knock the grime and coal dust, Dengler," said a woman's voice. "It's good camouflage, and unlike most things, it's free!"

The man chuckled and leaned the flashlight against a wall, allowing a splash of diffused light to orient the newcomers. They were in what had once been a parlor but now served as a meeting room, complete with a long scarred wooden table, chipped cups of cold coffee, and piles of maps.

Dengler was about thirty years old. He had

rugged good looks and an air of confidence, but his speech betrayed his lower class origins. "We have one full day to rehearse the plan," he said to the group. "You newcomers can take two hours for food and rest. I know there are friends and comrades who haven't seen each other in some time, but you'll have to keep the reunions short. Shultz; Ludwig. You have guard duty."

Adolf ran his gaze over the dozen or so members of Dengler's group. Several were exchanging emotional greetings with Adolf's companions from Reinhardt's group. Since there would be no old friends waiting for him here, Adolf began to look for food and a likely spot to rest. Then the world stopped as he tried to make sense out of a face that his brain told him was familiar.

"Well, Adolf, I was wondering when I'd bump into you."

"Frederic!" cried Adolf, as the voice and face materialized into a ghost from his past. "You're alive!" Adolf nearly mowed down several fellow revolutionaries in his haste to reach his old schoolmate.

"For the moment," said Frederic, throwing his arms around Adolf in an awkward embrace. "I knew you'd make it out somehow. But I never expected to see you with these ruffians."

"What are you doing here?"

Instead of answering, Frederic glanced at another young man, hovering at his elbow. He was a few years older than Adolf and Frederic, clearly Aryan, and looked vaguely familiar, though Adolf could swear he'd never met the man.

"This is Adolf Zelig," said Frederic. "Our

Brigitta was his sister."

Adolf felt his stomach tighten at the word *was*. Here, at last, was his chance to learn of the fate of his loved ones, and now he wasn't sure he wanted to know. He thought of the shy young girl, who had only been in their group for a few months. After an awkward silence, he turned to Zelig. "What happened to her?" he asked.

"She was picked up by the *Gestapo* before I could get to her. If I'd found out just a few hours earlier I..." Frederic squeezed the other man's shoulder and shook his head, as if they'd had this discussion more than once.

Zelig went on. "They sent her to a brothel somewhere. Not even an *SS* place, since they don't want her traitorous tendencies to be passed on to future Aryans." His voice shook. "The real irony here is that my whole family has been up to its eyeballs in illegal activities for years. Last year, things started coming apart, so I insisted we send Brigitta off to college so she'd be safe!"

"If he hadn't come looking for his sister— against all common sense I might add—I'd be dead now," said Frederic. "I was still trying to figure out what was going on and where to hide. Fortunately, Zelig's background was a bit more useful. He hid me in a cellar for three weeks before he decided it was safe to leave Berlin."

Adolf turned back to the other Adolf. "You mentioned your family's long time involvement in illegal activities. If I may be so bold, what kind were they? Were you involved with Jewish writing...?"

"I'd never even heard of the Jews, other than what we learned in grammar school! If I'd known

Brigitta was involved with that sort of thing, I'd have
pulled her from the school!

"Believe it or not, I'm a patriot. My family's
been trying to fight the corrupt leadership that's
invaded the *Reich* in recent years. I never intended to
destroy it, but I'm not left with much choice now."

"I know exactly what you mean," said Adolf.
He turned to Frederic. "Do you know anything about
the others? Krista? Franz? Ilsa?" Adolf gulped back
the last name, afraid Frederic might know something
more recent than her letter.

Frederic's face grew grim in the meager light.
"It was a well stocked hideout. There was a vid set;
and Zelig had a radio not tuned to government
channels. Krista was executed just a few days after
we were all denounced. It was a group execution.
'Sexual deviants' the announcer said."

"I guess a short, myopic lesbian didn't have
much of a chance for anything—not even a life in
brothel."

"You forgot to mention poor," said Frederic.
"No. She never had a chance. However, if a brothel
was the alternative, I'd guess she would have
preferred death.

"Franz was captured, but there's been no
official word on him. He's probably in some high-
level security prison somewhere. I heard that Karl got
pulled in for questioning, even
though he'd been out of contact with us for years.
They released him, presumably after seizing all
his assets and ruining his name. I don't know where
he is now."

"And...my family?"

"Still alive and free, last I heard. Your father

must have some major stuff on a lot of powerful]
people, to be able to hang onto what little he still
has—not to mention pull off that story about you!"

"What story about me?"

"You haven't head? Why, Adolf, you've been
kidnapped by terrorists! At least that's what your
grieving parents and their high level friends are
saying. That way, they can explain your
disappearance without denouncing a Goebbels as a
traitor or spending scarce resources tracking you
down. I expect that soon, your 'body' will be
discovered, all of Germany will mourn, your death
will be avenged—against whichever group the Party
wants cleansed at the time—and it will all be
forgotten."

"My God," said Adolf. He stared at his friend,
trying to make sense of it all. His family was safe, but
who knew how many innocents would soon die in his
name? "They're not even searching for me?"

Zelig shook his head. "Not officially. But
don't relax your vigilance for an instant. The Party
still wants to get its hands on you. And
once you're declared dead, it will be doubly
dangerous for you to surface."

Adolf nodded, still a bit numb. "What about
your family," he belatedly asked Frederic.

"Not so fortunate as yours," he said through
clenched teeth. "My father committed suicide, and
my brother's wife divorced him. I still have some
hope of finding him and my mother. That's one of the
reasons I'm with Dengler and Zelig. They have the
best intelligence in the underground."

"Or so we keep telling him," said Zelig. There
was an awkward pause. "Let's get some rest," he

added. "We have important work to do. And reunions like these can take a lot out of even the strongest men."

It was the stillness that Adolf would always remember.

For the longest time, nothing moved as he crouched by the train track with the other fifteen volunteers. *Don't move,* Adolf reminded himself. *Don't breathe. Don't grip your Mauser so tight you cut off your circulation. Or perhaps in my case, shoot myself.*

They had only the stars for light and wore black clothing as camouflage. To their left, the tunnel through which the train must pass was rigged with an almost laughably simple booby trap. As it was standard for all trains on official Party business to have one guard atop each car, a thin wire had been stretched across the end of the tunnel at what they all hoped would be the right height. As the train exited, the first guard would be knocked over—either off the train or into the guard behind him—followed by the next and the next, until, hopefully, all had been rendered "non combative" as Dengler put it.

Like dominoes. Like bowling balls. No one would have to fire a shot.

Burning garbage across the track just outside the tunnel would force the engineer to stop the train. Then there would only be him and a few guards in the caboose to deal with.

Adolf crouched in the wet grass, and wondered if anything ever went according to plan in this life.

The lonesome whistle of the approaching train

galvanized everyone into action. The tunnel created
an echo chamber, so any shouts for help that might be
coming from the guards atop the train would reach
neither the men inside nor the saboteurs on the
ground.

The train, when it emerged from the tunnel
was empty on top.

Dengler let out a victory yell that would have
done his Saxon ancestors proud and proceeded to light
the reeking fuel already placed on the tracks. They
could almost hear the frightened cursing of the
engineer as he maneuvered four tons of steel into an
emergency
stop. Dengler shot him before he could draw a
breath of relief at his narrow escape.

"Was that really necessary?" asked Adolf,
staring at the blank face that moments ago had been a
skilled engineer. "For all we knew, he hated his job!
He might have joined us if we'd asked!"

Adolf caught several angry glares as his
comrades hurried to their assigned box cars. "We
don't have time to do personality profiles," said
Dengler. "And you'd better get used to that fact."

Angry, but not sure at who, Adolf went to his
car and helped open the door. They were greeted by
the stares of several dozen people, crammed into a
space not even designed for humans. Some looked
terrified by this latest development. Others seemed
beyond fear; beyond any feeling at all. A few, the
youngest, thought Adolf, seemed to recognize the
newcomers as possibly here to help.

While Adolf had imagined himself heroically
guiding grateful prisoners from the train and into a
new and better life, the reality consisted of hustling

everyone roughly off the train and into the forest. He occasionally called out reassuring greetings and explanations, but the fact was, only a lifetime of ingrained obedience on the part of most of the prisoners allowed the mission to succeed.

Once the last victim was off the train, Adolf left Lena and Schuller to explain the situation to the refugees and joined the others in stripping the area of anything useful.

Maps, codebooks, weapons and heavily damaged radio equipment lay in a growing pile on the ground. "Adolf!" called Dengler. "Go help Werner's group with the uniforms."

Adolf hurried into the tunnel, now dimly lit with flashlights and torches. There, five of his teammates were busy stripping blood-soaked uniforms from the mangled forms of guards. Adolf swallowed hard as he stared at what had sounded like a comical bowling game just hours before.

"These won't be much use to us," said Emilie, fighting with the top half of a corpse for his jacket.

"There're ways to get the blood out," said an older woman.

"I wasn't thinking of the blood. Look, these are intestines wrapped up in here. Hey Adolf! Whatcha waiting for? I've got a lovely one for you..."

Adolf ran into the woods and threw up.

Back at base camp, no one said anything to Adolf about his unmanly behavior. Most were too busy being ecstatic. The raid had been a complete success without a single casualty—at least among the rebels--and the loot they brought home was enormously valuable.

The people they had rescued turned out to be a mixed lot. Some had useful skills and a strong desire to join the underground. Others remained in shock. A few seemed angry to have missed their appointment with the furnaces.

Whatever was to become of them, Adolf would never know. Before dawn the next day, Dengler ordered the base scrubbed clean, and broke everyone into small groups, with various covers and orders to disperse or regroup later. Adolf barely had time to finish his letter to Ilsa and give it to Wolf before they headed off in opposite directions.

"I'm so glad you were assigned to our group," Lena told Adolf as the crumbling factory town fell away behind them. Adolf, Lena, Schuller and a pock faced boy who had no tongue were on their way to France. Dressed in the rags of what had once been farmer's clothes, they carried papers that identified them as members of one family, 'rotated' off their land, and looking for work in the nearest city.

"It wasn't much of a choice," said Adolf. "I don't have the skills for any of the other missions. This way, I can at least make contact with another museum group."

He wondered if he would ever see Frederic again. Their brief encounter of just days before was already starting to feel like part of a dream. Perhaps he would meet more of his old friends in the underground. Or perhaps, he shuddered at the thought, he would meet them on the other side of a drawn weapon. He had learned of many such cases from the people he now met and worked with.

They were stopped and searched several times that first day, but their papers passed inspection and they had nothing worth stealing. They stopped for the night at a roadside camp, filled with other dispossessed people on the move.

They ate their meager rations in silence, and then spread their blankets. Adolf offered to stand first watch, expecting the others to sleep. Instead, Lena brought him a book and, to Adolf's amazement, lit their tiny kerosene lantern. "Won't you read to us please, Adolf?" she said. Schuller and the boy nodded eagerly.

Adolf glanced at the strangers gathered nearby. "Are you crazy?" he whispered.

"It's only a book of children's tales," said Lena. "No one here will recognize them--except for those whom we might want to meet."

Adolf considered her words. "Why not?" he muttered. Opening the crumbling, weather stained book, he found a story he remembered. "The Wise Men of Chelm," he began.

When they left the next morning, their group had grown to twelve.

CHAPTER 13

The first bites of winter were mild here in the south of France. Adolf sat in a small outdoor café, where it was almost possible to forget the horrors happening worldwide.

Polio and smallpox were killing millions. A weakening in the immune system—particularly among Aryans—was making it harder for people to fight lesser diseases as well. An earthquake had leveled most of Denmark, and the ocean was reclaiming what was left. A food riot in the Ukraine had been settled by massacring thirty thousand people. Heresy was once again a capital crime, and with all the cults springing up these days, the officers of the Aryan Church were very busy.

None of this was in the newspaper spread on the table before him. Adolf had learned what the Party didn't print from people he met in this café. The old couple running it—both café and underground cell—boasted that this place had been a resistance headquarters of one kind or another since the 1780s. Adolf wondered if something particular had happened at that time in France. If so, nothing of it been mentioned in his history books at school.

The best news however, was for Adolf's eyes only. Ilsa's latest letter lay hidden under the newspaper. It had arrived marked "postage due" and the young messenger who brought it actually held out her hand as if waiting for payment. Fortunately, Adolf was able to buy her off with a piece of bread

and a magic trick he'd learned from his Uncle Gustav.
He pulled out the letter and read it again.

Dear Adolf,

*Life continues to be interesting. I recently had
the rare privilege of attending a discussion panel with
several Torah scholars. I'm not sure which part was
rarer: serious Jewish studies in a world in which all
Jews are currently dead, or the fact that a woman was
allowed to participate in a discussion of a religion
which never allowed women to participate. How's
that for a riddle? Give me your thoughts in your next
letter.*

*As to your question about how a revolution
intended to help the masses can keep them safe in the
meantime? Especially if they're foolish enough to
provide us with aid and comfort? That one is hard for
me as well. Try suggesting they follow a kosher diet.
It's true that starving people don't usually take well to
dietary suggestions unless there's also food attached.
(And believe me, I know. Feeding people has become
a priority for me, lately.)*

*However, current events are taking an
interesting turn. Trichinosis is on the rise, and most
shellfish is highly toxic because of the pollution in the
oceans. Coincidence? Yet another interesting subject
for discussion.*

*In the meantime, know that I think of you
always, Adolf, and hope to hear from you soon.*

*Until we meet in a better world—here on
earth—I remain,*

Your Ilsa

As usual, the letter contained nothing that could reveal her location, or compromise her mission.

But Adolf didn't need Ilsa to tell him about her activities. His wife was becoming a legend. She had been reported everywhere from Iceland to Egypt, doing everything from preaching Judaism to blowing up military outposts. The latest intelligence had her back in Germany, collecting supplies for the underground—by raiding *Wermacht* supply depots. Based on the reference in her letter to feeding people, that last rumor was likely true. It was certainly Ilsa's style.

Adolf too, had traveled extensively. Since his flight from Berlin, he had seen a great deal of Germany, Holland, Belgium, and France. And while he had been to all of those countries before, what he saw and experienced now was very different from what the privileged young heir had seen. For all he had thought he knew about the poverty and injustice of the empire, Adolf had been amazed at how it actually looked, and smelled, up close.

He turned back to his newspaper, marveling again at the headline that reported the death of Rupert Finster. Someone had managed to rig an explosive in his bedside radio. It had gone off two nights ago at ten o'clock; right at the start of Mystery Theater.

"More coffee, *Herr* Schmidt?" the young waitress asked.

"Yes, please." Adolf took a thoughtful sip, then cursed as once again he tasted hair from his mustache. This new dye was making it fall out.

Scooping out the hair and sipping more carefully, Adolf hoped his contact would arrive soon. There would be the usual exchange of codes taken from Proverbs or Psalms, then he or she would escort Adolf to yet another meeting or cell or safe house. After seven months, Adolf was getting sick of it. He had yet to accomplish anything of real importance.

Except maybe for his contribution to Finster's death. And as far as he could tell, that hadn't done a damned thing for the suffering masses other than getting a few of them hauled in for interrogation and torture.

It had come as quite a surprise, but Adolf had discovered he didn't want to be part of the killing; any killing. Not even of someone as malignant as Rupert Finster. *I guess that makes me a failure as a traitor along with everything else*, he thought.

Someone was approaching his table. Adolf looked up, expecting his contact.

Two *Waffen SS* stood by his table.

Adolf had been detained often enough by now that he knew what to do. He drew his ID from his pocket in a bored manner, and remained perfectly calm until the older soldier spoke. "Adolf Goebbels?"

Then his blood turned to ice water. If they knew who he was, it was over. Still, he was not about to waste all these months of training. He muttered a protest in garbled German and waved his ID at them.

Fortunately, the soldiers were trying to avoid a scene. Just as they were about to manhandle Adolf out of the café, an explosion shook the street. In the middle of a crowded intersection, a private car was now burning. Whether it was a rescue from his contact or a coincidence, Adolf never knew. He took advantage of the momentary distraction, not by running, as any good soldier would have expected, but by dropping to the ground and rolling under the table.

Then several more tables.

And then he was up and running. Adolf knew he could never evade capture if he stayed in town. They knew the place better than he, and no one would risk hiding him now.

His salvation rode into view in the form of a covered transport vehicle that was forcing its way through the chaotic traffic jam toward the city gates. A government seal on the windshield promised that the truck would not be searched when it left the city.

Whatever danger awaited Adolf inside the truck was no match for what he faced out here. He dropped to the pavement and slithered along the street until he was just beneath the transport. At that moment, the road became clear enough for the transport driver to finally move.

Adolf caught hold of the tarp over the back, just as the truck accelerated. Cursing in every language he had ever heard, he struggled like a hooked fish to get inside the truck. Finally, it was not his own strength, but a large pothole in the poorly maintained street which catapulted him inside the vehicle.

The truck was crammed with people. Adolf tumbled inside, banging into elbows, knees, heads, shoulders and stomachs before skidding to an awkward halt. There were no guards watching the occupants; Adolf allowed himself a sigh of relief while he wedged himself between a middle-aged man and a young woman and regarded his surroundings.

The thirty or so men, women and children in the truck were a mix of Aryan and subject races. A few regarded Adolf curiously. The rest just stared vacantly, or slept. No one raised an alarm. Adolf could not believe his good fortune. Then he noticed that most of the people who sat listlessly in the truck looked ill, although with what he could not tell. There was certainly the smell of sickness in the stuffy air.

Adolf had "escaped" into to a quarantined transport.

"Where are we going?" he asked the man next to him. When the man did not reply, he tried again in French, even though everyone in the world spoke German by law.

Adolf's neighbor remained silent, but a teen-aged boy across from him grinned. In heavily accented German he said, "We're going to hell."

That was all Adolf got for the next hour. Then the truck lurched to a stop. The tarp was thrown back and Adolf cringed, shielding his eyes against the blinding light of afternoon sun. When he could see again, faceless guards in full protective gear had arrived and were now pulling out the prisoners.

Adolf leapt gracefully off the truck before a gloved hand could force him, but most of the others were too ill to move quickly enough to suit the guards. When all who could walk or crawl to the pavement had done so, the two suited men lifted the remaining bodies and tossed them to the ground. Only one of them groaned; none of them moved to get up.

Adolf forced his gaze from the ground and looked around. They were in a fenced compound, which contained two long, low barracks and a small administration building. A sign above the gate bore the standard Party Medical Insignia and the words "Lourdes Polio Colony".

"Welcome to hell," said the boy from the truck.

CHAPTER 14

"So you see," said Dr. Speer, "We can still serve a purpose. Everyone here: criminals, vagrants, inferior races—once exposed to polio, all become useful subjects for experimentation. Perhaps it shall be from this very colony that the Party finds the cure."

"And if not this one," said Adolf. "Then, one of the others."

"Exactly." Speer opened the single door of the administration building, and held it open for Adolf. "Coffee?" he asked as they went in, shutting the door on the November wind.

Adolf accepted a chipped cup of what passed for coffee and sat down on a folding chair beside a desk that groaned under the weight of papers, files, dirty dishes and an ancient typewriter. Dr. Speer took the lopsided sofa, rubbing his neck and rotating his head carefully.

Adolf copied the doctor's motions without realizing it. In the three days he had been here, he had experienced none of the fatigue, headache, fever, vomiting or stiffness that might indicate polio. But he had become intimately familiar with all the symptoms as he assisted Dr. Speer in his rounds.

The doctor smiled wryly at Adolf. "Incubation can take up to five weeks, you know. And it takes at least four days. If you have it, you won't know until tomorrow at the soonest."

"Thanks" said Adolf. "That's a real comfort. Anyway, you were saying? The lack of interest those in authority have shown for this place recently?"

"Ah, yes, that would be of special interest to you, wouldn't it? But you're safe—from the *Gestapo*, at any rate—regardless. They never come here."

"That could mean an even greater drain on their resources than anyone has previously thought," said Adolf. "If this new strain of polio is as deadly as you say, then finding a cure would have to be a top priority. The fact that no one has come to harvest subjects for new studies, or give you new experimental drugs to administer—"

Speer shook his head impatiently. "It could just as easily mean that they've found something really promising at one of the other sites. We're cut off here. And they'd certainly never tell *me* anything. Secretary Heydrich had little enough use for me—"

"Heydrich? Josef Heydrich?" asked Adolf.

"My, you really have been out of touch, if you haven't heard about the *Führer's* latest golden boy. He's in charge of the search for a cure. Not just polio. The other big killers as well.
He's going to save the *Reich*, according to his press agents at any rate. The rest of us just hope he doesn't kill us all in the meantime."

Adolf frowned. He hadn't kept up with Heydrich since his graduation three and a half years ago. Heydrich's decision to marry a girl from the Eichmann family a year later had been enough of a relief to dismiss the obnoxious bully from Adolf's mind. "I hadn't heard he went to medical school. Even if he did, how could he have finished already?"

Speer laughed. "He's not a doctor! Who needs a doctor to head up a medical operation? This is the *Reich* we're talking about! He's an efficient

administrator, feared by everyone, and has the
Führer's every confidence. What more do we need?"

"Of course. Silly me." Adolf sighed. "So Dr.
Speer, what did you do to get banished to this place?
You're obviously a brilliant physician. The Party
can't afford to disown many like you."

"I was agitating for a ban on human
experimentation. And for an inquiry into some of the
more questionable methods of some of Mengele's
disciples."

"That would do it," said Adolf. "So they sent
you here, to be half human subject, half administrator
of their experiments. Very artistic."

"Isn't it? Especially when you consider
that if I do nothing; refuse to give my patients the
drugs that randomly arrive here, I'll have to wonder if
maybe it's a cure I'm withholding. It makes it all the
harder when it turns out to cause cells to mutate
hideously, or children to die in screaming fits."

"That you continue to heal at all is a tribute to
your strength and courage," said Adolf. "Never let
them take that away from you."

Speer sighed. "I guess it's my own fault for
finding that damned copy of the Hippocratic Oath, and
then taking it so seriously. The Medical Corps had
good reasons for banning it." He finished his coffee
and gazed at Adolf. "Now it's my turn to ask
questions. What's a rich Aryan college boy like you
doing in a place like this?"

"Waiting to get polio."

Speer shook his head. "Come on now! I told
you my shameful secret. What about you? I know
you were running from the authorities; desperate
enough to not care which truck you jumped into. But

why the heroics? Why spend half your waking hours heating towels, cleaning up vomit, and running errands for me? Why spend your other half reading to patients and massaging joints in people you would never have been allowed to speak to as a child?"

"I have to do *something*. I've spent the past seven months on the run, lugging around the wisdom of the ancients—and I've accomplished zero! Now, here I am, surrounded by death, knowing that at any moment, I could be next. It feels like now or never. So I do what needs to be done. At least it doesn't take a lot of brainwork to figure out what that is in this place."

"Some of the boys are saying you're a prophet. Here to bring the word of God to the dying."

Adolf groaned. "Not again."

"If there's time this evening, I'd like to look at some of the notes you brought with you."

"Yes, yes." Adolf nodded. "I've been meaning to sort them for you. But it's been a little—"

"—busy. Yes, I know."

"Still, some of those notebooks I brought are medical journals. It might not mean anything at all, but I figure you need all the help you can get."

"Just the thought of reading another physician's notes gives me energy. Dead or inferior, it makes no difference to me."

"How many languages can you read?"

Speer laughed. "Ah, yes. I forgot that Jews were everywhere. I can read German, French and Latin."

"That will cover about half."

"We do have a language expert here," said the doctor. "But I doubt she'll help us."

"She?" Adolf felt a sudden irrational hope.

"Varina. Slavic girl. Younger than you, and amazingly bright. But pretty mad at the world."

"No surprise there," said Adolf.

Both men looked up as a young woman pushed the door open. One of two nurses currently assigned to the camp, she was already showing the symptoms of the first stage of polio. "Doctor, please come," she said. "Patient number 163 has stopped breathing."

Adolf watched as Dr. Speer tried to revive the boy. When he finally gave up, an attendant—himself a polio survivor—took the body to cold storage, to await the cart that transported the bodies to the colony's crematorium.

Only the cart wasn't coming around much anymore, and the bodies were piling up.

Adolf left the men's dormitory, laughing bitterly at the name. Few inmates were old enough to be called men. Like the original polio virus, this new version—a biological warfare experiment gone wrong—continued to strike children most often.

For those who had the Medical Priority Points, there were iron lungs and new therapies. For the rest: places like this. And if a cure had been found somewhere, or if civil unrest was actually, finally, threatening the *Reich*, then places like this could easily be forgotten. For now, the supply trucks still came. But that too could change.

Adolf paced the compound. Worn wooden benches bore testimony to warmer weather, when patients might be brought out to sit in the sun. Now, with winter fast approaching, most stayed in their beds. Though many who survived the disease were sound from the waist up, wheelchairs were not provided, and with the diminished staff, few besides Adolf had the inclination to transport anyone.

He stopped in front of the women's dormitory, and knocked. When no one replied, he tried the door. It swung open to reveal an arrangement identical to the one Adolf now slept in: three dozen white sheeted hospital beds, half of them occupied. Of the women and girls present, most slept or stared listlessly.

"I'm looking for Varina," Adolf said.

An older woman who could barely raise her head, shot Adolf a curious glance, then moved her gaze to the next bed, where a younger woman sat up, reading. "Go away," she said without looking up from her book.

Adolf didn't know if it was her reaction, or the fact that she had a book, but he burst out laughing.

That seemed to annoy the girl, because she looked up, and stared at Adolf as if he were a cockroach that wandered in.

Adolf moved closer and tried again. "What are you reading?" he asked.

"Nothing you'd be interested in, rich boy."

The old woman began to laugh. Adolf considered a retreat, but decided against it. Anyone who could care about books in a place like this was someone he wanted to know.

"I have a reading collection myself, but it's got more languages than I can translate. I heard you're the person to talk to."

She put down the book. "Did you now?" she asked. Varina was about nineteen years old. Her complexion was too dark to be considered attractive, but her raven hair and huge brown eyes were lovely.

Healthy, Adolf guessed she could have caught and
held the eye of any man she wanted. Now, pallor and
bitterness marred her fine features.

"Show me," she said.

"I'll go get them," said Adolf.

"Wait." Varina leaned to the side, and began
digging for something by the bed. Adolf noticed that
her arms were very well muscled. Varina sat up,
though with difficulty. "Don't you want to empty my
chamber pot first?" She thrust a covered, but still
reeking, porcelain bowl at him.

The girl was grinning with more malice
than Adolf had ever seen on a human face. And
he sensed, even without looking, that all the other
women in the room were wearing similar gleeful
expressions, as they waited for his reaction.

Although his first impulse had been to recoil,
he overcame it gracefully enough, and took the vessel
from her. Varina's expression changed to one of
amazement. Glancing around, Adolf saw other
women looking their way, toothy grins changing to
puzzlement and suspicion.

"I'll be right back," Adolf said.

He went to the latrine and emptied the
chamber pot, then to his bed for the books. When he
returned to the women's ward, Varina took the pot
warily, as if expecting a nasty surprise. When nothing
jumped out at her, she looked at Adolf, still scowling.

"Why did you do that?" she asked.

"Because it needed doing."

"And I'm supposed to believe that?"

"Believe what you want! Me, I'm just trying
to find a cure for polio before I get it, develop a
therapy that will fix your legs, and figure out the

meaning of life."

"Oh, I see," said Varina. "You're a lunatic.
They must be sending you guys here now, instead of
the incinerator."

"Right. Will you help me?"

Varina still glowered, but she was eyeing
the books curiously. Sensing she would never ask for
them—or anything else—Adolf set them on the bed
next to her.

Scowling, Varina picked up a notebook at
random, then another. As she became engrossed in
reading, some of her beauty peeked out from behind
the angry mask.

"Hmm. Hebrew."

"You can read Hebrew? You know about the
Jews? Where? How?"

"There's very little in print I haven't read,"
said the young woman. "I'm a mutant: a woman with
a brain."

"Yes, I know the type."

"Sure. I've heard that in Germany, Aryan
women are allowed an education. But I was born in a
little peasant village in Serbia. My parents had eight
kids to feed, even after the smallpox came through and
wiped out half the countryside. When I got through it
without a scarred face, they hoped I might improve
their fortune with a good marriage.

"But they hit the jackpot when wealthy
stranger—a Party scientist—came through the village.
He bought me from my family for twice what they
earned in a year."

Adolf looked away, ashamed of the society he
had once been part of.

"Don't feel bad, rich boy. It happens all the

time, and at first, it was great. He had more books
than most libraries, and since he kept me locked in his
house when he was away, I got to read them all."

"So what happened?" Adolf asked. "He found
out you were smarter than him?"

"Something like that. Oh, at first, when he
learned that I was reading, he thought it was terribly
amusing. Then, when he discovered I actually
understood what I was reading, he decided to make
me part of some grand experiment. He wanted to find
out how much I could really learn—sort of like
teaching a monkey to talk, you know? He was even
talking about publishing the results."

"What went wrong?"

"I turned out to be too smart for his own
good," Varina said bitterly. "He used some new table
he developed to measure my I.Q. When he got the
results, it stopped being funny. He put me through the
test five separate times, looking for the error. It turns
out I scored higher than he did. By a very wide
margin. Once he realized there was no mistake, he
sold me to a colleague doing medical research, and
here I am."

"That stinks," said Adolf.

"Hey, you're smarter than you look, rich boy.
Now, try living it."

"Someday, when you're not so pissed off, I'll
tell you *my* story, and maybe you'll see I already am."

Some of the anger slid from Varina's face.
"Sorry," she said. Looking back at the stacks of
papers she asked, "So, what exactly do you want
here?"

"How many languages can you read?"

"Everything I see here, plus a few more."

"Okay. We're looking for anything that's scientific in nature, even if it doesn't have any outward bearing on polio. If you're willing to, just go ahead and translate everything that's there into German."

Varina snorted. "Easy! Come back tomorrow with something hard."

"You can use Dr. Speer's office. I can carry you if you think you can refrain from breaking any of my bones."

"Thanks but I'll manage myself." Varina threw back the blankets, revealing one pale, but nearly normal looking leg. The other was a stick; shrunk to half its normal size. A shared gasp from the watching women told Adolf that Varina didn't often reveal her weakness to strangers.

With the help of a crutch, Varina pulled herself upright. Adolf was startled to see she was only about five feet tall, and probably less than one hundred pounds. She handed three notebooks to Adolf. "These are all part of the same influenza study. We'll start with them."

"This is great!" said Adolf. "We're going to find a cure here; I just know it!"

Varina snorted. "We'll see about that. But I wouldn't get your hopes up over the work of some dead American Jew named Salk."

CHAPTER 15

Adolf sat on a bench in the courtyard and gazed up at the bleak winter sky. Empty machine gun towers stood like black skeletons at the four corners of the Polio Camp. It should be comforting to be so completely forgotten by the Party. But to Adolf, it was simply depressing: the people here weren't even worth guarding. They were already dead.

And so was Adolf. It was official now; he'd just heard it himself on Dr. Speer's radio. Although the banished doctor had been left with a radio only for the convenience of the Party who might occasionally need to contact him, it still picked up the news station.

The badly burned corpse of Adolf Goebbels had been discovered in Italy, just weeks before his twenty-third birthday. His captors had tried to force him into bombing Party Headquarters in Rome, the sight of recent Catholic dissidence. The heroic young Aryan had made a valiant attempt at escape, and thus died rather than betray his race. His grieving parents were not available for comment.

It was this last part that worried Adolf. He didn't know if that meant they were dead, in prison, in hiding, or busy trying to denounce him.

He returned his attention to the letter he had been working on ever since he arrived here.

Dear Ilsa,
I've found useful work at last. It's physically

demanding, but leaves lots of time for reading and contemplating my future. I'm meeting interesting people. I'm so popular that some of them say they wish they could take me with them when they leave.

While I wish I could be wherever you are now, sharing your work with you, I've come to realize that our lives have taken different paths. I guess what I really wish for is your faith; your certainty; your ability to know that you're making a difference.

For myself, I've learned a few important things, none of which suggest I'm any sort of hero. I want to save the world, but I don't want to hurt anyone in the process. Cowardice or arrogance? Then there are days when I want to chuck it all, find you, and find a place where we can live quietly, if not happily, ever after.

What if I had to choose? Between having you and saving the world? Honestly, I couldn't say what I'd do—

Adolf stopped writing and reread the letter. Then he tore it up. There were some things you didn't commit to paper.

He considered beginning again, when the choking sounds of poorly maintained diesel engines broke into his thoughts. It had been over three weeks since the last transport. This morning, not one, but two trucks were approaching the gate.

Adolf quickly ducked into the men's ward while the trucks were unloaded, still more fearful of being recognized than of polio. Of course, after nearly two months without contracting the disease,

Adolf had begun to fear it less. And now that

he was dead, he should probably worry less about capture, and more about becoming anonymous.

After the drivers had dumped their human cargo and hurried away, Adolf joined Dr. Speer and the few other able bodied inmates at triage and transport.

The patients in the first truck were all from the same town in southeastern France. "Former town," Adolf heard some of them saying. Apparently, the new polio had struck suddenly, as it often did now, infecting nearly the entire town. However, a large number on the truck were already showing signs of recovery; others of only partial paralysis. Soil and water samples accompanied the orders to investigate any factors which may have contributed to either the virulent spread, or the unusually high rate of survival.

With a start, Adolf saw that several of the patients wore Hebrew letters sewn to their clothing, or in charms around their neck. He thought of Markus, who sold Jewish mysticism to the desperate. Apparently, there were others like him, and with desperation so much on the rise, business must be good. A man who had died en route clutched a crudely carved wooden symbol so tightly that Adolf couldn't pry it loose. Ironically, it was the *chai*; the Hebrew word for life.

Since so many occupants of the first truck were able to take over the job of transporting the more critical patients to the wards, Adolf went to help with the second. It was nearly empty when he arrived, and he stopped in his tracks at what he saw. This was a day for surprises.

Three African men, with skin like coal, and short, wiry black hair, stood apart from a small group of olive skinned Egyptians.

"Adolf? A word with you please?" Dr. Speer was beside him. Adolf nodded and followed the doctor a short distance, noticing the troubled look on his mentor's face.

"Have you ever seen a Negro before?" Speer asked.

"No. I've never even seen a picture! I had heard there were still some in Africa, but—"

"Quite a few, actually. For the moment. Adolf, I've just received a very disturbing report, along with a set of special orders for this group. I'm telling you this in the strictest confidence."

"Of course," said Adolf, feeling his stomach tighten.

"The Party scientists have noticed an unusually high resistance—possibly even immunity—to this disease in a few of the remaining groups of inferior races. It doesn't mean anything yet, but I am ordered to directly expose these subjects to the polio virus, and observe them for ninety days."

"And then?" asked Adolf. "If they don't contract it?"

"Whether they do or not," said Speer, "I am then ordered to terminate them, and attempt, through autopsy, to learn any pertinent information that can be gained."

Adolf felt his heart jump. "And...will you?"

"Exactly what else do you think I can do?" Adolf knew the anger in Speer's voice was not really aimed at him, but at those in power whom he could not reach. Still, he felt the man's pain; shared his helplessness.

"Are you a gambling man, Doctor?"

Speer smiled bleakly. "I'm letting you stay here, aren't I?"

"So why not go even further? Gamble on finding a cure in the next ninety days. Varina says you're close."

Speer shook his head. "That's a vaccine, not a cure we're working on. And that sort of timetable would be insane."

"A vaccine appears to be what the Party hopes to find."

"Finding a vaccine won't save the Africans, you know," said Speer. "And once it's discovered that I've disobeyed those orders, it won't save me. They'll just shoot me, and give the credit to some Party Scientist who's in favor at the moment."

"That's assuming any of us are still here when they come to investigate," said Adolf.

Dr. Speer sighed. "I'm probably going to regret asking you this, Adolf, but what do you have in mind?"

"Find the vaccine, then evacuate the camp." Adolf gestured to the deserted guard towers. "There's no one here but us! We don't even know if anyone's going to remember to come here looking for results in ninety days. The Party doesn't waste resources guarding this place, because by its very nature, polio renders its victims too immobile to represent a threat to Party Security.

"I know it's a huge risk, but if you think there's a chance you'll have something within three months, I say we take it and walk away."

"Walk away?"

"Ah, er, those of us who can," said Adolf, suddenly realizing how difficult transporting— and

then hiding—the crippled would be. But he knew it
could be done.

The doctor had that far away look that told
Adolf he was weighing things in his head. Suddenly,
he smiled. "Why not? I always did love the old story
of King Louis's horse."

"King Louis's horse?" asked Adolf.

"Don't you know the old story? There was a
thief, who King Louis of France—I don't know which
number—condemned to death. The thief told the king
that if he granted him a pardon, and gave him a year,
he'd teach the king's favorite horse to talk.

"A friend of the thief told him he was mad;
that no one could teach a horse to talk.

"But the thief said, 'Who knows? After all, a
year is a long time. The king could die, or the horse
could die, or I could die. Or, the horse could talk.'"

Adolf laughed. "You are a true hero, *Herr*
Doctor. I only wish we had a year, instead of three
months."

"Ah, well. Timing isn't everything. And who
knows? If I find the vaccine, they might not even
shoot me!"

Adolf sat alone in the courtyard, trying to read.
It was cold, but dry. For the moment, at least, Adolf
thought, staring into the low, steel gray rain clouds
that matched his mood.

As if things weren't bad enough already…

That was becoming a familiar phrase. Adolf
thought briefly about putting it to music. Everywhere
he went, he seemed to make things worse. For
himself. For his friends. And, in this place of death
where the rarest of doctors—a true healer—struggled

against impossible odds—here was Adolf, playing games with people's lives, and goading a good man into becoming a martyr. Why? What did he hope to accomplish?

Adolf thought of his family, as he had constantly since hearing word of his own death. He hoped that the circumstances of it all, as reported by the Party, would exonerate Helmut, and protect his position.

But it wasn't likely. The news broadcasts were for the consumption of the masses. The men who ordered those broadcasts knew the real story. And the shameful facts of Adolf's treason would be well known to everyone in the upper echelons.

Like any powerful man, Helmut had enemies. In the *Reich*, people moved up by pulling down whom they could and climbing over the bodies. Helmut wasn't the kind of man to live with disgrace. And if he was dead, what of Adolf's sisters? His mother? Uncle Gustav?

A chilling thought occurred to Adolf, one he hadn't had before. If *Herr* Goebbels had chosen suicide, might he have taken his entire family with him? Adolf shook his head, willing the nightmarish image away. It was too awful to contemplate.

The discovery that he had company came as a relief. Two children, boys, he judged by their shadows, were standing about a body length behind him. Adolf did not turn around, but sensed they were more interested in the book which lay open on the bench, than in him.

"It's easier to read if you come closer," he said.

Adolf didn't think he spoke loudly, but both

boys cleared the ground, bumped into each other as they landed, and began to run—squealing the entire time.

"Come back here!" Adolf called, this time conscious of his commanding tone. It had the same effect on the children as his father's voice had had on him.

Both boys approached, heads hanging. "Sorry to disturb, you *Herr* Adolf," said the older one. Adolf guessed he was about ten.

"Don't be. I needed the distraction. Did you want to see what I was reading? You can read it, if you know how. If not, I'd be glad to read some of it to you."

The boys exchanged a nervous glance. "Isn't that one of the Sacred Texts?" one asked.

"Well, I consider what's in it to be sacred, but that's just me. It's a book about an ancient religion called Judaism—"

Both boys jumped back. "See, I told you," whispered the younger one. "He's one of them."

"Jean Paul has a book like that," said the older boy. "Or, at least he did, back in the village. He and some of the other important men used to read from it."

Adolf's initial excitement turned to puzzlement. Sacred Texts? Important men? He recalled the Hebrew letters which some of these boy's neighbors wore as charms against polio.
"Did Jean Paul come to your village and tell you that there was magic in his book?" he asked gently. "Did he sell your friends charms that looked like this?" Adolf pointed to the right hand page; the one written in Hebrew.

Both boys were shaking their heads. "Jean

Paul isn't a peddler—"

"—was peddlers sold the charms—" said the
younger.

"He's secretary to the Party lazzanoffer—"

"You mean 'liaison officer?'" said Adolf.

"Right! Him and the other big men started
reading these books a few months ago. They're
supposed to…supposed to—"

"We don't know what they're supposed to do!
But Jean Paul says they're only for the Chosen Ones.
They wouldn't tell anybody else, or even let us touch
the books."

Adolf sighed. He knew he shouldn't be
surprised. This was, after all, a stratified society.
People naturally adapted anything new into
familiar patterns. Hadn't he and his friends found
what they wanted to find in Judaism as well?

But still… "It isn't like that at all," he found
himself telling the boys. "Jean Paul and his friends
are right—there is great power in these words, but
they are for everyone."

The boys looked at each other, then back at
Adolf. He read doubt and suspicion in their eyes.

"The people who wrote these books are all
dead," he continued. "They were all killed by the
Party, just for believing what's in these books that
Jean Paul and some others have found. Anyone who
wants to can read them and find out what they
believed, but there's no one left alive to tell us if what
we interpret is right or not."

"But Jean Paul says—"

"Look around you!" snapped Adolf. "Do you
see any Party members? Do you even see any Aryans,
other than the doctor and myself? Jean Paul doesn't

have any power here; he can't tell you what to do anymore. So I'm asking you: do you want to know what's so special about these books?"

Both boys nodded vigorously, nearly losing their hats.

"Sit down," said Adolf, gesturing with both hands to the bench on which he sat.

The older boy leaped to obey, but the younger one grabbed him by the frayed collar of his jacket and whispered something.

"Andre wants to know if we can bring a friend. He's back in the ward."

"Bring whomever you like," said Adolf. "Tell anyone who's interested that there's a... a *Torah* study in the courtyard."

The boys took off running. They returned a few minutes later, carrying a third boy between them, his body wasted from polio. Behind them, over a dozen other patients and test subjects walked, were carried or were dragged on blankets. Adolf nearly laughed as they settled down at his feet, apparently waiting for some great message. Then he sobered. The message *was* great, even if the messenger wasn't.

"I don't know what you've heard," Adolf began. "All I can tell you is what I know. Long ago, there lived a people known as Jews. They were different from other ancient people because they worshipped but one god—a god whose name and face even they didn't know, but whose spirit was all around them.

"They had a great civilization, and wrote about their beliefs, hopes, fears, passions—everything. Our illustrious leaders—" here, Adolf spat on the ground, to the shock and delight of his audience—"murdered every last man, woman and child who followed these teachings. But the truth cannot be killed. It lives, in books, and in the hearts of those who seek it. In fact, the Jews believed that God's words were written within every person's heart. And that it's up to each of us to find them."

Adolf opened the *Torah* to the first page of Genesis. "I can read to you from the beginning, or, if anyone has something special they would like to discuss, we can start there."

No one seemed inclined to speak, so Adolf began reading from the first chapter of Genesis. When he reached the expulsion from Eden he stopped. "Now, back at the museum," said Adolf, "we would stop here, and discuss what this story might be trying to tell us."

"Never talk to snakes?" said a boy in the front row.

"No, dummy," said the girl beside him. "That's just a symbol."

"What's a symbol?" asked the boy, looking at Adolf for an answer.

Impressed, Adolf looked back. "Don't ask me," he said. "Ask her."

The girl, less intimidated by him than most of the others replied, "It's like a truth that wears a fancy mask."

A few of the children laughed but Adolf applauded. "Excellent!" he said. "What's your name?"

"Mirielle." She was about eleven or twelve. About Marta's age, Adolf thought, if she was still alive. This girl, however, looked nothing like Adolf's last memory of his sturdy blond sister. Mirielle was thin and wraithlike, with dry, colorless hair and nearly translucent skin. He had the disturbing feeling that she would not be with them for long, though the polio did not appear to have left her crippled.

It took a lot of patience on Adolf's part, but slowly, people overcame their shyness or awe, and began to ask questions and express opinions.

Unlike the privileged college students who were his first colleagues, these people were from the lower classes; the kind his father felt existed to be stepped on. But they were soon arguing with Adolf as an equal, perhaps because so many were short on time.

"Where did they go when they died?" asked a young man.

"Good question," said Adolf. The question had come up before, and as always, he wished he had more comforting news to give the dying. "The Jews didn't seem to give much thought to what happens after this life. There are references to a place called Shoal, which seems to be a sort of netherworld."

"Like for ghosts?" asked Andre.

"Something like that. In the book of Daniel, there are some hints of a nicer place."

"But didn't they have some kind of Valhalla?" asked an older boy.

"Or heaven?" asked a woman.

"Not that I've seen," said Adolf. "Of course, we only have a fraction of their writings. Their faith in the one God was very strong. They expected him to take care of them—in this life, and in whatever came next."

"Yeah," laughed an old woman. "That God took really good care of His people, didn't He?"

"I guess they thought so," Adolf said mildly. "I've found records of Jews who were offered life by our illustrious leaders. Those who looked Aryan— and many did—and who had skills the Party needed, were given a chance to deny their parents and recant their faith in exchange for life—and none of them accepted."

"Wait a minute," said a bald man who was covered with skin lesions. "You mean, even without the promise of some sort of hero's paradise, they died for their religion."

"So it would seem," said Adolf.

"They were fools!" spat the woman who laughed earlier.

"Or maybe they just had something that no one alive today has ever experienced," said Adolf.

"He has a point," said the bald man. "Look at us! Look where life and our illustrious leaders have brought us! We're animals waiting to die. I, for one, would trade whatever time I have left, for that kind of faith."

"But how...?" The boy beside Andre gasped for breath and tried again. Adolf leaned forward, but Andre, with an ear to his mouth, translated.

"He says, 'how do you get it? How do you make their god your god? Luis doesn't have much time left."

Adolf felt himself shaking. How indeed? What he wanted to know at that moment was how did he get himself into these situations?

"I can only tell you what my friends and I used to do. Jewish prayer is like everything else in that faith. It's a personal connection with God. You close your eyes and concentrate on what is most important

to you right now. Don't worry about what anyone
else would think about it. Then, imagine a presence
more powerful than anything on earth, and know that
force cares about that thing as much—or more—as
you do. Whatever you find there will be God."

Adolf watched as one by one, everyone around
him closed their eyes. Men and women; young and
old; faces pinched with pain or worn down from a
lifetime of care. Most of those dying were children.
What was he doing to them? Selling them faith like
patent medicine?

"What's going on here?" a loud, imperious
voice demanded.

All around Adolf, eyes flew open and people
started like chickens in a coop. He turned angrily, and
saw a swarthy, thick set man of about forty. He was
flanked by a pair of larger men, who, Adolf guessed,
probably had more brawn than brain.

"Jean Paul, I presume?" said Adolf.

The older man looked wary, yet flattered.
"You know me?"

Adolf took a deep breath and bit back his rage.
Whatever his beliefs or motives, Jean Paul craved
acknowledgement from his Aryan masters. If Adolf
could use that to keep peace, then he would.

"I know that you and I share an interest in
ancient truths. I'm always glad to find fellow
thinkers."

"I knew I was right about you!" said Jean Paul.
"But why are you sharing sacred knowledge with
those not intended to possess it?"

"As far as I know, there's no real hierarchy in
illegal activities," said Adolf. "As I'm sure you've
noticed, the Party takes a dim view on digging up

truth they've worked so hard to bury. It seems to me
that anyone who has the inclination is welcomed to
the stories—and the risks."

Jean Paul stepped closer to Adolf and
lowered his voice. "Knowledge is power! Surely you
know that. This truth we've found could raise us up
and make us great. What will happen if you let just
anyone have it?"

"For starters, we'll have more help using what
we find. More minds, working together-"

"Minds?" Jean Paul gazed with contempt at
the crowd, still gathered, much to Adolf's relief, and
watching the confrontation with interest. "Their kind
can never grasp what's in these books! Most of them
can't even read!"

"But most of them would learn to, given the
chance. Jean Paul, these are your neighbors! You
were all brought here for the same purpose, by the
same morally bankrupt leaders. How can you set
yourself apart?"

Jean Paul drew himself up, though still
noticeably shorter than Adolf. "These people are
peasants! I can trace my lineage back to the
fourteenth century, when we were stewards to kings!
Before the Nazis, my great-grandfather ran our town,
and mixed with government leaders. Even now, until
I came here, I was Secretary to the Party Liaison
Officer. You can't compare people like us to people
like them!"

"I was actually hoping for a world without 'us'
and 'them.' That's why I like Judaism. It seems more
interested in helping people live with each other than
setting up a few with power over the rest."

"Then you obviously don't understand

Judaism at all!" said Jean Paul. "True, there are men
in the stories who start out small, but once they gain
God's favor, they are always set above those around
them."

"An interesting interpretation. Personally, I
see those same stories in a very different light."
Suddenly, Adolf grinned. "But let's handle this in a
traditionally Jewish manner. I read in someone's
diary that when you get two Jews together, you get at
least three opinions." He pointed to the group.
"Come join us. We're discussing Genesis; a book I'm
sure you'll agree has a lot to say about our
disagreement."

Jean Paul's lip curled. "You have *women* in
this group!" he spat. "What about the laws which
forbid women from studying *Torah*? The laws that
bar them from most aspects of religious life? Do you
think you can just ignore them? How can you teach a
religion if you don't even understand its most
fundamental laws?"

Adolf turned his back on Jean Paul's outraged
protests and returned to his bench. "I apologize for
the interruption," he told the group. "Since Jean Paul
has questioned your right to study this religion, I
suggest we deal with that issue first, and save prayer
for later.

"I'd like to discuss the philosophy I find
most attractive in Judaism." Adolf began reading
Genesis from where he left off, and continued reading
through the end of chapter ten. He occasionally
glanced at Jean Paul, who listened from the edge of
the crowd, refusing to sit, and glowering the entire
time.

"So what does it mean?" Adolf asked when he

finished reading. "First we are told that everyone on earth is descended from Adam and Eve. Then, a short time later, the human race is wiped out, and we start again, this time descended from Noah and his family."

Adolf looked at his audience, but no one said anything. "It says something very important about rank and status," he prompted. "So important their prophets told the story twice, so even the densest among us would have to get it." Still nothing.

Adolf was about to give up and explain it, when Mirielle tentatively raised her hand. "Go ahead," said Adolf.

"Does it mean that everyone is really the same? That since we all came from the same parents, we're all one family?"

"Yes!" cried Adolf. "That's exactly what it means! Now take it one step further: no one is, by birth, any greater or lesser than anyone else. It's only the choices we make; the things we do that determine what we become."

"But what about the Master Race?" someone in the back asked.

Adolf grinned. "What about it?"

"But we're taught in school—"

"Everyone knows the Racial Hierarchy—"

"And what if everything we've been taught is a lie?" Adolf asked quietly. "The Jews believed that all men—and women, though that's another argument— were equals. Status depended on what you did, not the blood in your veins—because everyone's blood is the same."

"Everyone's?" Adolf looked up to see one of the African test subjects, standing in the back of the study group. His voice was deep and carried well.

Adolf had no trouble hearing or understanding the accented German, but he was briefly surprised the man could talk.

"As far as I know," said Adolf, "all humans trace their ancestry back to the same two couples. As for when and how the different races came into being, I really don't know."

"How could you not know?" cried Jean Paul. "You're an educated man! You know that certain genetic weaknesses created..."

"I know what those who call themselves the Master Race have to say on the subject!" Adolf shouted. "And I know what the Jews said! And I believe the Jews!"

There was a moment of stunned silence. Then, what had been the courtyard of a polio ward just moments before, erupted into a debate that only vital, sentient human beings could take part in. Adolf crossed through the shouting, gesticulating patients until he came to the African.

"What is your name?" he asked.

"Jacques," he replied. "Of Algiers."

"You are welcome in our discussions. Your two friends as well."

"They aren't my friends, *Herr*. We just happen to be the same race. Truth is, I never met them before we came here to die."

"This might be a good place to start making friends," said Adolf.

"Yesterday, I wouldn't have believed that," said Jacques.

"And today?"

"Maybe."

Then Andre was tugging on Adolf's sleeve, and people were demanding answers to questions they had never even imagined asking before today. By the time the meeting broke up, Jacques was gone.

But he was back for the next meeting.

It was Jean Paul and his flunkies who refused to attend.

CHAPTER 16

"Adolf?" Varina's voice seemed far away. "Adolf, I'm sorry, but it's time. She won't last the night and she's asking for you."

"I know." Adolf lurched from his cot and tried to stand, but lack of sleep made him dizzy. He stumbled, clutched a supporting arm —and was surprised to find it was Varina's. She stood, all five ferocious feet of her, balancing her own weight and his with a little crutch and a lot of determination. Looking into her worried brown eyes, it was hard to remember the contempt he had seen there just a few months ago.

"I'm so sorry, Adolf," she said. "We really thought we had the vaccine. And we'll have it soon. You know that if Speer could have kept her alive any longer—"

"Of course I know! And why shed tears for one child, anyway, Varina? You've seen hundreds die! And no matter when we find the cure, it's going to be after too many good people have died!" He grabbed a pair of books from his cot and strode out of the men's ward.

The February wind was from the north, cold and fierce. Adolf had forgotten his coat, but he pushed on without it. He had forgotten his manners with Varina, but he pushed past her too. He couldn't stop to apologize; couldn't go back for his coat. He needed to rage against someone or something who

wouldn't get hurt if he was going to face a dying
child's questions tonight.

In the women's ward, Mirielle lay on her cot.
If she had been Aryan; if her father had the right
connections, she would be in a modern hospital on an
iron lung and antibiotics.

But at least here, she wouldn't die alone.

Although Mirielle had no immediate family in
the camp, everyone in the study group was with her.
In less than three months, Adolf had converted most
of the population to a religion he wasn't even sure he
himself believed in. *Why couldn't I have picked a
religion with a nice, pretty afterlife?* He asked
himself. *Then we could all just sit around singing and
clapping our hands until she died, and then go home
happy for her!*

Mirielle caught him in her gaze before he was
halfway to her bed. The soul that lived in those eyes
was old for her eleven years; huge in her wasted body.
Jacques, who was speaking to her and holding her
hand, turned to follow her gaze, and stood when he
saw Adolf, indicating the place he had just vacated.

Adolf nodded his thanks to Jacques, and sat on
the bed beside Mirielle. "How's my best student?" he
asked.

"You tell me," she whispered. He moved
closer to catch her words. "Tell me…" Her voice was
lost in a series of gasps. Adolf took the wet cloth
someone gave him and gently moistened her mouth.
"Tell me the truth. Where am I going? Jean Paul says
nowhere. I'm just going to…end."

"Jean Paul is a swinehund who should be more
afraid of where *he's* going," said Adolf, promising
himself a private "discussion" with the man who saw

fit to share such opinions with a dying child. "When he dies, he probably will just end, because there wasn't much of him to begin with.

"But you, *liebling*. You're going to be with God."

"But the books. I read as much as I could. There's almost nothing there about..." Her voice trailed off.

"There's so little in the books, because Judaism is a faith carried in the heart. And because, like so much else, the journey of the soul is a private thing, just between you and God. But you were with God before you came to this world, and you'll be with Him after you leave it."

Mirielle's brow wrinkled, making her look— for the first time-- like a frightened child. "I don't remember any of that."

Adolf took her hand. "You don't have to. You just have to trust me. You can do that, can't you?"

The little girl's face relaxed and she smiled. "Tell me what it's going to be like."

"Like a big, warm hug. Like that feeling you get when you solve a puzzle no one else could. Like being so strong you never have to be afraid of anything ever again." Adolf's breath caught in his throat and he wiped away a tear. When he could, he began to speak again, of a place he had never before believed in, but that was now very clear to him.

It was only when he ran out of words that he looked down to see Mirielle drawing her last labored breath, and hear the rattle as the breath left her body.

But the smile on her face was almost enough to make him believe in angels.

Adolf woke up without any idea how he had gotten to bed. Mirielle! But no, she was dead. Had he missed her funeral?

"Oh, good, you're awake." Luc, a young man who had been a neighbor of Mirielle's, and was currently one of Judaism's most fervent students, stood nervously by Adolf's side. "Can I get you anything?"

"How long have I slept?"

"Almost sixteen hours. *Herr* Doctor told us not to wake you. He said you've been working too hard with too little rest. Something about burning a candle at both ends?"

"The funeral?"

"It will begin as soon as you get there. You're going to speak, aren't you?"

Adolf found that the washbasin on the table had been filled with fresh water, a relatively clean towel beside it. The cold water felt good on his face, and he started to feel almost human as he combed his disheveled hair into submission. The dye was gone; except for the dirt, it was blond again.

"I'll read," he told Luc. "I think I'll leave the speaking to those who know her better."

"Oh. We were hoping you'd speak." Luc's eyes widened and he began to stammer. "Not that I meant any criticism, *mein Herr*—"

"Just Adolf, please." From the battered trunk at the foot of his cot, Adolf drew his last good shirt.

Or at least the less torn of the two. "And criticize me any time you feel like it. I keep telling you: I'm not one of the Master Race because there is no Master Race."

"Of course, *mein Herr*." Luc scurried away.

The funeral was simple, as they all were. The crematorium had been shut down three weeks ago. As usual, no explanation was given. It was just as well, Adolf thought, as most of the living and the dying in the camp had adopted a religion which insisted on burial. The graveyard he now stood in was just hard earth at the edge of the compound. No one got a coffin, but just by burying their dead at all, the people here were defying the Party and asserting their humanity.

Most of the camp turned out. Dr. Speer was missing, but he rarely left his lab these days. It was surprising enough that Varina was there, as she rarely left Speer's side. Jean Paul and his friends were missing as well, for which Adolf was grateful. He had said goodbye to Mirielle last night. It was for the living that he spoke now.

"We are gathered—yet again—" he began, "to bid farewell to a friend. Mirielle was a gifted child, who would have grown into a brilliant and insightful woman. But though her time with us was brief, she touched us all in ways that will never be forgotten.

"I'd like to read from the Book of Psalms." Adolf opened a crumbling leather bound volume, and read three psalms, all written by King David. Adolf always found the story of a man who was both poet and king; harp player and giant slayer inspirational.

After reading them in German, Adolf read them again in Hebrew. He had noticed that although no one here could understand the ancient language, they all seemed to revere the sound of it.

After everyone had left the grave, and Adolf paused to gather his thoughts, Dr. Speer approached. Adolf knew the moment he saw him what message the doctor brought, and for that moment, Adolf hated him.

Evidently, Speer could read Adolf as well as Adolf could read Speer. "Maybe you'll forgive me when you hear the whole story," the doctor said, sorrow not quite overcoming the triumph in his eyes. "It's not a cure, Adolf. It's a vaccine. It wouldn't have saved Mirielle, even if we found it the day you arrived.

"But for everyone on earth who isn't infected—we have the vaccine, Adolf! Polio is beaten!"

For a long while, Adolf just stood there, staring at Mirielle's grave, absorbing the doctor's words. Finally he said, "The vaccine: did you get it from...?"

"From sleepless nights of research; from crazy ideas from that Varina character; from tissue samples from the Africans, and yes, Adolf: from the influenza research that American Jew started seventy years ago. I couldn't have done it without him—or you."

Adolf slowly unclenched his fists, and repeated the words he had spoken just moments before: "Unto thee O Lord, do I lift up my soul. I trust in thee: let me not be ashamed, let not mine enemies triumph over me."

Speer nodded. "Whoever that god of theirs was, or is," he said, "I'd sure like to have him on my side." He took Adolf by the arm and led him away. "Come on, young man. Your vaccine awaits. After all this, I'm not about to let you turn into the last casualty of this charnel house."

The next morning, Adolf, Varina, Jacques and Speer sat together at breakfast.

"It's drastic," said Speer. "It's unethical. I just don't see any other way."

"Well, I don't see what's so drastic—or unethical," said Varina. "Of course we have to keep this vaccine out of the Party's hands! You know what they'll do with it!" Her eyes narrowed on Adolf. "You, especially, rich boy. They'll inoculate all loyal party members, and a few docile populations of peasants and slaves—then sit back and wait while this disease kills or cripples anyone they consider a threat."

"They may not sit back and wait," said Jacques. "Things are getting out of hand for the leaders. There have been uprisings in dozens of labor camps. Underground and partisan activity has been reported on every continent. Once they have the vaccine, they'll probably decide it's more efficient to introduce the polio virus directly into the food or water supply of any undesirable area."

Adolf's gut twisted inside him, but he refused to budge. "And if we use it as a weapon of the underground? How are we any different from them? The four of us? We're going to decide who lives and who dies? On a planetary scale?"

"It won't be just us four!" said Varina. "You said it yourself, and so has Jacques: the underground is everywhere! We can distribute it to every leader! Every partisan group! Eventually, it will reach everyone the Party would have allowed to die."

"Party members have children, too!" said Adolf. "Are you willing to condemn them all for the sins of their parents?"

"It's the word 'eventually' that bothers me, Varina," said Speer. "Although I see Adolf's point as well. We've already seen how miserably inefficient Nazi efficiency has become over the years. Consider how much worse the distribution of the vaccine will be in the hands of dozens of squabbling underground organizations—"

"I trust them over the Party," said Varina.

"Whatever we decide has to be soon," said the doctor. "The autopsies for Jacques and the other Africans are already ten days overdue."

"For which we are grateful," murmured Jacques.

"I've stalled for as long as I can. Very soon now, someone will arrive to investigate, and all this lovely philosophy will become moot."

Four pairs of eyes glowered at each other.

"Let me suggest something," Adolf said suddenly. "We evacuate the camp today as planned. We take the vaccine, and the formula, and distribute them far and wide. But we leave behind all the notes; enough to ensure that— eventually—the Party doctors will have the vaccine as well."

"I would agree to that," said Speer.

Jacques shrugged.

Varina eyed Adolf coldly. "I hope you realize that from every batch of 'innocent Aryan children' you save, there will grow another Mengele; another Himmler."

"Or perhaps," said Adolf, "Another like you or Jacques or the doctor here. Or maybe even the messiah that the Jews waited for all those years."

Varina snorted.

"We have to get moving," said Speer. "We have two working vehicles, which should be enough to transport all those who can't walk—"

"Thanks to last night's little cyanide party," snapped Adolf.

"It was their choice, Adolf," Varina said quietly. "We have no safe place to take them; no hope to offer for any life at all, outside the underground—and even that's going to be risky for those of us making the attempt. Can you blame them for not wanting to be here when the Party 'physicians' arrive to take care of the situation?"

"Still," he said bitterly. "In time, there might have been a cure; a treatment—"

"In time, there will be," said Dr. Speer. "Especially, if those of us in this room live to do what we're meant to. If we can get Jacques back to Africa with the vaccine, he just might be able to stir up a continent. Varina's brain will very soon be classified as a lethal weapon—wherever she chooses to take it. And your voice, Adolf, along with this ancient faith you've discovered, might just be enough to turn the world upside down."

"You didn't mention yourself, doctor," said Jacques.

"You're coming with me, aren't you?" said Adolf.

Speer smiled sadly. "I'm afraid I'm a bit old to play revolutionary. When they come, I'll be waiting."

"No!" cried the others—the first thing they had agreed on all morning.

"They'll kill you," said Adolf.

"Until a moment ago, I was perfectly content to die covering your escape. Actually, Adolf, it was your plan to let the Party have the vaccine that gave me this idea.

"I did quite a lot of theater in school. If I can
convince them I was overpowered and left
unconscious during your great escape, I may yet live
to add 'creation of a fifth column' to my resume.
And, since you've all agreed to leave our research
notes, I'll have a bargaining chip. As the sole creator
of the polio vaccine, I might even have a shot at
reinstatement."

Varina flashed an obscene gesture toward the
doctor, but Adolf just smiled.

The sun was still low above the eastern hills
when the last forty residents of the Lourdes Polio
Colony gathered for a farewell. The half who were
visibly crippled huddled in a group near the trucks that
would take them on a search for sanctuary; for
someplace that wouldn't "mercifully" end their
sufferings, and the discomfort felt by those taught to
hate anyone with physical differences. Varina, Adolf
noticed, was not among them.

The others stood in small groups, their few
belongings piled around them. It would be dangerous
for everyone: by slipping away without official
permission, they would all be fugitives. No one
seemed terribly bothered by the notion, Adolf thought
as he stood before them, to address them one last time.

As he opened his book, he heard the familiar
grate of Varina's crutch and footstep behind him. He
paused to wait for her. "Decided to attend the service
after all?" he asked.

Varina shrugged. "Everything I've read about
the Jews tells me they treated women just as badly as
the Nazis do. But I've decided that you don't. If you
do manage to create a new world Adolf, tell me one

thing: will you alter this religion enough to make it equal for *everyone*?"

"I won't have to," said Adolf. "I'll have you there, to make sure it never becomes an issue."

Varina smiled, and then hobbled over to stand with Dr. Speer.

"Jewish tradition," Adolf began, "is filled with references to new beginnings; to the scattering of seeds.

"What we few begin today, could turn out to be the greatest new beginning of all. We set out with nothing—nothing that is, except a vaccine that could change the face of the world. And as you scatter your tiny seeds of life and hope, remember that you are doing what no Aryan superman is capable of doing. You will be holding faith with life; giving of yourselves so that total strangers, of no immediate use to you, will live.

"You will be doing the work of God— whatever you conceive Him—" He glanced at Varina. "—or Her to be."

Adolf pointed to the west, where a pale rainbow faded in the aftermath of a predawn rain. "Even now, God gives us a sign. 'I do set my bow in the cloud, and it shall be for a token of a covenant between me and the earth. And it shall come to pass, when I bring a cloud over the earth, that the bow shall be seen in the cloud: And I will remember my covenant, and the waters shall no more become a flood to destroy all flesh.'

"The cloud that stretches over the world today is a dark one. But always, people of faith have endured, to greet the sun once more. Let us take the rainbow as a sign of our eventual triumph."

They prayed then, and soon after people began to leave.

"I remember a saying from my childhood," Varina said. "I see now that it came from that story about the flood. 'And the lord hung a rainbow as a sign. Won't be flood, but fire next time.' Adolf, my friend, you may very well have lit the spark that sets that fire."

Adolf nodded. He wished he knew whether to rejoice, or quake with fear.

Book III

CHAPTER 17

"'And the Lord called unto Moses and spoke unto him out of the taba...taber...?'" The little boy looked up from the huge volume spread across his lap, a familiar look of fear creeping into his eyes.

"Tabernacle," said Adolf. "It's a hard word, Daniel. Don't worry, you're doing fine."

"What's a tabernacle?" asked one of the bolder children.

"It was the tent that covered the Ark of the Covenant," said Adolf. He smiled at the smaller boy. "Go on, Daniel."

Daniel continued reading from the book of Leviticus. When he stopped, Adolf and the other children applauded. Adolf looked up at his guests with a proud smile, which faded when he saw their expressions.

"It's all very interesting, Rabbi," said the leader of the delegation. "But how is teaching a bunch of *missgeburt* to read going to win this revolution?"

Adolf strove for patience. The twenty-five youngsters in the room became very still, willing themselves invisible, as they always did when they sensed tension among those who controlled their fate.

"These children are not *missgeburt*, Walter,"
he said. "Every one of them was declared mentally
defective at birth! Uneducable, and suited for only the
basest forms of labor. When we rescued them from
their 'training camp'—" Adolf knew that spitting
when he remembered the conditions of the place was
inappropriate in front of fellow Aryans, brought up as
he himself had been, "—none of them knew the
alphabet! Or numbers! Or anything beyond basic
commands.

"Look at them now, just one year later!"

Walter Bormann and his two companions
murmured to each other. Adolf felt like a headmaster
leading the trustees on an inspection of his school.
Come to think of it, the comparison wasn't far off the
mark.

"It is very impressive," said Walter. "Everyone
admires what you've done here. Many of us owe our
lives to your polio vaccine, and I, myself am a
graduate of your code school."

"As is anyone who wishes to communicate in
the one language the Party doesn't know," said
one of the two men with Walter.

All four men took a moment to savor the irony
that the dead language of Hebrew had become the
underground's first unbreakable code.

"But the time is at hand for the revolution to
come into the open," Walter continued. "To challenge
the *Reich* directly. To do that, we need more than
misdiagnosed children and utopian communes."

"You're missing the point," said Adolf. "This
entire place is living proof of the mistakes made by
the Party—and their Cult of Science. Once we make

what we have here known to the public—"

"But we can't make it known to the public until we control communications!" said the man who had spoken earlier.

"And we can't do that," said the other one, "until we've consolidated all these squabbling organizations into a single army."

"That's where you come in, Adolf," said Walter. "Your reputation as a spiritual leader; this 'rabbi' thing; it makes you an ideal spokesman. This religion you're spreading is catching on everywhere. And no one feels threatened by you. Join us, and we just might be able to pull everyone together: the fringe groups, the Aryans like ourselves who know the current system is doomed, and most importantly, the desperate masses who will be doing most of the actual fighting. We could finally declare all out war on the *Reich*—and have a shot at winning."

"Under your leadership?" Adolf tried to keep his voice neutral.

Walter had the grace to blush. "Someone has to take responsibility for getting the job done. If you're wondering if I might turn out to be the next dictator, it's a reasonable concern, but I can assure you, it isn't in my future."

So then what are your plans for after you win? Adolf thought about asking, but he already knew.

Adolf always hated this part. He knew by now that he didn't want to throw in with this group, and whomever else they had behind them. But having decided that, the problem was always how to say "no" without convincing them they had to kill you to protect their security.

"Let me show you what else we've been doing

here," said a gravelly voice. Winifred, one of Adolf's
partners (although if asked, she would probably call
herself one of his followers) stood in the doorway.
The three visitors cringed when they saw her, but after
only a moment's shock, hurried to follow her. A point
in their favor.

Winifred had once been a beautiful woman.
But a fire had so badly disfigured her that no
perfection-worshipping Aryan could bear her
presence. Her family had mercifully tried to kill her,
rather than see her hidden away in an institution, but
Winifred had found her way to the resistance instead.

Now, while she took their visitors on a tour of
the commune, Adolf would have time to consider their
offer—and how to extricate himself from it.

"Did we do okay?" Daniel asked anxiously.

Adolf smiled, suddenly glad for the distraction.
"You were great; all of you. Just like I tell you every
day."

"Those men didn't like us," said one of the
girls.

"No, Rachel, they just don't yet realize how
important you are."

In reality, Adolf shared Rachel's view, which
further dissuaded him from an alliance with these
people. He dismissed his students and went outside.

Spring was just barely making itself felt this
far north. Here, in a nearly forgotten corner of
Denmark, small groups like Adolf's struggled to
reclaim land from sea, and workable farms from the
devastation of the big earthquake.

In the two years since leaving the polio colony,
Adolf had finally achieved enough so that even *he* had
to admit he was doing some good. The distribution of

the vaccine had gone better than any of them had
hoped. For months, it had been almost laughable as
hungry, oppressed people from lower classes and
lesser races showed a sudden resistance to a disease
that was dropping Aryan supermen like flies.

Dr. Speer had shown truly inspired timing,
when, just as it seemed their leaders would begin
vivisecting whole populations out of sheer frustration,
the vaccine was "discovered" by a "brilliant Aryan
scientist, formerly out of favor with the Party."

Adolf still worried about Speer, even more
than he worried about Varina and Jacques, whom he
hadn't heard from in months. The doctor had the
frightening job of living among the enemy every day,
while Adolf lived among friends and followers. He
had the luxury of speaking his mind, and following
any crazy notion that came to it.

He gazed fondly at the small farming
commune he and his friends had begun last year. It
wasn't so small anymore. While Adolf was no better
a farmer now than when he stayed with Stefan and
Anna, many of those who followed him here had a
true gift for coaxing a living from land that the Party
had declared unusable. Between their hard work, and
Adolf's success at freeing the *Reich's* oppressed and
integrating them into this commune, the place now fed
and housed over one hundred people.

Nothing that large or successful could escape
the Party's notice for much longer. Soon, they would
have to disband. Or, at the very least, Adolf and
certain other high profile activists would have to move
on.

He wished that fewer people knew who he had
been before he joined the revolution. It was true that

"Rabbi Adolf" enjoyed a reputation as a spiritual leader who shunned partisan politics, and whose advice was sought on everything from devising codes to performing weddings. But he suspected that it was Adolf Goebbels that people like Walter Bormann wanted to use.

Adolf sighed. Why did he do this to himself?

Because humility was his friend, and a revolutionary leader who started believing his own press wasn't likely to live very long.

And when powerful, self-confident leaders like Walter approached with dazzling visions of the future, it was easy to be swayed. And when desperate, broken people like Winifred or those kids he rescued looked at Adolf with adoration and put their lives in his hands, it was easy to swell with pride. None of which would help him right now.

"So, will you be leaving us to pursue greater destinies?" Winifred broke into his thoughts.

"Where are our guests?" asked Adolf.

"With Baldric, learning all about our water purification system. They may not have been too impressed with the kids, but they'll find enough to make the trip worthwhile."

"Good," said Adolf. "Because that's all they're getting from it."

Winifred's scarred face showed surprise. "You won't be going with them?"

"I don't trust them. Not that I think they're spies, or anything other than what they say they are. It's just…they're not who I want leading the world."

"They may be the best shot we have."
Winifred wiped her hands on her apron and sat down on a bench beneath the grape arbor. Adolf sat beside

her. "Look, Adolf, I don't think much of Walter as a person. To him, Judaism is a convenient tool. For that matter, so are you. But he's a damned sight better than what we have now."

"You're right, Winifred. But after all the bloodshed and loss and sacrifice—'better' just isn't good enough! I'm not signing on with anyone who I can't trust with my heart and soul—not to mention my back turned."

"I can't argue with you there. But that means trouble for the rest of us."

Adolf cocked an eyebrow. "How so?"

"Well, everyone wants what you just described. But for most of us, that means you! I wish you'd stop looking for a leader you can follow, and settle for being the one the rest of us want to follow!"

"Who guards the guardians, eh Winifred?" Adolf shot her a sidelong glance, hoping he could joke his way out of this one.

They were interrupted by a shout from one of the sentries.

Everyone scrambled to alert, then stood down as a single injured man was brought inside the compound.

"Get him to the infirmary," Adolf commanded.

"Don't bother," said Anton, a onetime medical student who now functioned as the colony's doctor. "Just try to make him comfortable here. He hasn't got much time, and he appears to be a messenger. Let's hear what he's trying to say."

The man, bleeding from a half dozen bullet wounds, was shouting incoherently. Winifred brought water and tried to feed it to him in small sips, while Adolf sponged the man's forehead. "Get a patrol out at once," he whispered to Anton, while smiling reassuringly at the dying man.

"Ten millimeter ammo," said Anton. "Only used by the Mauser 82S – sniper rifle. It's possible he lost them, rather than leading them here." As everyone would naturally worry about. Anton went to arrange for the patrol, while Adolf and Winifred ministered to the man.

"Adolf!" he shouted suddenly, his fevered eyes clearing slightly. "You're him! You're the rabbi, aren't you?"

"Who wants to know?" Adolf asked automatically.

Bloody hands clutched his shirt. "Come to the Pripet marshes. She sent me. You have to…" the messenger's words were lost in a fit of coughing.

"Who sent you?"

"Come. They need…we need…" Adolf pressed his ear closer to the man's mouth, but bubbles of blood were all that came out. His body jerked once and went rigid.

They couldn't cover the body with a sheet; supplies were far too scarce. Adolf led the burial party, after the body was searched for further clues to his identity or mission, and then went to join the waiting council to decide what to do.

"It smells like a trap," Baldric was saying.

Winifred snorted. "Baldric, to you, everything smells like a trap."

"That's because nearly everything is," the big man retorted.

Anton shook his head. "You're suggesting the Party arranged to shoot a volunteer in such a manner that he would have exactly enough time to reach our base on foot, tell enough of a message to tantalize Adolf, then die before an awkward silence sets in?"

"You don't think they're willing to do exactly that?" asked Baldric.

"I'm sure they've *tried*. I'd hazard a guess they've even been successful. But I examined that man's wounds, and I don't believe that the timing was planned. Also, the condition of his body as a whole: he lived a rough life; consistent with that of a partisan unit…"

"And maybe he was one! Maybe he was captured and…*persuaded* to cooperate…"

"With a suicide mission?" said Winifred.

"It's been known to happen!"

"All right," said Adolf. "Thank you all for your input. I think I've heard enough."

"You're going, aren't you?" said Winifred.

Adolf shrugged. "It gives me the perfect excuse to decline Walter's offer, without appearing to do so. Besides, I can't just ignore a mystery like this."

"That's what worries me," muttered Baldric.

"We all knew it was time for me to leave. We've reached the point where I'm a threat to the commune." Adolf looked at the three so very different people at the table. "I leave this place in your capable hands."

"We'll never get anything done now," sighed Winifred.

Adolf trudged through the snowy forest, following the broad back of Heinz, the bodyguard Baldric insisted accompany them. Two other devoted disciples trudged along behind Adolf. He would have preferred to make this trip alone. Companionship was nice, but for as long as they were with him, these people were his responsibility.

It's spring, Adolf thought for the hundredth time. *Too bad no one told that to this part of Poland.* The Party had done an admirable job of clearing out forest, both to reduce the hiding and provisioning of rebels, and to create new farmland. But there were some things that were beyond even Nazi efficiency. Adolf gazed through the primordial silence of the ancient woods, and saw trees older than the *Reich*; older, than the name "Germany." This forest, he realized, had seen the rise and fall of countless empires, and would be standing long after the *Reich* had been forgotten.

"Well Gerik," said Adolf, shaking off his melancholy, "we could walk on nice flat road, and stop trudging along this trail to the side of it."

"Sure. And get shot in the ambush. Have the whole war over with that way," muttered Gerik.

"The road turns soon. We need to find out where. I'd hate to get lost on top of everything else." Rufin started off to his right and slipped from tree to tree or bush, keeping in cover.

"Gerik, doesn't this road have a drainage ditch alongside it?"

Ruffin nodded. "Was built back in the 30's when they did such things properly."

"Shh…" Heinz signaled for everyone to stop. Properly trained, the bodyguards took positions behind cover. Adolf leaned against a tree.

Sure would be nice not to be threatened by every little bush, ditch, or bird. Adolf glanced around, bored with the silly exercise his bodyguards seemed intent on following. Heinz waved to the group and pointed with two fingers in the age-old gesture of "Look there". Adolf watched Gerik and Rufin take in the scenery with wary eyes. Adolf looked where they were staring so intently.

He remembered that snow was an easy thing to use as camouflage. The trick to spotting someone in camouflage was to watch for movement. After a moment, Adolf recognized that the slight rise he was staring at was the slope leading up from the drainage ditch to the road.

Heinz stood up and waved everyone to walk away from the road, back into the forest. "Turn's a couple of klicks up. Faster people, we are going way too slow. And next time, Rabbi, get down behind cover. Please." Heinz stared at Adolf until Adolf, uncomfortable, looked away.

Three more times, Heinz led the party back to the road. Three more times all anyone saw was the slope from the drainage ditch. Adolf yawned, tired, and cold as he stood up and started walking.

"Are we boring you Rabbi?" asked Heinz.

"No. Just tired," said Adolf. Not quite a lie.

The fourth time they approached the road, Heinz seemed even more tense.

"Problem?" Adolf whispered.

"Maybe. Curve in the road is classic place for ambush."

"Why would they bother?"

"Someone shot that messenger." Heinz motioned for silence and crept forward. Heinz, Gerik and Rufin took turns moving, getting into cover, and then watching in the direction of the road. Adolf crept, and felt like a real idiot for doing so.

He froze, aware he had sensed movement. Intently he stared forward and to his right. Movement again! This time it materialized into a man. Adolf stared at an all too familiar neck and hairline; this was beginning to feel like a dream. *What in hell is Heydrich doing HERE?*

Acting on an instinct he didn't know he had, he quietly slipped the safety off on his Sten Gun, and grabbed a hand grenade. Heinz looked back, his eyes widening in almost panic as Adolf placed the grenade under his arm pit and twist the cap. Frantically, Heinz waived his open hand in short chopping motions for "Cease Fire". Gerik and Rufin, alarmed started scanning in the direction of the road, silently slipping the safeties on their Sten Guns.

Adolf was oblivious to everything but the sight of Josef Heydrich in front of him. Holding the Sten in his left hand, Adolf stood, left shoulder aligned with Heydrich in the picture perfect style of throwing a potato masher, and threw the grenade. Time seemed to stop for Adolf, yelling as he brought up his weapon to fire.

Heinz turned to stare at the ditch, and could make out an entire squad on either side of the man Adolf was yelling at. And the platoon leader, a young *Leutnant*, and praise God, the platoon sergeant, a *Feldwebel*. In one motion, Heinz grabbed, set, and tossed a hand grenade while Adolf's grenade was still in the air.

The soldiers stared behind them as first one, and then a second hand grenade was heading toward them.

Adolf had the satisfaction of watching Heydrich's eyes go wide as he stared in Adolf's direction. He fired his weapon at Heydrich and missed. The entire world exploded as the Germans began firing back. Gerik and Rufin unloaded their clips into the backs of the would-be ambushers. The two hand grenades went off, fragments audibly whirring among the ambushers.

The concussions were enough to cause every tree within ten meters to shed the snow off their branches, obscuring everyone's view more thoroughly than any amount of smoke. For a moment, the firing stopped. The cries of the wounded echoed through the forest.

On the run, Heinz grabbed Adolf. Without being told, Rufin covered the group's rear as they ran back into the forest, away from the road. Adolf started breathing again, somewhere in the middle of what appeared to be a kilometer run.

In reality, Heinz stopped running after 100 meters or so, and threw himself and Adolf into cover. Gerik and Rufin caught up and found cover.

Out of breath, Gerik spoke. "Whew! Good shooting Heinz. I think you got the platoon leader and his *Feldwebel*. That should keep them from following."

Heinz cocked his head sideways, intent on what if anything he could hear. Softly, he could hear a single voice shouting, but he couldn't make out their words. "Who is Heydrich? Is he an officer?"

Adolf shook his head as if to clear it. "He was the damned *Health Secretary* last I heard! What was doing with the infantry? And here of all places?"

"Wanting you badly enough, that he's rallying what's left of that platoon to come after us. Alright, let's get out of…" Rifle fire finished Heinz sentence.

The group fell back at a run. After another 100 meters, they stopped, everyone but Heinz out of breath. Heinz placed Adolf in cover, and motioned for Rufin and Gerik to spread out.

"Now what?" muttered Adolf.

"We sting them to make them slow down their chase." On their left, Rufin fired into the trees. Rifle fire quickly found the tree he was hiding behind. Rufin fired again as a rifle grenade hit the tree in front of him. The grenade severed the tree four feet from the ground and threw the trunk into Rufin. Adolf looked away from the mess the falling tree made of his young guard's body. He changed magazines, got on his knees and fired into the forest.

Without warning, Heinz shouted "Fallback," and again dragged Adolf for another 100 meters. Heinz changed magazines on the run. Behind them, they could hear the shouts as their pursuers kept on coming.

Sensing their pursuit was almost on top of them, Heinz, Adolf and Gerik turned and opened fire. Off in the distance, they could hear an MG94 fire briefly, then stop. Gerik fired to his left, trying to fend off the closing flankers. Adolf watched as Germans alternately dove back under cover from his shooting, and then fired back as he paused to take aim.

Adolf changed magazines again. He fired, and watched as a man he was trying to hit pitched forward. Heinz started firing to the left as Gerik spun around, eyes wide, as blood spurted from his shoulder. Adolf ducked back behind a tree, prepared a hand grenade and tossed it in the general direction of the enemy. And saw yet another soldier pitch forward, part of his jaw flying in Adolf's direction. Heinz, out of ammunition took his last two grenades, and threw the first one. Again, the double concussion from the grenades caused tree canopies to dump their snow, creating yet another chance for Heinz and Adolf to run.

Heinz lost the race just as a sudden crescendo of Sten Guns rang out behind them, then stopped as suddenly as it had started. Adolf had covered 25 meters when he heard a familiar female voice yell in perfect Hebrew "*Sheket! Sheket*!!". Adolf turned and ran towards the voice, then came to an abrupt stop in front of a person with a Finnish combat parka, face shrouded by a fur hood.

Then their rescuer pushed back the hood of roughly tanned furs, and Adolf stood gazing across the silent battlefield at his wife.

CHAPTER 18

It was a while before Adolf remembered to breathe.

Adrenaline and shadows can confuse the eye, he told himself as the woman checked on Adolf's companions, methodically seeking signs of life—or useful information. It can't really be...

"This one's alive," she said, kneeling over Gerik's still form. It was Ilsa's voice. "Come on, Adolf, let's move! There'll be time for catching up later!" Adolf's training as a partisan took over, and he hurried to Gerik's side, his mind still whirling.

Together, they carried the injured man for what appeared to be forever. Shadowy figures moved cautiously ahead. Meanwhile, Ilsa and Adolf spoke together for the first time in three years.

"That was a full platoon that tried to ambush you," she said

"It was more than that. Heydrich was there."

"Heydrich? Damn. We found about a dozen bodies back where you hit them. The radio was destroyed by a hand grenade, so they didn't get word out. I'd guess about another half dozen or so escaped our running into them. That means Heydrich got out alive." Ilsa and Adolf dropped into silence as they considered possible implications.

At the edge of the forest, they reached a marsh. A short distance across the marsh stood alone cabin, so well camouflaged Adolf would have missed it without a guide. His practiced eye did, however, notice the guard on the roof, and the one behind the screen of tall grass.

Inside, about a dozen fur clad partisans huddled around a nearly smokeless fire. As Adolf and Ilsa entered with Gerik, conversation stopped. A babble of different languages asked and answered questions, and Gerik was borne away by whatever passed for medical personnel in this place. Ilsa barked an order to the radio operator, "To all bases: stay close to home. The *Reich* is starting to take us seriously." A typical day at a typical partisan base, thought Adolf—except for the woman in charge.

She had shed her outer garments, and Adolf got his first good look at his wife since their wedding night. She was thinner and darker than the last time he'd seen her. The sun that had tanned her once creamy skin had bleached her blonde hair to near silver. Her face was seamed by a long and frightening scar, but none of it could mar her beauty in Adolf's eyes.

"I'm glad you came, Adolf," she said, as if they'd been apart three days, rather than three years. "Sorry about the welcoming committee."

"I'm used to it," Adolf said. "To what do I owe the honor of a summons from the Valkyrie?" Adolf asked.

A smile twitched the corners of her mouth. "I would prefer a more Jewish title, but there don't seem to be many where women are concerned."

"Still, there's a lot to be said for the glory of irony," said Adolf. "The Party that once denied your humanity now has to hear you described by the greatest title awarded any Aryan woman."

Ilsa chuckled. Adolf grinned at the sound. It

was happy! Nothing at all like her brittle laughter those years ago in Berlin. "It's finally time for us to work together, Adolf. You interested?"

Adolf glanced at an imaginary wristwatch. "Well, I am rather busy just now, but maybe I could pencil you in for some time next year…" He swept her into his arms and planted a wet kiss on her mouth. To his great delight she not only responded eagerly, but no one shot him. In fact, judging by the whistles and cheers of those around them, her unit was happy to see them together like this. He wondered how much she had told them of her personal life, and what, if anything, these people knew about him.

"You've all heard of Rabbi Adolf," she said, addressing the group. "Well, here he is. And for those of you who speculated, but knew better than to ask," some of the old fierceness was back, but even it was softened, "yes, he's also my husband."

The freezing, half starved partisans broke into a new round of cheering and applauding, though Adolf could detect at least a few sighs of disappointment from some of the men. He was surprised at how good Ilsa's public acknowledgement of their union made him feel.

"Rabbi, we have need of your wisdom," Ilsa said formally, and now, Adolf could sense the urgency behind her mask of calm authority.

"I am at your service," he said, equally formally.

Ilsa gestured to someone in the back of the room, and a young Aryan woman, unremarkable but for a broken nose that had never properly healed, stepped forward.

"This is Berta. She's the leader of a cell which

recently disbanded. You need to hear her story."

Berta looked at Adolf with the same awe that was becoming uncomfortably familiar. She seemed to have trouble finding her voice. When she finally did, it was steadily enough. "You are familiar, are you not Rabbi, with the celebration known as Passover?"

"Oh, yes," said Adolf. He guided Berta to a rough bench against the wall, and drew up a camp stool for himself so he could sit directly across from her. "I celebrated it last year in Belgium."

"But not this year?" Berta's eyes held a strange intensity.

"I'm afraid not. We managed to figure out when it would be, but unfortunately, we were busy, ah, putting out fires at the time."

"We tried it this year," Berta said. "Last month. We had a Rabbi and three *haggadahs*—each in a different language. Most people in the cell couldn't read anyway, but there were pictures showing how the table should look, and everyone liked the part about drinking four glasses of wine." Berta blew a stray hair out of her face and took a deep breath.

"Rabbi, when you did your service, did you put out an extra cup of wine for Elijah?"

Adolf nodded. "That's part of the ritual. You set out an extra glass, and open the door—if you have one—for Elijah to enter. The year he finally shows up to drink the wine is supposed to foretell the coming of the messiah." Adolf smiled fondly at the memory. "Of course, in reality, it just means an extra portion of wine, and no one ever wants to waste *that*. I remember the most serious discussion we had all night, was over whether to drink it ourselves or pour it out at the end of the evening."

"Well, we didn't have that discussion," said Berta. "Because, near as I can tell, Elijah showed up."

"What?"

Berta hugged herself as if for warmth. "It was at the end of the *seder*. I'd just filled the cups for the fourth time. Elena opened the door for Elijah, just like the book said to. Rabbi Sol stood up and read the next passage, where it talks about greeting Elijah; the messenger of the redemption of mankind.

"Then, all of the sudden, this guy walks in. He went right over to the extra cup and dipped his hand in it, and then he shook out ten drops of wine on the table. He said the name of a plague with each drop— but I know they weren't the same plagues that hit Egypt; we'd just recited that list earlier in the meal!"

"Do you remember what they were?"

"It's not something I'm ever likely to forget: Rats. Weakened flesh. Storms. Burning rivers. Poisoned water. Leprosy. Fevers. Boils. Bleeding guts."

Silence fell heavily upon the room.

Berta was about to speak again, but Adolf said, "That's nine."

"What?"

"The plagues you just listed. You only named nine."

Ilsa's eyes widened in surprise, and Berta listed them again, counting. "But I was sure there were ten! Just like in Egypt."

"You must have forgotten one," said Adolf.

"But…" Berta shook her head violently. "No! I hung on every word."

"Perhaps the final plague won't be revealed until the first nine have run their course," said Ilsa.

"As I recall, God gave Pharaoh one last chance before carrying out the slaying of the first-born. But I'm surprised I didn't catch it the first time Berta told me."

"You were not at the *Seder*, I take it?" said Adolf.

"I was busy being pinned down by machine gun fire at the time. But I've known Berta for a long time. If she says she saw and heard this, she did."

Adolf wished he had something more to go on than that, but he was still intrigued. "What did this guy look like?" he asked.

"He was big. I know this sounds silly, but he seemed to fill the whole room. He had on a black cloak, with a hood that covered most of his face. But I could see a beard. Not long, but dark, and turning gray.

"Anyway, he drank the wine and said that the redeemer already walked among us. There would be ten new plagues, and then the Nazi reign of terror would be over. And after that, what happened would be up to us. Then, he walked back outside. No one ever saw him again."

"What did you do next?"

"Speaking from personal experience, I'd say some of us almost shit our pants. Oh, excuse me, Rabbi!" Berta blushed all the way to the roots of her blond hair, while around her, the room erupted with much needed laughter.

Adolf smiled. "Don't worry, Berta. If you didn't, I think I'd start doubting your story about now."

After several tries, the young woman picked up the thread of her story.

"Conrad ran out to ask the guards what they

saw, and to chew them out for letting an intruder get past them. Sol said the whole thing was just a joke. There were four people on guard duty; one of them must have thought it would be funny to put on a black cloak and be Elijah."

"That does sound more reasonable," said Adolf. "And I have heard of tricks like that being played."

"Do you think I'd have asked you to come all this way if I thought that's all it was? Look, I know you don't know me, Rabbi, but I know my people! Three of those guards were illiterate, with no interest in Judaism. The fourth is a short woman, with a squeaky voice and no sense of humor! And clothing and bedding are scarce around here. If anyone had a cloak like that, someone would have known.

"Besides that, it just felt real to me. That's what has me so shook up."

"Did anyone besides you have that reaction?" asked Adolf.

"Conrad believes someone was there, but not Elijah. He doesn't believe in ghosts."

"Elijah never died."

"What?"

"You said ghosts. Elijah never died, so, technically, he's not a ghost."

Berta stared at Adolf, as if to decide whether or not he was making fun of her. "Thanks, that really helps," she said finally.

"Sorry, I wasn't trying to be funny. It's just that…oh, I wish I'd been there!"

"I wish you'd been there too! Our rabbi is fine, but he's not you, Adolf. If you had been there, maybe the man would have said or done more, or maybe..." Berta shook her head in frustration. "At least we'd have known if he was real."

"I appreciate your faith in me," said Adolf. "Don't take this the wrong way, Berta, but I have to bring it up: you'd all had three glasses of wine already. Just what kind of wine was it?"

"Heavily watered!" she snapped. Then, more softly, "And yes, it was ordinary bottled wine from someone's cellar, not the home brew that puts people in comas, or the opium stuff that the rich drink. And no one at that table was drunk. I'd stake my life on it."

"You probably already have," said Adolf. "I believe you, Berta. I just wish I could explain it." After a heavy pause, he addressed the room. "Any thoughts, people?"

They were strangers to him, and had doubtlessly discussed the subject a great deal since Berta's arrival. Still, they reacted with pride and enthusiasm, because it was "Rabbi Adolf" who was asking. A gaunt man, who sat perched on a bench with his one remaining leg propped up in front of him, shook his head. "There's no end to strange occurrences these days. I say this is just one more."

"It's got to be a hoax," said a familiar voice. Adolf saw Gerik, resting on a cot in the far corner of the room. The medic was still working on his shoulder, but Gerik, as always, refused to be left out of the discussion. "Although, perhaps a valuable one. If enough people start believing that the new age is at hand, they might just believe it right into existence."

"It's no hoax!" shouted a new voice. "Elijah has returned. If you look closely, you'll find the signs leading up to this event are everywhere!"

Adolf turned to see a slightly built young woman—or perhaps girl, as she couldn't be more than sixteen—addressing the room. Long dark hair spilled behind her as she moved through the crowd to stand before Adolf. Her eyes seemed unnaturally bright. "We have to make the world ready, Rabbi, and there isn't much time! That's why it's up to you!"

Adolf glanced at Ilsa.

"This is Alina," she said. "She's been having…visions, lately."

Adolf sighed wearily. "Yes, I've run into a few—"

"And more often than not," Ilsa continued tightly, "They come true."

As far as Adolf was concerned, that didn't make listening to a fanatic any easier, but he was a guest here. "What have you seen, Alina?" he asked.

"I've seen a plague of yellow locust devouring all life on earth. I've seen insect-like men in black rubber suits, surviving the plague, only to die later at each other's hands. Then lately, just after Berta came to us, my visions began to change."

"For the better, I hope," said Adolf.

"Yes, thank God. You see, I've come to understand these visions are warnings; very specific warnings. The locusts are some kind of new weapon that the Party is working on. The black suites are some kind of survival gear. It's going to happen soon—very soon! But now I see that we have a chance. God has sent us prophets! If we can unravel the clues He's set before us, I believe we can avert the destruction of all life on earth!"

"Well, that would be good," said Adolf. "What do you think Berta's experience at Passover means?"

"First of all," said Alina, "it means we have to start keeping kosher. Next, we have to convince the rest of the world to do the same."

"Kosher?" said Gerik. "What's that?"

"A set of dietary laws—" Adolf began.

"An entire system of what you can and cannot eat, and how food has be prepared, served and stored," said Alina. She went on to explain the kosher laws, from the prohibition against pork and shellfish, to the laws against eating meat and dairy at the same table. Her knowledge, Adolf had to admit, was impressive.

"You're going to persuade starving people to do *that*?" Gerik stared at Ilsa. "Do the rest of you agree with this crazy notion?"

Adolf could tell from the expressions of those around him that there was a considerable difference of opinion regarding Alina and her prophesies. That, too, was typical of units that contained zealots.

"Actually," said Ilsa, "I'd considered something like it myself, much earlier." Adolf remembered a reference to that effect in one of her letters. "I saw it as more of an identity thing; a way to separate ourselves from the enemy. But now I see something that should have been obvious from the beginning.

"I didn't notice it the first time Berta told me what she saw and heard. Even when I went back and read the book of Exodus looking for clues, I was still trying to determine if Elijah was really in the room at Berta's *seder*.

"Now I see I was following a false lead. You see, in the original story, the Jews were spared the devastation of the ten plagues by putting the blood of the Passover lamb on their doorposts. That way, God recognized His own.

"I think what Berta's visitor was trying to tell us, is that something terrible is coming—you don't have to believe in visions to believe that—but there are ways for people to protect themselves."

"I see what you're getting at," said Adolf. The others in the room apparently did not, so Adolf continued. "Look at the plagues Berta listed. Most of them are already making an appearance: rats are becoming a problem everywhere, and thousands of children have been born with immune systems too weak to fight off illness—especially among the Aryans."

"Two rivers have already burned," said the man with one leg. "And everyone knows how toxic the oceans are becoming."

"Toxic enough so that few varieties of shellfish are safe anymore. And certain illnesses are on the rise: trichinosis for one, which specifically attacks pork—the mainstay of the German diet, but strictly forbidden by Jewish law. Two of the plagues Berta mentioned, fever and bleeding guts, are symptoms of trichinosis."

"And symptoms of at least a dozen other diseases as well!" said Gerik. "Look folks, this is all very interesting, but surely you're not suggesting that we go around telling starving people to give up their only sources of food—to avoid some kind of doomsday plague?"

"It wouldn't be the craziest thing I've heard yet," said Ilsa.

"Something else," said Adolf. "Most of those plagues reflect what the Party is actually doing to the earth. We're not just threatened by a totalitarian government; we're in danger of global ecological disaster. Kosher laws happen to be among the most enlightened environmental laws ever devised."

"They sound silly to me," said Berta. "Why should anyone have to worry about whether they're eating milk and meat together? And you'd have to be crazy during starving times to not eat anything you could get your hands on! Who cares whether a fish has shells or scales? And pork's as good as veal when I'm hungry."

"Granted, they're not very practical to the average revolutionary with a price on his head," said Adolf. "But in calmer, freer times, they're very nice. Some of the great Jewish teachers were vegetarians, and many others have encouraged people to at least limit meat in their diets. Early in Genesis, God said, 'See, I give you every seed bearing plant that is upon all the earth, and every tree that has fruit; they shall be yours for food.' Like maybe we're not supposed to have to kill to eat.

"Even if we do have to live off the flesh of other creatures, the idea of keeping meat and milk separate was originally to avoid the cruelty of mixing the life giving element of milk with the death element of flesh."

Alina nodded emphatically. "The idea of caring for the environment is kosher too. If you eat all the eggs, there won't be any more birds; kill all the fish and—"

"Yes, I think we all get the point," said Berta. "It's just not the way starving people are going to think. Surely Elijah—or whoever he was--must know that."

"I'm sure he does," said Ilsa. "But whatever really happened at your base, Berta I think someone is trying to send us a message."

"If nothing else," said Adolf, "we're being warned to think ahead. That one day, Nazi rule will end, and it's up to us to take better care of the earth than they did."

The assembled group murmured quietly to one another. They partook in the ritual of a shared meal; fish and bark soup, in this case. Afterwards, there were questions for the Rabbi, and a *Torah* reading, followed by more questions and discussion.

Finally, long after the sun had set behind an already dark sky, Ilsa led Adolf to her tiny, semi-private room in the back of the cabin. She normally shared the room with two other women, she said. Tonight, Adolf noticed, there was no one else here.

"It isn't much," she said, indicating her bedroll, a pile of clothes and a small desk with an oil lamp and a scattering of papers, and sheets of bark covered with writing. "But it's mine. And for tonight, it's ours."

Adolf set his bedroll beside hers. "Let's see if we can remember what to do with a private room," he said.

CHAPTER 19

Much later, as they lay in each other's arms in a tangle of blankets, Adolf and Ilsa caught up on each other's adventures since their last exchange of letters.

"Those code schools you started will probably be remembered as the most decisive factor in winning this war," Ilsa said.

"Let's win it first," said Adolf. "And leave the writing of history to whatever breed of historians we spawn. Besides, it wasn't any stroke of genius on my part. It was all those Aryan geniuses in our grandparents generation, who made sure no one in the Party knew what Hebrew was—then left all those books for us to find."

"Your modesty will probably be remembered as the second greatest factor."

"You'll have your own troubles, my dear," Adolf said, nibbling Ilsa's ear. "What with your feeding your troops by raiding military supply depots! You managed to feed thousands and boost morale in the movement at the same time." He turned to look her in the eye. "I just wish you wouldn't take so many risks."

"You knew when you married me I wasn't the type to stay home and bake cakes, Adolf." Then with a shrug, she steered the conversation back to lighter topics. "I heard all about your sojourn at the polio camp, and how you were involved with finding the vaccine. But now that you've told me the whole story, I must meet this Varina. For some reason, her part seems to have been written out."

"Ugh!" Adolf pulled a pillow over his head.
"Ilsa, you have to promise me you'll start spreading
the real story at once! If you don't, Varina will find
me and kill me before I get to see who wins the war!"

Ilsa wrapped her arms around Adolf's waist.
"There, there, *liebling*, I'll protect you from her," she
teased. Then she wound her long legs around his, and
he forgot about being humorous.

"Why did you send for me?" Adolf asked later.

"Three reasons," said Ilsa. "The first two you
met this afternoon."

Adolf nodded. "Tell me about Alina. What's
her story?"

"Near as anyone can figure, her parents were
into Judaism before any group that I've been able to
trace. No one knows exactly why, or what their plans
were, but they filled an old bunker with books, relics,
food, water—whatever they had in mind, it was for
the long haul. They were killed before they could go
to ground there, but they managed to get Alina
stashed.

"She thinks she was seven or eight at the time.
All we know for sure is she spent the next five years
alone, with no contact with anyone or anything—other
than the books and relics. Except, if you ask her,
she'll tell you God was talking to her the entire time."

"Not surprising," said Adolf. "Considering
what that kind of isolation does to people. But at least
it explains how she got to be such an expert on
Judaism. Prophet or not, I think we have to rate her as
extraordinary."

"When she was found by an underground cell,
they brought her to me—Jewish Central they called us

back then. She seemed harmless enough at the time, but if what she's seen—this doomsday weapon—is real, we have to find it."

"I hope you have a suggestion as to how. None of the places I hold sway in have the resources to investigate something like that." He thought about what would be needed for an operation like this: a large base, secure year round, educated people—no, trained *scientists*—communications array, organization..."

"Finland," whispered Adolf.

Ilsa kissed him. "Got it on the first try."

"But aren't they in a state of crisis right now?"

"They're *always* in a state of crisis. That's why they never accomplish anything."

"Well, yes, I can't argue with that," said Adolf. "Still, it's no small thing that they've gone from holding a 'privileged spot' in the *Führer's* glorious plan, to being the most discontented hell raisers in Europe."

"Gee, I wonder why?" said Ilsa. "Might it have something to do with the fact that anyone anywhere who's tall, blond and smart enough gets recruited by the Party for education and citizenship—"

"If they're deemed worthy at the end of their training," Adolf finished. "And of course, the Party's been pretty desperate lately."

"That's what comes from executing half your educated populace. Or driving them away, as in your case," said Ilsa. "But anyway, over time, the great honor the *Reich* was bestowing upon its provinces started wearing thin. They got tired of losing their women to *SS* brothels and their sons to hot spots on the other side of the world.

"So now Scandinavia's got several million irate subjects, several hundred educated men and women who washed out of University or some other training, a handful of old timers who still remember how to set up an underground—and some of the most difficult terrain on the face of the earth."

"Everything we need," Adolf agreed.

Ilsa nodded. "Do you remember Ludwig?"

Adolf smiled fondly at the memory. "I had the honor of serving with him briefly, about a year ago. Is *he* up there now, organizing the Scandinavians?" If so, there might be hope.

"He was," Ilsa said sadly. "Mustard gas to the lungs, one too many times. He sent out his last message three weeks ago, from Finland, naming his replacement. It's you, Adolf."

"Me! No, there must be some mistake. I'm no military leader!" *Just ask Heinz, Rufin and Gerik*!

"They don't need a military leader. They've got dozens already. That's their problem!"

"Ludwig spent his last six months up there, and discovered a unique situation: too many thinkers and too many leaders. Here, we've barely got one educated man, or ex soldier per cell. Up north, they've got plenty."

"So what do they need me for?"

"To get them working together. To get all their brilliant ideas—not to mention weapons— pointed in the same direction."

"They don't need me for that," said Adolf. "In fact, it sounds more like your line of work."

Ilsa wrapped a ragged blanket around herself and leaned against the back wall. "It is. We'll be going together. If you agree to it, that is. I'm supposed to play hard ball; come in like the general of all generals, or something." She half smiled. "It's quite an honor. I'm not the oldest, or the most experienced. I'm certainly not educated, or Scandinavian or a man. Ludwig said I'm 'unique.' And that's the only thing he could argue that they don't already have too much of."

Adolf's heart leapt at the thought of working with Ilsa, side by side. But he couldn't simply tag along as Ilsa's husband. Not when he was finally accomplishing things of real importance on his own. "So I repeat my question," he said. "What do they need me for?"

"They need Rabbi Adolf," Ilsa said simply.

Adolf laughed, then wrapped himself in one of Ilsa's blankets, since it seemed keeping each other warm wouldn't resume until after this business meeting was over. "To half this underground, Judaism is nothing more than useful codes and a quaint bit of historic symbolism."

"But to the other half it's a lot more than that," said Ilsa. "And there's plenty in the first half for whom it could be more, if they weren't so afraid to let their guard down. And that's where you come in.

"People are afraid of me, Adolf. I'll admit I enjoy the feeling, and it helps me get things done. But they *trust* you. In a world where no one can afford to trust anyone, somehow everyone has come to trust you. And right now, that's something we need more than anything else. It's what will get all those separate groups working together. Whatever Judaism means to each person in the revolution, the one thing everyone can agree on at this moment—is you, Adolf."

Adolf sighed. He thought back to the ambush this morning, where two more good people had given their lives for him. It felt like a trap with no way out: he didn't want people to die for him, but he didn't want to kill anyone either.

To date, his own confirmed kill rating was still zero. But right now he had to wonder, as he thought about throwing that grenade and spraying bullets all over the forest, if this time, he had killed someone. It wasn't the first time he'd been in that situation, and as always, he hated it.

But worse was that nagging fear that if he could just get over his revulsion of killing, more of his friends would be alive. And if he finally did get over it, what would he say to Ruffin and Heinz, and all the others who had died so he didn't have to kill?

That memory brought up another subject.

"Ilsa, what was Heydrich doing here today? You didn't seem surprised when I told you I'd seen him."

"I wasn't. You see, wherever the two of us are, so are men like Heydrich. A lot of ambitious men have promised the *Führer* they'd end our threat to the *Reich*. Some have even promised to personally bring the *Führer* our heads—that's yours and mine, specifically. Heydrich's the only one I'm currently worried about."

"I guess I'm really out of touch," said Adolf. "Last *I* heard of him, he was heading up the search for the polio vaccine."

Ilsa smiled. "And he didn't come out of that one looking too good, did he? So he switched careers. Now he's high up in the Department of Political Security. The guys in it are mostly *SS*. They run it like the Inquisition in ancient times."

The SS vs. Judaism. One religion fighting
another. And those fights were the worst kind of all.

"So how about it?" Ilsa broke into Adolf's
brooding. "You gonna team up with your wife and go
save the world?"

"Personally, I think you're all crazy. But I
certainly won't turn down a chance to see the famous
Finns. Or to wake up next to you every morning.
Three years of celibacy was hard enough."

Ilsa brushed a lock of hair from her face and
stared at Adolf. "Do you mean to tell me you haven't
been with anyone all this time?"

"Well...yes. You know, marriage vows and
all? How about you?" He tried to make it sound
casual.

"Yes, of course. But it's expected of me—
both the Jews and the Nazis agree on *that.*"

"Since when have *you* cared about what
anyone in authority expects?"

Ilsa shrugged. "It's also easier for me, Adolf.
Other than with you, sex has never been something
I've sought out."

"Are you...are you really sure about that
'other than with me' part?" Her past experiences had
never stopped haunting him.

Ilsa slid from her blanket into his. "Can you
doubt it?" she asked, rubbing against him. "Do you
need a refresher course?"

"Definitely," said Adolf, pulling her on top of
him.

A while later, just as Adolf was drifting off to
sleep, Ilsa murmured, "Do you think it's possible to

get the entire underground following kosher laws?"

"Not really, no. Why?"

"I was just wondering if we could ever be certain that no one on our side was eating pork. What would happen to the balance of power if just one of us slipped into the biggest pork processing plant in Germany, and introduced a bug…say…trichinosis into the storage facilities?"

Adolf jerked violently awake. "I would assume you are speaking hypothetically," he said calmly. "And that you would intend to keep it that way."

"Of course I am," said Ilsa. "But—hypothetically—what would be so wrong with it?"

"Well, for one thing, there's a difference between being a revolutionary and being a mass murderer." He struggled to keep his voice calm, reminding himself that this was Ilsa—his wife—he spoke to. But that was part of what scared him. "Our greatest ally of late has been the Party itself. They've become a living definition of Evil. Every day, more and more people see that.

"Ordinary people, people who never saw themselves as revolutionaries are starting to support us now—at least in their hearts.

"What would their opinion of us be if we did something like that? What would our opinions of ourselves be? And keep in mind, some of the best, most selfless people in the underground do not identify themselves as Jews, and won't be following kosher laws just because we tell them to."

Ilsa was silent for a time. Then she yawned and said, "You're right of course. It was a crazy idea.

We better get some sleep. Tomorrow will be a busy
day."

It was a long time before Adolf fell asleep.

CHAPTER 20

Three days later they arrived in the port town of Tallinn on the Gulf of Finland. Their instructions were to wait for a contact who would ferry them across to Finland in secret. While they waited, Adolf and Ilsa looked for work.

The little fishing town looked to be the most unchanged piece of land Adolf had ever seen. Here, men fished the same waters their grandfathers had, sailed the same boats, and even barreled herring the same way.

Labor was in high demand. Adolf found work aboard a herring boat, while Ilsa served drinks in a local bar. Smallpox and polio had so depleted the population that, for the first time in years, there were more fish than men could catch.

Adolf worked for five days, taking quiet pride in the newly developed strength of his arms and back; in his ability to learn quickly something so far outside his experience. And if anyone found it strange that a handsome young Aryan was working on a fishing boat, they didn't say so.

Davin Larson had once been the patriarch of a large fishing family. Now there was only himself, his youngest son, and the men he hired. Adolf spoke little, listened a great deal, and looked out for sign of his contact.

Relaxing in the bar one night, at one of Ilsa's tables, Adolf was amazed to see the normally taciturn Davin suddenly throw a drink the face of another

fisherman. The fight that followed was merely good
entertainment to most of the locals, but Davin's son,
Johan, and several neighbors, swiftly intervened, and
pulled Davin outside. Adolf lent a hand, and later
asked Johan what it was about.

"He probably said something about Katrina,"
the boy said bleakly.

Adolf considered what he already knew, added
what he could read from the boy's body language, and
took a chance. "Your sister?" he asked. "The one you
lost to polio?"

Johan leaned against the peer and stared
moodily at the black water. "That man," Johan jerked
his head toward the bar, where the other combatant
remained. "He was a neighbor of ours. Katrina was
supposed to marry his son."

Adolf glanced over at Davin. He sat sobbing
on a coil of rope, while two friends strove to comfort
him. "I take it this was more than a case of her
untimely death breaking a contract?"

Johan shook his head. "My mother; the baby;
my younger brother—they died quickly. Father and I
and my older bother—we never got it at all. But
Katrina got it and lived. She couldn't walk, but she
could sit up most days, and her hands were fine. She
would have been a good seamstress."

Adolf could see where this was leading. "She
could still sew? As good as before?"

Johan stared past Adolf; past the water, too it
seemed. "The epidemic was bad here; the Party
issued a temporary stay to the mandatory euthanasia
laws."

Adolf nodded. "Those who were still
productive could continue breathing—until they found

the vaccine and put all those laws back into place."
Silently, Adolf cursed himself a fool for thinking that
sharing the vaccine with the Party would somehow
turn into a grand humanitarian gesture. Would Varina
tell him this was more blood on his hands?

"Anders wouldn't let his son marry Katrina.
No one was really surprised, except father. Our
families go back a long way. But later, when my
older brother passed his exams, and had a shot at
citizenship—"

Adolf went cold. "A crippled sister would
have ruined his chances," he said calmly.

"Not just his!" Johan looked desperately into
Adolf's eyes, begging him to understand. "Our whole
family—what's left of it, anyway. If he does well, it
could mean citizenship for all of us! But Anders, our
friends, everyone said we had to do it; that she'd be
better off; that she'd never have a normal life!"

"Was it Anders who killed her, then?"

Johan shook his head, wiping away tears with
the back of his hand. "My brother did. But father
always blamed Anders. Maybe because he's the one
who gave Lars the poison he put in her soup."

"Well, yes, I can see how he might carry a
grudge."

"'Only by sacrificing the imperfect can we
achieve perfection,'" Johan recited hollowly.

"I never argued with that!"

Both Adolf and Johan jumped at the voice.
Davin shook off the restraining arm of one of his
friends and strode forward. "I've been a loyal subject
all my life! I've never questioned Party policy, never
even complained about my taxes! Out here, we do
everything they ask of us; our boys die in their wars;

our fish feed their children. And we're as racially pure as anyone in Germany!"

"Davin, come on," said his friend, a husky, weather-beaten fisherman like himself. "I'll walk you home."

The grieving man shook off the other's arm. "All I'm saying is that they didn't have to die! My wife, my son, my little Katrina! They got sick last summer! Everyone knows the Party has had the vaccine for over a year now!"

More like two, thought Adolf.

"We'll get it soon!" cried the other man. "But it could never be soon enough for those who—"

"When?" said Davin. "All our lives we hear promises! I'm a good loyal subject! All I want to know is when will our Illustrious Leaders start keeping their promises! Why do our children die and theirs live—"

The other fisherman grabbed Davin's head and urgently whispered in his ear, glancing at Adolf as he did. Davin deflated like a burst balloon. He sat down on the pier, no longer sobbing, but clearly distraught.

"You have to understand," Johan said to Adolf. "He's had a lot to drink. He doesn't mean anything—"

Adolf smiled wearily. "I'm not a spy. I know you have to be careful around strangers. Or friends for that matter. It's just that I understand what your father is saying. And so do a lot of other people I've met in my travels."

That was as far as Adolf would go towards recruitment for the revolution. At least for now.

The contact, when she finally showed up,

turned out to be owner and captain of a tiny skiff which could carry up to eight passengers—if they didn't mind getting cozy. This night, Adolf and Ilsa were the only passengers.

"We're crossing the gulf illegally," she told them, handing them each a life vest. "So stay down and stay quiet. Keep your eyes open for Z boats. They're trigger happy these days."

"Any particular reason?" Adolf asked, forcing his numb fingers to work the zippers on the life jacket. They stood on a deserted stretch of beach in the freezing night. Adolf was wearing nothing but the black pants and sweater his transport captain gave him. Ilsa wore the same thing, but as usual, seemed perfectly comfortable.

"Too many smugglers have been getting through. You know, people like me?" She wore a skin-tight outfight made of something black and shiny. Her hair was hidden under a knitted cap of some unidentifiable dark color. Adolf noticed that she wasn't wearing a life vest. She had probably decided that if things went badly, drowning beat capture.

"Are you in this for the money or the cause?" asked Ilsa.

"Bit of both I guess." And that was all they got out of her until they reached the coast of Finland, shortly before dawn.

The rest of the journey was short, but grueling as they went from contact to contact, costume to costume, check point to check point. Only the spectacular beauty of the rugged mountains, snow covered, even in early summer, and the endless cold blue sky took Adolf's mind off his exhaustion.

When told they would travel the rest of the

way by skiing, Adolf nearly balked.

"I haven't skied in years!" he told their guides, a husband and wife team who were both so burly and wrinkled he had trouble telling which was which. "And that was on nicely manicured slopes at a Swiss resort." He looked up at the jagged mountain range they proposed crossing and decided not to mention he had stuck mostly to the bunny slopes.

"Have to," growled the man—or was it the woman? "It's the only way in,"

"This isn't a resort you're going to," said the spouse. "The *Reich* would give a lot to know where our strongholds are, and how to get there. If it was easy for you, it would be easy for them."

Adolf gritted his teeth, and started up the slopes. The going was hard, as he had expected. Ilsa, who had never taken lessons at a mountain resort—never been on skis in her life until three years ago, he'd have wagered—kept up, if not easily, at least less clumsily than Adolf.

To make matters worse, both guides wanted to discuss various interpretations of Jewish writings throughout the journey. Adolf finally decided he could either keep up with them physically or conversationally, but not both. Fortunately, they decided that delivering the new rabbi to his destination was more important than gleaning his wisdom.

Several bruising hours later, when only pride kept Adolf from being carried by his wife and the old couple, they reached a cave. Gratefully shedding his skis, Adolf followed them down a tunnel and through a dizzying series of narrow passages. Ilsa followed silently behind him. The air was pleasantly warm. The tunnel walls were rough, but straighter than nature could have provided. Adolf often saw the mark of shovel and pickaxe. *No need for blindfolds,* he thought. *Without a guide, I'd never find my way out of this maze.*

At a challenge from a sentry, the man stopped and Adolf heard whispered voices exchanging passwords. Then they took the next turn, and found themselves in a huge stone chamber, like something out of a fairy tale about a troll king.

Lit only by torches and a small fire burning in a stone hearth, the shadowy cave was alive with activity. A cauldron of stew bubbled over the fire, tended by a lithe young girl whose old fashioned local dress enhanced her elfin features.

At a long wooden table, an old man was instructing a group of older boys and girls in the construction of something electronic. Probably a radio, Adolf decided. Near the hearth, another man, stripped to the waist, displaying a back more scarred than any Adolf had ever seen, drew a piece of glowing metal from the flames, and began to shape it with a large forging hammer. The cave rang with metallic blows.

Children scurried about, performing small tasks with obvious enjoyment. A group of burly, fur clad men, apparently just back from a hunt, were unwrapping a freshly killed reindeer from a plastic tarp.

At a few words from Adolf's guide, activity began to wind down, until all of the cave's forty or so residents were gathered around Adolf and Ilsa.

The smith secured his work, stripped off his gloves and strode to the front. "You are Rabbi Adolf and Ilsa the Valkyrie?" he asked in a voice that rang with authority.

Both of them murmured their assent. "Ludwig thought we might be of use to you," said Ilsa.

"We're pleased to have you." Through the shadows, he glanced keenly at Adolf. "I take it the trip here was a bit rough?"

Adolf smiled weakly. "If you happen to have a hot bath, a sauna and a good masseuse, I wouldn't turn any of them down. Failing that, a meal and a night's rest will probably put me back together just fine."

The assembled partisans laughed. Then a woman wearing mostly rags pushed through the crowd to where Adolf stood. She led him to a stool, bade him sit, and to his surprise, began to massage his aching shoulders.

"No bathtub, I'm afraid," said the man who led them. "But the hot springs that heat this place provide us with a sauna, of sorts. And you'll find Rika is the best masseuse around for miles."

"When you're done with him, I want to be next," Ilsa told Rika, as she sagged gratefully down on a nearby bench.

"Why wait?" asked a booming voice in heavily accented German. A large blond man, who could have passed for Thor in this mythically enhanced setting, began rubbing Ilsa's back.

"Sven, here, is a close second," said Rika.

Adolf reminded himself not to start trouble his first day here.

The girl who'd been tending the cauldron brought them stew in crude wooden bowls, and gave them sticks that had been sharpened to a point for spearing pieces of meat and vegetables. Adolf gulped down his portion with relish, and slowly felt his body returning to normal.

The partisans let them eat in peace.

Afterwards, there were questions.

"How are things for the peasants in Holland?" asked a sharp faced young man. "My family is there." An ugly wound on his scalp still looked fresh.

"Better than many other places," said Adolf. "Radiation has become a real threat to the crops all over Asia and the Middle East. The newest policy I've heard—and remember this is several months old, now—is to give the European farmers every possible assistance."

"We've been worried about that up here, too," said a woman dressed in a patchwork of fur and cloth. "We heard there was a hot strike not far from here, in northwestern Russia. Have you any further news on it?"

"Actually," said Ilsa, "that one failed to explode. Word is, some Russian partisans retrieved the nuke. A delegation left Poland the same time I did, to try to establish contact with them."

"Now there's something I'd like to see," said the smith. "As of now, all we have of Asia is rumor. Even the European groups are pretty fragmented, as you've probably noticed."

"True," said Adolf. "But that's part of why I'm here—"

"Might you know my sister?" asked a young woman. "Her name is Anika. She left for Germany with a group of girls posing as whores. They were trying to recruit from the lower classes and the *missgeburt*."

"Sorry, I don't believe I've—"

"Are you really a rabbi?" asked a little boy.

"What's a rabbi?" asked another.

"Good question," Adolf said to the first boy. To the second he explained, "'Rabbi' means 'teacher' in Hebrew. Rabbis were wise men who studied the holy writings, and made themselves available to their people for whatever needs they might have." To the first boy he added, "I like to think I'm in the process of becoming a rabbi. But people liked the title and it's sort of stuck."

"There's not a real big need for Hebrew scholars around here," said the smith. "But I'm sure we can put you to work."

"Speak for yourself, Seppi!" said a young man who stood among a group of other young people. He stepped forward and clasped Adolf's hand. "My friends and I would be honored to study with you, Rabbi. We're tired of going over the same few books we have between us. Even the discussions are getting repetitive. I'm Thoresten. These are Hans, Cullen, and Luisa."

Adolf took in Thoresten's Aryan features and natural grace, and grinned. "Let me guess," he said. "You've attended University somewhere in the *Reich*? A city that had a *Judenmuseum*? And the books, people and ideas you found there changed your life?"

There was a buzz of excited whispers among Thoresten's friends, while the young man himself looked amazed. "How did you know?" he asked.

Adolf was spared the need to reply when Seppi applauded, laughing. "Maybe Ludwig was right. Maybe you are just what we need."

Rika finished massaging Adolf's back and slid around to face him. "Is it true that you found the cure for polio in a magic Hebrew book?"

"I helped find the vaccine, but--" There was another buzz of excitement. Adolf tried to explain that all he did was deliver the notes of a Jewish doctor into the right hands, but no one seemed to want to hear that.

When the commotion subsided, two men hurried over, both talking at once. Since one was speaking German and the other Finnish, Adolf turned to the German speaker. They were both doctors, he learned, or at least the closest these people had. They had been the ones to distribute the vaccine in this part of the world, and were eager for anything more Adolf had to offer.

While he was handing over all the medical journals he carried, along with Speer's notes and a more accurate version of how the vaccine was discovered, another group arrived in the cave. Adolf was beginning to suspect that this hidden cadre was the size of a small town.

"He says his name is Adolf?" an oddly familiar voice was saying. "And he's about my age?"

"Adolf!" called Seppi. "I almost forgot! We've someone among us who you already know."

Adolf turned, and found himself face to face with yet another ghost from his past. His once carefully trimmed hair and pencil thin mustache were overgrown; his eyes bloodshot from drink. But there was no mistaking his identity.

"Karl!" cried Adolf, staring. "Karl, I don't believe this! What are you doing here?"

"Waiting for my chance to do this!" Karl punched Adolf in the jaw with enough force to land him hard on his back. Then, everything went dark.

CHAPTER 21

Adolf sat up a moment later, feeling dizzy and confused. He thought his ears were ringing, too, then discovered it was just the sound of Finnish being spoken by many shrill voices. Karl was being restrained by several locals, while two others had guns trained on both him and Adolf.

What a great first impression this must be making, Adolf thought.

He stood slowly, and though he made no move toward Karl, their eyes were locked. "Mind telling me what that was all about?" he said, rubbing his jaw.

"You son of a bitch!" shouted Karl. "This is all your fault! It was supposed to be a game! Forgotten races, ancient religions, museums full of relics. We were there to have fun! Look for answers. No one was supposed to get hurt…"

"I'm not arguing so far," said Adolf.

"But then you had to go and start believing in it!" Karl's face was twisted with rage and pain. "You turned it into a movement! Made our leaders afraid. Do you know what you've done? Do you know how many lives were ruined?"

"Ruined? How about lives that were *lost*, Karl?" Adolf's voice echoed in the stone chamber, and suddenly, everyone fell silent.

Anger surged within him. Adolf gave full voice to his commanding tone. "If you need a scapegoat, fine! Use me if it'll make you feel better! But you look very much alive to me, which is more

than I can say for Franz and Krista and I don't know
how many others!"

At that, Karl's face crumpled and he began to
sob. The partisans holding him exchanged uncertain
glances, finally turning to Adolf for direction.

"Let go of him," Adolf said gently. His new
comrades retreated, as did Ilsa, leaving Adolf and Karl
alone by the cave wall. Adolf steered Karl to a stone
outcropping; a natural bench than had been rubbed
smooth over years of use.

"What happened to you?" Adolf asked, with
more patience than he felt.

"I was working at the Department of
Commerce. It was about three years ago. I wasn't
moving up as fast as my parents had hoped, but at
least, you know, I had a life. I had a terrific
girlfriend—who I was trying really hard to turn into
my wife. Her family controlled over half the beer
industry in Europe.

"Suddenly, one day, I get called into my
commandant's office. I get there and find two
Gestapo agents wanting to talk to me." Karl's eyes
burned with remembered terror. "It was two weeks
before I got out! They kept at me twenty-four hours a
day! I didn't sleep; I barely ate! Always the same
questions: 'What did you do at these meetings?
Which other students attended? Think carefully, now.
It's important we have all the names.'"

"Which I'm sure you provided," said Adolf.

"Did you think I wouldn't?" demanded Karl.
"Do you think *you* wouldn't, if you'd been in my
place? Yeah, I've heard your hype: everyone here
thinks you're a hero! But I knew you back then.
When the scariest thing that kept you up nights was

the next day's math exam!"

"Things have changed a bit since then."

"You don't need to tell me! One, stupid, adolescent mistake, and I was a pariah. I lost my job; I lost my girl. Even my parents were being harassed."

"And for this you're blaming me?"

"Maybe not just you. Some of the others were going off the deep end with the Jewish thing. But I forgot all about it once I was out in the real world. To have it come back and haunt me after all those years..."

"So how'd you end up here?"

Karl leaned his head against the rough stone behind him and closed his eyes. "Shining shoes or washing dishes for the rest of my life didn't appeal to me. So I decided to kill myself. I went back to Stuttgart; to a bridge near my old neighborhood.

"I brought a bottle of bourbon. Unfortunately, it took the whole thing to give me the courage to jump. I was so drunk, I fell off the damned bridge; right onto a smuggler's boat, passing underneath at the time." Karl rubbed his eyes. "I'd like to think I'd have seen it, if I were sober."

Adolf couldn't help it: he laughed. After a moment, Karl joined him. It was harsh and ragged, but it was the first sign of healing Adolf had felt between them.

"And they recruited you for the underground?"

"Eventually, yes. First, they had to argue over whether or not to slit my throat. One guy wanted to hear my story first. Turns out, he had some customers in the underground who were interested in any inside information about the government, even as low level as mine.

"After that, I just wandered. I found out I have a knack for forgery—when my hand's steady enough."

"Doesn't your drinking count as a security risk?"

"Bastards here won't let me drink! I keep telling them my hand gets shaky when I *don't* drink, not the other way around. It's getting better though."

"Glad to hear it," said Adolf, wondering what to do next.

After a while, Karl spoke. "That blond with you? Is that the *missgeburt* from the museum?"

"Her name is Ilsa," said Adolf, realizing for the first time how little she had registered with Karl back then. "And yes, it's her."

"You *shtupping* her?" Karl asked with mild interest.

"I'm required to by law," said Adolf. "I'm her husband."

Karl's bloodshot eyes widened. "You *married* her? Wow, you'd do anything for attention!"

"Karl, I'm trying very hard to maintain a non-violent stand right now, but if you say one more word about Ilsa—"

"Okay, okay, forget I said anything. What are you doing here, anyway?"

"I was hoping to organize a revolution and spread a little Judaism. Now I'm not sure. Just how much have you poisoned them against me?"

"Me? I'm not that stupid. If I said a word against you, they'd have thrown me out or worse! You saw how they reacted when I hit you. These people think you're the messiah!"

"Messiah? Karl, I think you remember more

Judaism than you give yourself credit for."

Karl smiled sheepishly. "Well, knowing Judaism kind of sets you in the elite group here. And it really impresses these resistance girls."

Some things never change, thought Adolf. "Do you know what happened to any of the others? Or are you even interested?"

"I'm not quite as big a jerk as I seem," said Karl. "I know about Krista. I saw her execution on one of the broadcasts." To Adolf's surprise, Karl's voice broke. "I never knew 'till then how much I liked her," he said.

"Brigitta was sent to a brothel," Adolf said. "Frederic's somewhere in the resistance. Do you know anything about Franz?"

"In some high level prison, somewhere. That's all I know."

Adolf nodded. It was the same as he'd heard from Frederic.

Karl went on, in control once more. "The others, I never heard. Except for you, of course. You're dead."

"So they keep telling me. What about my family? Have you heard anything at all?"

"As far as I know, they're still safe." For a moment, Karl's expression was one of malicious glee, and he was about to speak. Then he changed his mind and returned to a look of sullen resentment.

"What aren't you telling me?" Adolf demanded.

"Nothing. Just rumors. And as little as you might think of me, I'm still not the kind of guy who spreads them."

"Tell me!" Adolf was a bit surprised to hear

his command voice echoing off the wall of the cave.

"It's nothing! Just that the Heydrich family has moved up the pecking order; very cozy with the *Führer*."

Adolf finally realized what he hadn't before: if the Heydrich family was that far up, his own must be on the way down. "Can you tell me anything specific?"

"If I knew anything, I'd tell you. I've never been a real font of wisdom, as you know." Karl brooded silently for a moment, then said, "I know you didn't mean for this to happen, Adolf. And it wasn't all your fault. I've just been so pissed off for so long. I…" Adolf waited. "I guess I'm sorry I hit you."

"Forget it," said Adolf. "What can you tell me about this place?"

"I've only been at this base since November. I helped blow up a tunnel the Army put in, about fifty miles south. I came here to give a report, and then got stuck for the winter.

"That leader, though. Seppi. He's someone I could follow."

"What's his story?" asked Adolf.

"He's from up north. The men in his family had been the village blacksmiths since— well, forever, I guess. The way he tells it, his people lived the way their ancestors had since the Vikings. The country changed its name, government, everything, and these guys never even noticed."

"Until the *Reich*, I suppose?"

"Even then, Seppi said, it didn't much matter, at least at first. He says the trouble first started when they refused to learn German. Even that, they might have survived. God knows other peasants have."

"So what happened?"

"Well, I thought it was kind of weird at first. You know how Scandinavia has been a major source of 'upgradable stock' for the gene pool? You've probably noticed that Finland has always been different."

Adolf nodded. Most people he'd seen so far were swarthy and compactly built—a throwback to invaders from Central Asia, a millennium ago. Adolf could guess where this was leading. "I take it Seppi's village was one of those 'anomalies' where children with pure Aryan features show up randomly?"

"One of the most interesting cases, they told the people. Nearly a third of the population had ideal looks—and unusually high intelligence to boot."

"Naturally, they were harvested."

"Of course," said Karl. "The women for *SS* brothels, the younger men for education, the children for testing and fosterage. You'd think their families would have been proud!"

"And they weren't?" Adolf asked innocently.

"No. Although I can sort of understand it. I mean, how would you like to wake up one morning and find out the only people left in town were short, dark and stupid?"

Adolf resisted an urge to laugh—barely. "What's this have to do with Seppi?" he asked.

"At first, nothing. Seppi's people were old stock, and as bad as things got with so much of their work force gone, people still needed a blacksmith. But then the whole region turned into a nest of resistance factions. They wanted their people back, and they wanted their taxes lowered, and they wanted German education out of their schools.

"Party Security identified Seppi as the lynchpin for the whole organization. Rolf Himmler himself took charge of the interrogation. He brought in a team of eager young *SS* boys. They caught Seppi at his forge, and when he wouldn't give satisfactory answers, Himmler had Seppi's entire family lined up in front of him. They shot them all, down to his youngest child, and still didn't get anything from him.

"Then, one of the young studs suggested that a man so reticent didn't have any need for a tongue at all. Old Rolf agreed, and ordered the guy to pull out Seppi's tongue with his own tongs."

"Wait a minute," said Adolf. "That can't be right. I heard him speak just a few minutes ago."

"I'm getting there," said Karl. "The poor fool pulled Seppi's mouth open—and Seppi bit off three of his fingers! Glove leather and all! Next, he head butted him into the forge—they hadn't put out the fire since they needed it for the hot irons—and brained two soldiers with an iron bar.

"These recruits, or whatever they were, panicked, and Seppi finished off most of them with his bare hands. Rolf and one of his guards made it out alive, but that was all."

"How did Seppi get out?"

"No one knows. He had at least a dozen bullets in him, and Rolf's rather the old fashioned type when it comes to interrogation: whips and hot irons. Seppi shouldn't have been able to walk, let alone run. But he did. And now he's a legend. I know people who'd follow him to the gates of Hell.

"But you want to know what's really funny about all this? Seppi wasn't even in the resistance back then! He didn't tell them anything, because he honestly didn't know! But now, he's the undisputed chief enemy of the *Reich* and everything it stands for. He says he won't rest until every last Nazi is dead."

"I'm so glad he didn't say 'German,'" said Adolf. "A lot of them do, you know." He shook his head. "And so once again, our Illustrious Leaders create their own downfall."

"How do you mean?" asked Karl.

"You said it yourself: Seppi wasn't the least bit dangerous to the Party, until they gave him a reason to be. And he's not the only one. Look at the two of us, for example."

Karl was thoughtful for a moment. "Do you really think so?" he asked. "I mean, do you think, if they hadn't targeted the museum crowds, if they had just left us alone, we'd never have become a threat?"

"I guess I always assumed that," Adolf said feeling surprised. "But maybe not. The principles of Judaism could never have co existed with something like the *Reich*. Maybe a clash was inevitable."

"Maybe they should have burned the books along with the Jews," said Karl.

"I'm sure right now, there are many powerful men expressing that very sentiment. But I think it wouldn't have mattered. I think Judaism would have resurfaced anyway, even without the props."

"You always were the mystic, Adolf. Do you really think it's going to happen? That a dead religion will somehow topple the Thousand Year *Reich*?"

"If it doesn't, something else will. It's inevitable now."

"Yes but when? Will we live to see it? And

how do we know it'll be any better than what he have now?"

"Good questions, Karl. Maybe if we live long enough, we'll find out."

The cave dwelling partisans, who by now were acting if this sort of thing happened every day, called Adolf and Karl to supper as soon as they finished talking.

"Will you bless the meal, Rabbi?" asked Rika.

"That should be the job of the youngest child," he said.

The younger people exchanged embarrassed glances. "We don't know any of the blessings," said Thoresten.

"Then I'll teach you," said Adolf. "Who wants to help me?"

Several boys and girls came forward. He recited each blessing, and had the children repeat them.

As always, he was moved by just how many people bowed their heads as he prayed, revering the act, the speaker, and possibly even the God he prayed to.

It wouldn't be easy, he reflected, but just maybe, in this place, they could all accomplish something.

CHAPTER 22

"It could just be misinformation," Thoresten said hopefully.

Ilsa exchanged a glance with the Eikki, the grizzled old radio operator, and shook her head. "It's from a reliable source. And really, it's not that surprising. We should have been prepared for it."

Adolf rubbed his pounding temples. Ilsa was right, but sometimes he wished she could be a little more tactful. Both agreed that they had seen and accomplished more in these past two months in Finland than in the previous three years. But neither had ever been part of so large an operation before—let alone, tried to lead one.

"Prepared for the Party to learn Hebrew?" said Rika.

"It was supposed to be unbreakable!" wailed one of the younger men.

"No code is unbreakable," said Eikki.

"But it wasn't just a code," said Thoresten. "It's a language. One that no living Party member should even know of."

"You were supposed to burn everything you didn't take out of the museum with you," Karl said with an accusing glare at Ilsa.

"No, I was supposed to doctor the records so no one would realize how much was missing," Ilsa said calmly. "Then *they* were supposed to burn everything."

"So what happened?" asked Thoresten.

"Nazi efficiency, most likely," said Ilsa. "They save copies of everything."

"But how did they realize it was Hebrew in the first place?" asked Rika. "How did they even make the connection?"

"Just as no code is unbreakable," said Thoresten, "No side of any war is safe from treachery. It was only a matter of time before the Party captured someone who knew the language, and got it from them."

"I'd hardly call breaking under torture treachery," said Rika.

"Whatever we call it," said Adolf, trying to move the discussion toward a solution. "We have to decide what to do—"

"—And soon," Eikki finished for him. "Our communications network has gotten too big to go back to using old-fashioned military codes."

Adolf pondered for a moment. "You know, it's never been just the language," he said. "The Party knows the language, yes. But the stories; the people from *Torah*—that's what they don't know."

"But they will," said Rika.

Thoresten shook his head, eagerly taking up the thread of Adolf's thinking. "They're only just learning the language. But the code depends on knowing Judaism. To break it fully, they'll have to think like Jews."

For a moment, there was silence. Slowly, almost against their will, smiles slid across the faces of the gathered partisans.

"It would almost be worth it, wouldn't it?" said Rika. "To lose the war—but know the whole Nazi Party had to half-way become Jews to beat us?"

"Almost," said Adolf. "However, I don't intend to lose the war. We have, at the outside, six months, before they can decode any message we send. I'd say that gives us three months to come up with something new, or..." He let the sentence trail off, unfinished.

"Or what?" Thoresten asked impatiently.

"Or be ready to take on the Party and win—in three months."

The silence that reigned was almost palpable. Adolf was enough of a leader to recognize an advantage when he saw one. Before anyone could speak, he divided his team into groups and assigned each one a task, ranging from new code ideas to obtaining the specs for the Party's worldwide broadcast system. They departed in silence.

"Ludwig was right," said a voice behind Adolf. He turned to find Seppi leaning against the rough stone wall of the cave.

"About what?" asked Adolf.

"You are the One."

"I wish people would stop talking about me like that!"

"Like what?"

"Like...there was a capital 'O' when you said the word 'one.'"

Seppi chuckled. "Most young men would eat up the praise and adulation! But then, I guess that's part of the deal. The ones who *want* the job, and all the worship that goes with it, are the ones you're better off not having. I guess the only good leader is one who doesn't want to be one."

"And don't forget the rest of the equation," said Adolf. "Those who make the best leaders in winning the revolution are not the people you want running the government afterwards."

"That's not usually a problem," said Seppi. "They generally manage to get shot by the time the war's over. Though I have to admit, sometimes it's by their own side."

"Well, like you said, at least it solves the problem."

Seppi didn't smile. "I hope that doesn't happen this time, Adolf. Because, I believe you to be one of the rare exceptions. And it's going to take someone very special indeed, to clean up this mess when it's all over."

I'll add that to my list of things to do, thought Adolf, taking a foot path out of the cave.

It was summer now in the land of the midnight sun, although Adolf rarely left the caves often enough to know it. Ilsa, who divided her time between hunting reindeer and keeping up with the news from all known forces of their ragged revolution, saw more of it.

Adolf had learned that this base did not, in fact, hold the population of a small town. It was more like a city. Since he was still not certain of every path in this place, he stopped frequently to ask directions, and at the same time, checked on the progress of each group in the vast network of caves.

There was an entire team of scientists who lived in one of the inner caves, and probably saw the sun less often than Adolf. Currently, they were poring over the medical notes Adolf had brought from the polio colony in the hopes of further breakthroughs. So far, none of them had found anything to support Alina's theories of new Party super weapons.

Soldiers were being trained in various outer caves. Medical teams came and went from the base infirmary, responding to calls for help far and wide, but usually arriving too late due to limited transportation. There was only so much you could do with sled dogs and skis.

When he finally reached open air, Adolf stood for a moment dazzled by the sun. Then he nerved himself for a look down the mountain. Despite the beauty of it all, the dizzying drop from where he stood always caused his stomach to tighten. The ledge he stood on was nearly at the tree line. Above him was only gray rock and snow. Below was the brilliant splash of green fir trees, snowy fjords and deep valleys, crossed with streams that looked like tiny blue threads from up here.

Children picked berries, clambering up and down the slopes like the mountain goats these people raised. Then he saw a truly amazing sight. A group of women were sunbathing on a small ledge—and one of them was Ilsa.

Granted, she was more modest than the others, with a small towel over her crotch. The other women seemed intent on capturing the warmth of Finland's short summer—with everything they had. Still, the sight of her there, relaxed, at peace—and natural— delighted him. Almost as much as the fact that she was actually taking time off from the war.

"Hello, Adolf," Ilsa said lazily, after he had stared for several minutes. "Care to join us?" The other three women smiled invitingly. No one seemed disconcerted by his fully clothed presence.

"I'm afraid the sun would be wasted on my poor, pale flesh," he teased. "Did we win the war and someone forget to tell me?"

"No," said Ilsa, sitting up, and stretching. "But with you setting that deadline of three months, I thought we'd better take a break while we still could. This might be the last one for quite some time."

"Actually," said one of the other women, "the real break for everyone will be next week at Litha. We're working on Ilsa now, since she's such a tough case."

"Litha is the Midsummer Festival these northerners have celebrated for thousands of years," explained Ilsa.

Adolf smiled. Any annual celebration that could survive unchecked through these times was bound to be good for morale. "So what will we be doing?"

The oldest of the three locals smiled. "Singing. Dancing. Making love under the midnight sun. Listening to the skalds recite the old tales. And—if the reindeer are cooperative—feasting."

"With Ilsa here to hunt with us, we'll have reindeer whether they want to cooperate or not!" said the youngest, one of Ilsa's many devoted followers.

"Normally there's a lot of drinking, too," said the third woman. "But now, with nothing but Garnet's homemade brew, you take your life in your hands if you do!"

"We've always been a people of risk takers," said the first. "And notoriously hard to kill—even with Garnet's home brew."

Midsummer Eve, when it arrived was everything the locals had promised. For a moment, it seemed, they were suspended in time. There was no

war. No hunger. No terror. Only the impossible
beauty of a summer night that seemed never to end.
And the rituals of a people as old as the Jews.

Adolf took part in the festivities with relish.
He could hardly help doing so. They were outdoors,
feasting in a mountain meadow so green it was nearly
blinding. There was roasted reindeer meat, goat's milk
cheese, nuts, berries and, for anyone brave enough,
Garnet's mead. He danced with Ilsa, and most of the
other women of the base, to the tunes of drums,
fiddles and flutes. When he was finally too tired to
dance, Adolf lay back in the grass, and listened to an
old man tell the great deeds of Thor and Odin.

Yet, for all the beauty and pleasure, and the
women who invitingly explained that for this one
night, marriage vows were null, Adolf could not shake
off pangs of envy.

These people were partaking in a ritual as old
as any Jewish festival Adolf and his friends had
imitated—but here, it truly *belonged* to the revelers. It
was theirs by birth and by blood. Perhaps, in the great
scheme of things, the difference was not really
important, but for the first time, Adolf became
painfully aware of the fact that there *was* a difference.

"Is this my husband, looking so grave and
serious at a festival?" Ilsa stood over Adolf, a
drinking horn in each hand.

"What's wrong with that?" asked Adolf.
"Afraid I'll muscle into *your* territory?

"Maybe." Ilsa sat beside Adolf, and handed
him a horn.

"I'm just feeling envious," said Adolf.
"Of who?"
"Of anyone born with actual blood ties to the

heroes who founded their religious tradition. Anyone who has a birthright to ritual, rather than stealing it."

"Is that what you think we've done with Judaism?"

"What else do you call it? We only found it at all because our grandparents kept the books as curiosities of a dead race. We celebrated some of their most sacred rituals as a game. Just because we've started taking it seriously—does that give us the right to claim the traditions? The covenant with God?" He took a sip of the mead, and then gagged as liquid fire shot down his throat.

Ilsa patted his back helpfully. "Take it slow. It grows on you."

"If it doesn't kill you first!" gasped Adolf.

"If you think about it, most things in life are like that. Anyway, back to your mood swings. Blood isn't the only thing that gives a person the right to claim a tradition. Take this festival—Litha. Nearly half the people in this compound come from outside Scandinavia, but they're celebrating it just the same."

"As guests," sighed Adolf. "Which is a fine, time honored tradition in its own right. But...I'm tired of being a guest! I want something that belongs to me—while at the same time, I belong to it! The only traditions my parents gave me were some neo pagan bullshit manufactured by the First *Führer's* Minister of Propaganda!"

"Not much of an inheritance," agreed Ilsa. "But then, how are you any different from Abraham? He wasn't born to Judaism any more than you were. *Torah* says the Lord called him. Isn't that what He's done with you?"

"Has He? According to *Torah*, God *literally*

called Abraham! He introduced Himself, and spoke to
Abraham in a language he could understand.
Established a covenant with him. Hardly the
stumbling around in the dark I've been doing these
last seven years."

"You sure you want the same covenant
Abraham had? I didn't think that circumcision thing
sounded all that appealing."

At that, Adolf laughed. "Good point." He
took another swig from the horn. "I just wish for
something equally clear and personal. You know?
Like an engraved invitation?"

Ilsa shook her head. "Be careful what you
wish for on a night like this. They say the walls
between worlds are thin."

Adolf laughed again and drained the horn.

Shortly before dawn, Ilsa helped Adolf find his
bed. He was eloquently continuing an explanation for
the universe and his plans for its future. The
frightening thing about a drunken Adolf, the
community agreed, was that he didn't slur his speech,
and sounded just as convincing as when he was sober.

After several protests that he could find his
own bed, Adolf allowed Ilsa to tuck him in.

He dreamed that night, that he was walking
with Ilsa through a meadow dotted with pomegranate
trees. They continued past a flock of sheep, tended by
a shepherd who was playing a harp. In the distance,
an old man and a young boy were descending a
mountain. On another mountain, in the opposite
direction, was beached a ponderous wooden ship.

They paused by a gurgling stream of milk and
honey. Adolf stopped and turned to kiss Ilsa, then

saw, over her shoulder, a strange flash, as if the sun was rising in the west. He stared for a moment in a puzzling silence as birds began to fall from the surrounding trees. Then, the trees began to bend, as if in a ferocious wind. All at once, the trees and everything else in the field burst into silent flames, crumbled into ash, and blew away. Horrified, Adolf grabbed hold of Ilsa, as if by his own strength he could save her. For a moment, he thought he had.

Then, very slowly, Ilsa turned to ashes in his arms, and began to crumble through his fingers. Just as her face began to blacken, she looked at Adolf and asked, "Why didn't you stop it when you had the chance?"

Then she was gone.

Adolf came awake, choking on non-existent smoke and gagging on a bitter metallic taste in his mouth. He cried out Ilsa's name, but heard only her sleepy response as she lay safe and whole beside him.

CHAPTER 23

A few days later, Adolf sat alone at a long wooden table. Spread before him were carefully organized sheets of paper. There were maps, lists of names, messages that defied decoding and, in the margins, a few scrawls in Adolf's own handwriting.

Since his nightmare, Adolf had become obsessed with all incoming messages, which, everyone had to admit, were becoming increasingly disconcerting. He had requested and received this workspace, along with unheard of amounts of privacy. He had cut back on teaching, assigning Ilsa and Thoresten to take over for him. Adolf even had strong, battery powered light to read by, rather than candles and oil lamps that the others had to make do with. At least, he reflected, he'd still have some eyesight left after he found whatever it was he was looking for.

He picked up a translation of a broadcast from the previous week. The first half contained a list of rebel supply depots with instructions on where the hungry could find food, and where those who had it to give could bring it. Meat to one place; dairy to another. There were warnings against stripping any natural area clean of anything. There were warnings against eating pork or shellfish. In other words, strict adherence to Kosher laws.

That much, Adolf did not find surprising. One of Ilsa's recent projects had been to find out if any other groups of practicing Jews had encountered

Elijah at Passover this year. So far nearly a dozen groups worldwide had reported events similar to what Berta had described. And now Kosher laws were taking effect—even amid starvation.

Then, there was the second part of the message. It was a list of names—with no further explanation. Adolf stared again at the familiar names, willing them to give up their secrets. Otto Mengele. Eva Eichmann. Adolf Bormann. On and on the list went, like a Who's Who of Nazi power brokers!

The only thing Adolf noticed, other than that he had once attended concerts and soirees with most of them, was that they seemed to be arranged in family groups. Eva Eichmann, he knew, was the married daughter of Otto Mengele. Adolf Bormann was related by both blood and marriage to the next two names on the list, and so on.

But what was the point?

He had rejected as wishful thinking Thoresten's suggestion that all these people were now members of the underground. Seppi believed that they were targets of assassination or kidnapping by one or another of the underground organizations. That certainly made more sense, since at least half the people on the list held key positions in the *Reich*. But what about the other half?

Adolf was certain it was something else. If he could just figure out what.

Other bits of information were painfully clear. Just yesterday, they had received word of Dr. Speer's death in Berlin, along with three other Party doctors convicted of the unauthorized dispensing of medical supplies to non-Aryans. Adolf tried to be happy for all the good his friend had accomplished in his life, but it wasn't easy.

But selfless doctors weren't the only ones dying. Two cabinet members had been assassinated in the past month. Neither of *their* names, Adolf noticed, appeared on the mystery list. A failed attempt on the *Führer's* life had had the unexpected asset of implicating several of his trusted advisors—including his own mistress.

And now, since the use of Hebrew messages with direct translations had been compromised, there were dozens of messages whose meaning no one could agree on. Words that would be lovely to discuss and analyze under different circumstances: instructions for Jonah to deliver his message to the people of Nineveh; requests for Esther and Mordecai to save the kingdom; an urgent plea for Jacob and Esau to forget their differences.

Adolf had already spent precious hours trying to figure it all out. Karl insisted that Adolf was making it overly complicated. "This is *Torah*, not Enigma!" he had said. "Try the simplest interpretation."

Adolf put his head down on the table and closed his eyes. *Just for a moment*, he told himself.

Someone was shaking him, and a voice was saying, "Rabbi, wake up!"

Adolf sat bolt upright, adrenaline washing away sleep. "How long was I out?" he muttered.

"I don't know," said the boy who woke him. "But Seppi's called a meeting. A message came in and he said it was important."

"All the rebel leaders in one place?" Karl repeated after Seppi finished explaining the proposed plan to the assembled community. "Isn't that sort of like what that American president did at Pearl Harbor? Lined all his ships up nice and neat for the Japanese to bomb?"

"It's risky, no question," said Ilsa. "But we can't win this war in scattered pieces. It's time to coordinate our efforts and plan the actual defeat of the *Reich*."

"Not to mention, figuring out a plan for the world in the event we actually win," said Thoresten.

"Like there's really a chance that might happen?" said Karl.

"I don't know what's possible or what's real anymore," said Adolf. "But things are moving faster than we can control them. This revolution has turned into a wildfire." He shivered as he remembered his dream. "If someone doesn't take charge of it soon, it's going to consume us all—rebel and Party alike."

"Naturally, that person is you," said Karl.

"Of course it is—" Thoresten began, but Adolf shouted over him. "You want the job, Karl? You're welcomed to it!"

"Calm down, both of you," said Seppi. "If it will make you feel better, Karl, we can put it to a vote."

"We both know how that will turn out," Karl muttered, never taking his eyes from Adolf.

Adolf took a deep breath and strove for patience. "The idea would be that any group that considers itself part of this revolution would send one representative. That person would bring the ideas and suggestions of his or her group, and would have the authority to vote and finalize decisions. I'll admit, I'd like to be the one from here, but it's up to you."

It was hard to keep the urgency out of his voice; hard to even sit still through this meeting. It was as if God really had spoken to him, and Adolf felt that if he didn't go to this conference, all they had suffered and died for would be lost. Was this how God called his prophets? Or was this how megalomaniacs were born?

"Small groups might be better than single individuals," said Rika. "Say, delegations of up to five people?"

"Or single ambassadors with authority to speak, but allow them a couple of assistants," said Ilsa.

"I like that idea best, Ilsa," said Seppi. "Does the message say where this is supposed to happen?"

"How do we even know the 'revolutionary committee' or whatever they call themselves is behind this?" asked Karl. "If I were in charge of crushing this rebellion, I couldn't think of a better way to get all the enemy leaders in one place."

Everyone shifted uncomfortably. The message seemed authentic. The coordinates were given in Hebrew, but the message itself was all biblical allusion.

"Where is it being held?" asked Rika.

"Russia," said Eikki. "A forest, somewhere near the old Polish border. The Free Russians wouldn't meet anywhere else, and the area is technically outside Party control."

"Not according to the Party, of course," said Thoresten. "Adolf, I want to go with you." Immediately, a dozen others were making the same request.

"All of you will have important jobs," Adolf
said. "Whether you attend the meeting or stay here.
And keep in mind, all it takes is one slip up on our
part, and the whole revolution could be over. Anyone
who goes could be walking to his own execution." He
could see that wasn't going deter anyone.

Adolf began assigning people various jobs,
until only he and Seppi remained in the great rock
chamber.

They sat in silence for several minutes, while
Adolf watched the partisan leader, who seemed
unaware of his presence. Tonight, Seppi looked every
one of his sixty years.

"It's an unbelievable moment," Adolf said at
last. "But I get the feeling you're not struck mute by
joy that victory may be within our grasp. What is it,
Seppi?"

"It is unbelievable," said Seppi. "And cause
for joy. But never once did I imagine I might live to
see it. And now, I suddenly realize that I wish I
hadn't."

"Why is that?" asked Adolf, not quite knowing
how else to answer to a statement like that.

Seppi ran a gnarled hand over eyes that Adolf
knew had seen far too much. "Fighting an Evil
Empire is easy. Blowing things up is easy. Dying is
easy."

"But, Great Odin, what happens if you actually
win? Do you ever think of that?"

"All the time," said Adolf.

Seppi looked at him, and Adolf could still feel
power in the weary, red-rimmed gaze. "I believe you
do, young man. So maybe there's hope for us yet.
But most of us...most of us old timers...it's been

enough for us to have a war to fight. Until now, everything's been so clear and simple. Kill the Nazis. Destroy the *Reich*. Use any means necessary. No decisions to make, beyond how and when. No ethical dilemmas.

"But winning? That changes everything. And to try *building* something—anything--out of the ruins of a vanquished Third *Reich*..." Seppi shook his head. "That's going to be hard."

"Or maybe impossible?"

"For me, and all the others like me? Yes. But maybe not for you, Adolf. You still have things alive in you that are dead in us. Compassion. Forgiveness. Faith in a species that did *this*—" Seppi waved his hand to indicate the world at large, "—to itself. But after all I've seen, and all I've fought for, I don't have the courage to face a new world order that very likely—barring a miracle—will be just as bad as the old one."

Adolf nodded. Seppi's words came as no surprise to him. He too, had seen things that made him well aware that, in the end, they still might leave the world worse than they found it. There were certainly enough examples in history of idealistic revolutions that ushered in unimaginable horrors.

Yet for all that, he still hoped.

"'What will we do if we win?' I had planned to put that second on the agenda at the conference, right after 'how to win the war'. Maybe now I'll put it first."

Seppi smiled. "I'm glad you came to us, Adolf. I'd hate to imagine leadership like this in anyone else's hands."

"Seppi, it's people like you that brought us this

far. And it would mean a great deal to me if you would give me your blessing."

Seppi looked at Adolf in surprise—an expression his features were not familiar with. Why?"

"Dying may be easy, but sacrificing your life for a cause is still a sacred act. And you've sacrificed more than just your life for this cause. If I'm to take up the torch, and try to build something from the ashes, I want the mandate from someone who made my job possible."

Again Seppi looked surprised, but Adolf decided it was a much nicer variety of surprise. He raised his hand, as if in traditional blessing, but changed it to ruffling Adolf's hair. "Bless you, young man," he said. "For all you've done—and will do. Now get some sleep. We've a lot of work ahead of us."

The thing that surprised Adolf most about the next few days was just how quickly everything came together. Everyone was full of energy. Not even the nagging fear that this entire operation could end in a mass grave could dampen their enthusiasm.

An unexpected benefit for Adolf was discovering that he would be seeing, or at least hearing from, old friends and comrades. Ghosts from his past, with names like Schuller, Lena, Markus and Varina began to pop up as messages came in from as far as South Africa and the Americas.

Adolf had mixed feelings about Ilsa coming with him. He was glad not to be separated from her, but couldn't shake the feeling this was somehow pushing their luck. Thoresten and Rika would be going as well, plus a large, silent bodyguard named Gregor.

Ilsa arrived just then, with the latest communication from their contacts. "If we can rendezvous with Miklos and his group of Free Poles ten days from now, we can travel the rest of the way with them," she said. "They claim they can get us authentic travel passes."

Adolf whistled. "That would certainly make things easier. How on earth did they come up with those?"

Ilsa gave Adolf her "don't ask, don't tell" smile. "We'll still have to weigh the risks of traveling in such a large group."

"How large?"

"They've got six—they say they're representing three different Polish groups, and couldn't make do with fewer."

"But with our five—eleven people. Traveling almost three hundred miles—"

"Ten people," said Ilsa. "I'll meet you on the other side of the border. I have some things to take care of first. Besides, my face has become almost as well known as yours. We can't afford any extra risks now."

Adolf felt a chill, as if a shadow had crossed his grave. "What kind of 'things'?" he asked. "And why now?"

Ilsa only flashed Adolf yet another enigmatic smile and went off to organize their supplies. Adolf hated the fact that she still kept secrets from him, although as a long dead friend had once said, her air of mystery was part of what drew him to her. It was just that now didn't seem to be the time for mystery.

Too much was riding on this meeting; on what

was discovered and decided over the next few weeks. To separate now seemed—irrevocable. He had the sudden overwhelming desire to change the entire plan, delay the meeting—anything to avoid being separated from Ilsa.

"Rabbi!" someone was calling. Rika burst into the chamber. "Oh, excuse me Rabbi, but there's another argument over the plans for after you leave, and Thoresten and Sven have found two entirely different departure ceremonies in the Talmud for tomorrow and everyone's at each other's throats."

"I'll be right there, Rika."

He was Rabbi Adolf, and he had a job to do. He didn't need a book to tell him that his duties as a leader came before his duties as a husband.

CHAPTER 24

Early the next morning, Adolf found himself yet again saying farewell to strangers who had become dear to him in a very short period of time. But this time, he prayed, it would be different. This time, he would return, with a cohesive plan to topple the Third *Reich* and live in freedom for the rest of their lives.

Yeah, right.

Rika and Thoresten chattered excitedly as they set out, but Adolf was nearly as silent as Gregor. His companions respected Adolf's need for silence, but that didn't help much either. Despite the enormity of the mission, it was being parted from Ilsa that weighed heaviest upon him. That, and wondering exactly what she was up to this time.

Whether in spite of or because of his worrying, everything went off without a hitch. Adolf, Rika, Thoresten and Gregor met up with Miklos, a Polish leader Adolf already knew, and his five companions. They set off together amid interesting discussion and exchanges of relevant news. They crossed the Polish frontier without incident, thanks to their travel passes. Then late on a moonless night, the party slipped past a drunken guard in a lonely tower, then across a rather unimpressive stretch of scrub into the "unoccupied" wasteland unofficially known as Free Russia.

The significance of the moment nearly drove away Adolf's grim thoughts. He was, for the first time in his life, physically outside the *Reich*. Realistically, it didn't mean much. A radioactive wasteland, with enough forests to hide the last few rebels, and terrain that would take more than the *Reich's* overextended resources to conquer was hardly a viable alternative to life under Nazi rule. Still, it had an emotional impact, and that, no doubt, was why the rebel leaders had chosen to meet here.

They had Geiger counters, good only for keeping them away from the worst of the hot spots. Everyone who came knew they were shortening their lives at least a little by staying for a just a few days. *Good way to keep the meeting short and focused*, Adolf mused.

They stopped for a few hours rest behind the cover of an ancient fallen tree. When they woke at dawn, Ilsa was sitting in plain sight, just outside the sentry's fire range.

Adolf greeted his wife formally, introducing her to the few members she did not already know— though Ilsa was known by reputation to all of them. "Planning on telling me where you've been?" Adolf whispered as the group set out.

"Every marriage needs secrets to keep it exciting," she said.

"I don't recall reading that in any of the Jewish writings," Adolf muttered.

They traveled for another three days without incident. This land had been sparsely populated before the *Reich*; now it was deserted. They passed the ruins of an abandoned village, then the crater that had once been a town. Other than that, there was no sign that anyone had ever lived here.

"Do you think they're watching us?" Thoresten asked glancing around the thin edge of forest they skirted.

"The Russians?" said Miklos. "Probably. I'd like to think they're watching our backs."

"I wonder what they think of the conference," said Adolf.

"You think they'll be there?" asked Rika.

"I hope so," said Miklos. "They're the only free men left on earth. I'm hoping we'll be working together."

Ilsa consulted her map. "The conference is supposed to start today, and we've still got twenty klicks to cover. We'd better pick up our pace."

They tried, but the uneven ground and the heavy forests made for slow progress—both physically and emotionally. Already, they were feeling like ants trying to scale a mountain.

They did not reach the ridge overlooking their destination until nightfall. The meeting site was the burnt out shell of a farmhouse—the only structure left in what appeared to have been an agricultural collective. Those who had already arrived were observing blackout rules, but the dark clusters of tents and gear were faintly visible in the clear, moonlit night.

"I don't see any sentries," said Adolf. "But they're sure to have them. We should probably wait until morning."

"But we've already missed the first day!" Thoresten sounded like a kid waiting for a candy store to open.

"We have passwords," said Miklos.

"We might even get to use them before they shoot us," said Ilsa.

Adolf was suddenly uneasy. He wasn't sure why, but he knew approaching the conference site tonight was a bad idea. He glanced at Ilsa and knew she felt the same thing.

The other members were beginning to get restless; they too sensed something was wrong. Adolf tried to think of something reassuring to say. After all, everything they had worked for years to achieve was waiting for them in the field below.

But before he could say anything, everyone stiffened at the familiar, though still barely audible sound of an Arado Ar.2000. Then the night turned into day, and the sky was alive with the whistle of bombs falling.

The farmhouse turned into a fireball. When Adolf could see again, paratroopers were landing to take charge of any survivors. Although the sounds of screaming couldn't reach the people on the ridge over the noise of the engines, they all heard it anyway.

"We were betrayed," Thoresten said stupidly.

"It's happened," whispered a woman from Miklos' group. "Just like we feared. With one strike, they've killed us all, and everything we've worked for."

"Maybe not," said Ilsa, peering intently into the woods below. "I don't know if everyone just got amorous and went for a walk in the woods or if the farmhouse was a ruse, but there's a lot of movement down there."

The others tried to see what Ilsa was seeing. Yes, there were survivors running in the shelter of the woods. The sounds of gunfire being exchanged confirmed it.

"We've got to help them!" Rika shouted.

"How?" demanded Miklos. "Against an armored division? All we'd do is get ourselves taken as well!"

"Then you'd better leave it to us," growled a menacing voice in barely recognizable German.

Then they were all surrounded by what appeared to be a group of walking trees.

Orders were rapidly given in Russian, and about half the new group disappeared down the slope. The remaining ten or so men waved decaying rifles—and a few new spears—at Adolf and his fellows, indicating they should come along. Nearly every man among them towered over Adolf, and even the ones who didn't looked perfectly capable of splitting him in half with their hands.

Adolf shrugged and walked as instructed. The others followed his lead.

They had met the famous Free Russians.

CHAPTER 25

"So you Aryan geniuses came to save us, huh?" The big Russian sneered at his guests.

The contempt of their rescuers didn't bother Adolf nearly as much as their smell. There were perhaps thirty or so Free Russians gathered around a nearly smokeless fire in a rough forest camp. Roughly the same number of resistance leaders—just under half of those who had come to attend the conference— were crowded into the far end of the hut.

"We were hoping to make contact with the legendary Free Russians, yes," said Adolf. "And we hoped by working together, we might save each other."

It was late afternoon, and no one had slept well recently. The Russians had led Adolf and the others on a difficult journey through the forest that lasted most of the night. Volunteers had returned in the morning to search for survivors, and report the position of the Germans who remained for the same task.

Yuri, the only member of the band who spoke German, acted as translator.

Another Russian spoke. "Ivan," said Yuri, "wants to know how you plan to overthrow the *Reich* when you don't even have enough security to hold a conference without it blowing up in your faces."

Adolf hoped the pun was unintentional. "Actually," he said, "I've been wondering that myself.

I think we all have." He glanced at what was left of
his fellow revolutionary leaders and continued. "I
know we're all pretty shook up right now. We're
wondering who betrayed us, or if this whole thing was
a set up from the beginning—and of course, the big
question: is there a traitor sitting here right now?"

From the reactions of those around him, Adolf
could tell he'd struck a nerve—several probably. The
sudden hush among their Russian hosts was a hopeful
sign as well.

"I think it's time we got to know each other,"
Ilsa said, her gaze taking in revolutionaries and Free
Russian alike. Slowly, they went around the room,
like kids around a campfire, and introduced
themselves.

"Rabbi Isabella of Portugal," said a small, dark
woman.

"Don't you mean Rabbina?" asked one of the
other delegates.

"No," she said. "I mean Rabbi. Letting
ourselves be divided and categorized is what got us
into this mess in the first place. I had hoped to change
all that—that is, until half of this the conference ended
up dead or captured."

"We still might do it," said Adolf.

"Ian MacKinnon of the Highland Freedom
Fighters. I came to offer my arm, heart and brain to
the cause, but also to beg for any help you might give
to my people. They're sick and hungry, and we fear a
new plague's been tested on our water supply."

Several of Ian's neighbors slid away from him.

"Rabbi William. Originally of northern
England; now a wandering preacher."

"Whom do you represent?" someone asked.

"Anyone and everyone who'd like a better life and who's sick of German tyranny. I have contacts in several underground organizations who could not otherwise be represented here today."

"I look forward to speaking with you, Rabbi!" said Adolf. Slowly, he could see people coming out of their despair, and reconsidering their options.

"Nikolai of the Greek Alliance. Uh, I think I'm all that's left of it."

"My name's Marla," said an Aryan girl, barely out of her teens. "I'm from Vienna, and I've been fighting this accursed government since they executed my father, five years ago. I brought the blueprints to the *Führer's* new summer palace. I was rather hoping we could blow the place up while he was still there, but now…" Her voice trailed off.

"Marla?" cried a voice from across the room. "I'm Felipe! It's great to finally meet you face to face!"

Marla perked up, and then pushed through the crowd to meet her long time radio contact.

"Gunthar of the South African Aryan Enclave. What's everyone looking at? Even *we're* feeling oppressed these days!"

"That's a bit hard to believe," said one of the Poles from Adolf's group. Again, suspicion flared.

"I don't know if anyone up here has heard yet," said Gunthar. "But you know those airborne viruses our Illustrious Leaders released to cull the black Africans? They're not just killing Negroes!"

"Father Bernardo, originally of Assisi, Italy, now representing any living Catholics who might make their faith known if it were to become safe to do so."

"What are the Catholics unhappy about?" asked Ian. "Didn't they agree to support the *Reich* in exchange for the right to worship freely?" Suspicion again became palpable.

"Catholics haven't been doing too well lately," said the priest. "In case you haven't noticed, we've become the most popular scapegoat in recent years. And even if the pope himself—if there was one anymore—were to declare it righteous to obey the *Führer*, I would refuse. My conscience demands that I be here, working for the overthrow of an unjust and brutal system."

"How do you feel about working with the New Jews? Isabella asked suspiciously.

"Fine by me," said Father Bernardo.

"How do you feel about taking up arms?" asked Marla.

The old man eyed Adolf thoughtfully. "I will put my life on the line gladly, but I will not take the life of another. That is something I'm told I have in common with some of the rabbis."

"Not all," said Isabella. "Some of us prefer action. Talk is cheap." She traded a smirk of disgust with Marla.

Thoresten leaned forward and whispered into Adolf's ear. "If this is typical of his relationships with women, I can see why he took an oath of celibacy."

Adolf jabbed Thoresten with an elbow, and applauded the priest.

There were a few others: a woman named Jessica from the North American Protectorate, a Muslim from Turkey, a pack of teenagers from Holland. Under any other circumstances, Adolf would have been delighted just to talk with them all.

As it was, however, he had to somehow find a way to get them working together, despite forty percent losses, and despite the fact they didn't know how many of their comrades were now in enemy hands, spilling their secrets.

"Thank you all," Adolf began, making eye contact with each of them. Then he turned to the Russians. "How about our hosts?" He tried to smiled winningly.

They were, he noticed, nearly all men. Three or four were definitely women, and a few he wasn't sure about. There were no children, nor any who seemed over the age of forty. Their demeanor had changed; they were looking a great deal more impressed with their guests. Several were eyeing Marla, and Adolf didn't think it was just for her looks.

"We've never had much use for grand plans and the work of intellectuals," said Yuri. "For us, it's been simple: keep to the forest. Scavenge enough to live on. Shoot any German who comes by. So it was for our parents, and their parents, who fought for Mother Russia.

"But things have changed. We're fewer than sixty able-bodied fighters. Most of us are sick from radiation and malnutrition. Few children are born living anymore, and those that do don't thrive. We must face the fact that our time is growing short." Adolf was not comfortable with the direction this was going.

"But we have one last card to play," Yuri continued. "Come and see."

Yuri led both groups away from the camp, a short distance through the trees, to a small hut. Some Free Russians they had not met guarded the unexceptional structure, while others from the main group brought torches. Rather than a door, a section of wall was rolled away so the visitors could see what lay within.

Adolf's first impression was of a bloated metallic fish with a short stubby tail. Amid the gasps and exclamations of those around him, the image resolved itself into an old fashioned, high yield atomic bomb.

"Where did you get it?" Gunthar asked.

"It fell out of the sky," Yuri replied, straight faced. A few people laughed. Yuri shrugged and continued. "We're still not sure if it was meant for us, or just happened to malfunction over our heads. It hit, but didn't go off. We've held onto it for two years, hoping we'll someday figure out how to fix it—and return it to its makers."

"How would you deliver it?" asked Marla.

"We have the rocket as well. In another location."

One of the Dutch teenagers squatted beside Gunthar. "When it went off course, it was probably given a lockout code, to keep it from going off where the Party didn't want it to. Breaking the code won't be difficult. If there's no damage to the device itself—it might be usable." Gunthar nodded slowly.

"This," said Yuri, "is how we can help each other. We have the weapon-but no knowledge of how it works. You, on the other hand…" He turned to the rest of the surviving rebels. "How many others of you can work on this?"

The American woman came forward. "I don't know how much use I'll be without my stash of illegal books, but I can try."

"What, exactly, do you have in mind?" Adolf asked Yuri.

The big Russian looked surprised. "Isn't it obvious? Our final blow for freedom! You girl," Yuri jerked his chin toward Marla. "Was it true what you said? You know the where the *Führer* is now?"

"I know where his vacation home is," Marla said carefully. "And I know he was there five days ago."

One of the Russians spoke urgently to Yuri. "Ivan says that if we could be sure of killing the *Führer*, every man here would gladly climb aboard the rocket and drop the bomb with his own hands."

"It may come to that if we can't fix the guidance system," Gunthar called from his place before the device.

"Good," said Yuri. "It would be the best way to go out."

"Wait a minute," said Adolf. "Now, I think it's great that you have this…resource." He tried not to think about how much radiation the thing was leaking. "But to use an atomic bomb to kill one man? Isn't that like using a hand grenade to kill an ant?"

"You have some hand grenades?" Ivan asked hopefully.

"You have an ant problem?" Thoresten said, trying for levity.

Isabella turned to Adolf. "Look, I know it sounds extreme," she said. "But I believe that under the circumstances, it would be worth it."

"And it could take out much more than just the *Führer*," said Felipe.

"Yes, it will," said Adolf. "Several thousand

innocent bystanders for starters. And probably more than one resistance cell, too. And if, as I would guess, his vacation home is in the Swiss Alps..."

"Austrian Alps, actually," said Marla.

"Yes, of course. Dropping a nuke on top of that kind of mountainous region..."

"The destruction would be massive," said Father Bernardo quietly. "And quite impossible to control."

Adolf nodded to the priest, grateful for an ally. "There are, I think, enough reasons already to sit down and discuss this plan. I'm sure that most of us already have too much blood on our hands to want any more—especially on this order of magnitude..."

"Speak for yourself!" shouted Nikolai. "I haven't got a problem with it!"

Adolf turned the full force of his gaze on the shaken young man, who Adolf knew was the only survivor of his delegation. "Is this what you and all your friends were hoping to accomplish when you came to the conference?" he asked quietly.

"No," said Nikolai, looking away.

"What were you hoping for?"

"A way to win. To defeat Nazi tyranny and build something better." He turned a bleak, and much aged face back to Adolf. "But that's all over now."

"He's right, Rabbi," said Isabella. "After all our great plans—this may be the only thing left to do."

"Do you always give up so easily?" Adolf swept his gaze across the both communities. "If so, I think I came to the wrong conference!" He noticed that even Thoresten and Rika seemed uneasy at his back. He was taking a big risk, he knew, but he had only one shot at turning the remnants of this conference away from a futile, suicidal gesture.

"What do you think you can still accomplish?" Yuri seemed genuinely curious now. "You've lost nearly half of your leadership! And you don't know how many were taken alive, so you have to assume that all your secrets are known! What can you do now, but join us? Killing the Führer is no small thing!"

"It may be just the signal those we left behind will need to launch a general uprising," said Marla. "Even if we don't live to see it, we can still be the founders of a new age."

"*Führers* have been killed before," said Adolf. "A new one is always found—usually after a great deal of blood-letting." Then, as he saw eyes light up with a new thought, he added, "And dropping this thing on Berlin in the hopes of talking out the cabinet won't work either! Nazi machinery is too spread out."

"All right then, smart guy," said Felipe, "what do you suggest?"

It was the opening he needed, if he could just make it work. "We came here hoping to forge a plan to overthrow the existing government. It was an ambitious goal then, and it's even more ambitious now—but it can still be accomplished."

"How?" asked several voices. *They were asking, not arguing. Good.*

"Those of us here still represent thousands of dedicated rebels all over the world. Those who were captured," Adolf swallowed around a lump in his throat and pushed on, "can only betray a few names and meeting places." He prayed he was right. "That leaves thousands more, primed and ready for the revolution—and now, to avenge their friends.

"Add to that the one thing our fallen comrades cannot betray: any plan we devise now.

"Thanks to our new allies," Adolf nodded towards the Russians and hoped he wasn't presuming too much, "we have more fire power than any of us ever dreamed of. My suggestions here are simple.

"One, we come up with a plan to seize control of the universal broadcast network in Berlin. Once it's ours, we can send out a coded message—something that will be understood by all members of the underground—telling them it's time to rise up. Our job will of course be made easier by our leaders' paranoid decision to have only a single worldwide network.

"Two, that we few here devise and agree upon some kind of...constitution...that will serve as the blueprint for a new government. That way, even if none of us survive the coming conflict, our dreams still might—endorsed by our blood."

Isabella shifted uneasily. "That was very much like the plan *we* came to propose. I just don't see that it's possible now. We're so few..."

"Not that it would have stood a chance of working had you been many," said Yuri.

"You seem very well prepared," Felipe told Adolf. "And very unruffled by our recent losses. Almost as if you were expecting them."

Ah, the need to uncover traitors in our midst, sighed Adolf. *What underground is complete without it?*

As if reading his mind, Ilsa said quietly, "You can hardly blame them for their suspicions, given the circumstances."

"True," said Adolf. "But they do get in the

way."

"Did you bring this constitution thing with you?" asked Ian.

"No. I had hoped we'd come up with it together."

Sighs of frustration filled the air.

"We don't have time for something like that!" cried William. "We're skating on thin ice as it is."

Adolf took a deep breath. Here was his chance, and he knew he could blow it all in the next few minutes.

"Then I have a suggestion for a model." He opened his knapsack and took out the battered, travel stained *Torah* he had kept with him for three years.

"In here," said Adolf, holding the book up for all to see. "Is everything we need, in a form most of us are familiar with."

Pandemonium erupted.

"He wants to replace Nazi tyranny with Jewish tyranny!" said Ian.

"Actually," said the South African, "it might be worth it just for the poetic justice. Think about it."

"Religious fads are good for launching a movement," said Marla. "But lousy for governing one afterwards."

Adolf stood in the middle of the circle. Glances at the faces of those who called themselves rabbis told him that they were interested.

"There are many here more learned in this book than I," Adolf began. "But, to put it simply, what we find here says that we are all one family. No one's blood is any better than another; no one's life is more or less precious. Equality is not an interesting theory. It is a fact of life.

"Add to that, there are laws that are designed solely to help people live together—something we desperately need to learn. Personally, I don't think they've been topped yet."

"If we follow this religion as a guide, we'll have made at least a start at those things so many have been willing to die for. Equality. Justice. Freedom."

"And would we all have to become Jews?" asked the Turk.

"There won't be any forcing or forbidding of anyone's faith in any world I become a part of!" Adolf said harshly.

"Yet a world under Jewish law could be a very good place to live," said Isabella.

"It's certainly attracted a lot of followers lately," said Bernardo. "Despite what happened to the original set."

"Lots of religions sound great in the beginning," said Gunther shaking his head. "Including Nazism. Any official, worldwide religion would just invite the very same repression we're trying to overthrow!"

"Actually, Judaism has specific laws protecting the rights of non-Jews," said William. "It has since ancient times. As far as I can tell, it was the first religion to practice such a thing. I'm saying that because I find it interesting, not because I'd like to see it become universally enforced. Personally, I share the South African's concern on that score."

"I think what we're seeing here," Adolf said, "is the need for further discussion. It's true, we don't have much time, but since being here at all is something of a miracle—even in these tragically reduced circumstances—I think we should really make history and go home with an actual plan.

"But whatever is decided here today, I will
state right now my own little quirk. I will not support
any plan that wantonly takes innocent life."

It belatedly occurred to Adolf that somebody
should probably explain to the Russians what their
discussion of Judaism was all about. He turned to
Yuri, only to find the Russian staring at him in
disgust.

"If you haven't got the stomach for a real
fight," he spat at Adolf, "then go join the rest of the
cowards." He addressed the crowd as Adolf had done
moments before. "Yes, we have them, too. Anyone
who wants to listen to this mad dreamer, go ahead.

"But I can see that some of you are warriors,
with the heart and guts to join us in our work. Those
who have the courage can remain with us, and
together, we'll send our would-be masters a message
from the sky that they'll understand—no matter which
gods they pray to!" He spoke to one of the women in
his command, and she in turned snarled something at
Adolf that indicated he should follow her.

He moved to follow her, not sure how or why
everything he had attempted had just fallen apart. To
his surprise, however, nearly every member of the
failed conference followed him—except for Ilsa, who
walked proudly by his side. Only Felipe, Jessica and
Marla and two of the Dutch youths stayed with the
Russians—and Marla looked torn.

"I just want to go over these blueprints with
them," she called. "Then I'll catch up with you."

"Are you sure you want to do this?" Adolf
asked them over his shoulders. Considering the
harshness of life in these parts, the possibility that

"joining the rest of the cowards" involved passage to a mass grave was serious.

No one answered. They just kept walking.

"Why are they following me?" he asked Ilsa.

She just smiled.

Dusk was falling, rendering the forest nearly invisible to the untrained eyes of the outsiders. When the trees opened suddenly into a clearing, Adolf could see stars emerging in the blackening sky. Before them stood a burned-out building of stone and timber. The roof was gone, but the walls still stood. A massive wooden door sagged open, emitting more light than could be accounted for by the stars. And from within came the sound of singing. The tune was strange, but the words were familiar.

It was Hebrew.

"Of course," Ilsa murmured. "I had forgotten that today was Friday."

CHAPTER 26

The Russian guide jerked her head toward the building, turned on her heel and marched back into the forest.

"I guess these are the cowards Yuri mentioned," said Adolf.

"Shabbat services?" Isabella was shaking her head in disbelief. "How could there be practicing Jews up here?"

"Any *Judenmuseums* ever placed in the Soviet Union?" Adolf asked Ilsa.

"None," she said firmly. "But then, this isn't the conquered Soviet Union. This is Free Russia."

"But that doesn't make any sense either!" said Gunthar. "Most of these people are illiterate. Not to mention too busy fighting to know what to do with old books and relics even if they had them. Where's the rhyme or reason in their resurrecting a dead religion?"

The singing ceased abruptly. Several people came out of the building.

"Don't be alarmed..." the Turk began, but his accented German seemed to terrify them.

"*Shabbat Shalom*," said Ilsa. In halting Hebrew she asked if they could celebrate the Sabbath together.

There was the whoosh of in drawn breaths and an excited exchange in Russian. Then an old man was beckoning them into the building. Adolf bowed respectfully and followed him inside. The others followed Adolf.

The interior of the building was not as primitive as Adolf had expected. There were wooden benches; enough to seat nearly one hundred, which was good since the newcomers brought the number up to about eighty. The Russian congregation included children and old people, as well as the burly men and women who resembled Yuri and the others they had met.

The visitors found seats and looked around curiously. On a cloth-covered table, a pair of candles burned in battered silver candlesticks. A *Torah* scroll sat beside them in a gold embroidered case. The old man who had led them in was apparently the Rabbi, for he stood beside the table and addressed the congregation.

"We welcome our visitors who would seem to come from far away," he said in perfect Hebrew. "And we look forward to hearing your stories. But for now, let us continue the service."

And for the next hour and a half, that is what they did. Adolf and his fellows learned how to put familiar Hebrew words to strange, yet lovely, tunes as the service progressed; tunes that Adolf realized were probably Russian folk songs. Then the Rabbi carried the *Torah* scroll around to be touched by each person in the room. With great ceremony he withdrew the scroll from its silken wrapping, slowly unrolled a portion and began to read in Hebrew.

It was from the book of Exodus. *Appropriate*, thought Adolf. As the words rolled over him, he looked up through the missing roof to the canopy of the heavens. Stars shone through a thin veil of clouds, the scent of candle wax blended with the summer night air, and Adolf knew a moment of peace.

It was unlike anything he had ever experienced.

And although this was not the reason they had traveled hundreds of miles, as Adolf gazed at the people who sat in family groups and recited the prayers of a dead language with practiced ease, he was suddenly very glad he had come.

At the service's conclusion, people exchanged hugs and whispered the words "Shabbat Shalom" with each exchange. The visiting rebels were not exempt from this familiarity, and while Adolf happily returned the greetings, he noticed several members of his party seemed to be in a state of guarded shock.

While some of his group had no knowledge at all of Judaism, all knew at least a little Hebrew, and could therefore converse with their hosts. There was something especially fitting on this magical summer night about the image of those who spoke no Russian and those who spoke no German all able to communicate in Hebrew.

Adolf disentangled himself from the warm embrace of a nearly toothless old woman and sought out the Rabbi. "I am called Rabbi Adolf," he told the old man.

"Rabbi Sasha," said the other, extending his hand. If he was surprised to meet an Aryan who called himself a rabbi, Sasha did not show it. "I understand you all came here for some kind of summit. I assume that the airplanes and shooting the other night was the German response to your plan?"

"You assume correctly," said Adolf.

Sasha sighed. "I'm sorry. I hope you won't think me ungracious if I ask you to keep your visit with us short. They will be back soon, looking for the rest of you."

"Grandfather," a young woman interrupted. "This is not the time to discuss such matters." To Adolf she said, "In better times we would have an *oneg,* a Sabbath meal now, and welcome you properly. Tonight, I am afraid, we can offer only our company."

"My granddaughter, Olga," said the Rabbi. "This is Rabbi Adolf. From Germany?" He glanced at Adolf.

"At one time, yes. You seem to know something about us, but we know nothing of you. I helped arrange this meeting, but nothing about Russian Jews was known to any of us. Were you planning to attend the conference?"

Sasha hesitated. "Some of us hoped to," said a new voice. A powerfully built young man loomed over Sasha's shoulder. He had the familiar glint in his eyes of an impatient young rebel. Adolf was surprised to see him here, rather than with Yuri.

"This is Mordecai," said Sasha. "You can probably tell from his name that he had great hopes for your meeting and your cause. We elders, on the other hand," Sasha indicated several of the old people, grouped together and listening to the exchange, "hold a different view."

"Jews who take up the sword against a powerful enemy are always the first to die," said a wizened old man, even older than Sasha. "In the end, it only hurts us all."

"I think Mordecai would disagree with you," said Ilsa.

"I already have," said the youth.

"I was referring to the one from the Book of

Esther," said Ilsa.

There was a roar of appreciation of her joke from those who understood. Rabbi William was busy translating for the rest.

"I understand what you're saying," Isabella said, with a little help with the Hebrew from Ilsa. "But I am surprised. Everywhere I've been, Judaism is a political movement; the fulcrum for change. Here it seems like more of a...well..."

"Religion?" offered Adolf.

Isabella laughed. "Well...yes, as a matter of fact. Imagine that."

"How long have you been Jewish?" asked Adolf.

His Hebrew was clear, but he was greeted with blank looks.

He tried again. "What I mean is, how did you come by this religion? Did one of you travel outside, to a rebel group perhaps?" It seemed unlikely that anyone here had been to a University.

Some of the others still looked confused, but Sasha smiled with sudden understanding. "What makes you think we were ever anything else?" he asked.

Adolf felt the ground shifting beneath him. At least this time he had company. A glance at his companions told him what his own stupefied expression must be.

Ilsa was the first to recover. "Probably we think so because all of the original Jews are dead."

"Do you believe everything your leaders tell you?" asked Mordecai.

All around Adolf people were whispering. Was it possible? Had, somehow, against all odds,

some of the true descendants of Abraham and Sarah
survived? And if so, what did it mean for those all
over the world who, perhaps playfully, perhaps in
defiance, called themselves Jews?

"We doubt everything our leaders tell us,"
William said. "But the extermination of Jews? That's
something I've never questioned. It's not just our
leaders—"

"How?" cried Rika. "How did you survive?"

"The same way we always have," said an old
woman. "By living quietly on the fringes. By never
calling attention to ourselves." She glowered at
Mordecai.

"This building was once a synagogue," said
Sasha. "Built over four centuries ago. It survived
tsars, pogroms, and even the Revolution. And,
because we choose to worship here in its ruins, you
could say it has survived the latest war as well."

"We don't have the means to rebuild it," said
Olga. "Perhaps if you join us, then—"

"It's late," said Sasha. "Time we were asleep.
Surviving in the forest is every bit as exhausting as
farming was for our ancestors."

The groups dispersed; the Russians to their
hidden homes, the visiting rebels to the temporary
camp that the fighters had allowed them. They
prepared for sleep in silence, each lost in his own
thoughts.

"What do think?" Adolf asked Ilsa as they
wrapped themselves together in their blankets. He
didn't bother to specify about what.

"That we're only just beginning to understand
our purpose for coming here."

"You think we still have one?"

"Oh, yes," said Ilsa. "Now more than ever."

*   *   *

"Maybe we should try something besides biblical names," Marla said.

"Biblical names are the only reliable code we have!" said Thoresten. "They're the only words that can be recognized by all resistance factions!"

"Unfortunately, that's not entirely true," said Father Bernardo. "Many of those whom I represent will not recognize these Old Testament references you are suggesting. Others may interpret them differently than you do."

"I think the more serious matter is the fact that the Party is holding several of our key people, and might very well understand this code before we do!" snapped Felipe.

"Will you please stop reminding us!" said Nikolai. "Now, could we get back to the plan for seizing control of the network?"

Adolf sighed and stood up, but this time it wasn't to speak. He'd done enough of that.

He couldn't blame the delegates for dragging their feet when it came to choosing a signal for launching the revolution. Because once you decided on a signal, you had to empower someone to use it. Hard enough in the best of circumstances. But now, with their recent losses? With the possibility that whoever betrayed the conference might still be among them?

Maybe it was impossible.

He wandered through the forest, remembering not to greet the sentries hidden in the trees—but secretly pleased he was able to spot them. Especially now, with so much on his mind. Pausing by a small stream, shrunken now to its summer trickle, Adolf spied Ilsa, sitting alone on the bank. The sight of her was more refreshing than the cool flowing water on this hot day. Silently, Adolf sat down beside her.

"How goes the conference?" she asked.

"Dogs chasing their own tails.

"Unkind, but accurate, I'm sure."

"Have you spoken with Rabbi Sasha?" Adolf asked her. "Or any of the…Jews?"

"Real Jews, you were thinking?" She shook her head. "Not since Friday night. Strange, don't you think?"

"What, that they're not interested in talking to us? Except for Mordecai and the other radicals, no, I don't think it's strange. They don't like our politics. And…they probably don't consider us Jews."

Ilsa raised an eyebrow. "That really bothers you, doesn't it?"

"I guess I'm just getting tired of thinking I belong somewhere, then finding out I don't."

"Is that what it means to you? We find out that a handful of Jews survived, and instead of calling it a miracle, you start feeling sorry for yourself?"

Adolf flinched at her words, but held his ground. "All right then, you tell me where it leaves us! Never in recorded history did the Jews seek converts—the orthodox didn't even accept them! You were Jewish by birth or not at all! As long as they were all dead, we could do whatever we wanted with the religion—even practice it! But now, if there really are living Jews, who can trace their bloodline all the way back to Abraham…"

Adolf stopped and glanced curiously at Ilsa. "If none of this bothers you, what are you doing here? Why aren't you out there with them?"

"Because something else is bothering me," said Ilsa. She got up from the dusty ground and began to pace along the riverbed. "You know I worked in that museum for almost eight years, right? I'm self-taught; my knowledge isn't perfect. But, there're a few things I learned. Things that don't fit with what Sasha and the others said."

It was Adolf's turn to raise an eyebrow. "Such as...?"

"The way they spoke Hebrew, for one. I learned that language from phonograph records—so did you and the rest of the museum crowd. Those were records made by Jews. There's something different about the way these people speak Hebrew."

"Couldn't it just be their Russian accents?"

Ilsa shook her head. "It's more than that. It's the way they use the words. '*Oneg*' for example. Olga said it meant Shabbat meal. But it really means 'delicious'. It was basically a dessert party after services. An *oneg* is superfluous to Sabbath services—but the communal sharing of bread and wine is sacred. Even the poorest Jews, in the worst of times had something that passed for wine and bread— even we did, back at the museum. But, the other night, these people didn't. They didn't even mention the two blessings that normally end a Friday night service.

"And there was something else." Ilsa stared into the water. "You remember when Sasha said how surviving in the forest was just as exhausting as farming was for their ancestors?"

"Yes."

Ilsa turned her grave blue eyes to him. "Adolf, Jews weren't allowed to farm land here. They were bankers, doctors and shopkeepers, but never farmers."

Again, Adolf felt the familiar shifting of the universe beneath his feet. "So you're saying…what? They lied about being Jews? Why would anyone do that?"

"I don't know." Ilsa returned her stare to the stream, as if she could force answers from the water. "Hatred for the *Reich* runs strong in these parts. Maybe it's just their way of thumbing their noses at the enemy."

Adolf shook his head and stood up.

"Where are you going?" Ilsa asked.

"To have a chat with our local rabbi. Rabbis are supposed to be teachers, right? I'm ready to learn a few things."

Adolf found the ruined synagogue empty when he arrived. It felt like a reprieve; he wasn't ready to talk to anyone just then.

The place was peaceful. Just as the crumbling façade of the *Judenmuseum* carried a kind of spiritual weight, so too did this centuries-old synagogue. It seemed not so much to be falling apart as seeping back into the earth; manmade and god-made holy places merging into one.

Adolf settled into a corner of the main room. Long ago, the floor had buckled, creating a low seat. Leaning his back against charred timbers, Adolf gazed through the missing roof—economy sky-lighting he decided—and watched puffy white clouds float lazily in a brilliant blue sky.

He had slept little the past few nights, nor would he have expected to, given all the recent stress. But here, he felt safe; secluded from the events that churned around him. It was very soothing.

He wasn't aware of when, exactly, the dream began, but he knew he was dreaming. It had the same vivid quality as the frightening nightmare he'd had on midsummer night—and at first, this seemed to be a nightmare as well.

He saw a Jew being chased by a mob. He knew the man was a Jew, not by any physical clues, but by the shouting of the mob.

They weren't in Germany, he realized, nor anywhere in Europe. North America, perhaps?

It had a grizzly ending, as mob actions usually do. As the man lay dying, he cried out to Elijah—the prophet who was to foretell the coming of the Messiah. The one, Adolf remembered explaining to Berta, had never died.

"I call on you, Elijah, to come here, not as a witness, but that the covenant not be broken."

Then, it was the man's body that was broken. Adolf watched him die, his dream-self able to block out the sounds of the cheering mob. Then, something seemed to detach from the hideously beaten corpse and rise above the scene. Adolf realized he was seeing a soul ascend to…where? That place mentioned in the Book of Daniel? Adolf hoped so.

And curiously, as he woke up, Adolf found himself hoping that whoever that man was, he had gone to the same place as Mirielle and had been there to greet her. There was, he reflected, something strangely reassuring, almost happy, about the dream.

He came fully to himself, and found Rabbi Sasha sitting across from him.

"I thought I'd find you here," said Sasha.

"You were looking for me?" Adolf asked.

"I knew we would have to speak eventually." The old man moved to sit against the charred wall beside Adolf. "You seemed to be in the throes of a dream when I arrived—or was it a vision?"

"You tell me." Adolf related his dream to Sasha.

For a moment, the old Russian was visibly shaken. Then he said in a quiet voice, "I believe you were a witness to an event that occurred in 1958, somewhere in the southern part of the North American Protectorate. I saw it myself in a dream, long ago. I later learned from an eye witness it was real."

"And what was it?"

"The death of the last Jew on earth." Sasha coughed uncomfortably. "You know how the Party loves closure. Real or not, they had to have some kind of official ending to the Jewish Question. Over the years, I have come to believe that this was it."

CHAPTER 27

They were both silent for a while.

"Well," said Adolf at last. "That answers my first question, anyway. You people aren't really…by birth, I mean…"

"No."

"None of you?"

"No."

"Okay, so I guess my next question is…"

"Why do we claim to be?" Adolf nodded.

Sasha leaned his head against the wall and closed his eyes. The sunlight coming through the broken roof showed every line on his wrinkled face. "My name, when I was born," he began, "was Vladimir Ivanovitch."

"Who was Sasha?"

"I'm getting there. My father died when I was six years old. My mother had five children to feed. The State gave her a job washing linens in our new hospital, which itself was one of Stalin's building projects.

"She worked for a doctor, who we all knew was Jewish—not officially, of course. We were all good Communists, and thus, free from religion. This doctor was a good man. My family always seemed to be in some kind of trouble; he always helped us out. And then, when my sister became ill, and everyone said she would die—he saved her."

"He'd have probably done that for anyone," Adolf said.

"True, but it didn't make me any less grateful. My mother, too—or so I thought.

"Sasha was the doctor's son; two years older than me. We became friends. Better friends than I had thought, because he trusted me with a great secret—his faith. Sasha, it seemed, was destined to be a rabbi." The old man smiled, his eyes still closed. "I remember the day he explained to me what that meant. We were both hiding from our mothers to escape chores, and he showed me his treasure trove: a box of books he had hidden behind his house.

"He had been studying in secret. I wanted to know what was so special about what was hidden in those books; what made it worth such a risk. So he told me—no, he *showed* me. He taught me Hebrew, and told me about the *Kibbutz* movement in Palestine, and shared his dream of someday moving there. He was going to leave this place, he said, and live where he could sing his faith to the world. And although I never told him, I was planning to go with him.

"When Sasha turned thirteen he told me he was going to celebrate his bar mitzvah, the passage into manhood. It was a serious thing. The fact that there would be no one there but the two of us—and God, I suppose—didn't worry him.

"But I was worried. You see learning about his faith got me curious about my own. I knew my grandmother had had each of us baptized in secret as children, and I knew a little about the Russian Orthodox Church that my family had been a part of for generations. So I gleaned what I could."

"And you realized that if Sasha dedicated himself to a faith other than Christian, he'd go to hell when he died," said Adolf.

The grizzled old Russian opened his eyes and stared at Adolf. A grin split his wrinkled face. "You are very perceptive, young man. Of course, I shouldn't wonder.

"Yes, that's exactly what I feared. But when I told Sasha, he only laughed, and asked me again to be present for the ceremony. So I thought about it, and finally thought to ask if he wasn't worried that that I would go to hell if I didn't believe the way he did. I suppose I was just fishing for an invitation to come with him—to Palestine, to Heaven, who knows?

"But I'll never forget his response: 'What kind of god would send someone to hell just for just for worshiping in a different way? It's what you *do* that matters; how you follow the laws God wrote on your heart in the beginning of time.'

"So, I witnessed his bar mitzvah, and made up my mind that I would have one of my own someday.

"That was the year the Germans came.

"My grandfather was mayor of our little town. It never really meant very much—until the soldiers marched in, and gathered us all together. They 'explained' things to us; shouted many frightening orders. Then they told my grandfather to tell them who the Jews were.

"And my grandfather said no.

"So they shot my grandfather, and made another man mayor, and told *him* to hand over the Jews. He did.

"I hid Sasha and his family in our house. But when they began searching houses, my mother panicked. She led the soldiers to them and they took them away.

"Later, as a courier for the Russian Army, I

came across a mass grave, not far from our town. It was the week before my thirteenth birthday.

"So I left a stone by the grave, because Sasha had told me that's what Jews do, and I wondered why heroes like Sasha and my grandfather were dead, while cowards like my mother and myself still lived."

"You were hardly a coward," Adolf interrupted. "You were a child, and you took a huge risk, hiding those people at all."

"But I couldn't save them."

"Neither could your grandfather."

"I know. It seems foolish now, but I simply didn't want to be Vladimir Ivanovitch anymore. I wanted to be Sasha—and everything he might have become.

"And as the years went by, and the people around me faced an endless war, without the comfort of faith or the hope of victory, they needed something. So I gave it to them."

"And here we are," said Adolf.

"Here we are," said Sasha.

"And the chain was truly broken." Adolf brooded.

"Maybe not," said Sasha. "Did you notice something unusual about the dream you had just now?"

"Other than the fact that I had it at all? Not really."

"Traditionally, most Jews recite the *Sh'ma* when faced with death. In your dream, the man— possibly the last Jew on earth—called out to Elijah. The prophet who didn't die. If Elijah did, in fact, come down to earth at that man's summons, then there is still one living descendant of Abraham among us.

And if what you and I and the others are doing is truly righteous in the sight of God…" Sasha shrugged. "Who knows?"

"It's possible," Adolf admitted. "He's been seen just about everywhere, lately. Of course, I can't tell you what he looks like, since he's never seen fit to show himself to me!" Adolf hurled a stone across the temple foundations in sudden furry. He didn't know why, but suddenly, all he could feel was anger.

There was a commotion in the woods behind them. Adolf and Sasha hurried from the synagogue. They found nearly all of the visiting rebels, along with several Free Russians, gathered around yet another small party of foreigners.

"This place is getting too crowded," muttered one of the Russians.

From what Adolf could gather in those first few moments, the newcomers had come in search of the conference, with vital information.

Members of both the conference and the Free Russians were suspiciously interrogating the newcomers, who were, in turn demanding proof that everyone here wasn't a *Gestapo* spy.

Ilsa solved the problem easily enough by stepping forward and calling out a phrase in a language Adolf was sure no one there understood. One of the men responded in the same tongue.

"It's okay," said Ilsa. "They're supposed to be here."

"But what happened to the conference?" asked the woman beside him. The blood stains on their clothing helped to explain why they were late.

While Thoresten and Marla hurried to explain, and Father Bernardo offered water and rations to the newcomers, Ilsa and the man she obviously knew were anxiously conferring. Suddenly, she signaled for Adolf to join them.

"This is Brun," she told Adolf. "A renegade Party scientist. Until now, I was afraid he had died in the attack four days ago."

"There was some trouble just as we were trying to leave," Brun said. "We were stuck in a safe house three extra days, then had to fight our way through an ambush—which I see now was actually a good thing…" The young man looked like he was about to dissolve into hysterical laughter. Adolf knew the feeling well.

"This is Rabbi Adolf," Ilsa said to Brun. "It's okay, you can trust him."

"I know," said Brun, awe calming the fevered look in his eyes. He produced a metal tube from a pouch inside his shirt and gave it to Adolf. "I stole this from the lab I'd been forced to work in for the past two years. It contains a toxin that the Party has been developing—or perhaps perfected. I don't know what part of the process this sample is from. I don't even know for sure what it does.

"But I believe that it is a genetically coded virus, designed to attack only non-Aryans."

"Attack how?" asked Adolf.

"Fatally," said Brun. "That much, at least, I'm sure of. You have to get this back to Finland. It's the only place with the resources to analyze this thing, and God help us, find a cure."

"Do you know anything about the Party's plans for this thing?" asked Adolf. "Timetable? Distribution? Anything?"

Brun shook his head. "Nothing. All I know is

that over the last few weeks, everything's been stepped up. More staff brought in, round the clock shifts, you know what I'm saying?"

Adolf knew what he was saying. They had to get back to Finland *now*.

He left Ilsa to learn whatever else could be gotten from the group, and hurried off to find Thoresten and Rika.

When it was assembled, Adolf found he was leading a different party than the one he left Finland with. Thoresten, Rika, and the silent bodyguard were there, but most of their Polish companions would be staying here—some to work on repairing the bomb, some to train with the Russians. Father Bernardo and Rabbi William would be joining them, as well as Brun and some of his team.

They were packed and provisioned so quickly, Adolf barely had time to say goodbye to Rabbi Sasha.

"Safe journey, Rabbi," Sasha said.

"For you as well, Rabbi," Adolf replied. He wasn't sure, but he thought he detected relief in the other man's face at Adolf's use of the title. "I hope we will meet again, someday. There's still a lot I'd like to discuss."

They embraced, and Adolf hurried after his friends.

They traveled in silence through the thick dark forests. It was only after they had emerged into open meadowlands that Adolf drew Ilsa aside for private conversation, leaving security to the others. "What do you think, so far?" he asked her.

"Hard to say. The Party deliberately starts rumors, just to keep us chasing false leads. But this...? Who knows? I agree we need to get back to

Finland in a hurry. But I'd like to stop at my old base and get Alina first."

"Alina?" Adolf had nearly forgotten about the crazed prophetess he'd met in Poland. Suddenly, she didn't seem so crazed. "She described the plague as yellow locusts. The only people who survived were wearing special survival gear. Brun!" The young scientist hurried over. They were traveling through the rocky gorge of overlapping craters created by an old carpet-bombing campaign. The bleak landscape suited Adolf's mood. "Was anyone working on new types of survival gear, while you were working on the toxin?"

"Possibly. They were bringing in a lot of engineers before I left." He rubbed the several days growth of beard on his chin. "But I don't see why they'd need survival gear, when the toxin's harmless to Aryans."

"Maybe it's for select members of other races," said Adolf. 'Protected Status' was the old term."

"Or maybe just a back up if something went wrong during testing," said Ilsa.

The three fell to pondering in silence. Adolf's instincts told him of Thoresten's approach, and he glanced at the younger man, who, grinning, pointed at William, Bernardo and Gregor walking quietly ahead.

"So a rabbi, a priest and a Russian bodyguard walk into a bar…"

Adolf's smile at Thoresten's joke turned to a look of horror as William, Bernardo and Gregor's bodies danced in death to the sound of submachine guns. Ilsa leapt into the nearest crater, and unslung her Mauser sniper's rifle. Thoresten knocked Adolf down in the crater in which they were standing.

"*Sheisse*!! Now what?" grunted Thoresten.

Adolf raised his head, finding himself fascinated that of the group that been in front, he could only see a worn boot resting against the far side of the crater where their bodies had fallen. He jumped at the crack of Ilsa's rifle.

A fusillade of submachine gun fire pinned down everyone's heads for a minute.

"There! She got one!" Thoresten pointed, grinning. Adolf raised his head, and looked. A gray haired man lay slumped against a tree, his helmet sitting in his lap.

"Adolf! See him?" called Ilsa.

"Yes." Adolf looked about cautiously.

"Look at his hair – he's old!"

"So? You got a *Feldwebel*?"

"No Adolf, I can see his rank – he's just an *Obershutze*!" Adolf jumped again as Ilsa fired her Mauser. Again, the Nazi soldiers tried to pin Ilsa with submachine gun fire.

Shouting over the sound of weapons fire, Thoresten called, "Great Ilsa, so we get killed by grandpa today. How does this make today different?"

"Don't you see – it's a *Volkssturm* unit! Nothing but kids and old men!"

Adolf's stomach turned at the thought of having to kill children in order to escape. If he could just think of another way…"

"How do we get out of here?" Thoresten was asking.

"Crawl." Adolf looked behind him, and saw Rika, several craters closer to the woods they had left, push Brun over a crater lip.

"Won't they shoot us?

"No, those old submachine guns they have don't aim worth a damn. I can keep them pinned down from here."

Adolf and Thoresten turned and followed Ilsa's advise. It was the hardest 100 meters Adolf had traveled, interspersed with hundreds of submachine gun rounds blindly fired over their heads as the Nazis tried to kill Ilsa and her sniper rifle.

"Ilsa! Come!"

Adolf was rewarded by the sight of Ilsa throwing herself over the lip of a crater, and then staying down as the soldiers fired their submachine guns. Grinning, Thoresten pounded Adolf on the back.

"See! She'll make it!"

Ilsa had covered 20 meters and four craters in her retreat back to the woods when the sound of ripping cloth was heard. Instinctively, Adolf and Thoresten looked up towards the sound and then covered their heads. The earth around them heaved as artillery fire exploded. Just as suddenly as it started, it stopped. Adolf pushed Thoresten towards the woods "Go, while their adjusting their aim! I'll cover Ilsa." Thoresten jumped up and in ten seconds was back in the woods.

Adolf surveyed the ground in front of him. Ilsa was nowhere in sight. Just as the ripping cloth sound heralded a new artillery barrage, Adolf saw Ilsa leap into the next crater. Again the earth heaved. Adolf spat out the dust and dirt that he had swallowed. Another pause in the barrage. Adolf jumped up and covered half the distance to the woods.

"Ilsa, hurry!" Adolf turned around as he

jumped down into the crater. Only then did he realize that some of the artillery fire had been smoke, not high explosive rounds. In horror, Adolf watched as Ilsa jumped into a crater and submachine gun fire started up again, this time much closer. Adolf fired blindly into the smoke, but he couldn't see any targets, and he was too far away to aim if he could see something.

Ilsa fired into the smoke, then turned to jump into the next crater when a hand grenade went off and knocked her down. Shapes emerged from the smoke – old men and a couple of boys. Adolf opened fire, but didn't hit anything or anyone. The ground around Adolf exploded with the impact of bullets, forcing him to fall backwards into the next crater.

When Adolf looked up again, he could see two men dragging an unconscious Ilsa back towards the smoke.

"No!" yelled Adolf, as he jumped up to defend Ilsa. The men in front of Adolf all jumped back into the smoke. For a moment, Adolf thought that he had managed to scare them off. Then he stepped forward, and heard the distinctive sound of incoming artillery. Adolf jumped back down into the bottom of the crater. Again the world heaved around him as shell after shell rained down. Each concussion filling Adolf with dread. Realizing that he had emptied his magazine, Adolf patted himself down, hoping to find another one. Instead, he felt the container that the toxin was being carried in.

Adolf knew what his options were: get the toxin back to Finland, or try to rescue Ilsa.

He looked around frantically for someone else to deliver the sample. Just once, he prayed, let me be a husband rather than a rebel leader.

There was no one in sight but the enemy, and precious few seconds to reach the woods.

"Goodbye, Ilsa," Adolf whispered as he clutched the toxin and turned resolutely toward Finland, and the people whose lives depended on him.

Shortly after dawn, Adolf was reunited with Brun, badly injured, but determined to go on, Rika, slightly injured, and Thoresten, untouched, but dangerously close to nervous collapse. Everyone else was dead or captured.

Adolf's initial attempt to hand over the virus and run off after Ilsa was prevented by all three. Without Gregor, Adolf guessed he had a shot at overpowering his friends and running off anyway, but he knew that Ilsa was probably out of the country by now.

His only hope of finding her lay in the intelligence now being gathered back—like everything else, it seemed—in Finland.

So onward to Finland he traveled.

CHAPTER 28

Adolf remembered little of the days that followed. Rika and Thoresten guided his steps, forced him to lie down at night—although they couldn't make him sleep—and kept him under close watch. Other than that, they could do little and they both knew it.

"They were married?" Brun asked.

"Yes," said Thoresten. "But please don't use the past tense just yet."

"Sorry," said the scientist. "It's just that in my cell, we don't let couples go on missions together."

Thoresten backed down. "Ours, too—usually. But Adolf and Ilsa aren't your average couple."

"So I noticed."

"I hope someday he can see just how much he accomplished." Rika glanced toward Adolf, who walked a few steps behind.

"Accomplished?" Adolf echoed. "And please don't talk about me like I'm not here. I'm *depressed*, not deaf. And I didn't accomplish a damn thing in Russia, except for getting this toxin, which could very well be a false alarm." His expression told them that it better not be a false alarm, considering the cost.

"You got the surviving delegates to start thinking about grabbing the broadcast network, and a code that will get everyone to rise up at once. More importantly, you got them thinking about what kind of government they wanted after we won. Using Judaism as the basis for a constitution was pure gold, Adolf."

"So what? No one listened."

"No, but they heard."

Adolf wasn't sure he knew what the difference was. He wasn't sure he cared. All he could care about now was the fact that he had abandoned Ilsa to the enemy so he could return to Finland with the toxin. And if this heroic gesture somehow turned into a bad joke, he was going to...

What? What could he really do? Kill someone? Sure, but who? Himself was the most obvious target. But that wouldn't do anyone any good, and would be an insult to all the people—both living and dead—who'd believed in Adolf and the message he carried. Ilsa, most of all.

He just wished he knew which group she was in right now.

They slipped back into Party controlled territory with relative ease, albeit a lot of anxiety, just north of the bomb crater that had once been Leningrad. South along the coast, they waited to board one of the few ships still available to common people. Adolf would have preferred a secret crossing in a smuggler's boat. Despite their impeccably forged documents, he was always nervous facing officials. He became more nervous when he saw how agitated the soldiers at the harbor were.

Fortunately, they were passed without comment, and after the usual nerve wracking wait, they sailed on the good ship Von Hindenburg. Adolf noticed fewer soldiers than usual on the transport, and took it as a good sign.

"Let's all try to get some sleep, Rika suggested, leading them below decks to the scanty accommodations, consisting of a flat wooden surface covered with snoring bodies.

"Ah, yes," said Thoresten. "The lovely smells of proletariat travel. Machine oil, fish and unwashed bodies."

"You should talk," said Rika.

Adolf left them to their banter and went back to the deck. There, the fresh sea air and the rocking of the ship calmed him more than sleep would have done.

They reached Finnish waters later that day. Suddenly, Adolf was seized by a vision of bloated bodies, their faces twisted in agony. There were thousands of them. The stench of rotting meat invaded his nostrils. Then it was gone. Adolf sagged against the ship's rail, gagging. Anyone who saw him passed it off as a late bout of sea sickness, and left him alone.

What's happening to me? Adolf wondered. *If this keeps up, I'll be just like Alina.* For the first time, he felt genuine empathy for the girl, and began to regret not following Ilsa's wishes and returning to her base in Poland for her.

But that would have taken too long. All Adolf wanted to do now was get the toxin to the Finnish base, learn all he could from Eikki on Ilsa's possible whereabouts, and go after her.

Alina could take care of herself.

When the others joined Adolf on the deck, he said nothing of his vision. They docked in Helsinki a short time later. This time, they were overwhelmed by a military presence. It was hours before they could disembark, and only then to the sound of frightening words from a jackbooted soldier: "A state of martial law now exists."

"How does a military dictatorship declare martial law?" whispered Thoresten. "Isn't that kind of redundant?"

Rumors flew, but no official explanation was given. Only the usual double talk of danger from crazed dissidents and the *Führer's* great concern for the welfare of his people. Cooperation would be greatly appreciated, they were told.

It took them days to reach base, by which time they had heard so many rumors, Thoresten joked that they'd never believe the truth when they finally heard it.

Yet when they reached the hidden base, all was as they had left it. Only the strangely subdued excitement emanating from the people in the cave was different.

"What's happened?" Adolf shouted as they joined the group that surrounded Eikki and his radio.

Seppi looked up from a pile of messages, a strange glow in his craggy, careworn face. "The greatest single blow ever struck against the *Reich*, that's what's happened! Someone got inside the three largest meat packing plants in Germany, and poisoned the pork. No other meat was touched. But over half that pork was destined for military bases."

"It is believed," Eikki said, slowly removing his headphones, "that twenty five percent of the active duty infantry is dead or dying. The civilian death toll is estimated in the tens of thousands."

CHAPTER 29

Adolf watched the activity around him as if across a great void.

"We've all been waiting for a sign," said Luisa. "A signal for all to rise up and bring down the *Reich*. Do you think this is it?"

"It's too soon," said Thoresten, pacing nervously. "At the conference we never finalized any plans—"

"The *Führer's* left his summer palace because of the poisonings," said Rika. "So that blows Marla's plan. No pun intended."

"That's assuming her new buddies care about little details like who they actually kill," said Thoresten.

"That's also assuming they get the thing fixed and loaded at all."

"If only we could have agreed on a date and signal for the general uprising!" wailed Thoresten.

"This is so frustrating!" said Rika. "It's like dancing on the edge of a sword! We don't know which way to jump, but we have to jump some way-- and soon."

"Multiply that by a hundred million people, and you've got the state of the world today," said Eikki. "Most of the groups are afraid to move, but dozens of hotheads have already gone out and done something stupid. Most of them will be dead soon. Or worse."

"Anyone who could pull off something like

this would surely have a plan for the rest of us," said Luisa. "I'm sure we'll be hearing from Ilsa soon."

"We don't know she did it!" Adolf turned on Luisa with such ferocity she ran away from him. Everyone was staring, but for once, Adolf didn't care. "Thousands of rebels heard her advocating a kosher diet! Any lunatic could have—"

"You act like it's something to be ashamed of, Adolf," said Eikki. "Whoever did this is a hero. Ilsa's your wife. Aren't you hoping she's the one?"

Rika quickly stepped forward to explain to everyone about Ilsa's capture; about the toxin and all the other recent news. Adolf curtly ordered one of the children to lead Brun to the scientists with the toxin that he himself had carried all the way from Russia. He found he wasn't interested in talking with the scientists, or watching them analyze the sample. He didn't even care now what the results were.

Adolf turned his back on all of them. He fled the cavern and into the tunnels. As he left he heard Eikki reporting, "Latest tally puts the death toll at two hundred thousand. Almost ninety percent of them, German."

"That's wonderful!" someone said.

"Now if she could just get the rest of them."

Adolf kept moving, the voices ringing in his head. *Ilsa is German,* he wanted to say. *I am German. Millions of people too young to know what's happening are German. Lots of dead people whose opinions were never asked were German!*

But nobody wanted to hear that. And probably wouldn't understand it anyway.

Fresh cool air blew in his face, ruffling the straggly new beard that was coming in and tousling his blond hair. Adolf stood in the rocky dell that hid the opening to the base, and offered refuge to a man who wanted to think.

He climbed one of the rocky outcroppings and gazed at the Finnish landscape. Gray fog shrouded the nearest mountains, matching Adolf's mood. Far below, a slash of green told of a fertile valley. Adolf stood, gazing into the cold mist, feeling again the sense of mystery; of the unknown waiting to be made known. Like the *Judenmuseum*.

Two hundred thousand dead. And more to join them soon, if he was any judge of how mass murder went in the *Reich*. And if he understood nothing else, Adolf understood that.

There would be those whose superior Aryan constitution would keep them alive and in agony for a few more days. Then they would add their numbers to Eikki's' tally. There would be those who might be saved, but lacked the Medical Priority Points to receive adequate care in the current state of crisis. There would be those who would have to die for this unspeakable crime—whether or not they had anything to do with it. And, if this brilliant poisoner had concocted something new; something the doctors had never seen, there would be yet one more group of deaths: those used in the experiments to learn more about this poison and find an antidote.

Oh, yes. There was much cause for rejoicing today.

And Adolf wished he could stay there, among the dead of his vision, rather than follow his thoughts to the next obvious subject.

Was this Ilsa's work? Was she even alive? Something in his gut told him she was. And it would be easy enough to tell himself that Ilsa had been with him the whole time for the past four months, and therefore couldn't have been responsible for this latest sabotage.

Except for those few days before they left for Russia. Those secret "things" she had to do, that she never told Adolf about. Could poisoning a few pork processing plants been on her list?

She had, after all, brought up the idea back in Poland, while they lay together in bed.

"Adolf?"

He jumped, and then settled down as Rika came into view. "I'm sorry about what they were saying back there. About how great it was that most of the dead are German."

"Not your fault."

"They didn't mean it—"

"Yes they did."

"What I mean is, no one here forgets that you're German. And so are plenty of other people in this movement."

Adolf shrugged. "Hate begets hate. I can't blame them for being human."

"Then what are you?" asked Rika.

"Come again?" He had a headache, and wished Rika would just leave him alone.

"What are you that you never give in to hate, even while you forgive it in others? What are you that you can grieve for the dead, yet sympathize with the killers? How do you keep on preaching and teaching, day after day, and never want to strangle us when we still don't get it?"

"Who says I never want to strangle you?"

"But you never do it. And now you're worried

that the woman you love has—on a rather large scale."

"I'd rather not discuss that right now." At
least, not with Rika. Adolf wished Karl was here; he
was the only other person here who'd known Ilsa in
the old days. But Karl had taken off with a couple of
equally unreliable young men while Adolf was gone.

"I'm sorry," said Rika. "It's just I…you
should know…we need you Adolf. Not just the
revolution. The whole damned world! And if we
manage to defeat the *Reich*, then we'll need you even
more. But we need the person who poisoned that pork
too! Without…that person, there won't be a new
government. And without you, whatever new
government we get will turn out just as bad as the old
one."

Adolf thought about that, just as the fog
around them began to lift, showing that light still
lived, even when it couldn't be seen.

"Rabbi Adolf!" The shout seemed far away.
Then they heard the voice again, and a little girl came
running up.

"Mina, what is it?" asked Rika, collecting the
shaking bundle of rags into her arms.

"Rabbi, you have to come! Karl came back,
but without my brother or Jules. He said he had a
message for you. Seppi told me to find you, but…"

"But what, *liebling*?" said Adolf.

"But when I left, Seppi was crying."

"Stay here, Rika," said Adolf. "Keep Mina
with you, and don't move until I come for you. If I
don't come by nightfall, find a place to hide,
then…just go. Whatever you do, don't go back
into the cave." Rika only nodded, bleak acceptance in
her face.

Then for a moment, Adolf just stood there. He desperately wished he was wearing a coat, just so he could take it off and give it to Rika. *Trying to leave something of yourself behind, or just being chivalrous to the end?* an annoying inner voice mocked.

He went back to the main cavern, feeling strangely calm.

Karl was there. He wore a new jacket and gloves, but at least they weren't military issue. If Adolf saw him in a uniform, he knew he would most likely grab a gun from someone and shoot Karl before he had a chance to speak.

"Adolf? I...I wish they'd grabbed someone else, but I'm sorry. I have a message for you." Karl held a worn leather briefcase in his gloved hands. Adolf looked into his eyes, expecting smugness; perhaps a gleam of triumph. To his surprise, the self-absorbed arrogance he'd seen there just a few months ago was gone. Karl seemed uncertain, even afraid.

Adolf nodded. "Of course. But first things first." He punched Karl in the jaw, aiming for the same place Karl had once hit Adolf.

He took Karl completely off guard, sending him sprawling across the floor. To Adolf's chagrin, it didn't make him feel any better. In fact, about the only thing he felt was the pain in his knuckles.

"Adolf, please!" Karl was on his feet in an instant, arms up to ward off further blows. When Adolf made no move towards him, Karl lowered his hands and rubbed his jaw. "Look, I know what you're thinking, but I didn't sell you out! Jules thought it would be a good time to 'forage' supplies, what with all the chaos. Jacco and I thought we could drum up some business—"

"What kind of 'business'?"

"My second line of work; the one between government lackey and rebel soldier. Forgery. I thought, with things so crazy, and official attention elsewhere, there might be a market for official looking documents.

"Okay it was stupid! We should have stayed here! We all got picked up. I got I.D.'d."

"And you gave them us!"

"Not them!" Karl swept a hand to indicate the dozens of freedom fighters watching in silence. "Just you! You're the only one they want."

"Oh, and naturally, if I just turn myself in, they'll leave this place untouched."

"As a matter of fact, yes."

Adolf laughed.

"I'm serious! Look, they didn't have the manpower to take this place before. You think they've got it now?" Karl opened the briefcase, and drew out some papers. "They put everything in writing and told me to let you read it. I guess they didn't trust me to deliver a simple message."

"Poor Karl. Underrated again. It's the story of your life."

"Just read the damned thing! I don't expect my opinion to count for much just now, but I'll give it to you anyway when you're finished. They're not telling you everything."

"What a surprise." Adolf picked up the first sheet, crisp with the official stamp of the Department of Political Security, and read it. For a while, Karl and the others ceased to exist.

The message was simple enough. Within three

days, Adolf was to report to the *Waffen SS* base in Helsinki, and offer his complete cooperation in rectifying the current difficulties faced by the *Reich*. *That probably means the revolution,* thought Adolf. If he did so, the writing promised, his family would be freed from their current accommodations at Heidelberg prison. More than that, they would be restored to their previous position and rank.

If Adolf failed to cooperate, they would all be shot in four days. Any stoic calm he might have regained by telling himself they were already dead was dispelled by the photographs included with the letter. There were four in all, beginning with one taken during Adolf's last visit home. Leisl had just gotten her hair styled to look like Lottie von Tripp's character in her latest movie. Kurt was wearing his uniform with its gold *Hitlerjugend* badge. Even his mother's expensive new designer peasant dress was one Adolf recognized.

The next three pictures were all taken since his flight. Adolf, who had learned a great deal about the deceptive uses of technology, knew in his gut the pictures were genuine.

Leisl's bright eyes had dulled, and her beautiful face was thin and pinched with worry, but it was still her. Adolf thought his mother had aged twenty years in the last three. The drab gray prison garb hung loosely on her gaunt frame. His father, on the other hand seemed to hardly have changed at all, other than to look older and meaner. Frieda had had another baby since he was last home, but their father was not in the picture. Something was wrong with Marta, her eyes vacant and staring.

If these pictures were meant to break Adolf's

heart, they succeeded.

The ultimatum ended with a promise not to interfere with those residing at the base. If, however, Adolf chose not to comply, a *Götterdämmerung* bomb would be dropped on this mountain to pacify the entire area, as it was too difficult to reach any other way.

Exactly how Adolf was supposed to save the *Reich* from the unwashed hordes wasn't made clear, but phrases like "returning to the Fatherland", "setting a good example for other misguided youth" and "extraordinary influence over lesser minds" gave some clues.

Adolf carefully returned the contents to the briefcase, and gave it back to Karl. "You said you would give me your opinion whether I wanted it or not. I find I want it."

"You're sure?" Karl looked like a man expecting an attack, but unsure from which direction to expect it.

"Maybe not. But I sure as hell don't know what they're talking about. Any idea what they think I can do?"

"They think that you can single handedly stop the revolution in its tracks."

Adolf couldn't help it. He laughed. He tried to stop, but the more the absurdity of it all played across his mind, the more he laughed. Karl waited with surprising patience, and even offered Adolf a hand up when the fit of laughter finally passed, leaving him exhausted on the floor of the cave.

"Why are you heroes always so damned self deprecating?" Karl asked. "You walk around on a goddamned magic cloud, then when

someone asks you to do something, you get this
look of pious innocence and say, 'who me?'"

"Yeah, I'm a real hero," said Adolf. "Just
ask Ilsa."

"Well, like it or not, the Party experts have
decided that you and you alone have the influence,
charisma and power of speech to convince the world
that Judaism is just a silly cult whose time is past—for
the second time, I suppose—and that the revolution is
a bad idea. And, they believe, that if you promise the
people better times ahead, and immediate easing of
their sufferings, they will believe you."

"And why, pray tell, do they believe that I
would ever even attempt such a thing? Not that it
would work if I did! But do they think I believe for
one minute I could really save my family? That I
didn't already bury them, like all the others in my
same position?"

"The problem is, Adolf, that there have been
way too many people in your position. I'm not talking
about me; when I went outlaw, I doubt they
particularly noticed.

"But you! You're everything Hitler dreamed
of: the handsome, blond, Aryan superman; a natural
leader; an I.Q. that's off the charts. But they were
counting on you to use your gifts for *them,* not their
enemies! This entire generation, it seems, has turned
against the *Reich.*"

"Maybe they should take that as, I don't
know, a *hint,* or something, and change what they're
doing! Anyway, I can't let them use me like that,
even if I wanted to! Besides, last I heard, I was dead!"

"So what? That sort of status changes every
day in the *Reich*! And coming back from the dead

will only increase your popularity with the masses.

"But…there's something else you should know." Something in Karl's voice made the hairs rise on the back of Adolf's neck. "When I was working for the government, I saw something I wasn't supposed to. Come to think of it, this is probably one secret they *wanted* to leak out. It was just a draft of an emergency plan for if the *Reich* were ever to be defeated. At that time, of course, I didn't take it seriously. I doubt anyone else did either."

"Karl, I'm sorry, but I don't have a lot of time just now."

"Got five seconds? The name says it all. 'Scorched Earth.'"

"Yeah, and what the hell is that supposed to…oh. *Sheisse.*"

"You got it. From the original dream of Hitler himself. If the Aryan Superman cannot maintain his supremacy over the earth, it would be better to end it all, here and now, rather than—"

"Forget the rhetoric! Just tell me one thing: Can they do it?"

"You have to ask?"

Adolf suddenly thought of what he had brought to the base—was it just this morning? All at once, he knew with terrible certainty what the rebel scientists would find when they analyzed it.

"That new toxin," he said at last. "It doesn't distinguish between Aryan and non-Aryan, does it? It just kills. Everyone."

"Afraid so," said Karl. "Quick and painless— at least I'm sure it's supposed to be. It probably won't even kill animals or plants. Our current *Führer* is such a nature lover, you know. Almost as much as the first one."

Adolf shook his head. "It's more than that. He'll want it all left behind. Animals, plants, buildings, monuments. Like some giant mausoleum to be discovered by whoever someday visits from outer space, or else evolves down here."

"So it's not just you're love for your family they're counting on. It's a basic choice between life and death for the human race."

Adolf nodded. Then he put on his coat and went to the food caches in the back of the cave. He stuffed bread into his pocket, and found a full canteen of water.

"Where are you going?" asked Karl.

"To the desert. Isn't that what all the other so called heroes used to do at times like this?"

"But—"

"I'll be back in three days. German punctuality is probably the only thing I can still count on.

He stopped only to send Rika and Mina back inside. Then he headed north, toward the wastes of what had once been called Lapland.

It was the closest thing to desert he could find up here.

Book IV

CHAPTER 30

"'And the Lord spoke unto Moses in the wilderness of Sinai…'" Adolf looked up from the book to the starry northern sky, and said, "Well, that's good. Now, would You mind speaking to me? I'm sort of in the wilderness too right now, and I could really use some help."

He waited, but no answer came to him across the desolate hills. He continued to wait, not knowing what else to do. At sunrise, he would have to decide: either begin the journey to Helsinki and the agents who awaited him there, or flee. Again.

Adolf kept the *Torah* open to the Book of Numbers, although it was too dark to read. No matter; he had memorized it all long ago. That fact came as a surprise to him, as he sat alone for the first time in longer than he could remember, and tried to make sense of it all.

"How did I get here? Can You at least tell me that?

"It started as a game; I know that. But does that mean that it couldn't turn into something real?"

It *had* turned into something real. Adolf didn't need a burning bush or a voice from on high to tell him that. The religion of a dead race, deemed inferior by those who had conquered a world, had returned to the world of the living. Perhaps it had begun as just a pastime for rebellious rich kids, but somewhere along the line, seeds were planted, and had taken root.

"Just call me *Herr* Fertile Soil," sighed Adolf. "Somewhere along the way, I started believing in You. And right now, I'd really like for You to believe in me. Tell me what to do. You know I'll gladly give my life for this world and for Your covenant—because I believe the two are connected, and will always be, if we can get through this current crisis. But I don't know how to make that happen."

He stretched out on the gentle hillside, his arms forming a pillow beneath his head, his coat spread over him like a blanket. The stars were so beautiful, the night so peaceful. There must be a message here somewhere.

But if there was, it was beyond Adolf's power to decode.

"Of course, there's always the possibility that I've simply gone insane," Adolf said to the sky. "I'm sure that's what my father is saying. If I'm lucky, I can even convince our Illustrious Leaders, when they bring me in. Then I'll just get a little brain washing, rather than full-scale torture.

"Of course, if I really am crazy, then so are the thousands of other former rich kids and educated men and women in this movement. And the tens of thousands of illiterate poor, who've given their life to this cause—and their faith to You. If You're even there."

Adolf found a surprising amount of comfort in the knowledge that the faith he had embraced was shared by so many. "We can't all be crazy, can we?"

He closed his eyes, trying to imagine giving himself up. Renouncing the cause; naming hundreds of courageous friends as "traitors" and "dangerous agitators". Declaring everything he learned in the *Judenmuseum* to be a lie.

He couldn't do it.

But to run again?

He was too tired.

"How long have I been on the run?" Adolf asked the sky. That, at least, he could figure out without divine intervention. He had fled Berlin in April of 2004. Now it was August, 2007. "Three years, four months. Hey! That's forty months! You're really fixated on the number forty, aren't You? Is this supposed to be a message or a joke?"

Adolf tried to pray some more, but found he had run out of words. Toward dawn, he dozed. Now, thoughts came easier and feelings found names. For so long, Adolf had been living in his mind; thinking, planning, trying to outguess the enemy, wondering if every face he met *was* the enemy.

Now, for the first time in far too long, Adolf could remember what it was he had first loved about Judaism; about this god with no name, whose face no living man could bear to look upon.

He remembered the loneliness. Not just his own, but what he imagined must have been felt by an entire people who were despised by everyone around them, condemned to wander without a home, yet at home anywhere on the earth, because God was there.

He remembered Ilsa polishing the brass *menorah*, that the people who made it and all they stood for would not be forgotten. And the message of

Hanukkah: the light of hope shines through even the darkest of nights.

The simple message of equality between all people; the idea that everyone should treat others as they would wish to be treated. Adolf felt again the longing to live in such a world.

As he slid deeper into sleep, Adolf could hear the psalms of David, and imagine the soul of the man who could write such words. "There's a guy who screwed up even more times than I have. Maybe not on so big a scale, though."

But David found strength in his faith. No matter that his own courage faltered sometimes; that his power to do the right thing lapsed more than once. He always found his way back to God.

But what did God think of you? Adolf asked David in his dream. *Did he love you throughout it all? Did he forgive your affair with Bathsheba and your murder of her husband? Did He give you the strength to forgive yourself when you killed your own son Absalom? When you acted like a madman and a tyrant, could He still see inside you the gentle shepherd boy who used to write love songs to Him?*

And David answered, "Yes."

Perhaps if Adolf had awoken then, he too, could have kept his fragile faith. But his dreams darkened, until he found himself gasping for air in a cattle car crammed with frightened people. He saw the souls that flew from the broken bodies of men and women as all they were was reduced to ashes in the ovens. He smelled the stench of death and injustice on a scale the world had never before known.

And he awoke knowing that the blood in his veins was the same as in those who helped create that holocaust.

     The sky was growing light in the east.
Adolf felt the weight that he had come here hoping to
lift, crash down on him again. How had he ever
imagined that God would speak to him; that answers
could be found in the last moment before all was lost?

     "I guess the final proof that You never existed
lies in the deaths of all those people." Adolf stood
wearily and wrapped his coat tightly around himself.
"What kind of god stands by and does nothing when
something like that happens? If You lacked the power
to save them, then You're incompetent. If You had
the power but didn't use it, You're a worse monster
than Hitler. Either way, I've got nothing left to build
from."

     But nothing left to lose, either.

     Going home suddenly seemed like the simplest
thing to do. Maybe it was that faint hope that he could
still save his family.

     "Or maybe," he said as he began the long walk
south, "I'd simply rather die where I was born than in
some ditch in a foreign country."

     Adolf reached the base at the appointed time.
Before he had time to identify the threat, four guards
were on him, stuffing him into an airplane. But they
didn't hurt him, nor anyone else that he could see.

     Moments later, they were airborne.

CHAPTER 31

Adolf had never traveled by air before. Few civilians did; children almost never. With his family, he had toured Europe in luxury train compartments and private automobiles. Air travel had always been restricted to the military. This plane was luxurious enough to convince Adolf it was some high-ranking officer's personal transport. There were no passengers besides Adolf and his six guards.

The windows, though bulletproof, were transparent and Adolf enjoyed the sight of the world in miniature, passing beneath him. Rivers, lakes, forests and farmlands all looked like some exquisite toy, perfect and eternal. There was comfort in that.

Then they flew low over a city, and Adolf could see the decay and the want; the pathetic stream of refugees leaving only with what they could carry.

"Where are we?" he asked the nearest guard. "What's happened down there?"

"I'm sorry, *mein Herr*," said the guard. "We have strict orders not to engage you in any conversation."

"Oh. Well, thank you for explaining that." Adolf continued his surveillance of the world his family had helped conquer.

Despite the Party's boast that no atomic weapons had ever been used on European soil, much of the countryside looked sick. Worldwide pollution was taking its toll even here. Some places were pock marked by craters from more conventional bombs.

Others bore the mark of fire; terrorist explosions and Party reprisals. Adolf began to wonder how much longer the *Reich* would have a world to rule.

He was grateful to be left in peace. Guards politely offered him food and drink, which he equally politely declined. Late in the afternoon, they arrived in Berlin.

At once, the pace of things picked up. The next set of guards were less distant and deferential, but still not directly hostile. He was subjected to a degrading physical exam, where doctors probed his every orifice for weapons, bombs, poisons and signaling devices, but even that was done matter of factly without questions or insults.

Next, they hustled him through a hot shower and into a beautifully tailored dress uniform of the *Volkssturm*. Adolf was impressed to see his rank was that of captain.

A skilled barber left him pink cheeked, with hair even blonder than before, and styled in the latest fashion: wavy bangs and a sleek braided tail in the back. "Good thing I've been wearing it long, huh?"

The barber smiled cordially, but said nothing.

Just when he was beginning to wonder if they hadn't mixed up his file with the latest movie heartthrob, Adolf was taken to an office whose door bore the standard Party medical insignia and the name Dr. Siegfried von Dymler, Chief Psychologist, *SS.*

His guards ushered him in, then left, closing the door behind them. Adolf looked around. He stood in a lavishly appointed office. Against one wall a silver tea service sat on an antique wooden table. Beside the tea service was a tray of tiny lemon cakes trimmed with slices of real lemon. Adolf's mouth

watered at the sight of them. Crossed cavalry sabers
hung on the wall, beside a landscape painting. On
closer inspection, Adolf saw that it was an original
Hitler watercolor.

Against the opposite wall was an array of state
of the art surveillance equipment. Computers, unlike
anything Adolf had ever seen, winked and chirped.

Between the two discordant room halves, *Herr*
Doctor Von Dymler sat behind an antique oak desk.
Adolf guessed the psychologist was in his fifties, thick
around the middle, but in good physical shape. His
rich mane of brown hair, graying at the temples had
clearly never felt the touch of bleach. Adolf stood at
attention while the doctor read from a file that lay
open on his desk.

Von Dymler looked up with a warm smile.
"Adolf! I'm so glad to finally meet you in person.
Please, sit down." He indicated a winged leather chair
opposite the desk.

Adolf sat, resisting the desire to relax into the
chair's soft embrace. He sat at attention, wondering if
it was the uniform that made him do it.

When the doctor said nothing more, Adolf
leaned forward to peer at the file. "Do I make
interesting reading material, *Herr* Doctor?"

"I find you fascinating." Von Dymler closed
the file. "I have been studying your case ever since
you left Berlin. I've written dozens of papers on you.
And I am hoping that, together, we can pull our world
back from the brink."

Adolf glanced around nervously.

"Quit looking for torture devices; you won't
find any. I've always believed them to be inefficient
anyway."

"Drugs, then? I mean no disrespect, *Herr* Doctor, but if you know me as well as you think you do, then you know I am committed to the downfall of this government and all it represents. Surely you know, at least I hope, that my heart cannot be turned from that purpose."

"Fortunately, your heart requires no change, Adolf. Only your misguided actions. And that is easily remedied. If you would stop for a moment and listen, you would see that your goals and ours are the same."

"This should be interesting," Adolf murmured.

If Von Dymler heard, he gave no sign. He got up and went to the tea service, and poured two cups. "American tea," he told Adolf proudly. "As clean as you'll find anywhere."

Adolf made no move to stand.

"Go ahead," said the doctor. "Choose either cup. If the tea is drugged, I obviously won't drink. If there were poison in one of the cups, I wouldn't let you choose." He helped himself to a cake and ate with great relish, while Adolf considered the situation.

Finally he shrugged and got up. He was going to have to eat eventually. He might as well enjoy one of his favorite confections. Adolf went to the table and chose a cup of tea, drinking only after Von Dymler drank from the other. Then he ate a cake. It was so delicious that he ate another, and then two more, barely restraining himself from finishing off the entire plate.

"Now that we're finished with that little dance of trust," said Von Dymler, "Let's sit down and talk."

They returned to their chairs. "The world, Adolf, is in serious trouble. Can we at least agree on that?"

"Sure," said Adolf.

"It wasn't supposed to turn out like this. You know it and I know it. But the principles on which our government is based, the natural superiority by which our race conquered a planet—those things are still sound. To save the world we need someone who can rally the people behind those beliefs, and then, help us rid ourselves of the corruption and mistakes that perverted those dreams, and brought us to where we are now."

"But why tell me this?" Adolf was genuinely puzzled. "You know I'm not that person."

"But you are!" Von Dymler radiated a certainty that Adolf found nearly as compelling as the cause he had been fighting for all these years. "All that is good in us, Adolf, all that the First *Führer* dreamed of when He began His mission, has reached its pinnacle in you!"

The doctor opened one of the many files that sat neatly on his desk. "Champion of the poor and oppressed. Zealous seeker of justice and truth. Incorruptible. Ready at any moment to sacrifice his life for what he believes in—or the life of a single child he's never laid eyes on.

"Who am I describing, Adolf? You? Or a Teutonic knight out of the Middle Ages? Is it possible they are one and the same?"

Flattery and manipulation, Adolf thought. But it was much nicer than threats and insults…

"You've always wanted to be a hero, haven't you? Known in your heart it was your destiny? Then, along came your father. Cold. Tyrannical. Always telling you you're wrong; unfit; a failure. Is it any

wonder your destiny was twisted in the wrong
direction?

"He made you believe you could never
become that hero in the real world. So you turned to
fantasy. And guess what? All the suffering of all
those desperate people out there made them—and
you—the willing targets of something called 'mass
hysteria'.

"You believed that the only way to save the
world was to bring it down and replace it with
something better. The role was right there. All you
had to do was step into it. And you did a masterful
job, Adolf. Nothing less than I would expect from a
true son of the *Reich*."

"Last time I checked, the word for what I did
was *treason*," said Adolf. He knew he could see right
through Von Dymler's line of manipulation if he just
looked hard enough. But it was hard to see past the
man's charisma.

"Your actions have been wrong; terribly
wrong. But you could no more be a traitor to your
people than I could grow a third arm." For a terrible
moment, Adolf ached to believe him.

"Are you saying, then, that after you shoot
me, I'll be buried with full honors? In my family
mausoleum?"

Von Dymler's laugh was deep and rich. "If it
comes to that, yes. I give you my word. But I'm
hoping we won't have to shoot you. Or your family.
Or any of the thousands of other fine young people
who've fallen under your spell."

"What exactly do you want from me?" Adolf
was more than curious. He was exasperated.

"We want you to make a network broadcast.

Live, to everyone in the world. Tell them this
rebellion was a mistake. Show them that the answers
can be found here, in traditional Aryan wisdom, not
crackpot religions or vanished races. Get the people
back behind our leaders and back into their appointed
places. Then we can start to heal the wounds."

Adolf tried to speak. *So much for my brilliant
oratory skills.* "Even," he croaked, and then took a
deep breath. "Even if I agreed to do such a thing,
surely you know it wouldn't work. There are millions
of people out there ready to die for this cause, and
hundreds of leaders more powerful than me! All
they'll see on the screen is a traitor who broke under
torture. Some will curse me; some will pity me. But
all of them will forget about me and go on with the
fight."

Von Dymler smiled. "I had forgotten about
your famous modesty. It really is one of your most
charming traits. Probably because it's genuine. You
honestly don't know your true worth.

"Adolf, I've made a career out of studying the
players in this rebellion. So have most of the other
great minds in the *Reich*. Everyone agrees that you
are the key; the lynchpin. If you speak to the masses,
they will listen. If you tell them to do something, they
will do it. If you lead them away from this senseless
death and destruction, they will follow."

"So I can lead them off a cliff or into slavery.
What a comforting thought."

"If you choose to see it that way. But I
believe; have, in fact, staked my reputation on the
belief, that once you've had a chance to think about it,
you'll understand why you must do it. And then
you'll do it, not because we've forced you, but

because it's the only choice."

"What about my father?" asked Adolf. "You seem to be painting him as the villain in this whole tragic affair. If I cooperate with you, won't I be signing his death warrant?"

"Not at all. Your father is a brilliant man, with many useful skills. And his loyalty to the Party is above question. It's only in parenting that he's a failure. Once you make the broadcast, and your family is restored to power, the only change in *Herr* Goebbels' life will be raising no more children." The doctor's mouth pursed, as if tasting something sour. "From what I've observed of Helmut, he won't count it as much of a loss."

Adolf thought again of his family. Would they ever forgive him for wrecking their lives? Could he ever make it up to them? Suddenly, he needed to know. Needed to see them one more time, to try to explain.

"I'd be willing to take a look at the speech you've prepared for me," Adolf said, trying to sound strong and detached.

Von Dymler grinned. "I should have known you'd say that. Still believe you're just a pawn in a fancy suit, eh Adolf? There is no speech. My research has proven that any script we give you would be worthless. The words have to be yours, Adolf. Anything else, the people would see right through."

Adolf shook his head. "This is all a lot to take in."

"I understand. Take some time to think about it. The broadcast is set for noon tomorrow. Sleep on it if you like.

"Oh, I have to warn you. The broadcast will

be time delayed about ten seconds. That means that if you decide on some kind of noble suicide, like shouting 'Arise now!', they'll shoot you dead, and no one out there will hear a thing." Von Dymler looked genuinely troubled. "I'd really hate to see it come to that, Adolf."

"So would I," said Adolf.

"So in the end, we really do agree on the important things." The doctor stood and walked Adolf to the door.

"Take him to his cell," he told the guard who opened it in response to his knock.

"*Herr* Goebbels is to have one more interview," said the guard.

Adolf sensed a sudden tension in the air. Von Dymler scowled. "I was assured that would not take place! I have repeatedly warned the committee that such a confrontation could be extremely detrimental—"

"And I have my orders, *Herr* Doctor. And you know where they come from."

Von Dymler stopped, was about to speak again, then disappeared from view as Adolf was hustled down the hall—this time by eight guards—and through a maze of corridors and tunnels whose musty smell and dim lighting suggested rarely used underground passageways. Then they were in an elevator going up. For all Adolf knew, that could have walked halfway across Berlin by now.

Once out of the elevator, they were joined by more guards, who escorted Adolf down a hallway bristling with surveillance equipment. No one spoke. As the resonance of over two dozen goose-stepping boots echoed down the hall, Adolf became aware that he was marching in time with the soldiers. Some habits were hard to break.

Outside a heavily guarded door, Adolf was again strip searched, this time with the help of some kind of portable x-ray device. When all was pronounced in order, a senior guard punched a fourteen-digit code into a keypad next to the door. With great ceremony, the door swung open, and Adolf was ushered inside.

For a moment, he could see nothing in the dim light. He was aware only of the music in the background—Wagner—and a variety of smells. Water and soap and something floral. Incense, was Adolf's next thought. No, he realized. Opium. And beneath it all was the sickly sweet stench of decaying flesh. And something more.

His eyes began to adjust. In the gloom of the richly appointed chamber, an old man was seated in a luxurious marble bathtub. He was wearing dark glasses, despite the soft lighting, but nothing else. The tub was an antique, and not attached to any fixtures, as the room was an office, not a bathroom.

On the far wall, six ornately framed paintings hung, barely visible in the shadows. The largest, resting above the others, was of Adolf Hitler, the First *Führer*. Below it, and each about half its size were paintings of each successive *Führer*. Hermann Göring, who reigned for just three years, then died in 1962. Baldur von Schirach, the third *Führer*, ruled the *Reich* for twenty-seven years, and created the first dynasty when his son, Adolf, became the fourth *Führer* in 1989. But the second Von Schirach died just five years later. In the thirteen years since, the fifth and sixth *Führers* had ruled, died and been immortalized on this wall.

And in the bathtub, sat Himmler Hanover. The Seventh *Führer* of the Third *Reich*.

"Young Goebbels?" asked a shill voice. "Step closer. Let me have a look at you."

Guards trailing, Adolf approached the bathtub. The *Führer* removed his glasses and peered at Adolf with swiftly contracting pupils in eyes set in decaying flesh. Putrid sores covered his entire body. A strong medicinal smell arose from the water, but not enough to cover the stench of the body within it.

Leprosy? Adolf wondered. But it felt like something even more sinister.

Hanover lifted a beautifully carved ivory pipe to his lips. "So you are the man who thought he could bring me down?" he said.

"It doesn't appear that you need my help for that, *Herr Führer*," Adolf said softly.

All around him, guards stiffened. Some twitched, eager to reach for side arms, but no one here would do a thing without a direct order from their *Führer*. These men were fanatics, chosen for their loyalty.

Hanover laughed. "They told me you were like that! That is why I insisted on meeting you for myself. So many stories." He sighed. "Some accounts place you at twelve feet tall. Others say you sold your soul for a voice that would ensnare anyone who heard you. They say you have more lives than a cat." He sighed again. "All I see is another pretty boy, and we have so many of those. I'll admit I'm disappointed."

"I find that I am not," said Adolf.

"Do you know why I really wanted to see

you?"

"I can't imagine."

The man in the bathtub scowled, looking dangerous for the first time. "I needed to look into your eyes. My advisors hatched this half-baked scheme, telling me you could be persuaded to call a halt to all this nonsense—and that you possess the charisma to pull it off.

"Now I see you, and I don't believe it."

Adolf felt his gut twist. He hadn't even decided to make the broadcast, and now he was terrified that this rotting lunatic would make the decision for him.

"Oh, I'll give you your shot at it. I promised them I would. But I don't think you can stop this avalanche now that it's started." He giggled. "In fact, I'm betting my physician ten thousand marks that you fail."

"And what will happen if you win?" asked Adolf.

The *Führer* turned away from some imagined conversation, as if surprised Adolf was still there. "If I win I won't need the money. No one will. If you and I together cannot preserve the supremacy of the Aryan race, there's really no reason for anyone to go on living, is there? In us, mankind has reached its highest stage of evolution. To lose it all to the lower orders would be an insult to the planet that gave us life. It would be our duty to cleanse it once and for all, wouldn't it?"

"Well, I haven't really given the matter much thought. What do your advisors say?" *Please, tell me someone is controlling this madman!*

Hanover stood up and grabbed a silken towel

from the desk beside the tub. Adolf gagged on the smell that wafted his way. "Cowards!" he spat. "Most of them want to live at any cost! Even if it means defeat at the hands of every degenerate race ever spawned! Do they give any thought to their children? What will happen to their daughters? No!

"Therefore, I must think for them. They are my people, after all. My responsibility. If the Aryan race is to be defeated, I have at least made sure we shall all reach Valhalla together." His eyes roved over Adolf's body. "Those who are worthy, anyway. The bombs are all in place: a few of the old atomic kind, mostly the new biological. One order from me, and bases all over the world will carry out Operation Scorched Earth."

Karl, thought Adolf, *you may be morally and intellectually challenged, but you certainly understand the minds of our leaders.*

"Even in the worst of times, there are men who know the meaning of duty and obedience," Hanover continued. "Even today, there are whole families of loyal Aryans who have served the *Reich* for generations. The Bormanns. The Eichmanns. The Mengeles. All proud lines, who have helped our race rule the earth."

"Does this mean the Goebbels have been dropped from that elite register?" To Adolf's surprise, he felt no shame at bringing that state about.

"I have no use for traitors! Nor any of their blood! I'll..." The *Führer* began to cough and wheeze. A man in the uniform of Party Medical Corps rushed from the shadows and pressed a ventilator into Hanover's mouth.

"Calm down," the doctor said soothingly. He

glared at Adolf. "You've seen him, mine *Führer*. Now send him away. You mustn't risk another attack."

The *Führer* nodded. "Just one more thing," he said. "I want you to know, Adolf, that your family will have front row seats at your speech tomorrow. Your gentle psychologist didn't think you should know, but I think you should. If you try any kind of trick on the air, I promise, you'll live just long enough to see your family die.

"Take him to his cell," said the *Führer* softly.

Adolf was hustled out of the room, back through the nearly comically overblown security system, into a hallway lined with clean, efficient looking metal cells. All of them were empty. That made sense; someone of Adolf's stature would have to be kept in complete isolation. He recalled that even his escort had orders not to talk to him.

So it came as rather a surprise when an oddly familiar voice dismissed the other guards. There was some consternation among some of them, but after a few moments, all had saluted and turned smartly out of the corridor.

Adolf found himself alone in a cell with the captain of the guard. The door remained open. "You're a very difficult man to find," the captain said to Adolf. "You have no idea how hard it was just to get a few minutes alone with you." Then he removed his black helmet and turned to face his prisoner, allowing Adolf to see his face for the first time.

Adolf found himself looking into the handsome Aryan features of Josef Heydrich.

CHAPTER 32

"Well," said Adolf. "What does one say in a situation like this? Congratulations on your promotion, I suppose, are in order. When we met a few months ago in Poland, you were an Infantry Officer. Now I see..."

"Shut up!" Heydrich's voice reached a dangerously high note. Adolf might be able to learn a lot about the man's weaknesses if he survived the next few minutes.

"I was then, as I am now," Josef continued, "a high ranking member of the Department of Political Security. A position which often requires complex undercover work. And never more so than now."

Adolf said nothing, but eyed the open cell door and empty corridor beyond with interest.

"I have disabled the monitoring devices in this cell," said Heydrich. "They'll go on again automatically when the door slams shut. I can be gone for perhaps ten minutes without arousing suspicion, so let's get down to business."

"Which is...?"

"Saving the *Reich*."

"Yes, I've already spoken with Dr. Von..."

"I don't mean *that* old fool and his hare-brained schemes! Although the broadcast is a good idea, the fools still loyal to the *Führer* only want you to do it to keep him in power. As if we'd be safer with him in charge than with you!"

Adolf was beginning to understand. "But

that's not what you want."

"Of course not! I've kowtowed to that heap of decaying flesh long enough. And so have quite a few other good men. Young and strong like tempered steel, and ready to take our places as leaders of the new *Reich*."

"And you're telling this because…?"

"Because that wreck of a *Führer* has finally proven himself useful to us—for the first and last time. By setting up this broadcast for you tomorrow, he's given us the perfect opportunity to launch a precision strike. Everything is in place, but for weeks we've worried over how to pull it off in a single blow."

Heydrich slid a folded piece of paper from his sleeve and gave it to Adolf. "This is your speech for tomorrow, dear boy. Since our *Führer* has so kindly arranged to have the entire world watching, it will be you Adolf, who will have the honor of setting it all in motion. Don't read it now, there'll be time for that when you're alone. And don't worry about what it says."

Adolf ignored Heydrich and scanned the brief message. "My God, who wrote this crap?" he muttered without looking up. "You'd have to be as demented as the *Führer* himself to think this says anything at all. And don't you think codes like 'the monkey howls at midnight' are going to be obvious to anyone over the age of six?"

Heydrich grabbed the paper and slammed it onto the gleaming metal desk beside the cot. "I don't expect someone like you to see the artistry of it, Adolf. Just read it. Oration has always been your one strong point."

Adolf smiled. "Yes, of course, Josef, but what's my motivation? Is this the part where you offer me a place of power in your glorious new *Reich*? Or are you going to use the old line about sparing the lives of my family? You should know Von Dymler's already offered both."

Heydrich smiled back, far too confidently for Adolf's taste. "Your family has been dangled before you far too often as it is. And you and I could no more work together on building a new world than we could breathe in the vacuum of space.

"But I have something of yours that no one else in this snake pit can offer you. Something that means a great deal to you. Come and see."

He led Adolf to the monitoring station at the end of the corridor. The central screen allowed the guard on duty to look into any cell on the block. Heydrich flicked a switch, and Adolf found himself looking at a tight angled shot of Ilsa.

Three years in the underground had schooled Adolf in keeping his face a mask of calm when control was called for, but he knew a gasp escaped him. He knew because of the way it echoed in the empty silence—and by Heydrich's smirk of triumph.

"No one but me even knows who she is," he was saying. "I intercepted her the day she was captured. She's listed only as Hilda Kraus, terrorist, with great powers of persuasion over men, hence the isolation. According to official records, that annoying woman known as 'The Valkyrie' is now dead. Killed by me, as a matter of fact.

"So it will be a simple matter for me to return your *missgeburt* whore to you in exchange for your cooperation. I've grown rather tired of her myself."

Adolf gritted his teeth. *That might not even be Ilsa*, he reminded himself. *A picture on a screen proves nothing.*

"I'll admit I was disappointed," Heydrich continued. "After all the stories told of her fierceness, she didn't even put up a fight when I fucked her. She just lay there like a corpse. Or maybe she learned that from you?"

Adolf looked Heydrich in the eye, his face betraying nothing. "Come now, Josef. You have lots of experience with partners who would rather be dead than with you—like all of them, for example. Just as they would all prefer *you* as a corpse."

Heydrich grinned. "Maybe not all of them. Why don't you ask your sister Leisl."

Adolf remained still, though his body shook. "Are you sure you want to play all your cards right now?" he asked. "Pushing a victim too far often results in the sudden death of the tormentor—as I believe several of your relatives have already discovered."

The blow hit home, and now it was Heydrich who struggled for control, while Adolf thought frantically for a way out. The first rule was to stay in control. Ilsa—if it was indeed Ilsa—had already demonstrated her ability to choose her battles. She wouldn't fight Heydrich in a skirmish she had no chance of winning. Adolf knew he had to do the same. The time for killing Heydrich would come later.

But it took all of Adolf's control not to leap at him right then and there.

"The picture looks real enough," said Adolf.

"But they always do on screen, don't they? You might even have had her here a few days ago. But until I have positive proof, I will assume she's dead, and you'll get no cooperation from me. Funny how desperately you seem to need it."

Heydrich dragged Adolf out of the cell and slammed the door shut. "Of course I wouldn't expect you to cooperate without proof," he said, and the change in his tone told Adolf that the monitoring devices were back on. "Come with me."

Adolf followed Heydrich through impressive security doors and down a flight of stairs into a much more dungeon-like row of cells. These too were empty save one. Heydrich stopped beside the occupied cell and keyed a code into the panel on the door.

The door swung open, and inside, on the same cot he had seen upstairs on the monitor, was Ilsa. Her eyes widened a little when she saw him, but other than that showed no reaction.

"I'll give you a few minutes to reminisce," said Heydrich. "But remember, we are short on time." Heydrich pushed Adolf into the cell and shut the door.

For a few moments, Adolf stood frozen, half expecting Ilsa to be shot before his eyes, to amuse one of the many sadists who ran this place. An even worse nightmare was that she could have been turned; that she was simply the next weapon in the campaign for Adolf's soul. He was, he realized, a fool to have worried about that one.

"Did you get back to base with it?" she asked, calling his mind back to recent history.

"Yes. But there was no reason for the rush. It doesn't distinguish between races. It just kills."

Ilsa nodded. "I suspected as much."

"You always were the practical one."

"That remains to be seen." Ilsa looked pained. "Rumor has it that you turned yourself in."

"It's true. They made me an offer I didn't refuse." He waited for her look of horror; of recrimination or betrayal, but none came.

"I think there's a purpose in your being here, Adolf. I don't know how I know, but you did the right thing."

"I dared to believe that. Once. But then I spent a night praying to a god who never answered."

Ilsa smiled. "I'm glad you prayed, anyway."

"Ilsa, are you a Jew? Truly and in your heart?"

"Adolf, I became a Jew a long time ago. Several times, actually. I've lost my faith and found it again so often I'm starting to think I'm deciduous."

Adolf grinned at the image of Ilsa as a tree that lost everything each winter, only to bloom again in the spring. "I envy you," he said.

"You have nothing to envy, Adolf. You were chosen by God to save the world. That before all else. Only after that are you my husband and my greatest love."

He wanted to bask in the moment; to let nothing but their deaths interrupt it. But there was something he had to ask, and right then he didn't care who heard.

"Those poisonings at the meat packing plants were very... effective. Ilsa, did you—"

"No. No, that wasn't me. But I did know about it. And it's just barely possible that I could have stopped it. And I didn't. Do you find that unforgivable?"

Adolf's breath whooshed out in a sigh of relief that struck him as comical even then. "Everyone I know wants to give a medal to whoever did it! They couldn't understand why I might feel differently. How I might not want to be married to someone who killed indiscriminately on a massive scale—as long as it was for the cause! I'm not sure I understand it myself. But I'm very glad you didn't do it, Ilsa."

"I wasn't so glad about it when they captured me." She shook her head. "Those kosher laws. I started that whole campaign as a way to differentiate us from them. I thought if I could get people to see themselves as separate from the Party, yet part of something just as real; give them a culture—"

"Then maybe they would find the strength to make changes," said Adolf. "In themselves—and in the world around them." Ilsa nodded. "It worked, you know."

"Oh yes, I know. It worked so well that I wasn't the only one to see the possibilities. I thought about poisoning the pork long before the men who finally did it—as you well know. And, if I'd gone ahead and done it *my* way, we'd have had double the death toll—and nearly all of it within the military."

"So why didn't you?"

"Because of you. I thought about the innocent who would die along with the guilty. Even on a military base, there are secretaries, clerks, whores, wives, and children who never asked to be there. People who get groped and slapped around and treated like dirt by the men who really do deserve to die. And I discovered that I didn't care. That I could live with a little innocent blood on my conscience.

"And then I thought about you, and I knew that you couldn't. That even if it would have guaranteed victory for the revolution, you would never agree to it. Because every life is precious to you. And I wanted to be like you in that way, even if I couldn't feel all the things you feel."

Adolf marveled. "How could you want to be like me? Since this whole mess started, all I've ever wanted is to be like you! To be worthy of you. Your courage, your strength. I've met plenty of brave people, Ilsa, but no one who just refuses to give in to fear like you. I can preach and make suggestions, but you can reach inside the whole corrupt empire and rip out its heart with your bare hands."

Ilsa laughed. "And I've lived with people who really *have* ripped out hearts—both literally and figuratively. I'll tell you, they're not the kind of people you'd want running the government after you win. And for a time, I was one of them.

"But you, Adolf! Do you know what people say about you? That you win followers by loving the hate out of them! That one on one, you could sway anyone up to the *Führer* himself!"

"People need their heroes, sure," said Adolf. "This year they chose me. But look where I've brought us."

"Somehow, Adolf, I think that where you've brought us is exactly where we need to be."

"What, choosing between global destruction and Nazi dictatorship?"

Ilsa shook her head. "No. I don't think it's as bad as that. Sure, I'd hate to see life on earth end, but even that wouldn't be forever. Nature would try again. And I'm sure we'd all wish Her better luck next time around.

"But as for the Thousand Year *Reich*?" Ilsa smiled, and her blue eyes shone with the zeal that Adolf remembered well. "That's over. These pathetic players may not know it yet, but they're already dead."

"But if we can't replace it with something better, it's not much of a victory," said Adolf.

"It's the biggest victory for the Jews since the first Purim. Think about it."

"I guess there's something to be said for poetic justice." He sighed. "Funny how everything gets down to irony and poison. The Party poisons the world, the rebels poison the pork. In just the five months since Elijah starting showing up at Passover *seders*, those nine plagues have been felt more and more."

Ilsa nodded. "Since I came here I've heard more and more about people dying from minor illnesses, because their bodies just can't fight back anymore."

Adolf tried to remember more of what the scientists had been saying before he left. "The waters are reaching the point where they can truly be called poisoned. And another major river caught fire while we were in Russia."

"Trichinosis was the basis for the poison that was used on the pork," Ilsa said. "Fevers and bleeding guts were part of the symptoms. Somehow, it makes me feel better to imagine that the meat poisoning was ordained by God."

"And I would have trouble worshipping a god who sanctioned something like that."

Ilsa fell silent. "What about leprosy and

boils?" she asked after a while. "I haven't heard of an increase there, and they'd be pretty noticeable."

Adolf sat up. "They're here!" he whispered. "In the *Führer*. I've seen him—"

"Boils and leprosy invading the body of the divinely appointed *Führer*?" Ilsa began to laugh. "If I could just see that with my own eyes, I could die a happy woman."

"I don't want you to die at all, Ilsa!" Adolf suddenly gave in to his emotions. "There are quite a few people I want to see dead—some I hope to kill with my own hands—but not you!"

"Shhh." She took him in her arms, crooning to him as if he were a child.

"I'm sorry I let you down, Ilsa," he murmured into the gray prison uniform that covered her breasts. "If I'd killed Heydrich back in school when I'd had the chance…"

"Heydrich isn't important," she said with almost no trace of bitterness. "Soon, he will be forgotten."

"I want to make love to you."

"So do I. Does the fact that we're being monitored bother you?"

"A little. That, and the fact that tomorrow morning, I'm going to get in front of a bunch of cameras, and tell the whole world that Judaism was just a silly joke, and the revolution was a silly mistake. And living under a Nazi yoke is just peachy, really."

Ilsa gripped his hands. "Say whatever you have to say, Adolf. You won't betray the cause or the faith, even if you think that's what you're doing." She stared into his eyes. "Remember their own words to you, and know that they have sealed their own fate.

Do you understand what I'm saying?"

Adolf understood well enough that the cell was bugged and that Ilsa was trying to tell him something important; something she could not say directly. But he was too tired for spy games.

She read the exhaustion in his eyes, and his need for a few moments peace. "It's all right," she whispered. "Just know that I love you. Let's seal it with a kiss." She kissed him then, with a taste like fire and honey.

At that point, they were interrupted by the noise of heavy booted guards marching in unison, and the screech of the door swinging open. A guard strode into the cell. Five more waited behind him in the hallway. Heydrich was nowhere to be seen.

"*Herr* Goebbels, you must come now to your own cell," said the leader. "I am told you are to be well rested for your great speech tomorrow." He leered at Ilsa. "Surely your charming friend will wear you out if you stay here."

Adolf took a last look at Ilsa, wishing he had time to say with his eyes all he could never put into words.

"Goodbye, my love," he said.

"God watch over you," she whispered.

Then he was being hustled down a corridor, the door to Ilsa's cell clanging shut behind him.

Adolf was returned to the cell he had been in just minutes before. A typewriter now sat on the desk, with a stack of clean white paper beside it. He found the speech Heydrich had written for him on the bottom of the stack—and probably typed on the same machine, in case anyone bothered to examine it too closely. On a tray beside the bed was a hearty meal of beef barley soup and fresh bread.

"You are asked to begin work on your speech before retiring," said the guard. "If you need anything else, call me."

Adolf sat on the bed and didn't move for a full ten minutes while he considered his situation. Finally, for lack of a better idea, he gave in to his now nagging hunger and devoured the bread and soup. Then he gave in to the crushing depression that had been waiting for him since he first arrived in this complex.

Adolf stretched out on the cot—the most comfortable one he had slept on in years—and hoped the food was poisoned.

CHAPTER 33

Disappointed, but not all that surprised to find himself still alive, Adolf awoke the next morning. He felt fine, having experienced no ill effects from the food, water or air in the cell. His brain was not muddled or confused, for which he was grateful. If his mind remained clear, his personality unaffected, perhaps he could still think his way out of this situation.

Yeah, right.

Guards came for him at seven a.m. and proceeded to bathe, groom and dress him without any mention of breakfast. This time, his uniform was a full dress version of yesterday's: gray wool trousers, gray jacket with gold piping, and a black collar with scarlet tabs. A gorget hung with a golden chain tried valiantly to remind anyone looking that the wearer's ancestors were once Teutonic Knights.

In a covered car, Adolf was conveyed to the primary studio of the world's single broadcasting station. Security here was nearly as tight as at the *Führer's* palace. Guards paraded around the studio environs, halting and searching already harried technicians and clerks as they ran back and forth with cables, clipboards and trays of pastries.

"The speech is scheduled for 1200 hours," a large, authoritative man was telling the chief guard. "Until then he's your responsibility."

The sergeant craned his neck, as if trying to see all possible danger in the passageways, alcoves

and dark corners that surrounded the military escort.
"We must have a room! Something small and easily
guarded!"

"I thought you boys like a challenge," the
civilian said with a sneer. Then he frowned.
"Volmer!" A breathless young man skidded to a halt
in front of them.

"Yes, sir?" he said, eyes widening at the sight
of Adolf.

"Show these men to green room three. And
get makeup in there. Fifteen minutes. Might as well
have him ready early. At least someone in the *Reich*
can show these politicians how a production is
supposed to be staged."

Adolf was taken to a small room, empty but
for a ragged brown sofa, and a battered wooden table
that held an empty pitcher and three dirty glasses. A
large glass window, soundproof and probably
bulletproof, overlooked the chaotic bustle in the
surrounding studio.

He went to the window and looked out across
the busy studio as they prepared for the Salvation of
the *Reich*. Soon Adolf, the misguided prodigal son,
would tell the world the rebellion was over. The
Golden Age of the Thousand Year *Reich* was just
around the corner; theirs to have if they would just
obey without question their Illustrious Leaders.

Or else he would read Heydrich's speech, and
launch an attack that would result in men like
Heydrich running the world.

Neither option was acceptable. And, he had to
admit, neither option would save Ilsa or his family.

He had to find another solution. The fact that
his own brilliant idea of grabbing the very same studio

in which he now stood was being handed to him on a silver platter was the only thing that kept him searching.

Like a rat in a maze.

The door opened, momentarily shattering the silence with a rush of noise from the studio. Dr. Von Dymler came in alone.

"How are you feeling, Adolf?" the doctor asked.

"Just peachy," said Adolf.

Von Dymler laughed. "Yes, I guess that was a stupid question, wasn't it? I noticed that you didn't make use of the typewriter and paper. Are you sure you're ready? Would you like to go over any of your ideas? There are some things that will have to be covered."

"Such as?"

"The people should hear the names of as many high ranking collaborators as you know of. It will be better for everyone—including them and their families—if it's all out in the open now. The *Führer* has agreed to grant pardons to everyone who comes forward in the first twenty-four hours after your speech, and agrees to follow in your footsteps.

"Unfortunately, I'm afraid that one day won't be enough. There are bound to be some holdouts; dreamers who'll need weeks, maybe even months to finally accept the inevitable defeat of the rebellion. Others, especially those from high ranking families like yours, might feel they're safe enough to remain hidden, just blend into the background, and keep their youthful flirtation with disaster as a dirty little secret. It won't work. They will all be caught and executed.

"Their only hope will be you, Adolf. Tell the

truth now, while there's still time."

They were interrupted by the arrival of a young man carrying a heavy makeup kit. "Later!" snapped Von Dymler.

"I'm sorry, *Mein Herr*," the young man croaked. "But I have my orders…"

"Yes, fine, go ahead!" Von Dymler clasped Adolf on the shoulder and said, "I have faith in you, Adolf."

Then he was gone. The makeup artist fumbled with the clasps on the case. "Please be seated and look up toward the ceiling, *Herr* Goebbels," he said. Adolf did so, trying once again to figure out what he was supposed to do. He was greatly annoyed when the makeup boy decided to start talking.

"I have an important job for you, *Herr* Goebbels, and not much time, so listen carefully." He began to clumsily apply the base on Adolf's forehead. "I'm not really a makeup artist; I was sent because they knew you would recognize me."

"Ouch!" Adolf pushed him away as the brush jabbed his eye. "I can believe you're not a makeup artist!" He stared at the young Aryan man before him. "But I don't know you."

"Bruno Schmidt!" he whispered urgently. "My sister Helga was a friend of your Leisl! You have to remember me, everything depends on it!" Aware that they could be seen by nearly everybody, Bruno continued to fling makeup onto Adolf's face.

"The Alliance is ready to put our poor *Führer* out of his misery and take over the government, but we need your help. We're prepared to offer you the role of Speaker for the Provisional Government. All you have to do is…"

Adolf shook off Bruno's hands. "You'll have to take a number and get in line," he muttered.

"What?"

"Go find my secretary and make an appointment. She's currently handling all my contracts with the various coups and conspiracies. I suggest you bring along some silk stockings to bribe her with, as there are already several factions ahead of you." He stood up. Bruno remained in shock just a second too long. "Get out of here!" Adolf yelled, loud enough to be heard through the soundproof glass.

When the guards opened to door, he shoved Bruno through it. "Get me a different makeup artist!" he bellowed to no one in particular. Then to Bruno he shouted. "If I discover you've ruined my face for the broadcast, you're dead!"

Bruno scampered away while the guards, who apparently found Adolf's outburst perfectly appropriate for an aristocrat about to go before the cameras, ignored Bruno and hurried to find another makeup artist.

A few moments later, a woman rushed in. While she had no messages from any new conspiracy, she was, to Adolf's surprise, an actual makeup artist. Adolf heard later that he looked marvelous.

The makeup woman left, the guards came in, and, after complementing his appearance, led Adolf into a small, brightly lit room and seated him behind a cheap desk with an elaborate ebony façade. A pair of crossed cavalry sabers with the Crest of the Third *Reich* hung on the wall directly behind. Cameras were all around him.

"Ten minutes until air time," someone shouted from beyond the glass walled booth.

And then Adolf was alone in a still and silent room.

The calm before the storm, he thought.

Then, from where Adolf never knew, came another thought. *The darkness before dawn.*

In the sudden stillness, Adolf felt a sense that could only be called...*hope?*

Absurd, of course, but there it was. An intense, irrational conviction that if he could find the right words, he could save the world. And the right words seemed to hover just beyond his sight.

Adolf closed his eyes, and silently addressed God—though exactly Who that was, he still wasn't sure.

"For what it's worth, I'm sorry for those things I said to You back in Finland. And I'm sorry I never had time to feel You in my life the way some of the others have.

"But I'm grateful to have known You at all. Because of You—or those who proclaimed themselves Your Chosen People—I've lived a life I never would have had any other way. I had the rare privilege of sensing what life outside Nazi tyranny might have been, and I've seen the goodness that's possible in the human race.

"Maybe if a better man had grabbed this role before I did, someone who could have spoken with Your voice; Your authority... Your...*seal?*"

Ilsa's carefully chosen words of the night before came back to him: twice she had used the word 'seal'—and she had mentioned the holiday of Purim.

From across the years rushed the memory of the first Jewish festival Adolf had ever led, and the story he had read while the others reeled in drunken oblivion.

Within the book of Esther was a code so simple, yet so obtuse, it just might work. Adolf wondered why he hadn't seen it before.

"But sending the message is only half the solution," Adolf continued silently. "Where's the switch that will disconnect the men in the bunkers from their sense of duty to the *Führer* and Operation Scorched Earth?"

Then, like a sun exploding inside his skull, Adolf saw that answer as well. An answer handed to him by both Ilsa and the *Führer* himself. "Remember their own words to you..." she had said.

The *Führer* had bragged about the loyal families entrusted with carrying out his final orders...the same families named and arranged in careful groups on the list he had received in Finland more than a month before.

"Sixty seconds," said a disembodied voice. Cameras rotated, lights shone in Adolf's face, and the whirring of electronic equipment sound like the roar of the ocean.

"*Herr* Goebbels, are you okay in there? You're white as a ghost! Makeup! What happened? Get someone in there—"

"No time! Five, four, three, two...you're on!"

And Adolf Goebbels came face to face with the entire world.

"People of the Third *Reich*," Adolf said, as he twisted the crumpled remains of the speech Heydrich had given him with sweaty hands. The power and certainty of his voice amazed him. "My name is Adolf Goebbels and I have a favor to ask each and every one of you. I humbly beg you to stop whatever you are doing, and listen to me."

He paused for breath, and in that moment, everything became clear. He knew what to say. He knew how to say it.

"Throughout the recent difficulties, many of you have turned to strange cults, in the hopes of finding answers and salvation. I, myself, have fallen into this trap. I too, worshipped the false gods, Esther and Mordecai.

"We are citizens and subjects of the greatest empire in history. That is where we must find our answers. At times like these, we must think of all the good our government has accomplished, of all the things that our leaders have done for us personally. Then we will know what we must do." Again he paused.

"Any further attempt to overthrow this government would be futile, and cost countless lives. In the end, it could cost all our lives.

"With the hopes of preventing that terrible end, I will now name all of my fellow conspirators."

From the depths of his memory, Adolf drew the names. The desk, the cameras, the entire world around him receded. Names tumbled from his mouth; a few of them had faces; most were just pen marks on a sheet of paper he had read in Finland.

"Dietrich Bormann, son of Joseph Bormann. Otto Mengele, son of Leopold Mengele. Katrina Schultz, daughter of Wagner Schultz, Eva Eichmann Mengele, daughter of Franz Eichmann…"

And so it went on. When at last the river of names ceased flowing, over forty close relatives of founders of the *Reich* had been named. As he spoke the last one, Adolf slumped back exhausted. He had barely enough strength to command his final message.

"Each of those I have named, and the thousands of others who watch me now, and understand my words, must do your duty, as followers of the Second Order.

"Thank you for listening. *Heil* the *Führer*."

With that, the speech was over. Adolf bowed his head as cameras shut off, and waited to die.

CHAPTER 34

The door to the booth flew open and the sounds of chaos poured in. Guards were everywhere, asking for orders, and seemingly afraid to touch Adolf until those orders were made clear.

"What did you do?"

Adolf looked up to see Von Dymler towering over him, looking angry and confused, yet more than a little awed.

"Why I merely followed your orders, *Herr* Doctor," said Adolf in a voice of bewildered innocence. "I told the people that resistance was futile and I named my co conspirators."

"Those people could not possibly have all been traitors! They are members of the most trusted and powerful families in the *Reich*! Some of them are related to the *Führer* himself! They hold the most sensitive positions—"

"Surely, Doctor, you of all people understand just how insidious this movement has been. Had it been anything less, the *Reich* would not be hanging by a thread now."

"And what did you mean by the Second Order?"

This man was more perceptive than was safe, thought Adolf.

"Merely a salute to our Divine Savior. One of his early books, as you may know, was called "My New Order—"

"Every school child knows that! But what of

this Second Order? A new government, perhaps?
With you in charge?"

"If you've studied me half as well as you think
you have, Doctor, you know I have no interest in
ruling the world." Adolf relaxed, grateful that for
once, he could speak the simple truth.

"Have you figured out what he did yet?" A
man Adolf recognized from the *Führer's* bath
glowered at the psychologist.

Von Dymler stared at Adolf for a long
moment. "No. But we'll know soon enough. Tell
your people to monitor all movement. I'm talking
planetwide, not just suspected hot spots."

"We know our jobs, *Herr* Doctor," the other
man said coldly. To the guards he said, "Keep him
here. Be ready to move him at a moment's notice.
And keep alert."

And Adolf was once again alone.

The world around him spun like a silent movie
shown in slow motion. In the dim lighting, he could
see the huge live audience, hidden from view during
the broadcast, buzzing around like an overturned
beehive. He tried to pick out his family, but could not.
It was probably better that way.

Adolf wondered how long he had to live,
whether it would be measured in minutes or seconds.
He wondered if his message had been understood, and
felt a pang of regret that he would probably never
know. Yet more than anything, he felt relief. His job
was finally over, and somehow, in those final minutes,
he had found faith.

A banging on the window caught his attention.
A young technician was pointing at the blinking and
beeping equipment around Adolf, and arguing with

one of the guards. After a long and boring debate, the guard shrugged, and opened the door for the technician.

The young man never looked at Adolf, only bent to his work of turning off and securing equipment. As he passed close to Adolf, however he whispered, "Shalom, Rabbi."

"Shalom, friend," Adolf responded, not really surprised to find that his own organization had an agent working here. After all, everyone else's did.

"You did it, didn't you?" The young man dared to sneak a look at Adolf as he wound up a length of cable. "You sent a message." Adolf read hope and awe in the boy's blue eyes.

He rolled his own eyes to indicate the lack of privacy in the studio.

"Privacy's been taken care of," said the technician as he knelt by Adolf's feet to unplug something. "You may not know this, but at least two of your own people have already tried to assassinate you before you could make the broadcast. But me, I knew you'd never betray us. And I knew you'd find a way to send a message. I had it all planned out, how I'd throw myself between you and the bullets. I'd already rigged my camera to keep filming."

"Sorry to spoil your plans."

"Don't worry about it. I'll have plenty more chances to die heroically. As soon as you called Esther and Mordecai gods, I knew you were telling everyone to disregard what they were forcing you to say, and listen for a code."

"But did anyone besides you understand it?" Adolf whispered.

"I'm not even sure I did! But I know the story of Esther. After Haman sent out the first order under the king's seal, calling for the murder of all the Jews, Esther revealed his plot to the king and begged him to rescind the order. The king couldn't, because a royal decree couldn't be revoked, but he agreed to send a *second* order, telling the Jews to arm themselves and fight for their lives."

"And they won," said Adolf. "For the first time in recorded history."

The boy's eyes grew even wider. "And that's what you told them to do! My God, you did it! You gave the signal—"

"If they understood it."

"They did! I'm sure they did. Something's happening out there, and no one's saying exactly what! But, Rabbi? What about all those names you listed? All those rebels?"

"They aren't rebels," Adolf said quietly. "They are the loved ones of those who man the switches for Operation Scorched Earth."

"Operation Scorched…? Oh. But how did you know…?"

Adolf glanced upward, and then watched as the boy seemed ready to faint.

"Hey you!" A screaming guard leveled a rifle at the technician. "I said no talking!" The boy bounded away like a frightened rabbit, and Adolf was left alone to his questions.

Something's happening. But what? We discussed Mordecai and Esther as code words at the conference, but we never had time to agree on them. So is everyone rising up to overthrow the Third Reich, or only a small fraction, while everyone else argues?

*Have I just sent millions to their deaths? And if I
have, will it be worth it? Can it ever be worth it at
that price?*

*Or, is human life on earth about to end,
because of what I said?*

Oh, God, I really need to know!

And suddenly, Adolf did.

He felt disoriented, as if he were floating
out of his body. Then, he seemed to see the earth
spread out before him, and hear thousands of
voices shouting at once. Adolf closed his eyes and
found that if he concentrated, he could distinguish one
voice from another, like tuning a radio.

Throughout the world, the cry was raised.

"Vikings to the longboats!"

"Let freedom ring…"

"Uhuru!"

"Banzai!"

"Jean has a long mustache."

In Johannesburg, South Africa, every
government building and Party residence was reduced
to rubble within one hour of Adolf's broadcast.

On an island in the South Pacific, deserted
except for a missile silo, rabid Party supporter, Ernst
Janning was unable to carry out his final orders when
Wagner Schultz, clutching a picture of his only
daughter, shot his superior officer as he attempted to
launch the missiles.

In a place once called China, workers in the
Party-operated nuclear plant overpowered their
"employers" and ran to liberate the nearby prison

camp, which they found already in the throes of an uprising.

On a mountaintop in South America, a deadly airborne toxin was not released, after three low level technicians engaged in a firefight with those who would have carried out their orders to release it. One of them was the brother of a man mentioned in Adolf's speech. The other two identified themselves simply as Jews.

In a cellar in the south of France, two partisan leaders shot each other in a dispute over what Adolf's message actually meant. In the chaos that followed, the remaining members of their cells finally just took to the streets, where they found the local townspeople already lynching Party representatives.

At a base in Greenland, no one died when the Commandant himself refused to carry out the *Führer's* final orders, saying only, "I always knew the bastard was crazy."

And in Unconquered Russia, where most of the sixty-five remaining freedom fighters were still busy working on their leaky atomic warhead, Rabbi Sasha heard the broadcast on his homemade radio. After a heated debate, the Free Russians decided to defuse their bomb, and head south to see what was going on in the outside world.

And then Adolf was back in his own body, in a cheaply decorated booth in a broadcasting studio. But now he knew: his message had been received.

And except for a lot of death and destruction, the revolution was, as Ilsa had said, already won.

Adolf relaxed, recalling the last chapter of the book of Deuteronomy: "And the lord said unto Moses, This is the land which I swore unto Abraham, unto Isaac, and unto Jacob. I will give it unto thy seed: I have caused thee to see it with thine eyes, but thou shalt not go over thither." Moses had led the people to promised land, but that was as far as he could go. Others would lead the people from then on.

Adolf looked heavenward and smiled. "That's all right by me, God," he said aloud. "You've given me the greatest gift I could have asked for. I've sown the seeds, and others will reap the harvest. I can die happy now, because You let me see what my words have done."

"How convenient!" snapped a familiar voice, this time choking with bitterness and rage, "Since your god can't save you from me!"

Josef Heydrich stood in the doorway. With his rumpled uniform, bloodshot eyes and uncombed hair, he hardly looked like a victorious Aryan Superman. Even the gun he had trained on Adolf did little to spoil Adolf's enjoyment of the picture.

"So soon?" Adolf raised an eyebrow in mockery. "Can't we raise just one toast to the victory of God's Chosen People over Aryan Supremacy?"

The gun shook in Heydrich's hand. "The only victory that's going to matter to either of us is me living just long enough to see you die! Sure you don't want to pray to your Jew-God first? Ask him for a miracle?"

Adolf laughed. "As if He'd ever let *you* be the

instrument of my death!" Adolf had been leaning far back in the chair when Heydrich entered. It was a simple matter to slide the rest of the way under the desk, and into Josef's knees.

Heydrich went down with a grunt. A kick from Adolf sent the gun flying across the booth.

Both men were up in an instant, facing each other with no weapon other than raw hatred.

Then Heydrich glanced at the wall behind the desk. "Perfect!" he cried, leaping for the crossed sabers.

Adolf followed and a moment later both men were armed. The weapons were ceremonial and showed signs of rust, but as was typical in the *Reich*, perfectly able to kill. The steel edges were sharp and the blood grooves on both showed use.

There was a loud clang as blade met blade. "I should have killed you back in college when I had the chance," said Heydrich.

"Funny, I thought *I* was the one who should have killed *you,* " said Adolf. "It wasn't *my* throat that was exposed that moment at the end."

"But you couldn't do it, could you?"

Adolf laughed, parried and caught his breath. "Do you remember what you said to me, after I spared your life?"

Heydrich parried and replied, "I told you that you'd never be one of us; that the *Reich* had no room for cowards. It's still true!"

"And coming from you, Josef, I can't think of a higher compliment! Just remember that the New World the rest of us have built has no room for incompetent, oath-breaking rapists!" With each epithet Adolf beat his opponent's blade back.

Heydrich was forced to retreat until his back was against the wall of the small booth.

Heydrich fought well from his new position, though he was clearly tiring. "So kill me—if you've somehow developed the stomach, which I doubt."

"Watch me," said Adolf.

"Forget it, Adolf." The voice came from across the room. "This guy's all mine."

Both men froze as Ilsa walked calmly into the room. She was wearing the same gray prison uniform she had worn when Adolf had last seen her. It was lightly splattered with blood—not her own—and she carried no weapon.

"How did you get out?" Adolf asked, realizing this wasn't the time for discussion, as he glanced at Heydrich's gun on the floor, just a few feet behind him.

Heydrich dove for the gun in the same moment as Ilsa. There was a blur of motion as they struggled for the weapon, while Adolf stood frozen. His heart stopped when he saw the gun in Heydrich's hand, but at that same moment, Ilsa plowed her foot into Josef's crotch. Heydrich dropped the gun with a screech, a half formed curse dying in his throat.

Then, the thunder of a gun firing, the smell of powder and the faint flash in the dimly lit room.

Heydrich lay sprawled on his back, bright red spurting from his stomach, and to the smell of powder was added the stench of voided bowels. Adolf ran to Ilsa who stood over the body.

"Gut shot," said Adolf as shock wore off and Heydrich began to scream.

"I was aiming a bit lower," said Ilsa staring down impassively at her fallen foe. "But I can't say

I'm sorry." She turned to Adolf. "Come on, we've got to hurry. All hell's breaking loose and our people need their leader."

Finally accepting that she was unhurt, Adolf nodded. But as Ilsa turned to the door and Heydrich continued to scream, Adolf called out loudly, "Ilsa!"

"What?" she sounded annoyed. "Adolf, come on, hurry!"

"You got him in the liver! For God's sake, finish him off! At this rate, it could take him hours to die, all of it in agony."

"And you think I have a problem with that?" snapped Ilsa. Then their eyes locked. "Oh, all right!" Ilsa sounded like a petulant child, but she fired the gun a second time. The bullet struck Heydrich between the eyes and the screaming stopped.

In the sudden silence, Ilsa once again turned to go. Then the cold distance was washed from her face in a flood of emotion. "I wanted him to suffer!" she cried as Adolf put his arms around her. "In my cell, I dreamed of ways to kill him; and all the things I wanted to say to him. I thought I'd feel something amazing when I took his life. But all I am right now is tired. Is this what victory is supposed to feel like?"

"I wish I knew," said Adolf. "Maybe sometimes you just have to settle for being the last one standing."

"I agree," said a new voice. "Which is why so many of us have been turning this place upside down, searching for the both of you!"

They turned to find an unarmed old man standing in the doorway. A very familiar old man.

"Professor Hoffman?" Adolf asked in disbelief.

CHAPTER 35

"It's good to see you too, Adolf," the elderly academician said.

"But what are you doing here? How did you "

"For the moment, let's concentrate on keeping the two of you safe until the shooting is over." And Adolf, too dazed to do anything else, followed his old History Professor out of the studio and down a flight of stairs. Ilsa, looking equally drained, stayed close by his side. All around them was the sound of gunfire; of the screams of the wounded and of rallying cries and curses from both sides.

"I should be up there with them," said Adolf.

"We already have enough dead heroes, son," said Hoffman. "We're short on live ones with the brainpower and charisma to lead us out of this mess once the shooting's done." They went down several more flights of stairs and came at last to a door, which Hoffman opened with an old fashioned key.

"What is this place?" Adolf asked.

"A bunker, built during the War. Legend has it that the First *Führer* himself had it constructed, in the event of Germany's loss. Of course, he never needed it, but it will suit our purposes well enough. Some of your friends are already here."

"Any of them planning to shoot me?"

"Not anymore. The ones who actually believed you'd switched sides are feeling rather embarrassed right now. You know, after years of study, I've come to the conclusion that in most wars, the winners are the ones who can get all their weapons pointed in the same direction first."

They reached another door, this one guarded by two young women. At a second glance, Adolf realized one of them was Emilie, the young woman he'd first met volunteering for a suicide mission in his first underground. Before he could speak to her, the Professor exchanged a Hebrew code word with them, and the door flew open.

About thirty people were gathered inside, many of them around a radio. Others lay in a makeshift infirmary, being tended by a medic. Emilie's face wasn't the only one from his past, Adolf realized. Alina was there, and Markus, the fortune-teller who had once been a *Judenmuseum* curator.

"It's Rabbi Adolf!" shouted someone with a vaguely familiar face, and a hush fell over the room. Everyone was staring at Adolf.

"Isn't there someplace else you can stash me?" he whispered to Hoffman.

"The people in this room were chosen for their absolute devotion to you, Adolf," said Hoffman. "It may be uncomfortable, but at least it's safe."

Then someone shouted, "Elijah!" That's when Adolf noticed that some in the crowd were more interested in the old man than in him.

"Rabbi Adolf," said a white-faced boy in his late teens. "I saw that man last Passover! He came into our room and—"

"Drank from Elijah's cup!" shouted a woman. There were more murmurs and whispers.

Adolf stepped between his beloved old teacher and the crowd that he feared might give the poor man a heart attack. "Really, people," he said. "You must do something about this need to create heroes. This man is a hero because he saved my life, and probably for other reasons as well. But I assure you, he's simply a history teacher named..." Adolf stopped and stared at his old teacher. "*Elias* Hoffman? Elias? Elijah? Professor, are you...?"

"I'm an old man who is getting tired of all these questions! Right now, we've got a lot of work to do, and whether you know it or not, the odds are still against us.

"Adolf, as soon as it's safe, we've got to get you back on the air. Once the rebels realize they've won, they're going to be drunk on their victory. If anyone's got half a chance of leading them down a road of healing and rebuilding, it's you. Are you ready to try?"

"Of course," said Adolf. "But I still want to know who you are."

"Only who I am. If you're expecting a message from the Almighty, you'll have to get it directly from Him. I quit playing messenger long ago."

"Then just answer a question, if you can. Why did God break his covenant with the Jews?"

Elias smiled. "Who says He did?"

"He stood back and did nothing while every last one of them was murdered. I'd call that breaking the covenant."

"So did a group of rabbis in a place called Auschwitz," said the old man. "In 1943, they put God on trial. It was a very serious affair; lasted for three days. In the end, God was found guilty in a unanimous verdict."

"So then what did they do?" asked Ilsa.

"They prayed."

Ilsa gave a bark of laughter, but Adolf only shook his head. "They prayed?" he said. "After finding God guilty, they prayed to Him?"

"Yes, prayed. And then later, they died. So maybe now, they have their answers. The rest of us still have to struggle for ours. Very soon, Adolf, you will be the leader of a new world government, and your title will be 'Rabbi'. And a lot of people will want to know the answer to the question you yourself just asked. Maybe someday, you'll be able to tell them."

"Wait!" said Adolf, as the Professor turned away to answer a question from an anxious guard. "What about the men who were supposed to be guarding me! At least tell me how so many people got past them!"

Elias shook his head, busy with the guard.

"You really sure you want to know?" Ilsa asked.

"Maybe not." This whole thing was starting to feel like a movie. Adolf only hoped it wasn't one of his grandfather's.

The next several hours were some of the longest of Adolf's life. After years of being in the middle of things, he now had nothing to do but hide, wait, and let countless men, women and children die for him.

He tried to lead a *Torah* study, but no one could concentrate on anything but the radio and the incoming messages. The fighting was desperate and bloody, but so far, there was no indication of any use of biological of nuclear weapons. In that, at least, it seemed Adolf had succeeded.

Towards morning, when the tide was clearly turning in the favor of the rebels, they heard the loud thumping of booted feet rushing down the many flights of stairs above the bunker. Guards tensed, and Adolf found himself whisked into a heavily guarded corner.

The sounds grew louder: a large crowd. And the discordant sound of someone taking the stairs with his entire body.

Ouch, thought Adolf. *That's a lot of stairs.*

The door flew open, and fortunately, since the proper codes were exchanged, no one was shot.

An excited group of men and women beamed at the sight of Adolf. "We got the last of them!" shouted their spokesman, a large, dark haired man in his early thirties, whom Adolf recognized from a mission in Belgium two years ago. Rolf, that was his name.

"The last of what?" asked Adolf.

"Would-be assassins," said Rolf. "There were three attempts before the broadcast, and two more afterwards. Two are dead, two got away, but this one," he indicated a body being dragged forward, "we got alive, and decided to bring him to you!"

Adolf looked down, and found he was staring into Karl's battered and bleeding face.

While Adolf stood speechless, Karl's eyes swam into focus, and he realized who he was seeing. He groaned.

"I couldn't even get this right!" It was more of a sob. "I guess I shouldn't be surprised."

"And I thought you and I were finally starting

to get along!" said Adolf.

"Me too," said Karl. "Which is why I went charging across Europe after you—minus the luxury transport you got!" Karl spat out a bloody tooth. "When I heard you were going to denounce the revolution I thought I'd finally be a hero and kill you before you could destroy everything you lived for. I thought it was what you would have wanted. But like I said, I couldn't even get that right."

One of arresting crowd kicked Karl in the ribs. He groaned again, but made no effort to move.

"Stop that!" cried Adolf.

Karl's assailant looked puzzled. "But Rabbi, you heard him: he thought you'd sell us out!"

"Anyone who could think that deserves to die!" shouted the girl who stood next to Alina.

"If losing faith was a capital offense," said Adolf. "I would have been executed long ago! Stop torturing this man and tell me why you brought him here like this!"

The rowdiness began to ebb out of the group. "We just wanted to prove our loyalty to you, Rabbi," said Rolf. "Look here—" he yanked an already torn sleeve clear of Karl's arm. "We branded him with the mark of a traitor."

On Karl's left shoulder was an ugly burn in the shape of a sideways "Y". It was the Hebrew letter Ayin, Adolf realized, as his empty stomach heaved and he tasted bile.

"The first letter in the word 'Amalekite," Ilsa said quietly.

The man showing off the brand nodded. "Enemies of the Jews," he said. "God commanded His people to kill them all—unto the tenth generation.

So? You going to kill him, Rabbi? Or do you want us to?"

Adolf looked down at Karl. The bleak resignation he saw in Karl's face made him want to hit someone—but not Karl.

Adolf met the eyes of the pack's leader. "Haven't you had enough killing?" he asked. One by one, he met the eyes of everyone in the bunker. "Haven't all of you? This man is my friend. And it may come as a news flash for some of you, but when I got in front of those cameras, I thought I was going to betray you all too! Would anyone care to brand me with an Ayin?"

No one said a word, though several mouths dropped open. Adolf was pleased that Ilsa's was not one of them. "Please help this man into a cot," he said to the room at large. "And get the medic! Now!"

While Karl's injuries were being treated, Adolf addressed the assembled crowd. "If anyone expects me to begin leadership of the new free world with witch hunts and purges, then you'd better find yourselves a new leader! I've had all the bloodshed I can stomach—and then some! If you won't join me in shaking hands with those of our enemies who survive, then please--just go home."

"Shake hands with them?" shouted Alina. "The Gestapo or the SS or the Führer and his minions? It's for you and our future that my friends are out there killing them!"

Adolf turned his back on his confused followers and headed for the stairs.

Elias blocked his path. "Where do you think you're going?" the Professor demanded.

"Back on the air. To tell everyone it's time for

the killing to stop. If they don't choose to stop, that's their privilege, but they're not going to do any more of it in my name."

"The station isn't even secure yet, Adolf! How much good can you do if you're dead?"

"How much good can I do if I sit back and let blood-drunk savages solve my problems for me?" Adolf shot back. "Besides, what are the odds I'll be alive in twelve months, even if we win the field today? You taught history, Professor, so tell me: what's the average life span for a leader in my position?"

"Not long, I'll admit. But there is such a thing as maximizing the odds."

"You're right!" said Adolf. "Everyone here is right! And if I just wait here until the shooting stops, I'll have a much easier job!

"All those in power, who might have posed a threat to my administration will be conveniently dead—and so will millions of people who didn't pose a threat. The surviving population will be so small that this battered world's resources might even be enough to feed them. We can avoid starvation and the need for War Crimes trials all at once!

"And all I have to do to pull it off is sit back, nice and safe, while countless people kill and die in my name.

"All I have to do is found our future on moral cowardice.

"Does anyone in this room think I'm going to do that?"

Adolf could hear his voice echoing from the walls and ceiling. Then there was silence. Ilsa was smiling. "You have to let him go, Professor," she said. "Even if you really are the prophet Elijah, you can't keep Adolf here, or he wouldn't be the leader we need. And clearly, he is." As her gaze swept the rest of the room she spoke softly. "Face it, people: you can't build a world with Nazi tools, and expect it to turn out any differently than the one that Nazis already built."

Elias looked deeply thoughtful. "I'll stand aside, Adolf, if you can answer one question. If we can, like you, somehow learn to forgive our enemies, who says they're going to forgive us? If you let them live, how will you stop them from destroying everything we try to build?"

"That's two questions," Adolf muttered. But he had the distinct impression that his first test of leadership was happening right now, in this bunker, before an audience of thirty judges, rather than two billion.

He stared at Karl, wondering how many more like him would have to be sacrificed, before the new world could not be distinguished from the old one. Before a Hebrew letter branded into human flesh took on the same meaning as the armbands and tattoos of the world his grandparents had made.

Then it hit him.

"You!" Adolf pointed at Rolf. "Do you know the Hebrew scriptures as well as you know the alphabet?"

"Uh, well, I think so."

"Then tell us please, how God handled the first case of murder in Torah."

"That was Cain, who killed his brother Abel," said Rolf. "God banished him from his family."

"What else?" asked Adolf.

"I don't remember. The book says he got married—I always wondered to whom, since the only human beings on earth at the time were his parents and siblings."

"I wondered about that too," said Ilsa. "But I believe Adolf is referring to the mark of Cain." She knelt beside Karl, and gently traced a circle around the burned and tormented flesh that held the letter Ayin. Karl sighed, as if her touch was easing the pain. "When God banished him, Cain preferred death, claiming that any of his family who saw him would kill him anyway. So God put a mark on Cain, as a warning to any who saw him to let him be."

She looked up at Adolf. "When I first read that story I wondered if God was giving Cain a chance to find redemption. It seemed such an odd thing to me at the time, living, as I was, in a world where killing was such a casual thing; carried out for so many crimes."

Adolf knelt beside her, and kissed her hand. Then he stood and raised both Ilsa and Karl to their feet. "I hereby declare," he said to those around him, "that any man or woman who actively supported the Reich, but wishes to atone for those actions or associations, and be part of the new world, will be given the chance to do so. This mark," he pointed the Karl's brand "will be theirs to wear for the rest of their lives—but will be universally understood to guard their lives. From all of us."

"And what about those who don't want to atone?" asked Markus.

"Those, I won't prevent you from killing. But I won't do any of it myself. And if I can find them a nice, deserted island somewhere where they can found their own colony, they can go there with my blessing."

Karl stared at Adolf like a drowning man pulled to shore after he'd already given up hope. "Are you serious?" he whispered.

"If you want me to be your leader," said Adolf, "then those are my terms. What say you all? Because if I can't persuade thirty devoted bodyguards, I'm not even going to bother with the rest of the world."

It started slowly, with people nodding their heads, then rose to a low rumble as hands began to beat against hands, and feet against floor.

"I think that's a yes," said Ilsa.

Later that day, Adolf led the way back to the studio. As Hoffman had feared, the fighting was still heavy, but the booth where Adolf had made his earlier broadcast was secure and ready for him. Someone had removed Heydrich's body. Adolf resumed his place behind the desk, then after a moment, shook his head, got up and moved to where Ilsa and Karl stood.

"I'd like both of you to go on with me, if you would."

Karl looked first suspicious, then as if he might cry. Ilsa merely shook her head. "They want to hear from you, Adolf."

"They need to hear from us."

For the first time, Adolf saw the quiet pride of accomplishment in Ilsa's blue eyes. "You first. Call us when you're ready, and we'll join you."

To Adolf's surprise, it was Hoffman who went first before the cameras, motioning Adolf to wait a moment.

"People of the world," the Professor said, "I

would like to introduce to you Rabbi Adolf Goebbels." He waved to Adolf, who stepped in front of the camera as if he had been born to it.

There was no Divine voice in his head this time, but that was all right. This time, Adolf knew he could wing it.

Book V

EPILOGUE

"'These are the words Moses spoke unto all Israel on this side of the Jordan...' Hey, give me that!" Adolf tried to grab his book out of Markus's hands.

"Adolf," said Markus patiently. "That was a great speech—but Moses already made it! For now, we need to come up with something modern."

"There are probably some parts you can quote," said Anna.

Markus shook his head. "This is an important speech. We're celebrating one year of freedom from the *Reich and* we're trying to sell the first free elections held anywhere on earth in over sixty years. You have to remember that not everyone on the planet is a practicing Jew."

"You wouldn't know it from looking at the place!" Varina said as she shot a spitball at Leisl who was trying to take notes. Leisl retaliated, but Varina spun her wheelchair out of the way and ducked just in time. "Everyone wears a Hebrew letter or a Star of David around his neck. I keep hoping some guy will shave his beard, just to be different, but beards and curled sideburns are all the rage. No change in sight."

"Those are fads, not faith," said Thoresten.

"True, I think the majority of the population really is starting to practice Judaism, but plenty of people are walking the walk and talking the talk just so they can fit in."

"Well, come on," said Leisl. "You can't blame them for wanting to be on the winning side. And since Adolf's new laws make religious worship just slightly more private than going to the bathroom, we'll never really know what *anybody* really believes."

A clerk appeared at Adolf's shoulder. "Excuse me, Rabbi, but you wanted to know when the figures came in on the toxin levels in the Mediterranean?"

Adolf took the sheaf of papers with a nod of thanks—which he instantly regretted, as pain shot through his neck and into his back.

"Adolf, I'm sorry, but I think the speech comes first," said Thoresten.

"Fine! You write this one!"

"You know that doesn't work! The words have to be yours."

"Like everything else, Adolf," said Varina. "Everything of value must come from your holy lips. Or purified brain. Or sacred ass. Or—"

"Time for a break!" Adolf hadn't intended to use his command voice, but his staff quailed. Even Varina busied herself with a stack of papers.

"Good idea," said Anna. "I'll go fix you some lunch, Adolf."

"I'm not hungry." But he knew that wouldn't stop Anna. His head pounded and he wished, not for the first time this past year, that Rika had survived the war. She and so many others.

And yet, as if in answer to his pain, gentle fingers began to massage his neck. They belonged to his sister, not the girl he'd been remembering, but he was grateful just the same.

When she'd finished, Leisl sat down beside him. "I just wanted you to know," she said, hesitation in her voice. "Uncle Gustav is coming over today. We're going to visit the graves. Would you like to come along this time?"

Adolf wished he could avoid this question, and so many other things as well. He shook his head. "I'm just not ready."

"You can't keep blaming yourself for everything that happened, Adolf. You know what the *Reich* meant to Father. Dying with it was the only option for him. And dying with Father was the only option for Mother."

"I don't blame myself anymore...for that." A heavy silence descended, as it so often did now, between Adolf and Leisl. But what could he say? That she had been forced to become Heydrich's mistress to keep her family alive? That her parents had died calling her a whore, and themselves childless. It had all been said. If Leisl could forgive them, why couldn't Adolf?

He opened his mouth to say something—he wasn't sure what—when Ilsa appeared in the huge room. Adolf's command headquarters were still located in what had been Berlin's largest gymnasium. And before that, a long time ago, it had been a synagogue. Throughout the busy year he had steadfastly refused to find something more permanent, hoping to remind the world that he was only a regent. They would be electing a president or speaker or prime minister or something very soon.

They'd better, thought Adolf. *I can't keep this up much longer.*

Ilsa glided toward him, and he saw the strangest smile on her face, and wondered what was going on. She hardly ever visited him in the middle of the day. Even at night it was hard to pull her away from her work.

"How goes the struggle for equality among the Sisterhood?" he teased.

For once, she didn't rise to the bait. "Well enough to do without me for a while, I hope. I've just come from Hannah the Midwife. Guess what, Adolf? I'm pregnant."

"Very funny—" he began. Then, like a lightning bolt from on high, realized she was serious.

"Ilsa," he said, trying to keep track of reality. "Does this midwife really know what she's doing? Did you do any tests…"

Ilsa carefully unfolded a piece of paper. "I saw a doctor, Adolf. Someone Hannah convinced me to trust." Adolf whistled. For Ilsa to willingly submit to any kind of medical testing was a major event.

"Take a look. It's a picture of our baby." Adolf took the paper Ilsa gave him and peered at it intently. Then he turned it over and tried again. All he saw were squiggles and blobs in black and white.

"Here," said Ilsa, turning it back to the way he had it originally. "It's about nine weeks along. Here's the head; this bony thing is the spinal column…"

Adolf stared at the tadpole on the paper. "Ilsa? How is this possible?"

"Are you sure you want me to explain it to you

in front of your entire staff? You see, about two
months ago, there was this night we actually had the
apartment to ourselves, and—"

"I mean," Adolf said over the laughing and
whistling of his staff, "How did we get to the page
where the barren woman gets pregnant? I haven't
seen any angels lately, and you don't look ninety years
old to me."

"Not a day over seventy," said Varina.

His headache was gone. He stared at his wife.
"We're going to be parents?"

"This is fantastic!" said Thoresten, as the news
spread throughout headquarters. "This is exactly what
we need!"

"You want to use this in tomorrow's speech?"
asked Leisl.

"Tomorrow, and the next day, and when the
baby's born and…Don't you realize what this means?
It's the closure we've all been looking for! Ilsa, you
didn't have your tattoo removed did you? Good!"
Thoresten grinned as Ilsa displayed her red bar code.

Markus nodded, and continued Thoresten's
line of reasoning. "It's the final proof that the *Reich* is
dead; that overthrowing it was the right thing to do.
To the faithful, it's a miracle from God, and a blessing
on our two so very popular leaders."

"And to the cynics," said Thoresten, "it's
objective proof that the exalted Nazi Science and
Medical Corps were all bullshit! That all the trust
they gave the Party and its scientists was misplaced."

"Wow," said Leisl. "What's that going to do
to the people who lost their jobs—lost their children?
Or weren't allowed to get married or got sent to labor
camps—all on the basis of those medical tests?"

There was an uneasy silence around the table. Adolf felt some of his joy diminishing. "Thoresten, find Karl and tell him to set up a meeting. We'll need to beef up security in the Amalekite districts."

The young man was about to run off, but Ilsa grabbed him by one of his curled sideburns. "And tell him to get ready to find a new Head Rabbi. Adolf is about to take early retirement." She fixed her husband with a frightening stare. "You will, won't you? I'm not planning to raise this child alone."

"You won't be. But I appreciate the seven months of warning. I always work best with a deadline." Adolf hugged his wife, nearly lifting her off her feet. "Let's get out of here! Let's go for a walk! I've heard it's beautiful outside!"

"It is," said Ilsa. "You really should see the city during daylight hours."

"Hey, Adolf!" Thoresten called as the leaders of the New Free World headed for the door. "If it's a boy, will you name him Isaac?"

"I haven't thought that far ahead yet!" Adolf called over his shoulder.

Varina gagged on the sandwich Anna had just brought for Adolf. "I hope not! I certainly wouldn't name a child after a jerk who favored one son over the other, then, when it really mattered, couldn't tell them apart!"

"Adolf, wait!" Anna was chasing after them with a glass of milk. "At least drink the milk! You know what the doctor said about your ulcers!" Adolf stopped for the milk.

Shouts of "*mazel tov*" followed them out of the building.

They stepped into the dazzling sunlight of a summer afternoon. Around them, people from all over the world worked to rebuild Germany. From where Adolf stood, Berlin looked like a giant patchwork quilt.

As they reached the park, shouts of "Dirty Amalekite!" brought them up short. Three teenage boys were chasing a small party of construction workers, whose armbands signified they had been members of the higher echelons in the old regime. Since "higher echelons" had finally been defined as almost anyone above the status of factory foremen, it included a lot of people.

One of the boys pulled back his arm to fling a stone. "Hey there!" called Adolf, freezing the boy with his tone. "Care to explain what you're doing?"

The lad gulped when he saw Adolf, and his two friends shuffled back a few steps. "Sorry Rabbi," said the one with the rock.

"Don't tell me; tell them!" Adolf pointed at the three men and two women who stood bunched together for mutual protection.

For a moment, Adolf saw outrage in all three faces. They all shared the physical features created by early malnutrition and torture. They had probably been born in a slave labor camp. Still, Adolf held his ground.

The boys mumbled half hearted apologies, then ran off to find what Adolf hoped would be more constructive play.

"We have got to get rid of those armbands," he told Ilsa.

She took his arm and they proceeded into the park. "I'd think you'd be pleased that our people were finally willing to settle for armbands instead of branding. They have to display the Ayin mark. It's the only thing keeping them alive."

"Doesn't the fact that those people want to atone count for anything? They could be living in Argentina with all the ones who said it wasn't their fault!" Of course, based on the latest intelligence reports, that colony wasn't doing very well.

"Or they could be dead," said Ilsa. "That's what a lot of people are saying. They can't understand why so many Party members and collaborators are still alive."

"Aren't twelve million suicides enough for them?" Adolf demanded.

"At least it was suicide. You were so worried the tenth plague would be the slaying of the innocents, like last time."

Adolf thought about all the children who had died in the loving embrace of fanatical parents. "I'd call it a slight improvement," he said.

"The armbands can probably come off in a few years," said Ilsa. "Although I must admit, I agree with Rabbi Simon that they should stay on until the tenth generation." She grinned at Adolf, as if expecting another debate.

But he only stopped and set an awkward hand on her belly, noticing now that it wasn't quite as flat as it had been just a few weeks before. "Will their children be born any less innocent than ours?" he asked.

Ilsa's face grew hard, then suddenly softened. "No, I guess not," she said, sounding surprised. "Wow! Hannah said motherhood would change me, but I didn't think it would be this soon."

They strolled through flower gardens that had survived three global wars and the rise and fall of empires. Even in the worst of the fighting, the park had been spared. Adolf saw lovers walking hand in hand, and vendors selling food that hadn't been tasted by German palates in decades. He saw children playing, and for the first time, allowed himself to imagine what it would be like to hold one of his own.

Ilsa was right. It was time for him to retire. Before the stress of the job killed him. Or before some disgruntled citizen suspected he wanted to keep the job forever, and got to him before the stress did.

As if reading his mind, Ilsa said, "Thinking you might finally live your dream of becoming a humble village school master?"

"Maybe. But the school will be a synagogue, and I'll be teaching people of all ages. But that's fine with me. I'd love to try it, and find out if I'm any good."

Ilsa rolled her eyes. "Like you haven't been doing it for years already?"

"Yeah. But what might it be like without anyone shooting at me?" Adolf grinned. He seemed to be doing that a lot all of a sudden. "What I really need to find out now, though, is where to get a crib, and how to change a diaper, and if we could move into a smaller place for just the three of us."

"Mmm. I like the sound of that."

They reached the end of the park. There, now a pile of rubble, was what had once been the white marble mausoleum of Adolf Hitler. It had had stood from 1959 until the mob had pulled it down last year. They hadn't opened the coffin, so somewhere down there, his bones still lay.

Now the place was a memorial. Paintings, sculptures, banners and poems filled the open area. The most impressive to date was still under construction. On a huge wall of black stone, a man with an armband carefully chiseled a list of names. Newly uncovered records of the extermination camps had provided them. Adolf judged the artist could squeeze one hundred thousand names on the wall. To record them all, he would need four hundred more walls.

Adolf turned back to the vandalized mausoleum.

"Incredible," he whispered.

"What is?" asked Ilsa.

"Hitler. History. The way everything turned out. I've heard people say that the First *Führer* and I have a lot in common."

"Bite your tongue."

"Well, there could be something to it. I'd settle for being half the genius he was—if I could just avoid his fall into darkness. If you consider all he did—"

"Adolf, if you start waxing sentimental over Hitler, I swear I'll move to Switzerland and raise this baby by myself!" She stalked away at an impressive clip.

"But Ilsa!" Adolf chased after her, to the delight of numerous passersby. "Look at it this way! If it wasn't for Hitler, the whole world wouldn't be Jewish today!"

Author's Note:

This book began more than twenty years ago, when I saw a documentary on Simon Weisenthal, which described Himmler's plan to create museums of dead races. I immediately saw the possibilities for an alternate history story (at the time I naively believed it would be a short story!)

Soon after that, in another documentary, I learned of how Joseph and Magda Goebbels poisoned their six daughters before killing themselves on the day Hitler died. I knew at once that my protagonist had to be the grandson of Joseph Goebbels: propagandist, fanatic, the kind of man who could murder his own children rather than let them live in a world without Hitler. (Admittedly later, when I learned more about the atrocities committed by Russian soldiers against German civilians, I began to see the Goebbels' actions differently. When my mother compared their actions to Masada, my perception did a complete turnabout.)

My first problem, however, was how to keep Adolf's last name Goebbels, after the documentary had clearly stated that all six children were girls. After agonizing with me for some time, my husband suddenly shouted: "If Joseph and Magda didn't die, they could have had more children!" Yes! Perfect! After all, the youngest was only four when she died in 1945. So I invented Wilhelm Goebbels, who became

Adolf's father. Then, after about twelve years, several
rewrites and the invention of the internet, I learned
that Goebbels actually had five daughters and one son.
(A member of my writing group thoughtfully sent me
several web articles and a whole batch of pictures.)

After uttering a few words which will not be
printed here, I sat down to begin the next rewrite. It
wasn't that big a deal, I told myself. Just hit Ctrl F
and Ctrl H: Find Wilhelm; replace with Helmut.
Except it *was* a big deal. Bringing a nine year old boy
back from the dead so I could turn him into a
convenient villain became a very big deal to me.
Maybe that child would have grown into the tyrant he
is in this novel. But we'll never know, because he
never got the chance to grow into an adult of any kind.
In an effort to show respect for this little boy, and his
sisters, I learned all I could of the real Helmut
Goebbels, and incorporated all five sentences into this
novel. So little, and yet it speaks volumes.

Also included are stories people have told
me over the years. Within the pages of this
fantasy of what might have been, I have incorporated
all the reality I could, even the most obscure bits. And
if you are one of the people who told me one of those
stories, my short "Acknowledgement" section is not
nearly enough to express my thanks.

Sandra Saidak graduated San Francisco State
University in 1985 with a B.A. in English. She is a
high school English teacher by day, author by night.
Her hobbies include reading, dancing, attending
science fiction conventions, researching prehistory,
and maintaining an active fantasy life (but she warns
that this last one could lead to dangerous habits such
as writing). Sandra lives in San Jose with her husband
Tom, daughters Heather and Melissa, and two cats.
Her first novel, "Daughter of the Goddess Lands", an
epic set in the late Neolithic Age, was published in
November, 2011 by Uffington Horse Press. From the
Ashes is her first Science Fiction novel.

Made in United States
North Haven, CT
07 May 2023